JUST DECEITS

JUST DECEITS

A HISTORICAL COURTROOM MYSTERY

To Shane

An up & coming lawyer

Here's a tale from

our amazing legal

history.

Enjoy!

Michael Schein

11/29/08

Michael Schein

B&H Bennett & Hastings Publishing

Bennett & Hastings Publishing
7551 A 15th Ave NW
Seattle, WA 98117

Book design by Geoff Gray
geoff@typegray.com

First edition.
Printed and bound in the United States of America.

ISBN 978-1-934733-21-9

To Mom & Dad, for encouraging law;
to my wife Carol, for encouraging writing.

Contents

Author's Note

What you are about to read is fiction based on actual events. Richard and Nancy Randolph were tried for infanticide in 1793, and they were defended by John Marshall and Patrick Henry. The basic outcome and aftermath of the trial are as reported here, and the main points of the witnesses' direct testimony (except for Jack) are taken from Marshall's actual trial notes. Jack Randolph really did send a vituperative letter in 1814, some of the main points of which are used in the version I have crafted. However, the particulars of what was said to whom, and certainly all the interior monologues, are merely products of my imagination. The villains were perhaps not as villainous as portrayed here, but neither were they quite as much fun.

At times in this book it has been necessary to portray the institution of slavery from the point of view of the people of 1793. Do not confuse uneducated speech with stupidity; the speech of most slaves was unrefined not for lack of intellect, but because the oppressive institution of slavery denied them an education. And please, do not confuse the messenger with the message. I abhor the epithet "nigger" and all that goes with it. Some have said that I should take these things out in deference to modern sensibilities, but it seems to me that racism is only papered over by such tactics. When we change our hearts, these things will not matter; until we change our hearts, it matters that we do not prettify our past.

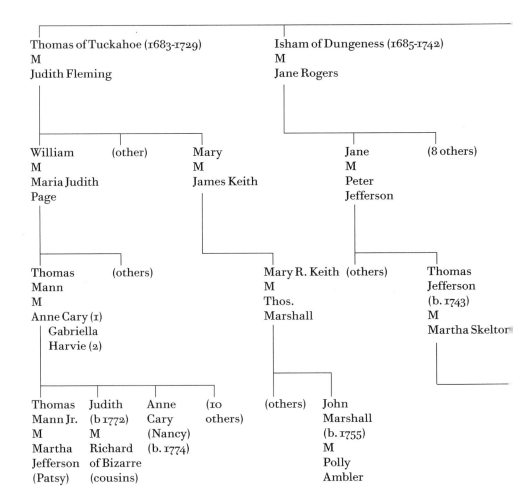

Thomas of Tuckahoe (1683-1729)
M
Judith Fleming

Isham of Dungeness (1685-1742)
M
Jane Rogers

William   (other)
M
Maria Judith
Page

Mary
M
James Keith

Jane
M
Peter
Jefferson

(8 others)

Thomas   (others)
Mann
M
Anne Cary (1)
   Gabriella
   Harvie (2)

Mary R. Keith (others)
M
Thos.
Marshall

Thomas
Jefferson
(b. 1743)
M
Martha Skelton

Thomas   Judith   Anne   (10
Mann Jr.   (b 1772)   Cary   others)
M   M   (Nancy)
Martha   Richard   (b. 1774)
Jefferson   of Bizarre
(Patsy)   (cousins)

(others)   John
            Marshall
            (b. 1755)
            M
            Polly
            Ambler

THE RANDOLPHS OF VIRGINIA (PARTIAL)

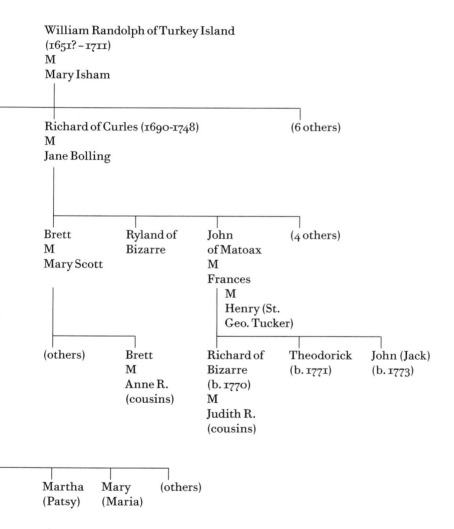

William Randolph of Turkey Island
(1651? – 1711)
M
Mary Isham

Richard of Curles (1690-1748)   (6 others)
M
Jane Bolling

Brett   Ryland of   John   (4 others)
M   Bizarre   of Matoax
Mary Scott   M
                                  Frances
                                       M
                                       Henry (St.
                                       Geo. Tucker)

(others)   Brett   Richard of   Theodorick   John (Jack)
               M   Bizarre   (b. 1771)   (b. 1773)
               Anne R.   (b. 1770)
               (cousins)   M
                              Judith R.
                              (cousins)

Martha   Mary   (others)
(Patsy)   (Maria)

Consider what you think justice requires, and decide accordingly. But never give your reasons; for your judgment will probably be right, but your reasons will certainly be wrong.

LORD MANSFIELD (1705 - 1793)
CHIEF JUSTICE OF THE KING'S BENCH

PROLOGUE

The First of October, sharply cold. Just a girl, really, she seeks comfort against the wrenching carriage ride in the warmth of her big sister's arms, and finds it as she always has. The rutted, half-frozen lanes leading to Glenlyvar are determined to shake out her bowels, but she fights back, sucking herself into a ball, focusing now on the blurred sunshine outside the window, now on the tempest within. Upon arrival she must lie down, not like this, not like that, not here, not there, for there is no surcease inside this skin. Up the narrow stairs, through the outer chamber, bolt the door to the inner chamber, muffle the cries between the spotless sheets.

The cries! Oh Lord such cries as fly unbidden from the entrails. Cries that would freeze a wolf in its tracks, sour milk in the teat, tauten vestigial hackles. *Sister dear, where are you? Laudanum, be quick about it!* So bitter it is sweet again then bitter then bitterest. No oblivion, just another ocean of nausea. *Sister, where are you? Brother, is that you? Medicine, now! No, not that, no – you know what I need.* Not so bitter, not so bad, it goes down greedy smooth then turns to broken glass in the womb.

Sister, hold my hand, sister? Brother? Take my hand and squeeze with all your strength. If you love me, really love me, you will help me now.

PART ONE
PRE-TRIAL PROCEEDINGS

COUNSEL FOR THE DEFENSE

i.

Straight in the saddle, at a canter not a gallop, he rode as a gentleman should. Boots spit shined, breeches starched, frock coat tight, waistcoat tighter, he took the ground between himself and the Cumberland County Courthouse like enemy territory. His sharp dismount tossed dark locks from darker eyes to reveal features at once frozen and roiling. Ignoring the handful of geezers stuck like toadstools to the courthouse's tobacco-stained stoop, he bounded up the steps and executed an abrupt about face, startling one octogenarian who stood too close. To the no one in particular assembled, and to all Virginia, which in 1793 was damn near everyone, he said with all the dignity he could muster through his rage:

"I am Richard Randolph of Bizarre. My character has lately been impugned by accusations of crimes at which humanity revolts. My wife is humiliated; the good name I would pass to my innocent baby son has been trampled in the gutter. I cannot refute these vicious smears by private suits against their authors; for every one silenced ten more would appear. Slander, to be refuted, must be confronted openly, here in the sight of God. If the crimes imputed to me were true, then my life and my sacred honor would justly be forfeit to the Commonwealth of Virginia. But I pledge that there is no truth to these slanders – none! Therefore I demand to be tried before a jury of this County on the charge of infanticide. And mark this well – I will clear my name!"

Done with this extraordinary declamation, Mr. Randolph produced a handwritten version of the same, to which he had not referred once while speaking, and shoved it through a link in one of the many wrist cuffs bolted to the front of the courthouse for use on auction day. He departed as smartly as he arrived, save only for the tobacco juice on his boots, and the triumph in his eyes.

"Damn fool," said the geezer he'd nearly trampled, "they'll hang him now, fer sure."

"Naw," said another of the courthouse gadflies, "that's a Randolph neck. It ain't never gonna stretch."

2.

"Mr. John Marshall," announced the butler, in advance of a tall, gawky fellow with a head too small for his body. Marshall bumped his homespun frock coat against the elaborately carved doorway of the study, sending up little wisps of road dust. In his pocket he could feel the eight words that had launched him from his modest Richmond home to Matoax, Judge Henry St. George Tucker's breathtaking plantation perched on a bluff overlooking the Appomattox River. "I must see you at once," read the Judge's scrawled missive, "urgent business." Marshall could guess the nature of the business: Judge Tucker was Richard Randolph's stepfather.

"Ah, Mr. Marshall, Mr. Marshall," said the Judge, a robust, trim fellow in his mid-forties, "welcome to Matoax. So glad you could come promptly – Do you see what I mean?" he added, suddenly addressing an overweight and apoplectic gentleman seated behind him, who looked to be at least fifty. "That's one thing you can count on Mr. Marshall for, over that other fellow – promptness."

"With all due respect Judge Tucker," said Marshall, bristling at the implication that he might be a second choice, "as no particular time was specified in your note, I could not fail but be on time."

"What'd I tell you, what'd I tell you," laughed the Judge to the corpulent gent, "logical as a watch spring; not like that other fellow."

The gentleman snorted noncommittally, apparently still loyal to "that other fellow." He looked from Marshall's homespun garments to his squashed keen face, and then quickly away, refusing to hold Marshall's eyes. Marshall could read the look: not what the gent expected of a fellow Randolph and a former member of the Virginia House of Delegates. Yes, it was true; his mother, a Randolph, had married "poorly," which meant for love. He himself had been out of the public eye for several years now, and had quickly slipped into obscurity. It rankled him that no one seemed to care any longer about his many services to the Commonwealth, or even that he'd stood by Washington's side through the endless Valley Forge winter that one in four hadn't survived. Now he was forced to hang out his shingle to feed his family. Well, let them look down their noses. No amount of family money would save young Richard – it was to him they had turned, John Marshall, a cousin who wasn't too proud to ply a trade.

"But where are my manners?" asked the Judge. "Mr. Marshall, this is Colonel Harlan Beauregard Randolph of Tuckahoe."

Marshall straightened instinctively at the mention of rank, though it be rank bought with cash, not blood. Of course, thought Marshall, striding to the brocatel easy chair supporting Colonel Randolph's girth to accept his diffident handshake, I should have deduced that this would be the compromised lady's father. "Colonel Randolph," he said with courtesy, "this is indeed an honor."

"Sir, indeed," affirmed Colonel Randolph, dropping Marshall's hand like a toad.

"Drink? Cigar? What can I offer you, Mr. Marshall?" asked the Judge.

"I'll thank you for a glass of milk to wash down the road dust," said Marshall, and then immediately regretted it when he detected amusement in the Colonel's eyes.

The Judge sent for the milk, and he and the Colonel refreshed their bourbons and lighted two Matoax cigars. After a long draw, the Judge looked up through the smoke and said, "Mr. Marshall, I expect you know why I've called you here." Marshall nodded his small head imperceptibly, waiting for the Judge to continue. He needed this high profile case desperately, but he was not about to show it. The Judge went straight to the point: "Colonel Randolph and I want the best lawyer we can get for Richard and Nancy, and I think that lawyer is you. I'd like you to take the case." That was it, plain and simple. Marshall liked Judge Tucker.

"I'm honored by your confidence, Judge, but," here Marshall focused on the Colonel, "what about that other fellow you two were considering?"

"Oh, that, well it's nothing, it's nothing – dash it, I can't fool you. I've seen your work, I know it's good, damn good, perfect to my Judge's eye. The only thing is, while that's just the kind of thing we'd want in a matter concerning mortgages, wills and the like, well, Colonel Randolph thought that maybe we'd need to find a lawyer with a little more, shall we say, fire and brimstone to his pleading."

At this, Colonel Randolph leaned forward in his chair. "Can you do whatever is necessary Mr. Marshall? Can you take the jury by the scruff of the neck, make them think up is down, like a real lawyer? Could you make them acquit the Devil himself?"

Marshall's milk appeared in a crystal goblet on a silver tray, but Marshall didn't touch it. He thought of his dear Polly, how she would love such a tray and goblet. He thought of his own reputation, how he had ridden high at the time of the ratification debates, but now was better known for mortgage foreclosures than eloquence, and little remembered for either. He chose his words carefully. "Colonel Randolph, do you believe that the earth is flat?"

The Colonel fell back in his chair, shooting the Judge an *I told you so* glance. "Of course not, the earth is round, like a ball."

"Then it follows, does it not, that what you call up is what another fellow on the opposite side of that ball calls down?"

"Well ..." Marshall had him there, but he wouldn't admit it.

"As for the Devil, he's just a failed angel same as any juror, so yes, of course, I could talk them into forgiving him most anything, just as they forgive themselves their own sins on a daily basis; but the question is: would I want to?" Marshall drank his milk.

"Why wouldn't you?" asked the Colonel. "Do you think they're guilty?"

"Do you?" parried Marshall.

At this the Colonel, for all his girth, deflated. "I don't know. I know she is an ungrateful wretch of a child. Her mother, my first wife - very fine family, you know, not Randolphs like us -" and here the Colonel graciously included Marshall - "but decent; she died when Nancy was fourteen, and I'm afraid she took it rather hard. I did what I could to console her, but somehow she came to blame me for, for," he paused, seeking just the right word, "the state of things," he said, with more emphasis than elucidation. "I thought perhaps she was getting better, until I remarried. That was three years ago, when Nancy was fifteen. A fine girl, Gabriella Harvie, perhaps you know of her grandfather, Gabriel Harvie?"

"Oh yes, a renowned lawyer," replied Marshall. And a renowned scoundrel. Any granddaughter of Gabriel Harvie was surely young enough to be Nancy's sister. No wonder she was hostile - her mother replaced by a strumpet. "If you want fire and brimstone, hire Gabe, right Judge?"

"Ha! That's right, that's right," laughed Judge Tucker. "I once had to throw his neighbor in jail for the night just to keep Gabe from killing him!"

"As soon as Gabriella arrived," continued Colonel Randolph, "there was no peace at Tuckahoe. Nancy was in a blind rage half the time, cold as ice the rest. Got so you couldn't have a word in her presence. Well, I couldn't stand it, and the new Mrs. Randolph couldn't stand it, so I had to ask Nancy to leave. I hated to do it, but it had to be done." The Colonel stubbed out his half-smoked cigar.

"Where did she go?" asked Marshall.

"To live with my elder daughter, Judith, and her husband Richard, at Bizarre Estate. Judith and Nancy have always been very close." The Colonel gave a wan smile. "Like shipmates going down together ..." he added, his voice trailing off. "But you haven't answered my question, Mr. Marshall, about –"

"Whether I'm too punctilious to defend a guilty client? Nor have you answered mine, Colonel Randolph," replied Marshall, enjoying the chance to flummox the head of a great house.

"Sir, you have the advantage. My old brain lets slip a thing or two these days."

Again, the Colonel was pinioned by a dark stare. "Do you think Miss Nancy is guilty, Colonel Randolph?"

"She's young, she's impetuous, she's beautiful, very beautiful. Do I think she's capable of illicit intercourse? I'm sure she is. But murder? No, I think not." He paused, and then added with a laugh that fell flat, "If she were, I'd have been dead long ago."

Marshall turned to the Judge, who'd been sitting with his feet up on a maple desk, staring nowhere over his fingertips through the haze of smoke, half-listening as if to a rhythmic master's report on the metes and bounds of a disputed parcel of property. Marshall startled him out of his reverie with an abrupt "And Richard?" Unaccustomed to being the target of the questioning, the Judge blurted out the simplest response. "He told me he isn't, so he isn't."

"With all due respect, Judge, that assumes too much."

Face flushing, the Judge rose and poked at Marshall with his cigar. "John Marshall, you are the most infernal machine. Richard's word is good enough for me, and if you want to continue to enjoy my hospitality, it'll be good enough for you, too."

Marshall rose, too, and executed a stilted bow. "Judge, I apologize. But it's necessary. Would you rather I be polite, or win the case?"

The two men glared at one another for a moment before the Judge relaxed. "You're right, you're right, confound it! It's just that, well, if you knew him ..." Here, the Judge's voice faltered. "He calls me 'father,' and I call him 'son,'" he added softly, as if that were enough.

After a moment of silence, Judge Tucker rallied. "We've answered your questions, Mr. Marshall. Now, you must answer ours. Will you take the case, and act with vigor?"

"Gentlemen," began Marshall, parsing the issues in his curious manner, "first, am I too punctilious to defend a possibly guilty client? The answer is that I am a lawyer, not a judge or a jury, and until the latter have spoken my client is innocent under the law, and innocent to me, regardless of the evidence against him. Second, will I undertake the defense? Promise me full control, and I shall defend them with all the energy I possess. Agreed?"

"Absolutely," said Judge Tucker, sticking out his hand to seal the bargain.

"And my fee shall be two hundred dollars," added Marshall, trying not to let his tongue cleave to the roof of his mouth at the mention of so princely a sum.

The Judge hesitated imperceptibly, then grabbed Marshall's hand with fervor. "So it shall, so it shall," he said with a grin.

"Colonel?" said Marshall, turning his way.

"One hundred dollars?" said the Colonel.

"Two hundred," said Marshall.

"One hundred and ten hogsheads of tobacco?"

"Two hundred," said Marshall, in a peremptory tone.

"Two hundred," said Judge Tucker, "right Colonel?"

"Hmph," grunted Colonel Randolph, reclaiming the dropped toad with reluctance.

CHAPTER 2

BIZARRE

I.

Bizarre.

Not a proper name for a respectable plantation house, thought Thomas Jefferson's daughter Patsy Jefferson Randolph, as she gazed from the window of her elegant phaeton at Bizarre House through the gathering twilight. As sister-in-law to Richard Randolph and his wife Judith, Patsy was familiar with the history of this house. She knew that it had been built here, outside the hamlet of Farmville on the banks of the sleepy Appomattox, about fifty years before by the first Richard of Curles for his third son, Ryland. She knew that the work had been done by Spanish laborers who drifted up from Florida, laborers who never grasped the preference of a Virginia gentleman for the sort of grandeur that piles one story on another, laborers who instead preferred to luxuriate in low, cool openness amongst the cypress and sycamore groves. Before her sprawled the awkward result: a flattened box that teetered between hacienda and colonial plantation house, unable to capture the grace of either. Any pretense of dignity was lost as the long staircase ascending parallel to the facade turned almost too late to join the portico. Accustomed as she was to the harmony of Monticello, Patsy had long ago decided that the twisted staircase was undignified, like a lion saddled with an elephant's trunk.

"Patsy, my dear, so good of you to join our celebration," and before she could say a word in reply she was enveloped in brother-in-law Richard Randolph's familiar warm embrace. She could see the doorman's gaze drift elsewhere to avoid the sight of the exotic dark gentleman entwining her awkward, angular frame. The most elegant gowns rested on her square shoulders tentatively, like birds about to take flight. Despite her ungainliness Richard always made her feel feminine. "And your husband, where is that rascal?" added Richard, as he looked about for Judith's brother, Thomas Randolph.

"I'm sorry, dear Richard," said Patsy, disengaging herself from her brother-in-law's arms as she cast an eye for Judith, "Thomas had to go to Williamsburg. More bric-a-brac ordered by Poppa for Monticello." She made a tiny exasperated purse of the lips. "He sends his apologies."

"Accepted and more!" cried Richard, giddy with catharsis after his trip to the courthouse. "Then we have you to ourselves, all the better!" and he offered his arm. As they ascended the lion's crooked snout, Patsy was able to return to her thoughts. She had heard the rumors about Ryland, the bachelor who had named the place *"Bizarro,"* Spanish for "brave." But Ryland's penchant for gypsies and mountebanks quickly suggested "Bizarre" to the local inhabitants, and the name adhered firmly as Ryland spent his reclining years cloistered in the Great House for weeks on end, shivering at what he called "the evil humors in the wind." Afraid to light a fire for fear the house might burn down, he went to sleep one frosty night and froze to death.

Bizarre – she turned the word over in her mind – not a proper plantation name like Monticello, Tuckahoe, Dungeness, Chatsworth, Matoax, and all the other great Randolph Estates of the richest, most powerful clan in the Commonwealth of Virginia; no, this name was more a quality, an essence, an ineradicable stain.

Silly, silly girl, Patsy scolded to herself, you've been here a hundred times before, these are your friends, your family, fellow Randolphs. Here, in a land settled but one hundred fifty years, caked with mud, squawking with chickens, full of empty wilderness, bound together by nothing more substantial than a handful of newfangled ideas and common enemies, where everything is rough and hard and squalid, Randolphs must stand together as a bastion of tradition, refinement, civility, culture.

But now this, the filthy reek of scandal, to distend their patrician nostrils.

Crossing the threshold, Patsy blanched momentarily against the sulfurous heat of the entry hall's grand hearth, before assuming a proper smile for the Bizarre branch of the Randolphs.

2.

"A toast," proclaimed Richard, rising, holding aloft a brimming goblet of burgundy. He stood at the head of the walnut dining table in the low-ceilinged formal dining chamber of Bizarre. The table was set for five but could easily have accommodated twenty-five. Fires blazed on each side of the room in tiled hearths bordered by fluted renaissance pilasters. The walls were heavily paneled and washed in a light green paint, which offset the indigo blue on white of the stuffed Queen Anne dining room chairs. From the gilded crystal chandelier to the fruit-laden Chinese punchbowl centerpiece to the gleaming silver wall sconces bearing the Randolph coat of arms, each detail breathed an elegance far beyond the ken of the ordinary Virginian.

"A toast," repeated Richard, his voice lowering respectfully, "to the memory of our dear departed brother, Theodorick, who is with us tonight in spirit." Richard's eyes, the only blackness not chased by the crystal and firelight, snagged the cat-eyed glance of his wife's sister, Nancy. "Would that he were here in the flesh."

"To Theodorick," echoed Nancy, and the party drank a quick draught of melancholy. Cupid, an Irish setter, detected the sinking spirits and bestirred himself from his place between Richard and Nancy to try to climb into Richard's lap. Rebuffed, he circled his quarry, and then collapsed with a bony sigh against the empty chair of the mistress of the house.

The melancholy was dispelled somewhat by the arrival of the roast beef. At least dinner is here in the flesh, thought Jack, younger brother to both the unfortunate Theodorick and to Richard. Born John Randolph nineteen years previously, he had a tongue like a dagger wrapped in a preternaturally smooth weasel face. For once he held it, not out of consideration, but gluttony.

"Jack," scolded Nancy, "can't you wait for Judith? I'm sure she'll be down in a moment."

"No," said Richard, "that's all right. This is a family party, and there is no need to stand on formalities. Please begin."

For a party, thought Patsy amidst the clinking of silver against china, it's rather morose. She looked about the table at Richard's shallow gaiety, Jack's devilish pout, Nancy's withdrawn pallor, and Judith's empty seat. All eyes were fixed on the meat. Patsy ventured into the silence. "I received a letter from Poppa this morning."

"Wonderful!" said Nancy, eager for distraction. "What's the news from Philadelphia?" Nancy leaned forward in genuine interest, as Richard and Jack both followed the close escape of the taffeta bowknot at her breast from a dunk in the roast's bloody juice.

"Everyone's talking about the President's second inaugural. Nothing like the first time in New York when it was oh so Republican. Now that the people have forgotten their fears about 'King Washington,' he begins to put on airs."

"How can a donkey put on airs?" sneered Jack.

"Jack!" scolded Richard. "I mean, after all, he is the President."

"And my stallion Damion is a champion, but none the wiser for it." They could not help but laugh.

"By the way," said Patsy, who could contain her curiosity no longer, "how is Judith?" Richard's reaction caused her to regret the question, though he did his best to conceal it in a spoonful of boiled salsify.

"Somewhat indisposed, I'm afraid," answered Richard. "She asked me to give you her apologies."

"Not too indisposed to resist the pleasure of dining with those whom I love most in this world," came a brittle chirp followed by Judith herself, wearing a carefully rehearsed smile on her puffy, plain face. Nancy flushed as Judith rearranged her bustle and settled herself into the seat next to Cupid. There she sat, as if upon a spider.

Georgeanne, one of the house girls, carefully served Judith a plate of roast beef, boiled salsify, and beans, as the party watched with exaggerated interest. Finally, Richard said, "Judith, dear, Patsy was just bringing us up to date on news from our nation's capitol." Judith seemed not to have heard, so Richard turned back to Patsy. "Go on, dear, what other news did you have from Philadelphia?"

"The talk of the capitol is the European situation," said Patsy, grateful to be of use. "According to the latest news from France, which is really no more than rumor at this point, the Revolutionary Government in France has declared war on Great Britain, Holland and Spain, and – well, here is the part that is most incredible; Poppa doesn't believe it, but he passes it on as an example of the kind of anti-French distortions promulgated by the Tories and even some Federalists – it is said, oh this is such nonsense that it is probably not worth repeating."

"Do go on," said Nancy. "I love nonsense."

"Yes," said Jack, "often it's the only thing that makes any sense."

"Well," continued Patsy, "the rumor is that the King of France and his Queen were guillotined by the mob!" Feeling somewhat awkward at making so horrific an announcement at so genteel a table, feeling, indeed, rather as if she had served up the heads on a platter, Patsy looked down at her bloody roast.

"This is wonderful news," said Jack, to whom a few heads more or less meant little so long as his wasn't one of them. "Long live the Revolution! A toast to the death of tyrants!"

As Nancy raised a goblet Richard grabbed her hand, sloshing the wine just over the rim, staining their hands crimson. "To the death of tyrants we'll drink, but not to the murder of women, nor to the murder of a friend of our Revolution." Judith's eyes narrowed, flashing from sister to husband and back again, as Nancy quickly withdrew her stained hand.

"Don't be so stuffy, brother dear," replied Jack with a grin. "Remember what Patsy's Poppa says: 'The tree of liberty must be refreshed from time to time with the blood of pompous asses and tyrants. It is its natural manure.'" He paused to admire his own cleverness. "Or some such manure," he added with a laugh, but this time no one else was laughing.

"Sir," replied Nancy, drawing herself to her full height and mustering all the dignity she possessed, which, despite her mere eighteen years, was not inconsiderable, "I raised my goblet in haste. Like any American, I stand for democracy against Monarchy, but I also stand against barbarism. In this, I am sure Mr. Jefferson would concur. If this rumor is true, then only the most unfeeling heart can fail to grieve for royalty who helped us in our hour of need, to hear that they have died so cruelly."

"Not so cruelly, I think," said Jack, who, if he knew when to quit, plunged on nonetheless out of spite, "at least the guillotine's quicker than-"

"John Randolph" shouted Patsy, "you bite your tongue!" But the damage was done. Richard looked scared, Nancy merely troubled.

Just then there was a pounding at the door, followed by voices and the approach of heavy boots. Four men appeared, armed with pistols and muskets. Cupid stood and growled, ignoring Richard's command to be silent. The men stepped menacingly towards the table, but were stopped by Cupid's bared teeth and feral warning.

The leader, a chinless fellow with more black hair springing from his ears and nose than his pate, leveled a musket at the dog. "Control that bitch or I'll kill her," he commanded.

There was a moment of frozen equipoise, broken at last by a quiet word from Judith that instantly transformed the setter from vicious beast to loving pet. "Take her out, Georgeanne," Judith said. "There's a man in here with no respect for a fine animal."

As soon as Cupid was gone, the leader said, "Richard Randolph?" though he knew Richard by sight.

"Yes, Sheriff," for he too knew Sheriff Dunby.

"Anne Cary Randolph, known as Nancy?" Startled, Nancy merely nodded. "By the authority of the Commonwealth of Virginia, I hereby arrest you both and seize your persons to answer at the County Court for the County of Cumberland to the charges of murder by infanticide, and adultery!"

Irons were clapped over the fine brocade velvet of the prisoners' evening clothes. Now they both looked scared.

"This is hardly necessary," protested Richard to the Sheriff, "especially with the lady. Release her at once!"

"Sorry sir," said the Sheriff, "but as there's two named in this crime, I'll take two prisoners."

"Crime?" screamed Judith. "What do you know of crime?" She clung fiercely to her husband. From the back of the house came Cupid's furious barking.

"Enough to know that I arrest them's that be named on the warrant, and then the Court decides what to do with 'em. So stand clear, or I'll take you as well!"

Judith would have gone, had not Patsy stepped in to gently disengage her desperate embrace. The prisoners were quickly led away into the chill Virginia night. Suddenly, Richard and Nancy were connected to their accustomed world of luxury by nothing but the finery on their backs and the fading sounds of Judith's uncontrollable sobbing.

– CHAPTER 3 –

INTRIGUES

I.

Marshall followed the Sheriff's lumpy head down a dark passageway to Nancy's filthy cell. Not a proper cell; it was really just an extra room in the back of the jail, windowless and dank. The regular cells were unsuitable for a lady, since they afforded little privacy. *So it is,* thought Marshall, *that my client is tortured by chivalry.*

"Miss Randolph," said the Sheriff, sounding a momentary warning before scraping the key in the rusty lock and throwing open the solid oak door, "you got a visitor."

Marshall caught a glimpse of creamy calf as the prisoner jumped up from her pallet, then averted his gaze once there was nothing more to see. "My apologies, Miss Randolph," he said to his boots, "perhaps you'd like a moment alone to compose yourself?"

Nancy shot the Sheriff a look that would melt pewter. But her eyes softened for the gangly man in a cloth redingote grasping a battered beaver top hat with hands that extended too far beyond his cuffs. "Yes, thank-you, Sir, it is indeed a pleasure to be once again in the company of a gentleman."

She no more belongs here than a nightingale in a pig sty, thought Marshall, drawing the door to afford Nancy a smidgen of dignity. Eager to prove his worth, he vowed to get her out that very day. "Tell Judge Allen I want to see him right away," he barked at the Sheriff.

"As you wish, Sir," said the Sheriff with a smirk that showed what he thought of Marshall's chances. Judge Archer Allen had the patience of a gnat and temper of a hornet. The Sheriff handed Marshall the taper and left him to contemplate its weak flicker.

"You may come in now," said Nancy. Marshall pushed back the heavy door. In the dim light, he could make out ringlet curls the color of honey framing a delightful face, well-proportioned and clear. Her large oval eyes melded from green to golden with each flicker of the candle, her nose was straight and noble, and her full lips tapered into a sensual suggestion of a smile when at rest. But even in the taper's poor light, Marshall could not fail to observe the dark stains beneath Nancy's lustrous eyes, and the spiderweb tracings of worry so foreign to her alabaster complexion.

"Permit me to introduce myself," said Marshall, with that queer jerk of his that passed for a bow, "I am John Marshall, Attorney at Law."

"How do you do, Sir?" said Nancy, with a graceful nod that elongated the exquisite arch of her white neck. She was indeed, as reputed, beautiful. All the worse for her considering the charge, thought Marshall.

"I have been engaged, Miss Randolph, to represent you and Mr. Richard Randolph in connection with the charges against you."

"By whom?"

"By your father, Colonel Randolph."

"By my father," echoed Nancy, her voice heavy with scorn, "that's very amusing. Why should he suddenly care what becomes of me; he never has before."

"The Colonel—"

"'Colonel' *ma dèrriere*, pardon my French; if he's a Colonel then you're the President and I'm the Queen Mother!"

"Miss Randolph!" exclaimed Marshall, somewhat exasperated.

"I'm sorry, Mr. Marshall, where are my manners? Squalid quarters are no excuse for vulgarity, and as long as I have a chair to offer, it is yours. Please, seat yourself."

"Thank-you, Miss, but it's your only one," remonstrated Marshall, who suddenly regretted speaking harshly towards this eighteen-year-old child of privilege who had been brought so low, so suddenly.

"I have my pallet, Mr. Marshall, and it suits me just fine. Please," said Nancy firmly, motioning to the chair, "I insist." And then she lowered herself onto the soiled pallet as if it were a satin divan.

"Miss Randolph, in order to defend you against these charges, it will be necessary for you to tell me every detail about yourself with perfect candor. Do you understand?"

Nancy inclined her head slightly.

"Good," said Marshall. "I think we'd best start with your relationship with the Colonel."

"The Colonel you know, or at least think you know," Nancy began, a trace of scorn still coloring her tone. "He is the son of William of Tuckahoe, who was the son of the first Thomas of Tuckahoe–"

"In whom we share an ancestor," interjected Marshall, just to be sure there was no mistaking him for a common tradesman.

"So you, too, suffer under the curse of lineage, Mr. Marshall!" Her laugh rang out like church bells. "My opinion of my father you have doubtless gleaned. I sha'n't bore you with the causes, but you may be assured they are adequate. He is not to be trusted."

"I must know the causes, Miss Randolph, if I am to help you."

"Sir, you are my lawyer, not my minister. My father can answer to God. In this particular matter, I will answer to no one."

"Very well," agreed Marshall, reluctantly, "please continue."

"My mother was Anne Cary Randolph of Ampthill. She was not a warm woman, Mr. Marshall, but I know she loved me. I didn't always deserve it, you know, the way Judith did. But I think she loved me the best anyway, even when I was wicked."

"Not too wicked, I hope," said Marshall, testing her.

"Wicked enough, Mr. Marshall," shot back Nancy, a warning in her eyes. "But all that came later. In the early years, I knew no cares. Tucka-hoe is a large and hospitable abode. I spent the long days horseback riding, picnicking and swimming by the pond, tending my own little flower garden, reading scandalous novels behind the slaves' quarters, and generally enjoying nature and freedom. Besides horseback riding, probably my favorite game was hide and go seek, which Judith and I played for hours in the boxwood maze behind the house. Eventually, we knew that maze better than the gardeners themselves, and, after Mother died and Judith was married, it got to be a handy escape. I do believe I even slept some nights among the boxwoods."

"Escape from what?" ventured Marshall.

There was a silence. "From missing Judith," said Nancy, staring at the dirty floorboards. "Of my nine brothers and sisters, I was always closest to dear Judith. We used to lie together all day in bed. We'd make tents of our sheets, heap in books, dolls when we were younger, play-ing cards, chessmen, needlepoint, apples, jugs of wine, astrological charts, anything and everything pleasurable, but our pleasure was really in each other."

Nancy looked up; Marshall looked down. "I see," he said.

"No, Mr. Marshall, you don't see. I don't mean just when I was five and Judith was eight. I mean when I was fifteen and Judith was eighteen, too, and every month of every year in between, year after year, Judith and Nance, sisters, best friends, two sides of the same soul, until this ..." She suppressed a sob. "We even had our own song, Mr. Marshall," and she began, in a high, dreamy voice:

> *Judith and Nancy are sisters*
> *like the sun and the moon above,*
> *We'll love each other till our days are done*
> *like moonlight sweetens the fiery sun.*
> *To Heaven we'll rise together:*
> *Sisters moon and fire breather.*

Nancy paused, her eyes misting. "I've made a mess of things, Mr. Marshall," she said at last.

"And I would like to help you fix it," replied Marshall brightly.

Nancy smiled to think that she had wasted so much truth on this angular lawyer who only wanted facts. Marshall appeared somewhat fidgety. "Do you see, now, Mr. Marshall, what drivel you get when you ask for every detail? A horse is a magnificent animal, but not so his fleas."

"Miss Randolph, Miss Randolph," sputtered Marshall, "I assure you that the details of my client's past are not drivel to me."

"Nonetheless, I will confine myself to the matter at hand." Just then there was a grating sound from the cell area, signaling the approach of the Sheriff. Marshall put a finger to his lips.

"Ahem, Mr. Marshall," came the Sheriff's voice.

"What is it?"

"Sorry to bother you, Sir, but Judge Allen says he'll see you now."

"Thank-you, Sheriff, I'll be right there." They listened as the Sheriff's footsteps retreated. "Please excuse me, but I should not keep His Honor waiting. Perhaps, Miss Randolph, we will be able to resume this most interesting interview in more hospitable surroundings."

Marshall paused for dramatic effect, reveling in the role of protector. "I am going to ask the Judge to release you pending trial."

"Wait," she exclaimed, grabbing hold of his shirt-cuff as he rose, then pulling back in embarrassment over her forwardness.

"Yes, Miss Randolph?" he said, anticipating her gratitude. But she surprised him.

"Have you talked to Richard yet?"

"No, I haven't had the opportunity." He'd tried when he first arrived, but Richard had another visitor.

"Mr. Marshall," she said in a whisper, taking his hand and pulling him close, "do not waste your efforts on me, but redouble them for Richard's sake. Remember, always, no matter what you hear, no matter what the evidence shows, that Richard is a good man, an honest man, and most of all, an innocent man."

The liturgical quality of this last, and the fire in her eyes as she spoke, brought "Amen" to Marshall's mind. "And you, my dear, are an innocent girl, I'm sure."

The fire went out, as Nancy looked away.

2.

Richard's other visitor was his brother Jack, who had set off before dawn on his Thoroughbred charger Damion to devour the sixteen miles between Bizarre and the Cumberland jail. No one in Prince Edward Counties could ride like Jack Randolph; he was an incorporeal wraith wrapped around his steed's neck, terrifying the beast to flight while hindering it in no bodily way. He arrived at Richard's cell door just as the first sunlight arrived at the tiny barred window, dissimilar visitors of unequal welcome.

"Good morning, brother, I trust I have not awakened you?"

Richard, in a plum habit that hugged his muscular torso, stood by the window of the dismal cell in a show of defiant elegance. He turned to face the cloaked apparition whose only sign of life was the quivering riding crop in its gloved right hand. "Heavens no, Jack," said Richard with a weary smile, "only criminals could sleep in a place like this. I'm glad to see you." Richard attempted to turn their handshake into an embrace, but the wraith slipped through his fingers. "Tell me, dear brother, how is Judith?"

Jack's child-like face darkened even beyond its natural duskiness. "Not well. Not well at all."

Richard lowered himself into a chair, and sat contemplating the indifferent furnishings. Two rough chairs, an unsteady table that could only be trusted after the soup was half spilled, a grimy pallet, a washbasin that dirtied its water, and a slops pail, constituted the cell's amenities. But when Richard looked back up, resolve had chased his anguish. "I must persevere, regardless. It's too late to turn back. Please, Jack, help Judith to understand."

Jack leaned across the table. "Help Judith to understand? How can I help her to understand what I don't understand myself?"

"Try," was all Richard could offer.

The leather riding crop whipped to within an inch of Richard's cheek. "Very well, I'll try," snapped Jack. "Here's my elder brother, whom I idolize, who has – or had, I should say – a reputation for honesty and a bright political future, locked up like a common criminal."

"Jack," began Richard, but he was cut short by the crack of the crop on the table.

"Here's my beloved sister-in-law, Judith," continued Jack, "her spirit so torn that I fear to look in on her in the morning lest I discover her hanging from the chandelier by a sash." Now he had picked up steam, and there was no stopping him. "Here's the Randolph family name, not six months ago the proudest in Virginia, reduced to skulking 'round street corners, serving as principal sport in every forum from the most elegant parties to the most squalid taverns." Again Richard moved to speak and again the crop slashed the air, leaving dark welts on the sunlight's bright dusty skin. "Here are the Randolph womenfolk, once justly viewed as the embodiment of all that is pure and refined, now seen as part of a great clan of harlots." Richard focused on the patterned spray of Jack's saliva in the light, numb to the shock of the words. "Here is our stepfather, Judge Tucker, who nurtured us and our affairs when we were little and fatherless, a man who stands for justice and the rule of law, bearing up under rumors that the foundling he so kindly took in has committed crimes against man and Nature herself."

Jack paused to draw a breath which, like a bellows, fanned the flame of rage in his breast. "And what is the cause of all this ruin, of the torment and unhappiness of a great family?" The crop struck the tabletop with a vicious crack. "One woman – nay, not woman, but devil in female form –"

"Stop, Jack," said Richard, reeling from this lashing perfectly aimed, as only blood could aim it, straight at his soft underbelly. "Please, stop."

"I wish I could stop, dear brother," and Jack's sinuous lips slipped back to reveal a smile more awful than any sneer, "but these are the facts, and so it is but filial duty that drives me onward. What is the cause of this ruin, this plague upon our family?" He dared Richard to respond, but Richard would not dignify the assault. "It is Nancy –" Jack spit the syllables – "Nancy and no other. Unless, of course," here he fixed Richard with a searching eye, "I am to believe the unbelievable, that Richard, my brother, is guilty of murder."

Richard met his look with one twice as fierce. "Jack, I am innocent of the charges against me," was all he said, and all he had to say.

"Of course, I knew it in my heart, but it is good to hear it from you. You and I have always shared our mother's gentle nature."

"Ahhh," said Richard, thinking of that time at the dinner table when Jack, in a fit of gentle nature, had thrown a knife at him with such force that it had shattered a vase of peonies and impaled itself three inches into the mahogany paneled wall. "But you're wrong about Nancy. She's quite innocent, and besides, she's Judith's sister, so she's our sister, and we've got to protect her." Seeing this had little effect, Richard added pointedly, "It was not long ago that you yourself thought much more highly of her, if I recall correctly."

Jack bristled at the reminder of that night alone with Nancy on the west portico. "I made a mistake," he said, coldly. "I may be the only one of us to survive that mistake."

"I'll survive, Jack. I've done nothing wrong. I love Nancy as a sister, that is all, as my wife's most beloved sister."

"If that is true, then it is to Judith whom your first loyalties lie. If you hang, Judith will not survive the loss."

"I think you overestimate our danger," said Richard, trying to pass it off lightly.

"I think you overestimate the capacity of a woman's heart to absorb pain," rejoined Jack, coming so close that Richard could smell the sour breath through his tooth powder. "I know, for I see her daily."

Despite himself, for the first time the possibility that he could cause Judith's destruction hit Richard, and he was humbled. "For this I am sorry, Jack," he said, but then, taking a deep breath, he shook it off. "Still, there is nothing to be done. I will not – I cannot – back down."

Jack studied his brother. For a moment, he wished for that easy familiarity other brothers share. "Richard, don't martyr yourself to an unworthy cause. You must think of your own life and honor, if not for your sake, then for Judith's, and if not just for Judith, then for St. George."

Richard's breath caught at the mention of St. George, his first child, born just after Theo's death in February, 1792. Jack pressed the advantage. "Richard, this is not a time for false sentimentality. You can't save Nancy, but you might still save Judith, St. George, and the Randolph family honor." Jack paused to let his words sink in, then added lightly, as if recalling a perfect near-side backhand from a polo match, "You could, for example, testify that Nancy was delivered of a mulatto, and that she broke its neck rather than face the shame."

"I could never," cried Richard, his face flashing fury, "it's a lie, one that would send her to the gallows."

"But don't you see," persisted Jack, "the way the people are stirred up, someone's going to the gallows, and better it be just her than both of you."

"GO!" screamed Richard. "Get out of here before we both discover a new and unwanted side to my character." Jack stood his ground, tapping the riding crop on his fingertips, lips split and moistened by his furtive tongue.

They heard the jangle of keys heralding the Sheriff's approach. "Somethin' the matter here?" he asked, alarmed by Richard's outburst.

"No, Sheriff," said Richard, "but my brother was just leaving."

The door to the cell swung open. "Think about it, Richard," hissed Jack, as he retreated.

"No!" yelled Richard after the dissipating form. But how could he not?

"What kind of mood's he in? Why, whatever do you mean, Mr. Marshall? I suppose he's in a proper sort of judgin' mood, same as always," allowed Mr. Critch, the Clerk of the Court. For Mr. Critch this was practically baring his soul, and when he realized he'd said anything, even though it was nothing, his upper tooth grabbed its accustomed spot on his lower lip and held firm.

"I'll tell you what kind of mood he's in," boomed Codrington Philip Binghamton, the County Prosecutor, propelling his grand domed frame through the doorway. "He's in a two-drunks-three-runaway-slaves-one-horse-thief-and-a-blasphemer-before-lunch mood, that's what kind of a mood he's in. And if you're not careful, John Marshall, he'll have you thrown in the stocks for impersonating a lawyer!"

"And if you're not careful, Codfish, he'll have you drawn and quartered for refusing to impersonate one!" shot back Marshall. Laughing heartily, the two men shook hands.

"I could do worse," continued Binghamton, wasting a wink on the parsimonious Mr. Critch. "At least I studied a little law on the way to the courthouse." Here, he turned to the Clerk in mock confidence. "I swear on my grandmother's grave, that this here 'Counselor' –" the word drawn out playfully – "spent the whole of his six weeks of legal training doodling the name 'Polly Ambler' in his notes!"

"A fine name it is too, on a par with Blackstone, wouldn't you say?" rejoined Marshall.

"Never would I besmirch Mrs. John Marshall, but still I think more law's to be learned from Blackstone than from your wife."

"Not the law governing me," Marshall answered with a grin. "Besides," he added, "it's your misfortune to have to study the law to know it. I have always known the law; it lies in here," and he thumped his chest.

"Are you sure you've got the correct part of the anatomy, Counselor?" teased Binghamton.

"Objection sustained," replied Marshall, "for the law is a tenant of the mind," and he tapped his squat skull with a crooked index finger.

"You don't mean to imply that the law is logical, do you?"

"No, no more than a cow is cow-like. The law is logic."

Binghamton laughed at his friend's quirky faith. "Well, that may be," he said, "but there's nothing logical about this case."

Marshall became suddenly attentive. "What do you mean, Codrington?"

"I hated to do it, John. I mean, don't get me wrong, I've got enough evidence to convict them twice over, but what of it? We're talking about Randolphs. Why, I've heard from the Attorney General of the United States already – you know, their cousin, Edmund – not to mention the Governor, half the State House, and every judge that ever broke bread with Judge Tucker. So, I could've left it alone, until that fool client of yours went and made a spectacle of himself down on the front steps. Then what could I do?" He shook his large head and looked imploringly at Marshall, seeking absolution for the sin of doing his duty. "Why'd he do it, John?"

Why, indeed? thought Marshall, who merely shrugged his shoulders. Because he's innocent? Or a fool? A well connected fool, at least, and that could prove useful. Marshall felt the heavy weight of expectation descend upon him. Would he be up to the task of doing whatever was necessary to win? He'd better be, if Codfish really had *enough evidence to convict them twice over.* Still, this business of trading on the Randolph name did not sit easy.

"His Honor will see you now relative to the case of Commonwealth versus Randolph," intoned Mr. Critch. "Right this way, gentlemen."

The Clerk led the two attorneys up the spiral stairway with its tapered steps that made treading the inside track treacherous, past the two conference rooms located on either side of the narrow landing, and through the heavy double doors into the courtroom. The high Judge's bench was deserted. Above it hung the portrait of George Washington, the flags of state and country, and the spiders clinging to their webs.

Marshall and Binghamton followed Mr. Critch through an inconspicuous doorway cut flush into the wall to the right of the witness box, that led to the Judge's private chambers. This meant that the Judge had decided that the business to be transacted on the case that day was not of great consequence, and could best be handled informally. As they entered, a servant was just clearing away from Judge Allen's desk some dishes containing the scraps of a meat pie. The Judge touched a napkin to his thin lips. He appeared not to notice their arrival.

"Good afternoon, Judge Allen, I trust you are well?" began Marshall, with forced good humor.

"Well enough," replied the Judge distractedly as he examined a wayward piece of stew meat picked up by the napkin, apparently more concerned with his chin than with the matter at hand.

"Thank-you for granting me such an expeditious audience, Your Honor," cooed Marshall. "I have come to ask you to release the Randolph girl to my recognizance, inasmuch as the jail facilities are totally unsuitable for the housing of a young lady of breeding, and there is no reasonable chance that the young lady will attempt to flee."

"Hmmph," snorted the Judge, "and if she does?"

"You'll have my bond against it."

"Your Honor," interjected Binghamton, "that would be most irregular, since murder, as a capital offense, is not bailable."

"What do you say to that, Mr. Marshall?"

"I'm not asking for bail, Your Honor. Simply deputize me and I'll hold the prisoner on behalf of the Sheriff."

"On what basis?" pressed the Judge.

"Because of the lack of proper county facilities to hold a young woman of gentle birth. It would be cruel and unusual punishment to continue to house her in that windowless storage room in the basement."

The Judge looked singularly unimpressed. "Mr. Binghamton?"

"Your Honor, no matter how 'gentle' her birth may be, Miss Randolph is accused of a brutal crime. For that, she belongs in jail, and no amount –"

"I agree," interjected the Judge impatiently. "The charge is infanticide, which is murder, and therefore not bailable –" but before he could utter another word, the door to his chambers burst open and in came Judge Tucker and Colonel Randolph.

Mr. Critch jumped up to bar the way, but seeing that it was not merely another judge but another judge with a Randolph in tow, he fell back. Judge Allen's demeanor snapped from disdain to obsequiousness. He rose and circled the large desk to warmly greet these uninvited visitors. Their easy banter was peppered with "Henry" and "Arch," but with great deference it was still "Colonel" for Harlan Beauregard Randolph. Within a few moments they were slapping one another's backs and laughing about some great favor the Colonel had done for Arch's pappy.

Mr. Critch, seeing which way the wind was blowing, quickly fetched up chairs for the gentlemen, and they got back to business. "Your fine counsel here, Mr. Marshall, was just presenting a motion for the release of Miss Randolph to his own recognizance," said the Judge, like some schoolboy reciting a lesson for his master. "Says we haven't got a suitable lock-up for her."

"You honor, may I remind you –" interjected Binghamton, but he was cut off with a wave of the Judge's hand.

"What do you think, Colonel?" asked the Judge. Marshall seethed at the way he was being preempted by this pompous man, totally unlearned in the law.

The Colonel took a little carved rosewood box from his waistcoat, and ceremoniously extracted a pinch of snuff between his stained thumb and forefinger, which he thrust up his nostril with a loud snort. Head thus cleared, he began with mock humility. "Arch, it's not for me to say, what with all you fine legal minds workin' it over. I have nothing here but a father's tender concern, as I'm sure you'll understand." Archer Allen, the bachelor, nodded sympathetically. "But without approaching the legal niceties of it, I could say this: that I have it on good authority that this unfortunate situation has helped to focus the attention of the State Assembly on your little problem of inadequate jail and courthouse facilities, and perhaps some funds could be located to help you out down here –" the Colonel cleared his throat – "in the interest of justice, you know."

The Judge studied the Colonel intently. Likewise, Marshall cast a sharp glance towards the Colonel, but like the piano player at the whorehouse, he figured it was his job to keep his mouth shut. Binghamton started to sputter, but knowing he had to get himself reelected in a Randolph-controlled county, he never really hit the mark.

"A Southern gentleman should not be blind to the suffering of a lady, no matter to what depths she has fallen," declared the chivalrous Judge Allen. "Mr. Critch, enter on the docket that the prisoner, Miss Randolph, is to be released to the custody of Mr. Marshall, as special deputy to the county Sheriff. Take a bond for the faithful execution of his duties. Counsel, will there be anything else?"

"No, Your Honor," they replied in unison.

"You'll be ready for trial one week from Monday, on April 29th?"

Marshall, already humiliated by the way in which he had been upstaged by the Colonel's maneuverings, had no mind left to consider that a week was precious little time to prepare. "Yes, Your Honor," he muttered.

"The State will be ready," added Binghamton.

"Good. Good day, gentlemen," said Judge Allen, rising once again and extending his hand, "and may I say Colonel, Henry, it has been a pleasure seeing you here today."

As Marshall paused at the Clerk's desk to pick up a freshly inked copy of the docket entry to present to the Sheriff, and to sign his fidelity bond, he was pulled aside by Binghamton.

"'The law is logic,' indeed! That was a nasty trick, John, and I better not find that you had anything to do with it."

Marshall, tarred by the Colonel's underhanded dealings, yet duty-bound to support the man who had, after all, just snatched victory from defeat, bit down hard. Slowly, he managed to meet Binghamton's accusing stare with a cool look. "I said that the law is logic, Codrington. I never said anything about the players." But as the words dropped from his lips, he felt ashamed.

Chapter 4

Jack's Wrath

I.

The fire burned low in the main hearth of Bizarre that Friday evening, but Judith made no move to fuel it. The dim light deepened shadows cast on the paneled walls by the generous stuffed leather armchairs. Two tall windows, covered in crimson brocatelle, winked like the bloodshot eyes of a drunkard. The house servants had been sent to their quarters, St. George was asleep, Jack was out for a moonlight ride, and Cupid was collapsed in a heap at Judith's feet. Spring was in the air, but to Judith its cherry-blossom scent was a false seduction, so she sat indoors by herself, listening to the pop of the embers and the click of her knitting needles.

She believed in Richard; he was everything she'd ever wanted. Nonetheless, she couldn't help thinking of how things might have been different. Was this a curse for the way she'd treated that Scottish tutor from the University of Edinburgh? Suddenly, across five years and an ocean, she could smell the wool suits he favored that rubbed his neck so red that it matched the tangled shock of hair atop his freckled face. She smiled as her eyes met once more his cornflower blue squint. Yes, he was brilliant, but his shy, pensive brogue made him the clumsiest of conversationalists. Except that time at Cousin Edmund's ball, when he'd found his tongue for her sake. She felt a twinge as she recalled the way she'd treated him. "Only a Randolph is suitable for a Randolph!" she'd said, and though she believed it – believes it still – the words had curdled on her lips when she saw how badly she had hurt him.

"Seen a ghost?" came a voice of indeterminate sex from the foyer, causing her to jump in her seat. It was Jack, back from the stables.

Judith smiled weakly, and resumed her knitting. "No, dear. I've just been thinking back to finer days."

"Weren't they all finer?" Jack asked rhetorically, helping himself to a brandy. "Like the time our two-year old won the Richmond Stakes," he added callously.

Judith pursed her lips. "That's just like you, Jack," she scolded, "all history reduced to a succession of horse races."

"Horse races and cockfights," corrected Jack, settling himself into the yellow silk damask of the large sofa across from Judith. He held up the crystal snifter to the fireplace, and watched the liquor sparkle as it made graceful circles in the air. "I visited Richard this morning," he remarked offhandedly.

"Did you?" exclaimed Judith as she dropped her knitting and sat forward. "Oh, I wish I'd known you were going, I would have sent provisions."

"Why don't you bring them yourself?" asked Jack, pointedly.

"Oh, I know you must think me a faithless wife for not visiting, but I can't bear to see him in such an awful place." She flicked absent-mindedly at the limp, tangled hair covering her pasty cheeks. "Did he seem well to you – I mean," she corrected, in response to Jack's reproachful look, "as well as could be expected?"

Jack took a long swallow from his snifter. "As well as could be expected for a man hell bent on destroying himself."

"Oh dear," cried Judith, alarmed, "whatever do you mean?"

"I mean that he won't do the first thing necessary to protect himself."

"What should he do?" asked Judith.

"Say Nancy had a darkie. She's always been too chummy with 'em anyhow. Once that gets out, no one will listen to a word she says."

Judith's nails dug into the rolled arms of her chair as she recoiled from the horrid image. "But John Randolph," she cried, "that's just not true –" She stopped herself abruptly.

Jack put down his brandy and leaned forward. "You were there," he urged, "what color was it?" Judith averted her eyes. "I don't understand you, Judith," prodded Jack, "how can you protect a sister who would steal away your husband? She has brought it upon herself, and anything you say against her would be simple defense of home and hearth, the right of every married woman." He picked up the snifter and downed the remaining spirits in a single gulp.

The last residue of color drained from Judith's face. "I'll admit I have suffered. But I know from their own lips that they are blameless – both of them. In this is my solace."

"Your solace, or your folly?" sneered Jack. "Do you honestly believe them?"

"I do. I must," she added, clinging to the promises like flotsam in a deluge.

Waving the empty snifter in Judith's face, Jack dashed her illusions. "It doesn't matter what really happened, Judith," he hissed, "who is innocent, who is not. The people are hungry for a sacrifice, and no one will believe the dutiful wife who says that she saw nothing. However, if you do as I suggest – well, people are always eager to believe the worst."

"It matters to me, Jack," protested Judith, her lips trembling. "I can't swear it was colored. It would be my own sister's death warrant."

Jack sprang up and hurled the crystal snifter into the coals where it shattered into a thousand fiery fragments. "Fine, then, hang them both!" he shouted, and strode the length of the parlor, turning with a flourish just under the arching pediment of the doorway. "If I may be so bold as to make a suggestion: do not be overzealous with the truth. Truth is not half as well regarded as people claim. It has killed more good men than lies ever will. And it is not worth dying for."

"Is there anything you would die for, Jack?"

"The last laugh." And he took it with him, echoing into the Bizarre shadows.

2.

Richard awakened Sunday morning refreshed for the first time since his arrest. After a breakfast much enhanced by victuals from home, he took up a quill and a sheet of the family writing paper, robin's-egg blue with the Randolph crest emblazoned at the top. In a steady hand, he wrote a brief note to Judith, signing it "Your faithful husband, Richard." Out of caution he added a postscript: "Destroy this note." Sealing the message carefully with candle wax, he took it to the window where his faithful Syphax, a youthful forty-year-old mulatto passed down from his father, awaited orders from the ground below. "Syphax," he called.

The large, light-skinned servant scrambled nimbly to his feet. "Yassuh?"

"Deliver this note in hand to your mistress. It is important, and must be delivered by you personally directly to Miss Judith. No one is to see it except Miss Judith, understand?"

"Yes, Massa Richard. No one sees it 'cept Miss Judith."

"Right." He paused. "Thank-you," he added, and his servant smiled and looked down at his feet, embarrassed for him.

Richard watched as Syphax mounted Basil, a sweet dappled gelding kept near the jail at Richard's request for the daily correspondence, and plodded down the road towards Bizarre. Richard lingered by the cell window, his attention drawn to a group of children, barefoot in the morning dew, who were reveling in the advent of Spring. "I'm the King!" shouted one little boy. "So what, I'm the President!" replied another. "I'm sending my ships to destroy your ports! Boom, boom go the cannons." "The Redcoats are coming, the Redcoats are coming," shouted several of the children, scattering before the King and his followers. "Patriots to arms!" shouted some others, "scalp 'em and roast the bodies." Then they all began to chant:

> *Cut off their heads like old King Louie,*
> *Chinaman used it to make chop suey,*
> *Salted it 'n said this ain't done yet,*
> *Till we add the head of Marie Antoinette!*

Richard turned away from the grisly field of play. From the sweetest of wombs comes the savage fruit of our love. He thought of his mother, Frances Bland, so gentle, so easily moved to tears by the suffering of any little creature. Thank God she's dead, he thought, thank God she's spared the agony of watching her sons die, one by one. When she died five long years ago he thought no God could let the sun come up again upon a world in which one so fine could die so young. But now he saw the mercy, the hand of God; that it is not in death He is cruel, but in life.

3.

Syphax felt good trotting like a freeman down the open road through the sweet blossomed air. He remembered the parting words of his Mama the day they sold her to the man with the black mustache.

"Remember, son," she'd cried to him, straining against the shackles as the wagon pulled away, "you's an Ashanti warrior." Today, for the few hours between Cumberland and Bizarre, he was free, like an Ashanti warrior.

Suddenly Basil's nostrils flared and he reared his head back, just as a dark-cloaked figure in black boots with a riding crop galloped across the lane directly into their path. "Whoa, steady boy," soothed Syphax, stroking the gelding's neck. He reined him in, and they came to a halt.

The black-booted figure coaxed Damion forward, and fear of the unknown deteriorated into fear of the known. Syphax forced a smile and a nod. Jack regarded him coldly.

"Stealin' a horse, boy?" he spat.

"No suh, Mistuh Jack, doen you know Massa Richard lets me ride Basil?"

With a lightning strike, the riding crop left a welt across Syphax's cheek. "Don't you dare ask me what I know. I know he lets you despoil that fine beast with your black ass from time to time, but I don't know you're out with his permission right now."

"Yessuh. With respect suh –" he near choked on the phrase – "Massa Richard, he ask me to delivah a message to Miss Judith, an' he give me Basil to ride."

"Prove it."

Now Syphax was trapped. Richard had said no one was to see the message but Miss Judith. Well, he figured, it wouldn't harm anything to just give old Jack-ass a quick peek. Slowly, he withdrew the note from the pouch around his neck. "See, Mistuh Jack, dis here's the note." He gave Jack the sweetest smile he could muster.

"That could be any old scrap of paper. Give it to me."

"But Massa Richard said I's to give it straight to Miss Judith. 'No one sees it 'cept a Miss Judith,' dat's jest what he says."

Jack's voice, abnormally high anyway, scraped like train wheels just before impact. "You're not disobeying my direct order, are you boy?" From beneath his waistcoat he produced a dueling pistol, and leveled it straight at Syphax's heart.

"No suh," replied Syphax quickly, and he leaned towards Damion with the paper extended. But just as Jack reached out to take it Syphax expelled a wad of saliva straight into the Thoroughbred's eye, not four inches away. Damion reared up in pain as Jack's pistol discharged. The ball whistled by his ear as Syphax snatched back Richard's note and dug his heels into Basil's belly. As Jack landed on his coat tails in the dirt, he saw slave and mount disappear down the road to Bizarre. Furious, he reloaded and gave chase.

"Oh Lord, Basil, we done it now," yelled Syphax into the terrified gelding's ear. "We ain't got far to Bizarre, but if'n we doen fly Jack-ass gonna shoot me dead, dat's fer sure. Run boy, run!" Syphax plastered himself against the gelding's heaving neck, urging him on, but Basil was past his prime, and soon Syphax glanced back to see a black cloak rounding the bend behind him. Horse and terrified rider thundered down the long straight hill, heading for the half-mile arch through the north pastures leading to the gates. Even if he made it to the gates, Jack would surely get him when he stopped to open them. But perhaps Old Franklin would be there at the gate, and maybe Jack wouldn't kill him in front of a witness, even a black one.

Syphax was strong, but heavy, while Jack was wasted and light and one with his steed. At the bottom of the hill, Syphax could hear the impact of a second set of hooves on the hard-packed dirt. By half-way round the arc of the field, the stones kicked up by Basil were ricocheting off Damion's proud chest, but the stallion didn't care, for he was bred to race. Head methodically thrusting and rising, thrusting and rising, Damion lunged forward as if the breath of life always lay just ahead. Now the distance was closed to three lengths, but the field slipped behind them and they were again in the woods, just shy of the gate.

Just one more bend in the road, thought Syphax, Franklin you old coot I love you, as Jack pulled his pistol and tried to aim against the furious jarring of two galloping steeds. There! The gates! Syphax's heart leapt and sank all at once, for it was deserted and closed. He rode right past it as the shot rang out. Basil gave out a terrified cry as he collapsed, the ball searing his hindquarters. Syphax was thrown into the bramble, as Damion tried and failed to avoid the fallen gelding. Down went Damion, down went Jack, who landed with a crack and was still.

Bruised and bleeding, Syphax ran towards the great house of Bizarre.

4.

"Miss Judith, Miss Judith, come quick, dere's been a accident, come quick!"

Judith was in the nursery, trying to coax something intelligible out of St. George's babblings. The gibberish of other fourteen month olds was almost intelligible, but St. George's efforts amounted to no more than inchoate grunts, at times startling in their intensity, but never vaguely like English – indeed, rarely even sounding human. This strange child worried Judith, but for now she put it out of her mind, handing him off to his wet nurse. "What happened, Syphax? Has some one been hurt?"

"It's Mistuh Jack, M'am, he an' Damion gone down out by da gate."

"Jack fell off a horse?" exclaimed Judith incredulously. She'd sooner believe a horsefly fell off a horse.

Syphax was not inclined to elaborate. He just nodded, figuring he'd done his part and any further delay would simply make Jack that much deader when they got back. The blood on Syphax's face and his torn clothes simply escaped Judith's attention in the rush of the moment, accustomed as she was to looking past the colored help. Richard would have noticed, thought Syphax, but not this 'un.

"All right," said Judith, springing into action, "Syphax, tell Junior to saddle up Smart Boy and ride for the doctor. I'll get Georgeanne to fetch some bandages and laudanum. Meet me by the front stairs as soon as you can with a gig and take me to where he fell. Oh dear," said Judith, the impact beginning to be felt, "I do hope he's not hurt too badly."

"Me neither, M'am," said Syphax. *Just dead.*

They went off to carry out their tasks, and the household hummed in anticipation of tragedy. "We's closer to Heaven now, Syphax," said Junior as he saddled up Smart Boy and Syphax hitched Sally to the gig. "'There the wicked cease from troublin', and there the weary be at rest,' says Job."

But Syphax was a skeptic. "I ain't 'spectin' no rest outa this. You 'n me's gonna be out there diggin' a hole for him, and draggin' some slab o' rock half a mile to mark the spot, just wait and see." He paused thoughtfully. "But anyhow, if'n he's dead, mebbe dat Christ God the white folks is always squalkin' about ain't so bad after all."

Syphax spat for emphasis, and with a "Giy on!" he trotted smartly to the front stairs to pick up Miss Judith. She was waiting anxiously with a basket of wet towels, and as soon as the wagon pulled up she sprang aboard next to Syphax without waiting for assistance. Nothing like trouble to bring the races together, thought Syphax. He flicked the reins hard and they were off with a lurch and a shower of pebbles.

It was only as the gates loomed into view that Syphax began to get a queasy feeling in his stomach. Suddenly the euphoria of the escape wore off, and he was back in the zone of danger, again the quarry of a hunter unbounded by any law. Naw, he thought, shaking it off, dat boy's down and out, and even if he ain't dead he sure ain't in no shape to make trouble now.

Syphax sprang down and opened the gates, peering into the late afternoon shadows. He could barely make out the form of a fallen horse, indistinct in the distance. All was quiet. "Let's go, Syphax!" said Miss Judith, breaking the silence, and as Syphax took the reins of the gig he was relieved to see Junior ride up beside them. Safety in numbers, he thought.

Syphax urged the mare forward through the gates and down the lane. As they approached the dark shape on the ground, Sally spooked and began shying away, emitting little strained whinnies and snorts in defiance of the scent-blind masters egging her on into the death smell. After a few more reluctant steps she just stopped, and Syphax could tell that further prodding would be futile. "She's a sweet Bay, Miss Judith, she'll stay put, but we cain't ask no more from her," said Syphax, setting the brake and dismounting. Junior followed on foot, leading Smart Boy. It was quiet, too quiet.

"Ohhh," said Syphax, for he saw that the dark shape was Basil, dead on the ground, shot in the rump. He scanned the area for Jack, thinking maybe he'd dragged himself into the bushes. No Jack. No Damion. No sound. *No Jack.* Then he saw it. A red hole behind Basil's ear. He was shot in the rump, and again behind the ear. *Again behind the ear!* Jack was up, and armed.

Syphax froze for only a moment, but it was a moment too long. He felt the barrel of the pistol against the back of his neck. "Down on yer knees, nigger, and prepare to die," in that sing-song, sickly sweet, unmistakable voice, the voice of a fevered child.

"Jack, no!" screamed Judith, as Syphax heard the hammer click into firing position.

"On your knees," Jack repeated firmly.

Syphax's head reeled, his body tense as a bear trap, but he could never kneel for this bastard. He could barely make his thick tongue work, but he peeled it off the roof of his mouth to choke out what he had to say. "You wanna kill me, Mistuh Jack, den you kill me standin', cause by killin' me you set me free, an' a free man doen kneel to nobody."

Jack paused, then laughed. "Disobedient to the end, eh boy? What good are you?" And he pulled the trigger.

The discharge blew Syphax right over on his face in the muck by the side of the road. Judith screamed, Sally reared back, Smart Boy bolted, Junior doubled over trying to contain his rage without attacking Jack and earning a quick trip to the gallows. Then Junior ran to his fallen friend, turning him over gently, brushing away the muddy blood.

Syphax opened his eyes and saw Junior jump back in fright. His head was spinning, his neck burned, and he smeared some cool mud on it. There, miles above him, was Jack, laughing. "I used the last ball on Basil, nigger boy, so I guess this is your lucky day." He bent over and plucked the robin's egg blue note from Syphax's pouch, folded it into his wallet, and turned to leave.

Syphax felt the anger well up in him, powerful and uncontrollable, the anger that he'd felt as a young man when he'd seen over and over again that he and the people he loved weren't worth shit in the white man's world, the anger he'd repressed time after time at every *boy* and *nigger* and *Massa* and lashing and a thousand other indignities small and large, spoken and unspoken, breathed, looked, felt, dreamed, tasted, till his own soul, that last reserve of dignity that he'd thought too private and too deep to be touched, was stained. The anger was too powerful now, he couldn't repress it, he didn't care what happened, he was going to strangle Jack Randolph, a white man, right now with his bare hands. With all his strength and fury he pressed upward, but the world spun around his head and he fell back. Flat on his back, the treetops swirling above, his anger gave way to unfathomable sadness. He was alive, a slave again. He began to cry, softly, so only Junior noticed. They cried together.

Chapter 5

Deeper into the Maze

I.

Monday morning never dawned, but poured out torrents of rain in place of sunlight. Through it all in his covered phaeton came John Marshall, heading down the hill towards the jail from the direction of Richmond. Richard, wet from watching for him, turned to his cell door in anticipation.

"Mr. Marshall, how do you do?" said Richard brightly, as the Sheriff admitted his lawyer. Before Marshall stood a young man of twenty-three, whose dark complexion, dark eyes, straight black hair, and high cheekbones carried the kiss of distant kinship to Pocahontas. The only imperfection was the slight weakness of his chin. *It is that chin that may save him,* thought Marshall, *for it softens his face and makes him worthy of pity.*

"Quite well, thank-you, Mr. Randolph. I hope you received my note, and once again please accept my apologies for not seeing you sooner. I would have come last Friday, but one thing led to another –"

"Rather brilliantly, I hear. No need to apologize, Mr. Marshall. I am most impressed." Marshall held his tongue. *Was it his fault that laurels were being heaped upon him for the machinations of the Colonel?*

"Please, be seated." Richard motioned him into one of the rough hewn chairs in the cell, and took the other. "For Nancy's release, I am deeply in your debt, Sir," said Richard. "For myself, it matters little what happens. After all, I did challenge the authorities to try me, although I could hardly expect that they would abuse a gentleman in this manner. But as for the lady –" here Richard paused, at a loss for words – "that they would stoop to making a prisoner of her, my God, it is inconceivable!"

This speech, like the one Nancy had made on behalf of Richard, was delivered with such transparent devotion that Marshall began to fear the truth of the allegations. "Mr. Randolph," he said, "before we discuss your case, my professional obligations require me to ask whether, in your mind, you believe there to be any divergence between Miss Nancy's interests and your own."

Richard paused, measuring his response. "I am not sure that I understand what you mean. What could be the nature of such a divergence of interests?"

"The most serious would be some fact which could be damaging to one of you at the expense of the other. This could take the form of evidence for or against Miss Nancy, or evidence for or against yourself."

Richard focused just beyond Marshall and said, "There is nothing."

"Are you sure?" probed Marshall, disquieted. "It is essential that you be completely candid with me now."

"You may be assured, Mr. Marshall, that Miss Nancy and I are as one in this matter."

"Very well," said Marshall, with a growing conviction that Richard was hiding something, "if you'll have me, I'll take your case." But as Marshall asked the first routine questions, he could not help but wonder whether his need for this case was blinding him to his own misgivings. He put the thought aside to focus on his client's story.

"I'm afraid that if this year is to be my last, my life won't be remembered much afterwards," Richard was saying. "I was born in a snowstorm in the month of January, 1770, eldest son of John Randolph of Matoax and Frances Bland Randolph. In that lineage were reunited two strands of the blood of William of Turkey Island, making me doubly a Randolph." Richard thrust his little chin out as far as possible, clinging to lost pride. "A year after I was born came my brother Theo, to whom I was very close, and then Jack, who was born on a hot day in June, 1773. Like most boys, our primary play for our first ten years was beating each other mercilessly, and as the eldest I always fared well. Theo could hold his own, but Jack couldn't, and he soon withdrew from our close circle." Marshall thought he detected a note of regret in Richard's voice.

"Relatively speaking, of course, we were well off, but a secure early childhood was not to be my lot. Momma's next child was premature and soon died, and then, thirteen days later, Father died too. That was October 28, 1775. I still remember the funeral, hiding in my mother's skirts, terrified, watching Uncle Ryland, who was drunk or worse, wailing that this was the first time childbirth had ever killed the father." Richard rose and crossed the few steps to the window.

"Then the War began in earnest, and though at first, like most of Virginia, we were untouched, as it dragged on the privations increased and it drew closer. You may recall that Benedict Arnold invaded Richmond in December, 1780, and by the next May he and Cornwallis converged practically on our doorstep. I remember well being awakened in the middle of the night and bundled off in a carriage. As we sped through the dark towards Bizarre, my nose pressed to the window, I was unsure whether to be more afraid of the Traitor Arnold or my Uncle Ryland, whom I'd last seen pissing behind the gravestones at my father's funeral."

Marshall remembered that shameful time in Virginia's history all too well. When Benedict Arnold marched on the State Capitol it fell without a fight. Advance warning had reached Governor Jefferson, who chose to scamper home to the safety of Carter's Mountain, tail between his legs. To this day Marshall could not forgive Mr. Jefferson for spending much of the Revolution at Monticello hobnobbing with British officers, while he and his fellow soldiers exchanged deadly grapeshot with the Redcoats.

"My mother," said Richard, "was a woman of great beauty and intelligence, yet even that pales beside her kindness. One of my earliest recollections is of riding with her some fifty miles by carriage to rescue a runaway slave from the cruelty of our overseer. She was, and must now truly be, an angel." Richard paused, holding back a tear.

"During the war, in September, 1778, mother married the eminent Bermudan jurist, Henry St. George Tucker, with whom you are acquainted. Judge Tucker has been a true father to me, a kindness which, I fear, I have repaid by bringing scandal to his doorstep." The sorrow burst forth, and Richard collapsed in the splintery chair.

Marshall gave him but a moment to collect himself. "Mr. Randolph, please focus on Glenlyvar, last October. I need your complete candor."

Richard rose and returned to the window. "Nothing happened, Mr. Marshall. Servants gossip, people gossip, that is all."

"You are trained in the law, are you not, Mr. Randolph?" asked Marshall, though he already knew it to be so.

"What of it?"

"Then you must know that a trial is a sort of battle, and we need every piece of ammunition we can lay hands on."

"Ah, yes," said Richard, turning back with an air of disdain. "I have never practiced my profession. I am a private and peaceable man, and I value honor; as you say, the law requires quite different arts, with which I am sure you are familiar." Marshall did not flinch. "Still," continued Richard, more to himself than to his lawyer, "before these events, there had been talk of a political career. Alas, that is all gone by, and whatsoever I may yet accomplish must be done in other ways."

Richard sat heavily once again, pondering his future, the weight of his changed fate bearing down on his shoulders. From outside the bars, came the sound of the children, taunting and fighting and laughing, tender and cruel all at once. Then a deep, resonant voice wafted in, singing:

Sun, you be here and I'll be gone
Sun, you be here and I'll be gone
Sun, you be here and I'll be gone
Bye, bye, don't grieve after me
Won't give you my place, not for yours
Bye, bye, don't grieve after me
Cause you be here and I'll be gone.

Their dark eyes locked. Richard reached across the table, took Marshall's hand and squeezed hard, searching for grace in Marshall's gaze, but finding only its closest legal counterpart, equity. "You must know that I am not guilty of the charges against me," he said at last.

"Excellent," said Marshall. "Now tell me exactly what happened that night."

Richard released his grip, jumped up and began pacing the cell as the story poured forth. "You've heard the rumors no doubt, but what really happened is nothing like what they say. Judith, Nancy, and I, along with our cousin Mr. Cedric Randolph, embarked early that morning by carriage to pay a visit on our old family friends, Mary and Grant Harrison of Glenlyvar. The carriage ride was uneventful, if somewhat unpleasant due to the rough roads. By the time we arrived, just before dinner, we were all thoroughly shaken, as well as chilled to the marrow owing to an unseasonable cold snap. Nancy had her greatcoat wrapped tightly around her, and a foot stove beneath her, but nonetheless she was feeling the worse for the trip.

"Upon our arrival we were greeted by the Harrisons and shown into Glenlyvar, their cramped little country cottage."

Probably no smaller than my house, thought Marshall.

"Nancy immediately complained that she felt unwell, and she lay down briefly on a settee in the foyer. Then she went off to bed before dinner."

"Were you concerned, at that point?"

"Concerned?" echoed Richard, trying to get the measure of where the question was headed. "No, not at all, for Nancy had often been subject to fits of colic."

"All right," said Marshall, "please continue."

"We had a fine dinner, stewed rabbit I think it was, lots of wine and good cheer all around. Grant Harrison, though a bit gruff, is full of fascinating stories of the frontier from his days as a surveyor in the Ohio territory. The three of us – Grant, Cedric and myself – spent a few hours talking after dinner, and what the ladies did I couldn't tell you; perhaps fussed over the Harrisons' baby girl. We retired around ten o'clock, Cedric and the Harrisons downstairs, along with a white housekeeper named Mrs. Woods, and Judith and I upstairs, just outside Nancy's chamber."

"What do you mean, just outside Nancy's chamber?"

"The stairs led directly to the door of the chamber that I occupied with Judith, and directly opposite was another door inside our chamber, that led to Nancy's chamber."

"Were there any windows in either chamber?"

"Her chamber had a window."

"So anything that went into or out of Nancy's chamber had either to go through your chamber, or through her window?"

"Nothing could go through her window because it was covered over with tanned hide, nailed firmly in place."

"Excellent," said Marshall. "Continue your account."

"I'm afraid you won't think it sufficiently dramatic. Shortly after we retired, we were awakened by cries coming from Nancy's room. Judith asked me to see what was the matter, and when I did so I found Nancy in the throws of an hysterical fit. I sent Jenna – that's Nancy's girl – for a pitcher of water and some rags, and when she returned I tried to sooth her with them. She was complaining of stomach cramps and a headache. I sent Jenna for some laudanum, and she returned with Mrs. Harrison and the medicine. I took the laudanum from Mrs. Harrison, administered it to Nancy, and sat with her until the combined effects of the medication and exhaustion permitted her to sleep. I then returned to my dear wife in the outer chamber, found her awake and concerned, allayed her fears by reporting that Nancy was now resting peacefully, and we went to sleep."

Marshall weighed the story in his mind. Was its slickness due to fabrication, or merely frequency of repetition?

"The next day Nancy was somewhat better, though still quite weak. She rested all that day and the next, and by Thursday, October 4th, she was up and about. We were able to bring her home to Bizarre on Friday, and within two weeks she was her usual horseback-riding, dancing, vibrant self. A few days after that, however, we were stunned to hear that some of the slaves had created an adulterous birth from this innocent malady, and even more aghast that the slander was being repeated by respectable people. The accusations have grown more vociferous ever since, till the latest has me dashing the poor bastard's brains out, and drinking its blood. Needless to say, I do not dignify this with a response."

"Do you deny that there was a baby born that night?" asked Marshall, aiming for the heart of the matter.

"I do," replied Richard, without hesitation.

"And you will so swear in a Court of Law?" pressed Marshall.

"Just a minute," said Richard, looking alarmed. "I know my rights. I cannot testify."

"More precisely," said Marshall, "you cannot be compelled to testify against yourself, but there is no reason that you may not voluntarily testify in your own defense."

"I cannot."

Marshall had feared as much. "Why not?"

"I cannot say."

Marshall rose ominously. "Then I cannot help you, and you will hang for ministering to a sick sister."

"Perhaps," was all Richard said.

Marshall bristled at the insolence of this child of privilege, secure even in this bleak gaol that family and money would protect him. "Don't be a fool," thundered Marshall, trying to startle this foundling out of his romantic notions of duty, but feeling genuine anger tincture his calculations. "You are young, and death lasts forever."

"I have faith," replied Richard, his voice quavering.

"Then you need a minister, not a lawyer," snapped Marshall. "Tell me the truth, and I can help you. Otherwise, I must go." It was a bluff, and he prayed it would not be called. But Richard said nothing, so Marshall had no choice but to stand and call for the Sheriff, who came jangling over to unlock the door.

At the last moment, Richard pulled Marshall aside. "You need to know only one thing," he whispered fervently, "neither Nancy nor I am guilty of the charges against us. That is the truth. The rest is our own affair. There are no saints in this world, but I've studied enough law to know that what it requires is not innocence, but the absence of guilt. We are not guilty. Will you judge us, or defend us?"

Marshall studied Richard's too handsome face, trying to read it for sincerity. It was the weak chin that pulled him in – how could such a face hide a cold-blooded killer?

"Defend you, damn it." But how to do it, he could not fathom.

2.

Syphax awoke in the slave quarters between the stables and the pig pen, an area aptly known as 'Mudtown'. His neck stung, his ear was ringing, and his cuts and bruises throbbed, but his first thought was anguish over losing the note to Jack. He had never known Richard to resort to the lash, but for such a failure he would have to impose some form of punishment. Might he be sent to the fields? Syphax shuddered, imagining the rest of his years consumed in the crippling monotony of the fields. He'd have to get that note back. But how?

Painfully, Syphax rose from the damp straw pallet on which he had collapsed, put on a heavy cloak, and ventured out into the rain. Mudtown was awash in its namesake, a perfect spot for the pigs rooting freely about. Syphax saw smoke coming from the chimney in the front shack, so he went in. There, sitting in a chair by the stove, wrapped in a blanket, was Jedidiah, the oldest slave at Bizarre. He had a pipe whittled out of a corncob stuck where his teeth used to be, and he was smoking and humming and staring with his useless eyes into some other world.

"Set yerself down, Syphax," said Jedidiah. Syphax always wondered how he did it; he'd hear you right through his humming and smell you right through his smoke quicker than a hawk could spot a rabbit. Maybe he used the hum and the smoke instead of eyes, part bat, part squid. Syphax sat.

"I hear you had a run-in wi' Jack-Ass yessaday," said Jedidiah.

Yesterday? He'd been out cold an entire day? "I guess so."

"What fer?"

The heat from the stove was making Syphax's neck burn even more, so he pushed his chair back. "Fer not showin' him a note Richard give me to delivah to Miss Judith." And he told Jedidiah the whole story, from when he first got the note till when he landed on his face in the mud.

"Hmph," was all Jedidiah said, and he looked like he was swallowing his whole face as he sucked on his pipe and furrowed his brow in thought. "Smoke?"

"Doen mind if I do," said Syphax, who rarely got to use the luxury weed for which his people broke their backs. Somehow Jedidiah always had a supply. Folks said old Ryland left it to him in his will. Syphax packed a cob with care, then withdrew a faggot from the stove and lit up, blowing great puffs that tickled his nose and relaxed his mind. He put his feet up on another chair, and began to feel good for the first time since his run in with Jack.

"You still got dat note?" asked Jedidiah.

"Naw, Jack got it."

"What'd it say?"

"I doen know. I cain't read."

"I kin read, but I cain't see," said Jedidiah, and they shared a short laugh. Then Jedidiah fixed his eyes about where he figured Syphax to be, and said, "What you care 'bout dis stuff fer? Dat's white man's business. Doen go stickin' yer neck out fer no white man, never, y'hear?"

"I doen know," said Syphax, "Richard's been good ta me, an' before that his father John was my friend."

"Yo frien'," said Jedidiah, his voice filled with scorn. "You ain't got no white frien's. No colored man's got no white frien's." He paused, nursing bitter memories.

"Anyhow, I wanna get that note back."

Jedidiah snorted. "What you gonna do? Say hey, Mistuh Jack-Ass, Sir, kin I please have dat note back?" The old man cackled at the thought of it.

"I dunno," said Syphax. "What you think I oughta do, Jedidiah?"

Jeddidiah's nicotine spit sizzled against the stove. "Nothin'. Jest go back to Richard an' tell him what happened. He wants dat note so bad, let him figure it."

Syphax finished his pipe, then dragged his battered body back out into the rain. That's right, he thought, what business of his was it? He'd done all a man in his place could do. More even. Risked his burning neck. He looked around at the patchwork timber scraps slapped into tumble down shacks, with their leaky grass roofs, dirt floors, and the perpetual oozing earth all around no better than slops in the sty. Then he looked up to the Great House, the embodiment of elegance and permanence, hewn from oak and chestnut, nestled gently between flowering fruit trees and carefully terraced gardens, atop broad sloping lawns.

Syphax knew Jedidiah was right, just as sure as he knew he'd be finding a way to get that note back.

3.

It was past nine on Monday, just one week from the trial date, when Marshall slogged into the entry way of his modest clapboard colonial on Richmond's respectable State Street, a block up from the new capitol and three from the James. The familiar clutter of their small parlor was a welcome sight after the rutted miles of dark rain. Marshall flung off his cloak and grabbed at one muddy boot which slipped off easily and then at the other which didn't, so he found himself hopping in circles on one stocking foot in the general direction of the sofa, which caught him just behind the knee knocking him into its threadbare lap just as the boot jumped free.

"Have some okra soup before you kill yourself," said the stern figure in a high-collared flannel nightgown watching through the low doorway of the dining room. But no matter how hard she tried, Polly's severity lacked its accustomed bite when addressing her husband. Two lovebirds, Polly and John, neither had loved another nor ever would. They were married in Richmond on January 3, 1783, he at the age of 27 and she only 17, yet by then they'd already been in love three years. With her large nose, full lips, fleshy cheeks, and the mole behind her ear sprouting hair a shade darker than the sensibly cropped straight brown hair on her head, Polly had been grateful for John's attention, and clung tight in a maternal way. Yet much of the nurturing had been sucked from her just two summers before, when they'd lost five-month-old John Jr. to the pox, followed in a matter of weeks by Rebecca, gobbled up by fever in the song of her third year. Since then Polly had carried the weight of shattered hopes everywhere she went, and it was only John's tender devotion and florid poetry that held her back from the abyss.

"Not yet, Polly," said John, pulling himself up from the sofa. "I'm afraid there's more work to be done tonight."

"Oh no, Cookie, so late?" 'Cookie' was her private name for him, an affectionate diminutive for 'Lord Coke,' the famous Seventeenth Century British jurist and philanderer, whose name was pronounced in accordance with the epigram it engendered, 'if there's a bun in the oven, there's been a cook in the house.' Marshall had been distressingly fond of quoting him during their courtship, and Polly had chided him gently with the sobriquet which, strengthened by the variant 'Polly wants a Cookie,' had stuck.

"Yes, I'm afraid so. If something good's to come of this case, it'll only come from me turning it upside down and giving it a good shake. Tomorrow I'll have to head for Bizarre, and then to Glenlyvar, so I may be gone for a few days. Before I go, however, I need to hear what Miss Randolph has to say, so we'd better get her down here."

"What do we have to have her here for at all, that's what I'd like to know?" fumed Polly. "Were you daft, dragging home a criminal for me to wait on?" She crossed to the sofa and pleaded, "Let's send her back, Cookie. Think of the children."

"Now, dear Polly," replied Marshall in that especially calm manner that drove her wild, "I need this case. *We* need it, Polly. This is the kind of case that makes a man. Besides which," he added, playing to her piety, "remember what Reverend Jenkins said in his sermon yesterday: 'Judge not, lest thou shalt be judged.'"

"The Bible also teaches that we must cast out the devil in our midst," retorted Polly, never to be outdone on quoting scripture. "How are we to do that, if we cannot judge him? Or her."

"Her?" came a soft voice from the stairway. It was Nancy, looking more angelic than diabolical in a casual chemise with her long hair hastily pinned back. "Surely you don't mean me, Mrs. Marshall?"

"Miss Randolph," said Marshall, rising –

"Don't get up, Sir," she interrupted, waving him off, "I'll leave tonight. I'd rather sleep in a prison where I'm welcome than on silk sheets where I'm not."

Marshall caught Polly by the elbow and half dragged her around the sofa towards Nancy. "Miss Randolph, I'm sure my wife did not mean –"

"Not that I don't understand, Mrs. Marshall," interrupted Nancy. "I wouldn't have me, either!" And she went to grab a shawl from the entryway.

"Polly?" said Marshall, wrenching her elbow slightly in an effort to squeeze out some ameliorative phrases. But he was lucky to get only a silent glare, before she pulled her arm free and retreated upstairs in a huff.

Marshall placed himself across the doorway. "Miss Randolph, please accept my deepest apologies for my wife's behavior. She has a good heart, but it has been sorely tried, and she can be difficult. Please, you say that you understand; if so, you will forgive her, and stay." Nancy pondered this with her eyes lowered, until he raised her chin with one hand so that she met his gaze. He watched as the resolve drained from her features, leaving an exhausted shell. "Besides," he said, taking her arm and leading her back towards the fire, "it is raining and dark, and there is no place out there for a lady of breeding."

She relaxed on his arm, and he lowered her into a warm chair by the hearth. Marshall sat across from her on the sofa.

"How is Richard faring in that awful jail, Mr. Marshall?"

"He is faring well," lied Marshall.

Nancy scrutinized him for a moment, then turned sadly away. "No he's not, but thank-you. I must ..." she stopped herself suddenly.

"You must what?" asked Marshall.

"Oh, nothing," said Nancy, giving him a quick smile.

"You must do nothing, Miss Randolph, but trust in me and tell me everything. Is that clear?"

"Yes, of course, Mr. Marshall, I understand."

"Excellent," said Marshall. "Could you answer some questions for me tonight, or are you too tired?"

"All right," she said, sitting up and smiling.

"When did you leave your father's home?"

"In '91. I was sixteen. You probably know about Miss Harvie."

"You mean the second Mrs. Harlan Beauregard Randolph?"

"I mean Miss Harvie," she repeated, unwilling to dignify her step-mother with her mother's title.

"What about Miss Harvie?" prodded Marshall.

"She was jealous of me, and very possessive of the attentions of my father, as if I were interested in them! One day I caught her abusing my old Nanny, berating her because her corselets didn't come out stiff enough, and I'm afraid I said something rather obscene to her. She came after me, but it was she who ended up with a black eye!"

"My dear Miss Randolph, this is horrible!"

"Oh no, Mr. Marshall, I assure you, it was wonderful. Haven't there been certain times, with certain people, where you've wished you could have done the same?"

"Definitely not," replied Marshall, pushing the name Jefferson out of his mind. "And even if I had, well, this is not what we expect from a lady."

"Gabriella's no lady," replied Nancy, oblivious to the alternate implication.

"Tell me about life at Bizarre," prodded Marshall, eager to press forward.

"Oh, it was so much fun at first, Mr. Marshall," she cried with youthful glee, "you can't imagine it against the gloom that hangs there now. The brothers were outrageous. Richard was robust, gallant, and exceedingly witty; Theo was frail, tender, bright and sweet; and Jack was Jack, funny, smart, nasty as an adder. We performed plays, pageants, created whole worlds together, Judith, the brothers, cousin Cedric and I, and for that one summer I really felt alive."

Nancy's exuberance died with the fire. Marshall crossed between her and the hearth, seized the large brass poker, and began stabbing at the coals beneath the andirons. "I'd like to put this as delicately as possible, but it's something that I must enquire into, Miss Randolph," he began, watching the sparks shooting towards the flue. "As a young woman of some means, and, ahem, beauty, I might add, out on your own, I suspect that you attracted a certain amount of attention from young men." Having said it, he turned to face her, casting a flickering shadow across her face.

"Yes, I suppose I did."

"From what quarters, may I ask?"

"I'd rather you wouldn't." Nancy shifted in what seemed like embarrassment.

"But I must, Miss Randolph. The allegations are crimes of the heart, and they force this indelicacy upon us."

Nancy sat still for a long time. At last she took a quick breath and said, "I was the object of the attentions of my cousin, Cedric Randolph, and of Mr. Jack Randolph."

"Can you tell me something more of this?" Marshall prodded.

"Cedric was," she tasted the air for just the right description, "Cedric." Marshall's unenlightened eyebrows shot up. "I'm sorry," added Nancy. "Cedric is the son of my Aunt Jane. He's blond and sweet with a face that will be lovely if his pimples ever clear up. He's not very grown-up, I'm afraid. He thought he loved me, but I think he loved mostly himself. He brought me flowers by the armload. Perhaps I led him on too much, for fear of hurting him, or," she added with a flippant smile, "for love of flowers. Anyway, I never took him seriously."

Nancy paused, and Marshall took the opportunity to add a log to the fire. As the room darkened before it caught, Nancy's expression turned cold. "Unfortunately, during this same time period, Jack had been pressing his unwanted attentions on me, both in person and in a series of increasingly impertinent letters."

"Do you still have any of the letters?"

"No. I burned them in disgust."

"A pity. Go on."

"I spoke to Theo and Richard of the annoyance, and together we devised a rather elaborate scheme to dissuade Jack. Under the pretense of pursuing a course of study in the law with his cousin Edmund, Jack had gone up North on a binge of mortification of the flesh – you know, bourbon, poker, ladies of the night." Marshall blushed. "Richard wrote to him there, and told him that Theo had a prior claim on my affections, and that brotherly consideration counseled that he desist."

"And was this so?" asked Marshall.

"Theo and I?" laughed Nancy. "He was my friend, Mr. Marshall, not my suitor. We shared true friendship, something too rare between men and women, don't you think?" She smiled coyly.

"Perhaps, Miss Randolph," said Marshall, avoiding the flirtation though his pulse quickened. "So how did Jack respond to Richard's letter?"

"The honorable course upon receiving such a communication is obvious. Jack did the opposite. I was visiting Monticello when he showed up on the doorstep, making no pretense whatsoever that his object was anything other than to woo me. Suddenly I found myself pinioned by Jack against a pillar on the west portico, under a harvest moon. I prepared myself for the inevitable stream of sweet nothings that unimaginative men feel obliged to recite on such occasions, but instead there spewed from his lips the most vile calumnies imaginable. And whom do you suppose to have been the object of his scorn? Why, none other than Theo, and Richard too, both of whom I knew from experience to be far better men than he.

"The disparagement of his brothers, his stormy passions, his selfishness, his dissolute air, all combined to render his attentions most disagreeable, and I told him so in the clearest possible way. He then affected a martyrdom, claiming great reluctance at the disclosures he had made, and that he was simply trying to protect me."

"When did Jack make these advances?"

"This was in the late autumn of '91."

"And has he pressed his attentions upon you since that time?"

"He's tried. But Richard –" She stopped herself.

"Yes?" coaxed Marshall, but Nancy was saved from any further examination by Polly's abrupt entrance.

"Cookie?" mewled Polly, a dwindling taper illuminating her night-cap. "It is time for bed." As if on cue, Marshall's prize Swiss cuckoo commenced chiming eleven o'clock.

"Perhaps, Miss Randolph, I ask too much of you to go through all this old heartbreak at so late an hour."

"I am rather tired," said Nancy, looking down to conceal a smile.

"That's fine. Go ahead up to bed, and we'll talk more tomorrow morning, before I leave for Bizarre."

"Oh, you're going to Bizarre?" said Nancy, brightening a little. "Would you do me a great favor, Mr. Marshall?" she asked, laying a soft hand on his forearm.

"Cookie?" insisted Polly.

"Just a minute!" cried Marshall, instantly regretting the sharpness of his tone.

"Oh, I'm sorry, Mr. Marshall," said Nancy, rising.

"Nonsense," said Marshall, rising with her like a puppy to a biscuit. "Anything, dear girl."

"Would you please have Judith send my girl Jenna here with some more of my clothes? I want to look my best next week. I'll write a note specifying the items that I want, and give it to you in the morning."

"Certainly, Miss Randolph. And, by chance, could one of those items be the greatcoat you wore to Glenlyvar last October 1st?"

"I doubt the weather will be cold enough for that, Mr. Marshall."

"That's all right. Just humor me and send for it anyway. Would you do that?"

"If you wish."

"Thank-you."

Nancy turned for the stairway. "By the way," called Marshall, "where was that coat made?"

"Why, in Paris, of course," said Nancy.

"Of course," said Marshall, half to himself, already deep in thought. "I'll be right along, Polly dear," he added distractedly. Recognizing the tone, Polly gave up on him, instead content to herd Nancy up the stairs before her. As tongues of flame danced and then dwindled to embers behind Marshall's fingertips, a defense began to take shape in his mind. "Of course," he echoed, as the cuckoo chimed midnight.

– CHAPTER 6 –

GUM GUIACUM

I.

Tuesday morning at the Marshall residence was no more chaotic than any other non-Sabbath morning, so a stampede of wild horses might have been noticed. The Marshalls' eight-year-old son was teaching his younger brother a very important if not entirely painless 'lesson', accompanied by war whoops. When the lesson at last abated, the younger took up the refrain of a tuneless and incoherent song, which he sang over and over, delighting more in each repetition, until at last his elder brother could take no more and attempted to silence him with a hand clasped firmly over his mouth and nose. Simultaneously, the baby upset her oatmeal, but she was crying for unknown reasons, since upsetting her oatmeal was usually a source of delight to her. Polly was trying to quiet the baby, quell the fight, prepare breakfast, coordinate the activities of their house girl, and help John pack for the journey to Bizarre. Clearly, she was outnumbered.

"Allow me to give you a hand, Mrs. Marshall," said Nancy, and without awaiting a reply she had a rag in hand and was wiping up the oatmeal. Polly tensed as Nancy picked up the baby, but relaxed somewhat when she saw how expertly Nancy cleaned her and quieted her with soft coos and nuzzles. Placing her back gently in her high chair, Nancy said, "I think she had some hot cereal on her," and she rinsed the rag in cold water and returned to dab at a red spot on the baby's leg. Happily, the baby teased the remaining oatmeal from her fingers into Nancy's hair.

Marshall and Nancy needed to talk, but the setting was hardly conducive to a frank dialogue between attorney and client in a case of murder, so they adjourned to the study. Marshall drew the door closed on his eight-year-old's warning that "if your eyes get gouged out and thrown away, you spend the rest of your life looking at the inside of a wastebin." "Whew!" said Marshall, turning towards Nancy, "I do apologize, Miss Randolph."

"Mr. Marshall," she replied warmly, "I think they're adorable. You and Polly are truly blessed."

Truly blessed. We were blessed by little Rebecca, too, thought Marshall, seeing once again the terror of a child without hope. *We are cursed, we are blessed, all in a single breath.* "Thank-you, Miss Randolph, it's very kind of you to say so. Indeed, if the jury could have seen the way you handled little Mary in there, this whole nasty business would be over in a flash, I'm quite sure."

"I've had a lot of practice recently," said Nancy, and when she saw that this drew a look of distress, she added, "with my nephew, St. George, dear child of Judith and Richard."

"Ah, yes, St. George, of course."

"Why, Mr. Marshall, you didn't think I meant –"

"Of course not, my dear," said Marshall, flustered and at the same time cursing this girl's capacity to bewilder him at will. "But now, you really must continue your account."

"Where was I? Oh yes –"

"Hot cakes!" commanded a voice at the door, and in marched Polly with a tray of hot cakes and loganberry jam, a plate of bacon, and a pot of tea. "Just because you'd rather work than eat, John Marshall, doesn't mean everyone would." She cast a critical eye on Nancy's lithe belly. "You want a little non-legal advice, Miss?"

"Polly –" warned Marshall.

"No, it's all right," said Nancy quickly.

"Fatten up. You're too thin. It's not natural."

Nancy blushed. "Thank-you, Ma'am," she said, pleased to see that Mrs. Marshall was beginning to mother her in her own gruff manner.

Polly bustled out as quickly as she had bustled in, leaving the tempting tray between them. "After you, Miss," said Marshall.

Nancy poured them each some tea, and then she took a hotcake, paused, took another, paused, took two slabs of bacon, smeared jam over the entire thing, and then took a lusty bite. "I fink, Misser Marsall," she said with a mouthful, "that this business of being a prisoner may haff its good points."

"I'm glad you think so," Marshall replied, as he fished about through the ruins of the platter in search of adequate sustenance.

"Now, please, before I leave, I must hear everything. You were telling me of Jack Randolph's advance in the autumn of '91. Did anything further transpire?"

"Nothing *transpired,* Mr. Marshall," replied Nancy, speaking more to her plate than to her attorney. "That autumn turned to winter in a most pleasurable, uneventful sort of way, a blur of riding, dancing, dining, and long afternoon walks. Oh, Mr. Marshall, it's not right, is it, to be nostalgic at the age of eighteen?"

Marshall said nothing, forcing Nancy to fill the silence. "Finally, a year ago December, I felt strong enough to go back and face my father. Theodorick was kind enough to accompany me. We rode together back to Tuckahoe one stormy day, and I recall my sense of dread as we crossed through the columns of the entryway. As luck would have it, Gabriella herself answered the door, and when she saw me she turned white as a corpse, obviously convinced that I'd come to finish her off. But Theo covered it over, saying how he had heard such wonderful things about her from me, and that she was even more beautiful than he had been led to believe – all the usual rubbish – and while I don't think she believed a word of it, at least it got us in the door.

"It was intoxicating, being a grown woman in the house of my childhood, safe to reexamine the phantoms that had terrified me as a child. Soon enough the King of the Phantoms himself appeared, pretending that he was glad to see me and affecting the role of the wounded paterfamilias. All right, I thought, I can stand this hypocrisy, for no one is fooled and he only makes himself a fool." Marshall shifted in his chair, uncomfortable that whenever he spoke with Nancy her focus returned to the Colonel, the very man who'd hired him, and on whom he depended for his future advancement. Should he steer her to the crime? Or was this the crime? He pushed the thought from his mind.

"When my father was finished drinking his dinner, his cowardice duly fortified, the conversation turned to my prospects for marriage. Considering that to be far too delicate a subject to lay before his drunkenness, I avoided it. Taking this to mean that I was somehow deferring to his authority, my father advised that he could arrange my betrothal to the finest lawyer in the State of Virginia, save Patrick Henry himself."

"And upon whom did he bestow this honor?" prodded Marshall, with professional curiosity.

"Mr. Gabriel Harvie!"

"No!" said Marshall, astounded by the Colonel's gall. To drive a wedge through the family by marrying a girl not half his age, then to try to marry off his own daughter to the child-wife's irascible old grandfather!

"I was enraged, and said some things that were better left unsaid."

"Such as?"

"Mr. Marshall, doubtless you know me well enough by now to realize that I speak my mind. You ought not press to hear what I said."

"Believe me, I would rather not. But I must insist."

"Very well." She took a deep breath. "I said that, unlike a certain young lady with whom we were both acquainted, I would not prostitute myself to senility merely to purchase comfort."

"No!" Marshall hid his smile behind a teacup.

"The Colonel struck me, of course, but I didn't care. At that point I am afraid that dessert degenerated into a brawl, in which the Colonel and Miss Harvie were trying to kill me, and poor, frail Theodorick was trying to hold everyone apart. At length, he prevailed upon us to revert to more civilized methods of violence, and we retired to our separate chambers to stick pins in voodoo dolls.

"Of that night, the less said, the better. It was a nightmare to be once again in the grip of that house. All the strength I had felt earlier seeped away with the setting sun, and I lay, vulnerable and terrified as a child, jumping at every creak in the floorboards. I didn't sleep a wink, and as soon as the first rays of dawn showed themselves over the boxwoods I dressed, ran to Theo's chamber, and woke him so that we could depart before anyone else arose. We rode off into a bitterly cold dawn, but to me it felt warmer than a full blaze in the grand hearth of Tuckahoe.

"Alas, it was not so for poor Theo. In our haste to depart we had failed to replenish the coals of the footstove, and he felt the cold deeply. Perhaps it was that, or perhaps it was that the Colonel and his concubine have a more direct line to the Devil than we, since their curses have borne fruit. On the ride home in the twilight, Theo caught a chill that aggravated his consumptive condition, until it seized the very breath from his throat. Richard, Judith, Cedric and I took turns sitting by his bed from just after Christmas until February, and each day he got thinner and more transparent. It was as if he were vanishing instead of dying." Here her chin began to tremble, but she managed to say the words. "He died on Saint Valentine's day, just last year." She buried her face in her hands and cried.

At long last her guard is down, thought Marshall, *and I can get to the truth.* But he was foiled by a commotion at the doorway, which filled with the corpulent form of the Colonel himself. Marshall was stopped half-way to his feet with a peremptory wave, as the Colonel crossed to his daughter and bent to peck at her cheek. Her last-minute flinch left his kiss suspended in air.

"Don't mind me," boomed the Colonel, "no real business here, just a chance to comfort my poor girl." The poor girl bristled, but held her tongue.

"Colonel, you are of course most welcome," began Marshall, silently cursing him a thousand times over. "May we get you something to eat?" Polly was hovering by the doorway, awaiting the Colonel's order.

"Well, I had something at the public house," and Marshall didn't doubt it, because he could smell it on his breath, "but I can't say it would be disagreeable." Mistaking Marshall's plate for the serving tray, the Colonel helped himself to Marshall's breakfast. As the silence grew palpable, the Colonel seemed to be enjoying himself more and more.

"Now," he said at last, "seeing as I'm payin' for this damned circus, I want to get a few things off my chest." He chewed and swallowed. "First off, I been pretty tolerant to this here girl, and raised her best I could after her mother, God rest her soul, departed." Nancy stared at the floor. "I just wanted to make sure there's nothin' else going on here – nothing else going to be said," and he looked quickly from Nancy to Marshall and back to Nancy. Seeing as no one had any desire to help him out, he continued. "Also, well, there's been enough damage to the family name already. That's got to stop. Understand?"

Marshall thought hard. Did he understand? He might, but he didn't like the implication. Still, this man already doubted his ability to do what had to be done. Would it be prudent to question him now? Probably not.

"Well then," said the Colonel brightly, "I just want to be sure that we are all paddling the same direction." Once again his greedy eyes darted from daughter to lawyer and back, like a fly afraid to light. "I mean, I'm paying the bill, I've got an interest."

Marshall saw pain in Nancy's face, intermixed with something else he couldn't quite identify. "We're paddling the same direction," she said flatly. "There was no child born, Father. It's all a big lie." Marshall thought he heard one small clenched sob escape, but it could have been just the scrape of the Colonel's fork.

"Well then," said the Colonel again, "I suppose that's settled. Go on with your work, counselor." And he stuffed the remains of Marshall's breakfast into his busy mouth.

Marshall knew he could not interview his client with the Colonel sitting in the room. Not only would it destroy the confidential privilege between attorney and client, but he had no chance of getting anything worthwhile out of her.

"Perhaps we have done enough for one day," suggested Marshall diplomatically. "I have heard Miss Randolph's denial of the essential charge. Her testimony will be quite helpful."

"Testimony?" cried Nancy. "Oh no, Mr. Marshall, I cannot testify. You must believe me when I tell you that I am not guilty, but I cannot testify."

Marshall felt his face flush. "But Miss Randolph," he pleaded, "you must."

"That is not possible, Mr. Marshall." This time it was not Nancy, but the Colonel. "If you're any kind of lawyer, you ought to be able to get my daughter off without exposing the family honor to any further ridicule on the witness stand."

Marshall could take no more. "Dammit!" he exploded, knocking the tray and the enameled teapot to the floor, chipping the spout. "Oh no! Curse the day I took this case! Polly!"

In rushed Polly, and when she saw the teapot, she gave a sharp cry. "All the way from London intact, John Marshall, and you can't even get it from the tray to your cup in one piece!" She bent down to examine it, and Nancy knelt beside her, looking for pieces on the carpet.

"I'm so sorry, Mrs. Marshall," said Nancy. "We have a floral Staffordshire service at Bizarre that I would be happy to send for to replace this one," she suggested.

Polly stiffened. "No thank-you, Miss Randolph, we don't need your fancy china here," she replied coldly. "I think this might be repaired with a touch of glue, and if it pours crooked then Mr. Marshall will just have to adjust his aim."

"That's right, Marshall," said the Colonel, amusement gathering in rolls of fat by his eyes, "adjust your aim."

2.

The art of litigation combines the skills of dramatist, analytical scientist, philosopher, politician, and minister of the gospel, but in addition it requires attention to the mundane. No one can effectively try a case without a cozy place to drag one's battered hopes at the close of the day's hostilities. In Cumberland, Mrs. Biddlesworth's lodgings provided the sole oasis within an hour of the courthouse, and Marshall knew better than to fail to book in advance. Marshall's reliable steed, Jurisprudence, steered on her own towards Mrs. Biddlesworth's as soon as they came into town.

Curiously, Mrs. Biddlesworth was not a very hospitable person, having been thrown into the lodging business by necessity after her husband was killed in the Revolution. Thin to the point of shriveled, she begrudged any indulgence to her guests, on the theory that sustenance beyond the bare necessities constitutes profligacy. Somehow this attitude had gained her a certain cachet among the lawyers of the area, who delighted in goading her on by dragging in fat gooses for her to cook, and vats of port for her to serve next to her spare pitcher of rain water. She suffered this because she knew that lawyers have been abandoned by God to enable them to do their work, and therefore the mortification of attorney flesh was a matter of no more consequence to Providence than the rutting of goats.

Marshall arrived late in the afternoon to find the notorious inn-keeper on her knees scrubbing the plank floor of her pantry. "How do you do today, Mrs. Biddlesworth?" he asked cheerily, anticipating a suitably gloomy retort.

"Same's I do everyday, Mr. Marshall. I'm content to do real work, as that's the Lord's plan, and I do it." 'Real work,' as Marshall knew, was physical labor, often employed by Mrs. Biddlesworth in contra-distinction to 'whatever it is you lawyers do.'

"And you do a masterful job of it, too, Mrs. Biddlesworth, if I may be so bold," said Marshall, who knew when to pander. This elicited a suspicious grunt from its intended object, and a fresh splash of her scrub-brush into the bucket. After a respectful pause, Marshall continued, "If I might trouble you for a moment to look at your book, I'd like a room for tonight, and two rooms for next week."

Mrs. Biddlesworth scrubbed on for another minute, just to make sure it was understood that Marshall's request was not the most important item on her busy agenda. Then, with a sigh, she wiped her hands on her apron and relinquished one chore for another. Marshall followed at a respectful distance as she dragged herself into the front parlor, where she kept the book. This she studied intently but distastefully for a time, like a doctor searching for pox, until at last she looked up and said, "Yes, Mr. Marshall, by some miracle tonight will be acceptable. As for next week, I'll be quite busy on account of that scandalous trial of yours, but I still have two rooms. Whom shall I expect?"

"They shall be for myself, and Miss Nancy Randolph."

At this, Mrs. Biddlesworth's quill froze. "This is a respectable boarding house, Mr. Marshall, not a jailhouse," she said with quiet venom. "I won't have trash in here."

"If you receive Miss Randolph, you certainly will not," rejoined Marshall coolly. "She is of the finest family, and a perfect lady," *if perfect ladies give their step-mothers black eyes.* "When I attain her acquittal next week, all Virginia will be ashamed of how it has treat-ed her, and those few with the Christian fortitude to have shown her mercy in her hour of need will be blessed."

"Well, Mr. Marshall," said Mrs. Biddlesworth, an easy mark for his persuasive powers, "it's not me, you understand, but what of the other guests?"

"Cancellations could only come from persons not capable of living up to the high standards of righteousness set by your example, Mrs. Biddlesworth," said Marshall. He studied his quarry, and, when he saw that the vestiges of doubt were not dispelled by righteousness alone, he added, "and besides, I shall pay full rental on any room vacated by such uncharitable souls."

"All right, Mr. Marshall," said Mrs. Biddlesworth, "I suppose that having lodged lawyers all these years, it's too late to get choosy now."

3.

Patsy Jefferson Randolph was resigned to living with the constant sounds of banging, clanking, sawing, and hollering, not to mention the smoke and stink of the brick kiln. Ever since her father had returned from Paris in 1789, he had been obsessed with the renovation of Monticello, which, when measured in his mind's eye against Madame du Barry's *Pavilion de Louveciennes,* the *Hôtel de Salm,* or even Roman ruins such as the *Maison Carrée* at *Nimes*, seemed hopelessly provincial. Upon his return, therefore, he determined to double the size of the main house by adding rooms to the east, and to raise the ceilings throughout the public rooms to a respectable French Noble mansion's height of eighteen feet.

On most days, Patsy sought solace from the interminable construction in the westernmost room of the house, the parlor, with its sumptuous fireplace and semi-octagonal exterior wall with gracious floor length windows opening onto the west lawn and gardens. Once a day she insisted that all construction come to a halt so that she could play fortepiano unaccompanied by the cacophony of construction, which she deftly supplanted with a euphony of Bach, Vivaldi and Mozart. When her father was home he accompanied her on the violin, and then turned his hand as easily to produce what to him was equally sweet music, the whiz-bang of the saw and hammer.

But today Patsy had things other than music and construction on her mind. She'd just had a visit from one Codrington Philip Binghamton, and he expected her to testify against her sister-in-law. Taking quill in hand, she sought her father's advice.

Dearest Poppa,

Thank-you for your most entertaining correspondence about the coronation of our own King George. Thank God for your steady Republican presence in Philadelphia, without which I am sure Mr. Hamilton would have instituted crowns and thrones by now. I miss you terribly, but I do not begrudge your absence to the Republic that needs you.

I am afraid this is not to be a lighthearted letter full of news of the family, though I hasten to assure you that all are well. You are, of course, aware of the scandal that has enveloped the Richard Randolph family, and crept so near to our own. Their trial is scheduled to begin this Monday. Richard and Nancy are defended by Mr. John Marshall, whom I haven't seen, but this morning I received a visit from Mr. Binghamton, the County Attorney. Mr. Binghamton said that he had heard from Mrs. Carter Page – you know, Peggy Page, Nancy's busybody aunt – that I'd given her some gum guiacum for Nancy. It's true, I did, just a week or two before that infamous October 1st of last year, but I hadn't thought much of it until today. I didn't say I did or didn't to Mr. Binghamton, for you've taught me well how to handle lawyers, but Mr. Binghamton says that it is now regretfully his duty to subpoena me into court to testify for the prosecution! This is the last thing that I want to do, but I cannot see how to get out of it. Of course I cannot violate the oath, but perhaps I should not remember things too clearly? The alternative is to help Mr. Binghamton send Richard and Nancy to the gallows. I am torn in a thousand directions – Poppa, what should I do?

Oh! In rereading what I have written I see that I have relied on your thorough knowledge of herbs and medicinals, but since gum guiacum is so often a women's remedy this may be asking too much. Gum guiacum is quite useful in treating colic, but it is also, I am afraid, an abortifacient.

Please help me if you can.

With Love and Respect,
Patsy.

Patsy sealed this correspondence and gave it to a trusted servant for delivery in hand in Philadelphia. Somewhat more at ease for having shared her burden, she joined her husband Thomas and several younger sisters for a pleasant game of lawn bowling under a canvas tent on the west grounds.

Chapter 7

Jack's Golden Rule

I.

The night's rain let up mid-morning on Wednesday, and Marshall saddled up Jurisprudence and headed for the jail. It would not do to be in town and fail to pay a call on his client. The words of his law professor, George Wythe, echoed in his mind: "Forget Chitty, forget Coke, forget even Blackstone if you must, but never forget your client, for he is the source of all truth." Marshall was determined to pry a little truth from the source.

He found Richard in a morbid mood. "It's been two days with no word from home. Have they forgotten I exist?" Marshall began putting on his best version of a sympathetic face, but Richard would have none of it. "You have no idea what it is like being a prisoner, shut up while the world goes on about its business. I feel as if I've already been condemned and executed, without the formality of a trial." Richard collapsed into the chair opposite Marshall, cradling his face in his hands. "Why hasn't Judith come to see me?" The plea seeped like tears between his long, delicate fingers.

"I'll ask her this afternoon, when I see her. I'm on my way to Bizarre right now."

"Good. Go quickly! Judith is the only one who can help us."

"She is hardly the only one. You could help yourself."

"I cannot."

Marshall weighed a plan in his mind. Was he willing to do what was necessary? Randolphs or not, this case could only be won if he could get to the truth. He decided to take the chance. "And I know why you cannot," he said.

Richard tensed. "What do you mean?"

Marshall sprang the trap. "Nancy talked. She admitted to the pregnancy."

"What!" cried Richard, his face emptying of guile for a crucial moment as he leapt from his chair, knocking it over, and turned away from Marshall's prying eyes.

"Nancy has told the truth, now it is your turn," said Marshall, pressing the advantage. But it was too late. Richard turned, his features suddenly clouded with anger.

"Mr. Marshall, since I know that it would not be in Nancy's power to forswear herself in a matter of such gravity, I can only conclude that you are deliberately deceiving me. Good day." He turned away again, this time with his arms folded across his chest, closed to all entreaties.

"I apologize, Mr. Randolph," said Marshall, unsure once again what to believe. "What I did was motivated only by my desire to represent you zealously." He paused, but received no reply. "Please understand, Mr. Randolph, I must have the truth, and you know as well as I that I have not yet heard it."

Richard neither admitted nor denied it. After an uncomfortable silence, Marshall stood to go. "May I carry a message to Bizarre?"

"I would not trust you with one," said Richard tersely.

Marshall trudged from the jailhouse, cursing himself for forgetting Wythe.

2.

It took Syphax until midday Wednesday to work up the courage to face Richard. Junior gave him Batwing for the ride back to Cumberland, a mule known around the stable as 'Fat Thing.' "Sorry to do it," he says, "but Mr. Jack's orders. Says you ain't to be trusted with a decent mount." Syphax didn't care. The trip back to Cumberland couldn't go slow enough to suit him.

Batwing limped up to the courthouse steps late in the afternoon and deposited its mournful burden in a lingering puddle, much to the delight of the courthouse geezers. "That's quite some mount ya got there, boy," taunted one of the old men on the porch. "You ever think of entering her in the Stakes?" "She got any of Messenger's blood in 'er?" asked another, referring to the famous English trotter stallion imported for stud in 1788. "Hell yes," said the first, "why that there's Messenger's great-grandmother!" The geezers laughed, but Syphax, knowing how quickly the baiting could turn vicious, just stared at the dirt, nodding his head and grinning.

The laughter subsided, and the old men squinted hard at Syphax, sizing him up. Then the first geezer said, "This here's a good boy. Go ahead in."

Too dead inside for anger, Syphax was simply grateful that nothing had come of the confrontation, and he nodded and smiled some more as he dashed quickly by – so quickly that he didn't see the outstretched leg of the last man in the gauntlet. His momentum carried him forward into the door which held fast. He got his hands up in time to protect his already-bruised head, and was lucky to land with only a scraped palm. He heard the laughter behind him, and knew that now was the time to escape; he'd paid the price of passage with flesh, his only currency. He turned slowly to face the idle whites, looked them in the eye one by one, rose to his full height, and slowly brushed himself off.

"Clumsy boy, though, ain't he?" said the man who'd tripped him.

"Excuse me, Suh," said Syphax quietly, "but I did not fall."

The men exchanged glances of anticipation. They'd got one riled. "Not fall, boy?" said the same man, cocking his ear forward as if he hadn't heard it right. "Why I'm sure I saw you flat assed wit' yer face in the tobacca juice down there." The others nodded in agreement.

"That's right, Suh," said Syphax, "but I dint fall. I was tripped."

The air changed from April to Hell in an instant. The white men rippled towards him menacingly, coils of a single albino cobra. "Maybe I didn't hear you right," it hissed, "but did you accuse me of trippin' you, boy?"

"Oh no, Suh," said Syphax, and the serpent relaxed, "I guess it was a accident, you havin' such long legs an' all, I musta just tripped right over 'em where they lay."

The serpent pondered this for a moment, looking for offense. At last it said, "That's right, boy. Now git!" and Syphax scooted through the door.

Richard was not pleased that he'd had no word from Syphax since Sunday, but one look at his servant's battered face told him to hold his tongue. "Good to see you, Syphax," was all he said as he sized up the fresh wounds. Richard motioned to a rough-hewn chair, and Syphax carefully lowered his bruised body. In doing so he rested his bloodied hand on a copy of the Gazette that was lying on the table, leaving a red smear across the headline, "RANDOLPHS HELD FOR MURDER."

"You're bleeding, Syphax," exclaimed Richard. "Let me get you some water." He poured water from a pitcher on the windowsill into the washbasin, and set it before Syphax. Syphax hesitated, and looked up at Richard. "Oh go on," said Richard. "The damn color is not going to come off on me."

Syphax chuckled and then grimaced as he lowered his raw palm into the water. "That's right, Massa Richard. If'n it did, we coloreds would jest go fer a swim an' you white folks'd hafta do all yer work fer yerselves." They shared a laugh.

"Now tell me," said Richard, "what happened?"

"Oh, dis here's nothin'," said Syphax. "Jest some ole boy out dere on the porch who's ma musta sired offa Messenger, so's his legs growed so long they trip people."

Richard laughed grimly. "What about your face?" he asked.

"I had me a little run in wit' Mistah Jack. He wanted that note you give me fer Miss Judith. I tole him no an' he chased me. He done shot the horse right out from unner me, and he woulda blowed my head off too, but he run out of shot."

"That God-forsaken little runt!" exclaimed Richard, furious. He jumped from his seat, smashed his fist into his hand, and began to pace again, like a caged cat. "Did he get the note?"

Syphax swallowed hard and looked at the ground. "Yes Suh."

Richard paced some more, tearing his fingers through the disheveled black mane that fell to his shoulders. Many masters would have lashed out at this point, well within the law to whip their disobedient chattel. But Richard held his temper. Slowly, he lowered himself into his chair, then stared at Syphax for the longest time. Finally, Richard took him by his uninjured hand and whispered, "I'm sorry."

"Oh, I'm sorry too, I really am. I'll never fail you again, Mistah Richard."

Richard just nodded, and then he took another sheet of robin's-egg blue Randolph writing paper from a leather satchel. He wrote in silence for a few minutes, then sealed the document with candle wax. "There is a lawyer in Campbell County to whom you must deliver this message without delay." Syphax stood, eager to redeem himself. Richard gave him the lawyer's name, and instructions on how to locate him. "I know you will not fail me in this," said Richard, pressing the letter into Syphax's good hand.

3.

While waiting to be announced to the lady of Bizarre Estate, Marshall received a thorough sniffing from Cupid, who apparently found no cause for alarm, since he promptly lay down and fell asleep on Marshall's briefcase. Marshall was still in turmoil over his blunder with Richard. Perhaps it was true that he was not up to the challenges of such a high profile case. Affecting a calm he did not feel, he began idly to examine the paintings on the wall. Soon, his attention was captured by a large oil of a clearing in a primeval forest in which a wolf was devouring a fallen king. Marshall was so absorbed in studying it that he did not notice Jack's entrance.

"That's my favorite, Mr. Marshall, so I am pleased to see that it interests you."

Marshall startled slightly, turned, and saw the diminutive apparition that was Jack. "You must be Mr. John Randolph. How do you do, Sir?"

"Dying, Sir, dying. And you?"

"Not as bad as all that, I hope?" parried Marshall. "I detect a philosophical, or perhaps metaphorical, bent to your comments."

"Natural philosophy only," corrected Jack. "What has come to be revered in this day and age: scientific fact. Merely an inconvenient one." Jack approached the painting of the wolf and the king slowly, intently. "What do you see in this picture, Mr. Marshall?"

"What do I see? Why, a wolf eating a king, of course."

Jack cast Marshall a quick glance to determine whether he was being deliberately obtuse. "Now I am speaking metaphorically, Mr. Marshall. What do you see?"

"Metaphorically? I see an independent America, the wild spirit of the New World, devouring the old forms of monarchy. The problem is, what's left? After the king is devoured, who shall contain the beast?"

"That's not what I see at all," said Jack, and he turned and tapped his shrunken breast. "I see a portrait of myself. The wolf is me."

"Oh really," said Marshall, "and who is the king?"

"You are," replied Jack. "You and your fellow Federalists, always prattling on about order, propriety, and law."

The two men stared at one another in silence, Marshall quite stunned by Jack's ill graces, Jack savoring the moment.

"I see you two have met." Judith's innocent voice cut the fresh antagonism, forcing Marshall to reel from anger to civility in an instant. "How do you do, Mr. Marshall?"

Accepting the Lady's outstretched hand, Marshall unclenched his jaw long enough to bestow a light kiss, and with a bow he lied that he was doing very well thank-you.

"Mr. Marshall, we would be most delighted if you would join us for dinner, and be our guest for the night. Isn't that right, Jack?"

"Quite right, Judith. Mr. Marshall, Bizarre extends her warmest hospitality to you tonight. Please accept."

"As it is your wish, Mrs. Randolph, so it is my command," said Marshall to Judith, ignoring Jack and his bizarre hospitality.

"Excellent," said Judith. She turned and called to Jenna, a muscular, attractive young Negress, who was setting the table in the dining parlor. "Jenna, please show Mr. Marshall to the Essex chamber, and fetch him some water and towels. Then see if you can find Jackson to assist him."

"That's all right, Mrs. Randolph," said Marshall, his tradesman's pride showing, "but I don't require a manservant, thank-you anyway."

"Very well, Jenna, you may leave Jackson out of it. But be sure Mr. Marshall has everything he needs."

"Yessum," said Jenna with a curtsy, figuring that 'everything' would include her sweet behind. She dutifully led the way up the dark stairs. When they reached the entrance to the Essex chamber, Marshall whispered conspiratorially, "Jenna?" Oh Lordy here it comes already, thought Jenna, and she turned around, leaned against the wall, shut her eyes and began to lift her skirt.

"Put that down, girl!" Marshall commanded in a hoarse whisper, "that's not what I want."

"I'm sorry, Suh, I didn't know, please doen tell Miss Judith on me, I jest thought dat's what you wanted, same's th' others."

"That's all right, calm down, let's just go on into my chamber and talk for a minute. I won't tell Mrs. Randolph."

Relieved, Jenna led Marshall into the Essex chamber, a spacious high-ceilinged room with an arched fireplace, flanked by floor to ceiling pilasters and richly paneled yellow walls. The furniture was mostly of burnished cherrywood, including the square fluted four-poster bed on the edge of which Marshall sat, and the Chippendale side chair into which he guided Jenna.

"I have news for you from Miss Nancy," Marshall began. Jenna's face immediately brightened, but she remained silent and cautious. "At Miss Nancy's request, I will be asking Mrs. Randolph to send you to my home in Richmond, so that you may tend to her needs during the trial. Your Mistress has sent along a list of the garments that she wants, which I will give to Mrs. Randolph to read to you."

Jenna couldn't believe her good luck. Richmond! Any place was better than this gloomy old house, but Richmond was heaven. And Nancy was her friend, maybe her best friend if a colored girl could have a white best friend. She wouldn't say so, but Marshall did not need to have someone read the list to her – she could read it herself, all because Nancy had been brave enough to defy the law against teaching a slave to read. She'd been worried sick about Nancy but now, whatever happened, she'd be there right by her side. "Oh thank-you, Mistah Marshall," she said. "Doen you worry, Suh, I'll take care of dat girl."

"I know you will, Jenna," said Marshall, "but before you go there's just one little favor I need to ask of you."

"Anything, Suh," said Jenna, who'd begun to trust this ungainly squash-headed benefactor.

"I need to know whether Nancy gave birth to a child that night at Glenlyvar."

She fell back as if confronted by the corpse. "Oh, no Suh, I dunno, doen ask me!" she exclaimed.

"But you do know, because you were there."

"I cain't say, I cain't say nothing, Mistah Marshall."

"Why can't you say, Jenna?"

"Cause Mistah Richard an' Miss Nancy, dey both ordered me never to talk 'bout dat night, an' I'm their's, Mistah Marshall, you know that, dey say jump an' I jump."

"Yes, Jenna, and you're a good girl for it, but you see, I'm their lawyer, I represent them, so you can tell me anything that you could tell them."

"I doen need to tell dem nothin' 'bout it cause dey already knows. An' I doen know why you bein' a liar changes anything."

"Not a liar, Jenna, a lawyer. A lawyer is a man hired by someone in trouble to plead their case to the court, and to try to save them from punishment."

"You gonna talk to de Judge den you best off not knowin' nothin'. I'll shave yer face, polish yer shoes, clean yer clothes, rub yer back, an' lay in yer bed if'n you want, I'll even jump out the window if'n I can fit, but I ain't sayin' no more 'bout dat night, whup me if you gotta." And with that she stood up straight, crossed her arms in front of her chest and shut her mouth tight as a bear trap.

Lord deliver me, it's a black Nancy, thought Marshall. "Go get me some hot water," he said to her softly. "I reckon I can shave my own face."

4.

Judith stared at herself in the dressing room mirror as if the reflected world might be free of the fear and humiliation she felt everywhere else. There she was, only twenty-one years old, and already her face looked flaccid. That's what comes from not having cheekbones, she thought, as she dabbed powder and rouge into the offending vacancies. And there was her hair, just a shade darker than Nancy's, which made it mousy instead of honey blonde. It was thin and dry, it had no curl, and what's more the puffy eyes it framed were brown to match. Altogether a forgettable face, not one the gentlemen of the jury will go out of their way to believe. She tried to apply the lip cream but her hand trembled so. Steady, she whispered to herself, steady, *"STEADY!"* she cried out loud.

"What's dat, Miss Judith?" shouted her maid from the adjoining room. "You ready?"

Oh shut up you fool, you did it again. Words just leak out of your head these days, may as well split it open with an axe.

"Miss Judith?" asked the maid, peeking her head in, concern in her voice.

"Oh nothing," snapped Judith through smeared lips. "I was just fixing my face."

"Here, honey," the maid offered sweetly, "let me do that fo' yah."

"I can do my own face just fine," Judith growled.

"Yessum," said the maid coldly, backing off.

"And don't call me 'honey.' It's insolent."

"Yessum." The maid retreated biting her tongue. *Call ya gopher droppings instead, cause yer just as ugly an' twice as foul.*

Judith took a gob of cream to wipe away the smears. A vision of wiping her mouth right off her face appeared in the mirror. The things we do with our mouths, she thought. Devour flesh, tell lies, kiss in forbidden places. What does Nancy do with her prettier mouth? Devour flesh, tell lies, kiss in forbidden places? Gasp for air to no avail, the rope tight around her neck? *Would it be worth doing as Jack says to have Richard back safe, just for myself?* Judith lay her head down to weep, but no more tears were left, so she sat up and was startled to see a real card shark staring back. Nothing betrayed, everything betrayed. Holding close the crazy hand dealt her, she rose to go down to dinner.

Judith descended Bizarre's curved staircase in an ochre taffeta gown with pagoda sleeves and lace ruffles at the elbow, trimmed from shoulder to hemline in a profusion of lily-orange ruches and embroidered pearls. Cheekbones or no cheekbones, she knew her station in life. Marshall greeted her with the deepest bow his waistcoat would allow, and she reciprocated with the most gracious curtsy her whalebone corset would permit. Jack, dressed in a dusty old riding habit, parodied them both with a bow so low that his pony tail slapped the carpet. They distributed themselves about the dining table, castaways marooned between great gleaming expanses of polished walnut. Georgeanne presented them each with catfish soup in a gold-leaf tureen.

"Did you have a pleasant journey, Mr. Marshall?" enquired Judith.

"Very pleasant. A lovely change from yesterday's downpour. Indeed, I even had an opportunity to stop in and see Mr. Richard while on my way here."

"Oh," said Judith, leaning forward, "I do hope he is bearing up all right."

"Frankly, Mrs. Randolph, I do not think that he is. He feels that he has been abandoned by those closest to him."

"But I've sent him food and necessities from home, and Jack has visited. It's only that I, I –" Here she broke off, looking for the words to express why she could not visit him. Was it to punish him?

"– would be overwhelmed by the sight of the beloved Gentleman in such circumstances?" prodded Marshall, helpfully.

"Yes, that's it," said Judith, looking deep into her tureen.

"If I may be so bold as to make a suggestion?"

"Please do," said Judith, genuinely in need of guidance.

"Go to Richard. He needs you now more than ever, and, unless I miss my guess, you need him, too."

Judith was pondering this when Jack cut in. "What he means, Judith, is that a man in Richard's position, accused of improprieties with his wife's sister, appears less guilty if the wife is not giving signs of offense."

Damn it, thought Marshall, for of course Jack was right, but he ignored him. "Mrs. Randolph, I do implore that you visit Richard. Will you promise me this?"

"I'll try, Mr. Marshall," she replied evasively, as she pushed her soup away untouched.

Georgeanne cleared and brought out the roast goose, with apple dressing. As Jack took up the carving knife, he said, "Perhaps our esteemed visitor would care to give his opinion on the recent developments in Europe."

No, the esteemed visitor would not care to be drawn into a political discussion with a self-proclaimed wolf, but as his dining companions turned their patient attention his way, he could not refuse. "It seems to me that the situation in France is most unfortunate, and is indeed bordering on that most intolerable of political conditions, anarchy."

With a thrust that severed the goose's thigh from its carcass, Jack parried, "Anarchy's not so bad, Mr. Marshall. No tyrannical regime was ever broken politely. I'd rather live without government, than live under the tyranny of Federalists like Mr. Hamilton."

"You're a dreamer, Mr. Randolph, uttering fine phrases as you carve that fat goose – which, incidentally Mrs. Randolph, looks positively delicious – but under which system, anarchy or this constitutional republic, do you suppose you'd be more likely to keep your goose?"

"Aha, Mr. Marshall, I am beginning to see your point," said Jack with a smile. "Your political philosophy is grounded in gluttony." And with that he broke the breastbone, splitting the bird in two.

"Jack!" said Judith. "You'll have to excuse him, Mr. Marshall. He is this rude to everybody; it's not just you. It's his way. He doesn't mean anything by it."

"Quite all right," said Marshall, who had decided to try not to give Jack the satisfaction of riling him. "In fact, Mr. Randolph, you are quite right, in a way. My political philosophy, like yours, is bottomed on self interest, and if you want to call that gluttony, go ahead. The difference between Federalists such as myself, and Antifederalists such as yourself – may I be so bold?"

"Why not?"

"– is that we admit it, whilst you and your partisans always feel this uncanny need to dress up your selfishness in the cloak of idealism – 'the Rights of Man,' 'All Men are Created Equal,' *'Liberté, Egalité, Fraternité'* – nonsense like that."

Jack turned to appeal to Judith. "Do you see how it is with these Federalists? They scoff at the ideals for which we fought the Revolution."

"'*We* fought the Revolution?'" cried Marshall, instantly cursing himself for letting Jack back under his skin. "Did you fight it in swaddling clothes? I actually fought the Revolution, so don't tell me why 'we' fought it. I froze by General Washington's side, as did Lieutenant Hamilton. We saw men die, and we saw other men turn and run, and it taught us that all men are not created equal."

"May I say a word?" asked Judith, who had been quietly nibbling at the turnips at the edge of the sauce.

"Please," said Marshall, calming. "I would welcome a woman's voice."

"Well, I'm not much for politics," Judith ventured and, seeing that no one was aghast at this revelation, she continued, "but it has always seemed to me that there are good people, and not so good, and some of the good people are Federalists or Tories or Monarchists and some of them are Antifederalists or Jacobins or Republicans, and the same is true of the not so good ones. So I guess what I'm saying is that the political label doesn't matter much, but adherence to God's Golden Rule does." And she smiled sweetly at them both.

"Well said," Marshall began, but Jack cut him off.

"You adhere to God's Golden Rule, but I'll feel safer adhering to Jack's Golden Rule."

"Which is?" asked Judith, never one to resist Jack's bait.

"'Do Unto Others Before They Do Unto You.'"

"I shall always remember the basis upon which you are operating," said Marshall, fixing Jack with a withering glare. They finished their dinner with barely a word between them, until Jack left the table before coffee.

Judith, quite perplexed that her effort at peace-making had ended so badly, said, "I'm afraid things would have gone better had I kept quiet. Please accept my apologies."

"There is no need for you to apologize, dear lady," said Marshall. "Mr. Randolph would have found some other source from which to launch a display of depravity had your remarks not come to hand, and indeed, yours seemed a less likely point of departure than many."

"I am relieved to hear you say so," said Judith. She leaned forward in her chair. "Now tell me, Mr. Marshall, how do you intend to secure the acquittal of my husband and sister?"

Marshall pushed away his plate and leaned back, carefully observing Judith down the length of the table in the flickering light of the chandelier. "I do not intend to," he replied, but before panic could set in he added, "only you can do that, Mrs. Randolph."

"I?" Judith clutched at her bare throat with one hand.

"Yes, you." Marshall leaned forward and fixed her in his gaze. "I am told that you occupied the chamber immediately outside your sister's last October 1st, and that ingress and egress without passing in front of you was impossible. Is that correct?"

"Yes."

"Did anyone carry anything past you that night?"

Georgeanne got awfully quiet by the corner buffet, where she'd been preparing the tea for service. "That's enough, Georgeanne," said Judith, "you are dismissed. And close the dining-room doors. Mr. Marshall and I do not want to be disturbed, do you understand?"

"Yessum," said Georgeanne, and she closed the oak double doors behind her.

Judith watched as Marshall rose and came around the table towards her. There was something rough about him that his evening clothes could not hide, an intense skepticism that burned through the carefully cultivated respectability of the Randolph home. He grabbed the heavy Queen Anne chair nearest Judith as if it were a plough, and scraped it along the carpet to within inches of his hostess's wild profusion of taffeta. There he sat, intent on squeezing out the truth by sheer physical presence. "Mrs. Randolph," he whispered, "did your sister have a baby that night?"

"A baby?" she asked, as if surprised that the awful thing on everyone's tongue might be known by such a pleasant word. "No, of course not."

"And will you so testify?" pressed Marshall, fearing the evasions he had met from Richard and Nancy, pressing in even closer to where he smelt her over her civilizing unguents.

She nodded once. "If I must." She wrinkled her nose, as if she'd detected her own disagreeable flavor in the air.

At last. Marshall had his witness.

Chapter 8

The Shingle Pile

I.

Marshall began his Thursday in a dispatching mood. First, he dispatched an appreciable chunk of bacon, four eggs and a quart of tea. Then he dispatched a letter to Polly, explaining that, regretfully, it would be necessary for him to be away one more day so that he could inspect Glenlyvar first hand, but that he trusted all was well under the firm guidance of her capable hand. Next, he dispatched Jenna to Richmond, along with the letter and a large trunk full of gowns, bonnets, scarves, corselets, gloves, petticoats, slippers, stockings, boots, sandals, and every other means of covering (and artfully not covering) the human frame known to woman. Finally, he dispatched himself, with a reassuring handclasp for his star witness, who had planted herself under an ostrich plume headdress for the occasion.

As Bizarre faded into the morning mist, Marshall could not help but think that his clients' fate hung by a thin reed, even with Judith's testimony. He knew that the jury would be quick to discount the exculpatory evidence of one so close to the defendants. Perhaps he could prop up Judith's story by stressing the fact that no body had ever been found. But had anyone seen a body, or had it left traces – a bulge in the tummy, cries in the night, blood on the sheet? Perhaps these questions could be answered at Glenlyvar, scene of the crime, if crime there had been.

As Marshall took the right fork in the field above Bizarre to follow the undulating Appomattox towards Glenlyvar, the sensation of being followed came upon him. Pulling up sharply on the reins, he spun about to find himself confronted by Jack on a chestnut Morgan. "How do you do, Mr. Marshall?"

"Living, Sir, living," was Marshall's reply.

"Living, dying, two sides of the same coin," responded Jack. "May I ride with you a ways?"

"If you wish," answered Marshall, assuming that he was about to be pumped for information.

"Did you have a nice chat with Judith last night?" Jack asked diffidently.

"Very pleasant," said Marshall.

"You know, of course, that she would do anything to protect Richard and Nancy?"

"Would she really?"

"Oh yes, definitely, anything." When he saw that Marshall was not biting, he threw out a little more bait. "Do anything, or say anything."

"And what about you, Mr. Randolph? For what purposes would you do anything, or say anything?"

Jack chuckled appreciatively. It would not be so easy with this fellow Marshall. "You imagine you know me, Sir. But hear me out, for no man can be as thoroughly despicable as you must think me to be."

"Go ahead," said Marshall, curtly.

"If Judith told you that no baby was born that night, then she is lying. I have proof."

Marshall reined in Jurisprudence to look Jack square in the face.

"What sort of proof?"

"A document. Ask Richard; he is aware of it."

"May I see it?"

"No."

Jurisprudence began shying away from the Morgan's fierce dominance. "Why not?" he asked, struggling to hold her in line.

"Because of your scruples, Mr. Marshall. You can't be trusted with it." Jack's hyena laugh rang out. "Isn't that delicious?" he said.

Marshall was not amused. He decided to shift his tactics. "If what you say is true, it means the gallows not only for Nancy, but also for your brother Richard. With Theodorick dead, that would mean Bizarre estate would be yours, if I am not mistaken. Are you so desperate for that debt-ridden plantation that you would turn on your own brother for it?"

"You misjudge me, Marshall," said Jack. "I have absolutely no intention of harming my dear brother. You need only tell Richard that if he and Judith will testify to the facts as we discussed them, then I shall have no cause to impeach them."

Marshall gave up, and let Jurisprudence fall back. "And how, pray tell, does that line of testimony proceed?"

"Ask Richard." And with a flick of his riding crop, he was gone. Marshall continued towards Glenlyvar, ever closer to the scene of the crime, if crime there was, ever farther from the truth, if truth there was.

2.

Nancy followed the green velvet bustle of her plump jailor as she hustled down the cobblestone way towards the shops of Richmond. Reluctant though she had been to bring her, Mrs. Marshall could not very well leave her home with the children and the servant girl. As they passed beneath an ancient profusion of medieval chestnut trees, two gentlewomen of about Mrs. Marshall's age approached. They recognized Polly and began to smile, until they got close enough to recognize her walking companion. Smiles stillborn, the women averted their eyes in unison.

"Oh, dear," said Mrs. Marshall, who was unaccustomed to being snubbed. She scowled at Nancy, and then pressed on, redoubling her pace.

Margaret Hunter's Millinery was one of the few enchanted windows onto other worlds that was to be found in Eighteenth Century Virginia. Miss Hunter herself was born in London and had traveled throughout Europe and the Near East as a young woman, establishing valuable contacts for the import of exotic goods, before opening shop in Virginia just prior to the Revolution. By 1793 even the ceiling was crammed with treasures. Hats, of course, were the primary stock in trade, but to say 'hats' in relation to her inventory is to say 'chapel' in relation to Notre Dame. Doubtless Marshall's beaver top hat and Judith's ostrich plumes had originated here, as did sundry coy dormeuse bonnets of sheer muslin with taffeta ribbons, flamboyant calashes of black silk shirred on wire hoops, conservative beaver-skin Pennsylvania hats ringed in a single modest ribbon, and various elegant formal headdresses bedecked by pearls, flowers and feathers.

The latest fashion rage, however, was the French Revolution. For the gentlemen, the felt bicorne or tricorne were the most popular styles, usually decorated with a tricolor cockade. For the ladies, the *bonnet du populace* decorated with a tricolor band and rosette, or the bonnet of tulle and taffeta, were *de rigueur.* All were available at Margaret Hunter's, in endless shades, fabrics and variations, along with jet necklaces and earrings, black love ribands, sleeve knots, women's and children's riding habits, dressed and undressed dolls, Scotch snuff, and a thousand other delightful oddities.

"Good day, Mrs. Marshall," said Miss Hunter in Queen's English that twenty years in the backwaters of civilization had not flattened an iota. "May I be of assistance?"

"Good day, Miss Hunter," said Mrs. Marshall, squirming under the strong hand of social convention which called for an introduction of her companion. "Miss Hunter, this is Miss Nancy Randolph, who is staying with us for the week."

Miss Hunter inspected her as she might a viper imported from deepest Africa. "How do you do?" she said, well aware that Nancy did not do well at all.

"Very well, thank-you. Miss Hunter, I think you have a perfectly marvelous shop."

Miss Hunter inclined her head, acknowledging the obvious to the minimum extent necessary. "If you need any assistance, I am at your service." With that she retired to her accounts.

While Mrs. Marshall shopped for the sturdiest Republican broadcloth with which to clothe her family, Nancy indulged herself, trying on every conceivable mode of head-gear, and rummaging through the accumulated wonders of the age. She bought a tricorne and a puzzle block for the Marshall boys, and special gifts for Richard and Judith. For herself she bought an antique silk parasol with matching silk mask from the seventeenth century, a *bonnet du populace* for her Revolutionary moods, and for her aristocratic moods, a sheer therese with a black satin band encircling it and a royal purple bow in front. Mrs. Marshall frowned at the girl's extravagance, but said nothing.

"Well, Miss Hunter, that should just about do it," said Nancy, piling her treasures on the counter. "Would you be so kind as to have these items delivered to Mrs. Marshall's?"

"As time permits, Miss," said Miss Hunter.

Nancy was unaccustomed to insolence from tradesmen. "Your shop is quiet enough, M'am. I expect time would permit my request to be carried out today."

"It is quiet now, Miss," replied Miss Hunter pointedly, "but I am expecting a marked increase in business momentarily." She nodded towards the knot of busybodies gathered by the front window.

Nancy felt her stomach tighten, and began to swoon. She was rescued by Mrs. Marshall's firm hand on her elbow. "Let's have lunch."

"I'm afraid I'm not very hungry," said Nancy, but Mrs. Marshall brushed away the feeble remonstrance.

"You need nourishment to restore your courage, child. Come with me," she commanded, and Nancy was so grateful to detect the wisp of maternal concern that she happily followed Mrs. Marshall towards the Blue Goose Tavern.

The motto inscribed over the entryway to the Blue Goose was *"Hilaritas Sapientiae et Bonae Vitia Proles"* – "Jollity, the offspring of wisdom and good living" – and the tavern rarely failed to live up to this inscription. At the threshold the ladies were overcome by the establishment's distinctive din, a concatenation of political debate, risqué jokes, gossip, clattering dishes, shouted orders for food and drink, and fiddle music. As they stepped into the low-ceilinged dining room, they were blinded for a moment by the transition from sunshine into darkness, then stunned by silence, as first the politics subsided, then the jokes and gossip, followed by the orders, the dishes, and one last scrape of the fiddle. By the time their eyes adjusted to the dim, the room was perfectly hushed and devoid of jollity. Nancy again felt the hot blood of shame in her ears.

The proprietor, a Frenchman named Doux, sidled up to them. "Ah, *bonjour,* Madame Marshall, how are you today?"

"Just fine, Mr. Doux," said Mrs. Marshall with all the verve she could muster. "May we have a table, please?"

Mr. Doux would have rather given them his liver. "Oh, I am so sorry, Madame, but I am quite full." He smiled, revealing his wooden dentures.

"Full? But Mr. Doux, there is a table right over there," said Mrs. Marshall, pointing to a rectangular structure with legs by the back wall that was, undeniably, a table.

"Ah *oui,* Madame Marshall, but you see, zat table ees *reservé,*" said the resourceful Mr. Doux, rolling his 'r's and resorting to his native tongue to aid in the obfuscation.

"Oh come now, I've never heard of such a thing," said Mrs. Marshall. "We'll take that table right now, Mr. Doux, or you'll be hearing from Mr. Marshall as soon as he gets back."

Mr. Doux's wheels spun behind the veneer of a wooden smile, and then he executed a resigned little bow. "This way, Madam." Nancy, who had been doing her best to disappear, followed reluctantly. Three score pairs of eyes dissected her every step, and there was not a smidgen of forgiveness among them. Nancy focused on Mrs. Marshall's hemline, clinging to it with her gaze as she navigated between tables. The blood which previously had been so quick to rush to her face had deserted it just as suddenly, and she felt dizzy, unconnected to her own feet. She kept telling them to move, and they moved, but she wasn't quite sure how or why or whether they were doing what they were supposed to. Whack! her leg struck a chair, she reeled, looked up, held on, gathered herself together with the help of Mrs. Marshall's steadying hand. *The leg goes crack, this girl's a wreck, but it don't mean nothing without the neck, neck, neck ...*

"Here we go, young lady," said Mrs. Marshall, leading her dazed charge a few more steps towards the back wall, "here's our table." Nancy literally fell into one of the chairs. Slowly, she rejoined her body, while shutting out the pain rushing from her bruised shin. She sat up straight, and cast a determined smile into the venomous sea of faces.

A gentleman at a nearby table stood, and addressed the lady with whom he was dining. "I am sorry, Miss, I had thought this was a fit tavern for ladies. Shall we go?" He extended a crooked arm, which was accepted by a mousy thing in pink chiffon, and the two departed. Then another party rose, though their meals were not half finished, and, casting a collectively righteous glare at Nancy, they too walked out. In a moment, half the room was on its feet, but rising along with them was Nancy herself.

"Already have you forgotten Reverend Jenkins's sermon of Sunday last?" Nancy challenged. Her hands were trembling, but her voice was clear as a summer sun-shower. "Please, Mrs. Marshall," she whispered, "if ever a soul was in need of a little Christian charity, it is I. You know the Bible. What was it that Jesus said about mercy?" Nancy pleaded with her eyes as Mrs. Marshall looked first to the vilified girl, then to the hostile faces of her neighbors, and finally to her soul. How like my lost Rebecca's eyes are Nancy's, she thought, willing to bear any torment if given but a little comfort. Slowly, she rose to face the bitter townsfolk.

"Neighbors," began Mrs. Marshall in a quiet voice, but when she saw that they were not listening her voice rose till it rang out clear as any church bell, "you must heed what the Bible says: 'Blessed are the merciful: for they shall obtain mercy.'" Nancy's eyes shone with grateful tears.

A resonant hush left the diners confused, standing, leaving, sitting, half-standing, staring at their hands. One or two more walked out. A few who had reached the doorway turned back, returned to their lunches, and resumed eating as if nothing had happened. One by one, those caught standing regained their seats, and gradually the jolly din returned, sweetened with a dash of charity.

3.

Glenlyvar seemed an odd place for a foul deed. A simple two-story farmhouse with whitewashed clapboard siding, it sat prim and proper amidst beehives and fruit blossoms, looking like Grandmother in a new starched apron. Gathered around it were a tidy barn, a stable, a forge, a cookhouse, a shack for a few slaves, and two outhouses, like so many grandchildren in their Sunday best, hair pinned back and noses wiped. This was a place where the inhabitants matched the bees for industry, where each tool had its hook, where even the rain obediently followed furrows into the beds of waiting vegetables. This was not a place for discarding a body, even a tiny one.

The tiny body of Elly, the Harrisons' daughter, was full of life, so she spit out the mouthful spooned into her by Mrs. Wood, the white housekeeper. "Come now, Elly, eat your meat, you want to grow up pretty like your Mama, doncha?" Apparently not, for the meat was everywhere but where it belonged, and she kept shaking her head so that the chances of any finding her mouth were slight. "Werries," she said, "werries."

"No strawberries if you don't eat your meat," said Mrs. Wood. "You don't want Mr. Marshall here to think you don't eat your meat, do you Miss Elly?"

Marshall, who had been abstractly enjoying the scene for its power to transport him homeward, didn't care to become a wedge between Elly and her werries. "That's quite all right, Mrs. Wood," he said. "My little Mary would eat the hat off your head some days, and then suddenly she won't eat a thing. I understand. Do you like to eat hats, Elly?" said Marshall, taking a step closer to her so she could enjoy the joke. Bursting into frightened tears, she clung to Mrs. Wood, preferring the known beast to the big hat-eating man with the squashed head.

"I'm sorry, Mrs. Wood," said Marshall, backing awkwardly to the entryway as Mrs. Wood deftly quieted Elly. "It must be hard enough here, so little help, without me scaring the child. Do you have any colored help?"

"There's just Old Esau and a couple of boys for the fields, Mr. Marshall, but don't you worry 'bout a thing, I got wash and candles and baking going, and I can handle it all. We used to have a fat young nigra girl name of Lou, but she was more likely to be underfoot than any help, always beggin' off sick, and she weren't no good for liftin', neither. Anyhow, she run off, so now it's jest me in the house."

"When did that useless girl run off, Mrs. Wood?" asked Marshall, casually.

"Oh, a week or so after the visit."

"What visit?"

"Why, Miss Randolph's visit."

"Do you know why Lou ran off?"

"Who knows with them darkies, eh, Mr. Marshall? Beats workin', I guess. Now, if you don't excuse me, you won't be able to chew your bread tonight."

"Just one more thing, please, Mrs. Wood."

"Yes Suh?"

"Did they catch Lou?"

"That's the funny thing, Mr. Marshall," replied Mrs. Wood, as she headed out the back door with Elly in arm, "Mr. Harrison, he didn't even try. He just let her go." And she slammed the door shut with her foot.

Pondering this, Marshall surveyed the dining parlor, a spartan room dominated by a long walnut sawbuck table and a massive walnut schrank that were doing their best to devour any sunlight that might sneak past the thick blown-glass panes of the two tiny windows. He imagined the party that October night, the precise Harrisons producing a perfect meal and serving it up with dutiful good fellowship, the men swapping lies, the women swapping recipes, and Nancy upstairs with the colic – or worse. What was Richard thinking of as he listened to Harrison's tales of the Kickapoos and Shawnees of Ohio? Did he drink too much? Did he cast his eyes upwards? What did Judith think when she saw the look in Nancy's eyes, saw the sweaty fear, the pain, and heard the moans, those unmistakable moans remembered from a time beyond memory?

Marshall retraced the movements from that fated night. There, in the foyer, was the settee upon which Nancy first lay down, an unwelcoming slab of polished walnut covered in thin goatskin, as unforgiving as the Harrisons to imperfections of the flesh. She could not have been very comfortable here, small wonder that she went upstairs, and Marshall followed, up a narrow, steep stairwell, no railing, just white-washed walls on either side to facilitate the fall of sinful guests to Hell. At the top, a door that opens by lifting the iron latch, to enter a middle-sized chamber, sparsely furnished with a double bedstead on the right, a window stool with no window on the left, and on the far wall, a hearth, a small dressing table, and between them the door the next chamber – the tiny chamber where it all happened. The double bed in the outer chamber was not curtained, and from it Judith could have commanded an excellent view of anyone – or anything – that passed.

The door to the inner chamber was unlatched, and the thin corporeal luminescence cast by sunlight oozing through taut buckskin shown around the frame. Marshall crossed briskly to the ruddy glow and stepped inside, drawing the door behind him. The latch failed to catch and pulling the bobkin from the inside did not help. Marshall opened and slammed the warped door, but it stubbornly creaked back open with a will of its own. Marshall was just about to fix the inner bolt to hold it shut, when –

"Our guests normally wait in the parlor, Mr. Marshall," barked a voice accustomed to scolding, and his hand jerked back. It was the lady of the house, Mary Harrison, just in from the garden, arms laden with daffodils. She was a striking young woman with unblemished skin and eyes yellow as lanterns, but she held her face hard in a way that contrasted sharply with the soft beauty of her load. Now was the time for picking daffodils, so she picked them; soon it would be time to chop the head off the chicken, so she would chop it. She did both with the same joyless precision.

"A thousand pardons, Mrs. Harrison," squeaked Marshall in his raspiest twitter. He stepped back into the outer chamber and executed a small bow. "I thought you would not mind if I took the liberty to inspect the scene of the – what shall we say? – alleged offense." He looked back longingly towards the inner chamber, all the while surreptitiously running his hand over the contour of the door.

"You will be sleeping downstairs, because Mr. Harrison is not partial to creaking overhead," was the tart reply, and with that Mrs. Harrison executed an about face with total assurance that he would follow. Marshall peeked back around the door, caught a glimpse of a narrow bedstead with a feather mattress, and reluctantly followed his hostess.

Back in the dining parlor, Marshall caught sight of Mr. Harrison striding in from the fields, with a gray-haired slave at his side, Old Esau. They had just finished mending fence, a task they performed together every Thursday afternoon, rain or shine, visitor or no visitor. With them, as always, was Lemon, Harrison's prize retriever. Old Esau, loaded down with wire, posts, and a post hole digger, headed for the barn, as Mr. Harrison approached the house, Lemon at his heels.

"How's dinner, Mrs. Wood?" shouted Mr. Harrison, two steps before he got inside.

"Ready in two hours," hollered Mrs. Wood from out back, accustomed as she was to providing precise information from any location at any moment.

"I'll get the chicken," said Mrs. Harrison, grabbing a cleaver and turning towards Marshall, to his discomfort, "or perhaps two, how is your appetite, Mr. Marshall?"

"Just as you like, Mrs. Harrison," said Marshall, coaxing her out, "whatever you think is best." With a grunt she departed to wreak havoc at the coop.

"A fine looking dog you've got there, Mr. Harrison," said Marshall, trying to be friendly.

"She's all right," replied Harrison, though he knew she was better than that. Suddenly inspired to show her off, he grabbed his flintlock, took aim at the branch of a lone oak, and with one shot he brought down a fat crow. Lemon wheeled and flew to the spot where it fell, returning in less than a minute. "There ain't nothin' she don't get," bragged Harrison as he eased the limp black carcass from between the eager dog's jaws.

"Very impressive," said Marshall.

Harrison returned the crow to Lemon, who retreated with her prize. "Now why don't you and I set a spell out on the porch while we're waitin' on dinner?"

"An excellent idea," replied Marshall, who was exhausted as much by the frenetic industry of the household as from his own travels. Relieved to find that even Mr. Harrison needed to rest once in a while, he followed his host to the front porch, settled into a nice, comfortable crook-footed chair, and began to rock contentedly.

"Lucky for you," said Mr. Harrison, handing Marshall a wooden handled device with a blade coming out at a right angle and a cylindrical club with a furrow in the middle, "I've got two frows and frow-clubs, so's you can help me cut some shingles." He shoved a block of cedar in Marshall's direction, grabbed one for himself, and, perching himself on the edge of an upright log, began rhythmically riving shingles by pounding the frow through the block with the frow-club. Resigning himself to this most utilitarian form of 'relaxation', Marshall hunkered forward and began to pound.

"I 'spect, Mr. Marshall, that your call on us is not entirely social," said Mr. Harrison at length. He was a frontiersman at heart, and though he'd married well and gotten a place in Petersburg as well as this place in the country, he still spoke plainly. "You'll be wanting to know about the visit, won't you?" 'The visit' was how the Harrisons referred to it now; with all that had transpired since, it had taken on a life of its own. There was the Family, Glenlyvar, the Church, and the Visit. These were the things of importance, around which their lives were ordered.

"That is correct, Mr. Harrison. As counsel for your friends, Richard and Nancy Randolph, it is my duty to find out whatever I can about what happened that night."

With a whack of the frow-club, another shingle flew off of Mr. Harrison's block. Our friends, he thought, but he didn't say anything.

"Can you help me help your friends?" urged Marshall.

Mr. Harrison seemed to be considering something for a while. At length he said, "Mr. Binghamton's already been here. He says we're s'posed to testify next week." He stopped, as if this were quite a revelation.

"Yes," said Marshall, when he saw that he'd get no more just by waiting. "I figured you would. What have you got to say?"

"Mr. Binghamton says we ain't s'posed to talk to you. He says you should not be tempering with the witnesses. He says we should jest come to court and tell our story, plain as day, good or bad, and let you hear it then jest the same's any other feller."

It was Marshall's turn to split a shingle, and he pretended it was Codfish's bald head. Damn him, playing the old 'just tell your story' game. That's fine for him now that he's heard it, but there isn't a lawyer alive who wants to hear anything for the first time in front of the jury, unless it be his opponent's star witness admitting he'd like to marry a sheep.

Marshall reined in his temper, and split another shingle neat and square, just like Harrison. "Of course you should, Mr. Harrison," said Marshall, smooth as silk. "I would never dream of trying to change one word of what you have to say. I'm as interested in having the truth come out in this matter as you are," he added, relying on Wythe's dictum for his definition of truth.

"That so?" asked Mr. Harrison, in between shingles.

"Of course," said Marshall. "It's just that, in order to help me find all the relevant evidence and to be sure that it all gets presented to the jury, I need to hear your story."

"I don't see why," said Harrison, and he really didn't.

"Well, you know, there are always two sides to every story, right?"

"I don't know 'bout that," said Harrison, eyeing Marshall with suspicion.

"Well, at least under our system of law, both sides are allowed to present evidence and arguments."

"Why?" asked Harrison, sincerely puzzled.

This may be harder than expected, thought Marshall. "So that the real truth comes out," he said triumphantly, convinced that no one, not even Harrison, could fail to see the unerring logic in that.

Mr. Harrison pondered this long and hard, at length even stopping his shingling. Marshall stopped too. Finally, Mr. Harrison said, "You want to see some real truth, Mr. Marshall? Grab your shingles, and I'll show you."

Puzzled, Marshall did as he was told. They walked in silence around to the back of the house, each carrying an arm load of fresh-cut shingles down a short path to a wooded spot at the edge of the forest, with Lemon sniffing around their feet. Where the tidiness of domesticity met the twisted beauty of the wilderness, there was a pile of shingles, a jumble out of place in both the ordered and the wild world. They dropped their load at the front of the pile, but when Marshall turned to go back he was stopped by Harrison's hand. He followed that hand as it pointed to a spot at the back of the shingle pile, by the edge of the wood. Lemon sniffed where her master pointed, and then came over to lick his hand.

"There," rang out Harrison's accusation. "Right there under them shingles. That's where Richard Randolph hid that poor little baby."

Chapter 9

Gone!

I.

On the Friday before trial, Richard was not pleased to have his reveries disturbed by the counsel he had so firmly banished. But Marshall had urgent business to discuss, so Richard deigned to admit him to his cell.

"You know, Mr. Marshall, so much in our lives is determined by our perspective."

Marshall, having made such a mess of his last visit, felt compelled to play along. "Is that so?"

"Yes, it is so. Take this cell, for instance. To the jailor, and to all you people who gad about on the other side, it seems a perfect device to hold me in. But from this side of the bars, it seems that you've got it all wrong, that the cell is just the perfect thing to keep you out. True, I've admitted you, but at my pleasure, and perhaps for the last time. Or perhaps when Judith comes I won't see her, then what? Then who's the prisoner?"

"I wouldn't recommend that," responded Marshall. "Remember, she's your star witness."

"Oh, we don't need witnesses to win this case, Mr. Marshall," sneered Richard. "It will be won on the pure force of our advocate's eloquence."

Marshall did not appreciate the mockery, but he knew he'd earned it. "Be that as it may," he said, "there are certain matters that I must bring to your attention now, since this may be the last opportunity we will have to discuss your case before the trial on Monday."

"You have my complete attention."

"Mrs. Randolph will testify that there was no baby carried through her chamber that night, and that no child could have been born without her knowing of it. This evidence is helpful, although the jury will doubtless discount it to some degree owing to its source. In my opinion it constitutes the foundation of a defense, but one which would be immeasurably stronger if bolstered by your testimony."

Richard shook his head curtly, so Marshall continued. "If Mrs. Randolph's testimony were strictly in conjunction with a case in which there was no evidence of a body, I could say that we might have a chance. However –" and here he locked onto Richard's eyes, "– I am afraid that this will not be a case in which there is no evidence of a body."

"What – what do you mean?" stammered Richard, as his mouth went dry. "Is this another one of your ruses?"

"No, Sir, I swear. I've just come from Glenlyvar, where I learned that Mr. Harrison will testify that he saw a body out in the shingle pile behind his house."

Marshall had seen so much in people's faces, so many things that they'd never tell, much of which he'd later found to be true. There is always that precious moment between consciousness and self-consciousness, in which the soul lays itself bare before slipping into its next skin. Marshall saw it in Richard's face, and he did not like what it revealed.

"So what are you going to do about it?" was all that Richard said.

"Do? I'll do what I can. First I'll argue for dismissal, since there is no evidence to link any supposed body with you and Nancy. If that doesn't work – and it won't, mind you – I'll just have to cross-examine Mr. Harrison to attempt to make it look like he does not know what he is talking about."

The barest suggestion of a smile flitted across Richard's face. "That's right. You do that."

My God, the fellow had not even bothered to deny it. "But then there's your brother, Mr. Jack Randolph," added Marshall.

"What about Jack?"

"He says that Judith is lying if she says there was no baby that night."

"How would he know? He wasn't even there."

"He says he's got proof."

"What kind of proof?" asked Richard, but he already knew.

"He says to ask you. What kind of proof does he have, Mr. Randolph?"

"He's got nothing!" thundered Richard, all bluster and frustration. "What in the Devil's name does he want from me? What kind of brother have I got?"

Perhaps just the kind you deserve, thought Marshall, but he held his tongue. "He wants you and Judith to testify 'as to the facts as you discussed them last Friday,' is how he put it." He watched Richard as a boy might watch a fly while picking off the wings.

"And what does he mean by that?" asked Richard, once again knowing the answer.

"I asked him that myself, but he said to ask you."

Richard was growing increasingly desperate and confused. "And what if I won't?" he asked, choking back his frustration.

"Then I expect he will use the evidence that he claims to have to discredit Judith's testimony."

Richard turned apoplectic with contained fury, but Marshall was not inclined to comfort him. "Mr. Marshall," he said, "I know we haven't always seen eye to eye, but I'm not the monster you think I am. Jack wants me to save myself by testifying that Nancy gave birth to a colored child that night, and that she killed it to cover up her shame. Naturally, I refused."

"My God," exclaimed Marshall, "that's horrendous." Then he checked himself. It all fit. The mysterious refusals to testify, the evasions, the body in the shingles. Could it be that he had it all mixed around? That it was sweet Nancy who was the guilty party, that Richard was sacrificing his life for her wasted honor, that twisted Jack was a beacon of truth in a tempest of miscegenation, devotion, and perjury? "Horrendous if false," he continued, his voice edged with steel, "but equally horrendous if true. Is it?"

"Of course not," screamed Richard, fury contained no longer, "it's just Jack's final valentine to the woman he couldn't defile." Richard stopped, trying to decide how much Marshall should be told. How he hated to expose the soft underbelly of his family pride before this priggish distant relation.

"Now listen to me, and listen carefully," said Richard solemnly. "Jack is in love with Nancy, or rather he was in love with her, and desperately so. I am afraid that he made rather a fool of himself in front of her, it wasn't her fault, but it happened. Now he hates her, for she is a walking reminder of that moment. For this, he has seized upon our present misfortune to attempt to get rid of her. You know, Mr. Marshall, the perfect murder, with the Commonwealth as executioner. That is what you are assisting when you ask me if it is true." He paused, searching for the words that would make a sufficient impact. "You must see, Mr. Marshall, that if we succumb to Jack's deceptions we become accessories to Nancy's murder."

Richard's tale jibed with Nancy's, but would it be sufficient motive for so foul a perjury? Marshall forced himself to withhold judgment. "So," he said, "it is clear that you will not testify as Jack wishes. But what's to stop Jack? Will Nancy testify to what you have just told me?"

"I doubt it very much, Mr. Marshall. But I wouldn't think that would actually be necessary, so long as he thinks she might. Perhaps you could suggest that to him?"

Although Marshall desperately wished to avoid further antagonizing his client, he was not eager to cross the line into blackmailing a witness into silence with a threat to reveal such lascivious – and inherently unverifiable – evidence. Then the Colonel's voice echoed in his mind: *Are you willing to do whatever is necessary?* Was he?

"Let's suppose I were to suggest that to him," ventured Marshall, buying time to think. "What is this evidence that Jack claims to have?"

"Mr. Marshall, that is an area where lawyers are not wanted. It is between brothers."

"Mr. Randolph, you make my position impossible. I cannot be a party to a conspiracy to suppress evidence."

"But I have already told you, Mr. Marshall, there is no valid evidence to suppress. It's a bluff."

Richard's dark eyes opened up to Marshall, inviting him as into a deep pool on a hot day. *This does not feel right.* But that's your client speaking, Professor Wythe reminded.

"Is it settled?" pressed Richard.

Marshall nodded curtly. "I will speak with Mr. Jack Randolph Monday morning, to inform him that his spurned advances towards Miss Nancy will be made public if he does not back down. Do I understand you, Sir?"

"Perfectly."

Marshall was ready to do what was necessary.

2.

"There now, Cookie, have a nice glass of hot spiced cider, and tell Polly what's the matter." Polly placed the potion before her brooding mate, and the sitting room filled with the pungent smell of fermentation and nutmeg. The aroma explored the contours of the fireplace, with its plain brick mantel, and the framed portrait of Marshall's parents, Thomas and Mary Randolph Keith Marshall, caught forever with the stern, discomfited look of pioneers in search of the next chore. The aroma doubled back to tickle the nostrils sprung from their utilitarian loins, and found them impervious to seduction. "Cookie," prodded Polly, "you're not listening," and he wasn't, for it was only just then that he perceived the elixir before him. "Please, Cookie, it will help you feel better."

"I doubt it," he muttered, but he took a sip. It tasted like nothing, and had no effect on him. "Here it is Friday night, just three days from trial, and I feel as if I know less about what really happened than I did when I was first retained."

"Tell me about it, Cookie. It may help to talk it out."

"Anything I tell you is covered by the oath of attorney-client secrecy because we are one person in coverture, and therefore in the eyes of the law it is not a disclosure 'to another.' Do you understand?"

"No, Cookie," answered Polly with a twinkle in her eye, "but if you want me to sign a mortgage on my heart, I'll do it."

"It is well for you to laugh," pouted Marshall, exhausted from the strain of too many revelations, too little insight. "But really, Polly, I don't want to burden you with legal matters. Why don't you just send Miss Randolph down for a moment?"

"Oh, Cookie, must I?" asked Polly.

"I'm sorry, dear. I just want to try again to convince her to testify. You know," he added to prod her along, "if I can win an acquittal, I'm sure Richard's cousin, the Attorney General, will take notice."

Polly relented, gave her Cookie a peck on the cheek, and went upstairs. Marshall settled back like a big cat seeking refreshment in a moment's nap before the hunt.

"John!" Polly's scream jolted his eyes open just as they shut.

"What is it, dear?" he called, rising unsteadily to meet the crisis. He loped to the stairs, and looked up to see his wife at their head.

"It's that Miss Randolph; she's more trouble than she's worth!"

"Just send her down, dear."

"I can't," cried Polly. *"She's gone!"*

3.

Nancy paused at the crest of a rocky knoll to admire the full moon. The moon looked down with the worn face of her mother, its milky light suckling her. Nancy's mount, a dappled grey, felt it too, so akin to the moon was she. Nancy lay forward against her great neck, and warmed her hands in the mare's steamy breath. "I do not know your name, dear one," she whispered, "so I will call you 'Chance', since that is what you have given me. Away now, take my full heart where it must go!" And with a flick of the reins, they flew off together under the moon's watchful gaze.

The same moonlight slipped effortlessly through the bars of the jailhouse window, casting pale stripes across Richard's unquiet sleep. He was in the master suite of Bizarre, but there were no walls or ceiling, and the bed slid dangerously from one end of the floor to another. Someone cried out, and he knew it was Nancy, so he got up to bring her some medicine. Suddenly Judith was there, wearing Nancy's embroidered nightshirt, the one with the butterflies. There were hundreds of butterflies spinning cocoons all around her face, and as he looked he could not tell if it was Nancy or Judith. He offered her the medicine, but instead of taking it she spit in it and it began to boil. Richard felt afraid, and then he was in bed, and the Judith/Nancy woman was there, caterpillars and worms crawling around her collar, as she offered him the bubbling potion. He did not want to drink it, he was terrified of it, but he could do nothing and say nothing to stop it. He just watched in horror as it approached his lips, his mouth opening against his will. "Richard," said Judith/Nancy, "Richard," and he saw that it was just Nancy, and he felt relieved, "Richard," and he smiled, "RICHARD!" and she plunged a knife into his belly and he felt the searing pain and awoke with a cry.

"Richard," came the urgent whisper, "be quiet, it is I, Nancy," and he was awake, unharmed, and Nancy was there at the window, the real Nancy, without potions, knives or worms.

Richard flew to the window and their fingers entwined between the bars. "Nancy, you fool," he laughed, and they made fish faces so that their lips might meet between the bars, "you utter impetuous fool, I'm so happy to see you, but you must go back at once – as it is you'll be lucky to beat the sun to Richmond."

"Oh, Richard, don't talk to me about going back. Where are your manners? Why don't you invite me in?" Her eyes, more gold than green in the moonlight, flashed the challenge. This was too much fun! She'd never go back.

"How are they treating you?" asked Richard.

"We've been shopping and dining and dancing all up and down Richmond," she lied. "I declare, Richard, that you and I are the life of the ball these days, you'll see as soon as you get out. Oh, but before I forget, I've brought you a little present." She produced from a pouch at her waist a neatly wrapped package, which she handed him through the bars. Richard unwrapped it eagerly, and discovered a smooth, curved mother-of-pearl handle, with a slit in one side. It fit nicely in his hand, but he had no idea what it was.

"Thank-you, its lovely," he said haltingly, examining it closely, "but what is it?"

"Reach over by the end, and pull that metal piece out, you'll see," said Nancy. Richard did as he was told, and a four-inch knife blade appeared. He shuddered, remembering the nightmare.

"It's a new invention," said Nancy. "It's called a 'jack-spring knife.' I thought it might come in handy if you wanted to break out of there." She gave Richard a searching look, and when he said nothing, she added, "Of course, if you haven't the courage, you could always use it to slit your wrists. I hear that lengthwise is most effective."

"Stop it, Nancy," said Richard. "You seem to forget that I asked for this trial. If I run away now, people would think me a coward –" He checked himself, seeing the implied criticism. "I never believed that they would arrest you too, so I am glad to see that you've gotten away," he added hastily. "I couldn't bear it when I knew you were in jail."

"And I can't bear to see you caged like some animal, when I know how gentle you are," she said softly, tears welling up in her eyes. "How can I go free and leave you to suffer? Our fates are entwined. I'm so sorry, Richard, so very, very sorry. You say that you never foresaw, but what of me? To have dragged you down this way, I really never intended ..." Here she had to stop, to fight for breath between sobs. "Who could have foreseen, that you and I could be brought so close, to share such a fate? I just want you to know, Richard, no matter what happens, I will always ..."

"I know," he said, putting his fingers through the bars to her lips. They were silent for a time.

"You must go, Nancy," Richard said at last. "Go far away. Jack has set a trap for you." And he conveyed to her the nasty details.

"Oh, dear Lord," cried Nancy, "how could he! Haven't I always been sweet with him?" Richard nodded, searching her face for clues to just how sweet, but the moon was setting and the answer was lost in shadow. "What betrayal!" Nancy continued. "Where is he? I'm sure I can persuade him to desist in this folly if I can but speak with him."

"No!" Richard cried. "Jack would likely turn you in for the reward money they'll be posting. I am afraid that you will be safest up North until this thing can be smoothed over. You may rest assured that I will never capitulate to Jack's scheme."

Nancy's spirits sank with the setting moon. "I don't know, Richard, I really don't know. What is the use of running, me a single lady? I thought perhaps if we went together, then there would be some hope, some chance of future happiness. But alone? Where would I go, in whom could I place my trust? How would I get food and lodgings? Where would my support come from?"

"Maybe the Colonel would foot the bill. He'd be happy enough to have you gone."

"I'd never take a penny from him," said Nancy, twice too loud. "In fact, his wanting me gone is a good enough reason to stay in Virginia, where I can rot right under his nose."

"Don't say such ghastly things, Nancy! Where do you think the funds for your defense are coming from? He cares enough to try to keep you off the gallows."

Nancy harrumphed, as she thought that one over. "To keep me silent, is more like it. If it was private, I swear he would string me up himself."

Richard let her cool off a moment in the dew. Then he asked, "Nancy, you haven't told a soul, have you?"

"Of course not. And you?"

"I never will," said Richard, resolute.

The graying night air traced the outline of their illicit rendezvous, warning them of the imminent need to part, pulling them ever closer. "I had a thought," said Richard, laughing slightly, "a daydream, really. We are tried and convicted, sentenced to death, but then for the unjustness of our plight we are sent an angel, who causes the ropes to snap each time they try to hang us, till at last they just give up. We are imprisoned together in a great deserted mansion where, as Lear says to Cordelia, 'we'll wear out, in a wall'd prison, packs and sects of great ones, that ebb and flow by the moon.'"

Nancy shuddered, remembering Cordelia's fate. "Do you believe in angels, Richard?"

"Yes, of course. Don't you?"

"Is that how you can face death?" asked Nancy, avoiding the question.

"I suppose so. It helps. A little."

"Theo didn't believe in angels, or heaven, or anything like that, but he was so brave at the end. I just don't know, Richard. How can a person be ready for death?"

Richard considered the question carefully. "By having made peace with God."

Nancy looked disappointed. "I haven't forgiven God," she said.

"That's not how it works," replied Richard.

"It's getting light; I must go."

Richard admired the dawn in Nancy's eyes. "Where to?" he asked.

"I don't know," Nancy replied, but she did know. She kissed Richard lightly on the fingertips, then vanished into the mist towards Bizarre.

4.

The mist had barely burned off when Judith arrived at her husband's cell, bearing kisses and provisions. Sweeping aside the Sheriff's standard gruel, their servants laid before Richard a breakfast of bran muffins, goat cheese, strawberries and broiled pigeon, then melted away to leave the happy couple to their pleasure.

Their pleasure, at first, was to sit in awkward silence. Judith sniffed at the air like a hound on the scent, as Richard toyed absent-mindedly with Nancy's smooth, oblong gift. "What have you got there, Richard?" Judith finally asked, and Richard covered it up with such a guilty look that "Oh, it's nothing," rang quite hollow.

"Why, Richard, look at you – you're all flustered. It is too something, and I'd like to see it."

Sheepishly, Richard produced the precious contraband, waving it under Judith's nose for a second before snatching it back. "If you must know, Judith," he said in a conspiratorial whisper, "it's a jack-spring knife, a handle with a little blade tucked up inside. If the Sheriff caught sight of it he'd confiscate it, so that's why I'm not eager to show it off."

"Well then," said Judith, ever practical, "you'd better stop fondling it and slip it somewhere where no one can see it, or it won't last the day. Where on earth did you get such a thing?"

"Syphax," said Richard, and he immediately regretted saying it, for where would Syphax get a knife, especially one so unusual?

"Syphax! Oh dear, the niggers are armed now, are they?"

"Judith!" scolded Richard. "You know I can't stand that word. God made us all; they are Negroes, not 'niggers'."

She hated it when he lectured her like that, as if he was the only Christian on earth, yet she liked it in a way, too, for it showed that he still cared enough to want to improve her. "Just the same Richard, where did Syphax come by a fancy contraption like a jack-knife, or whatever you call it?"

That's it! Thank-you, Judith, I can always rely on you. "From Jack, of course. He gave it to me; Syphax was only the messenger."

"I can't believe that," said Judith innocently, not because she didn't believe it, but because it surprised her. "Why would Jack trust a knife to a boy he'd just punished for insolence?"

Richard squirmed, convinced that he was being found out. "Dammit, Judith, I don't know," he snapped, and his vehemence caught her off guard. "What is this, an inquisition? Ask Jack why, who ever knows why Jack does anything? Probably just to rile things up, to make you suspicious of me, to get you asking all these questions, I don't know."

She wished she hadn't asked. "But darling, I'm not suspicious of you, don't say such things, I'm sorry," said Judith, realizing that they were headed for one of their arguments, that they were always heading for an argument these days. She reached from the rickety chair to the pallet where he sat, all folded in upon himself, and tried to caress the midnight cool of his dark hair, but he pulled away so that all she touched was the space between them, and it felt so slippery and unfamiliar that she wanted to cry. An inquisition, he'd said, who does he think she is, the prosecutor? She is his wife, the only one who will stand up for him, the one person who would do anything for him – anything? Well no, not anything, of course not, there are limits, but what are they? There are limits, like one does not ... does not ... do what? She once knew what one does and does not do. Now all she knew is that there are limits, *but she no longer knew what they are.*

"Tell me, Judith, how are things at home?" Richard asked, clumsily trying to change the subject. But Judith could not bring herself to speak the swaddling little words of daily life.

"Without you, Richard, there is no home. There is only gloom, and beams, and furnishings that don't know what to do with their arms and legs."

"Oh, Judith, please don't say so. What of little St. George, how is he?"

Judith shifted uncomfortably, feeling suddenly the need to cuddle St. George, yet knowing that she was already too disconnected from herself to nurture that strange fruit of her womb. "He's fine," she lied. "Yesterday he sat up on his own and there's no doubt he'll be crawling soon." Fourteen months old and perhaps he would be crawling soon.

"Excellent," said Richard, who failed to grasp the portent of this report. "And at least you must have visitors –" she shot him a look –

"I don't mean it like that, thank-you for coming, but you know what I mean, real visitors, company."

"Like your lawyer."

"No one else?"

"Who else would be seen calling on a house so compromised? Your stepfather, who told me to come here. And my father." *Who told me not to.*

"And what did the Colonel want?"

"He wanted to know what everyone wants to know: whether I saw Nancy with a baby at Glenlyvar."

"What did you tell him?"

"I told him that nothing happened, Nancy was ill and the Nig – *Negroes* will gossip about anything."

"So, he's been trying to turn you against me."

"No, no, not at all. He said he was pleased that I would say there was no baby born that night. 'We've had enough scandal for five families,' he said."

"I'm sure he rues the day he consented to our nuptials," said Richard bitterly.

Judith slid down from her chair to sit beside Richard on the pallet. The odor of slops and mildew assaulted her delicate nostrils, but she fought against the rising nausea. She put her arm around Richard's waist, and felt his muscles go tense. "I don't know and I don't care; what's important is that we never do," she whispered, as she moved her hand up to stroke him between the shoulder blades. "Richard, look at me." She stopped the stroking. He turned and rested his gaze in the soft cushion of her brown eyes. "If what I suspect is true," said Judith, "then you know you have placed me in an impossible position." He moved as if to speak but she put her fingers to his lips. "No! Don't deny it; don't apologize. I have already forgiven you." Surprise and admiration glowed in his dark eyes. "But in exchange for my humiliation," she said, "you must promise me one thing."

"Anything, my love," he said.

"Once you and Nancy are acquitted, we must find another place for Nancy."

"No, Judith!" protested Richard. "How can you turn on your favorite sister? She is one of the most wronged people in all Virginia, and you wish to add to her burdens by throwing her out of the only place she can call home? Do not be so quick to judge her harshly."

"But I do judge her harshly," replied Judith, her lips trembling. "How can I not, for we have given her our love and shelter and she has repaid us by bringing scandal upon us, and testing our sacred vows to the limit. Do not judge her harshly? Many would say I could claw her eyes out, and not have judged her too harshly."

Judith's tears began to fall, but the words kept sputtering out between sobs. "If she had confided in me, treated me like the loving big sister I always tried to be, well then ... but of course, she did not. She snuck around, playing her games, hiding the truth from me. She used her wiles to toy with you and look at the result." Now her trembling hands were pressing softly against his chest. "Please, Richard, do not force me to go on living with her. It will not end well. Already I am not half the woman I once was. I dread the coming trial. I babble crazy thoughts out loud. Why, just this morning I could have sworn I saw Nancy herself astride a dappled mount, staring at me out of the wood. If you add to these sisterly apparitions close confinement with Nancy in the flesh, nothing good will come of it. I mean it, Richard. I am at my wit's end over this matter."

Richard took Judith's hands in an effort to steady them, as he looked deep into her eyes. How like the brown eyes of a faithful dog, he thought, loyal and strong, able to absorb kicks and return them as love. "My life is in these hands, Judith." He kissed them, first one, then the other, slowly, with great tenderness. "You won't let me down, will you?"

"Of course not, Richard, but –" He took her in his arms, and suddenly she knew what the limits were. The limits were to lose this embrace.

Chapter 10

Resting in Peace

1.

Marshall's thighs chafed, his back ached, and his rear was sore from too much contact with Jurisprudence, but what could he do? Friday night he'd grilled the girl Jenna, from whom he'd learned that yessuh, Nancy had been there at dinner time, and no suh, it sure looked like she wasn't there now, but beyond that she couldn't say. After squandering thirty minutes on that he talked to the stable boy, from whom he learned that Jenna had come for a horse for Mrs. Marshall around dinner time, which he'd thought strange since she didn't want a rig with it, but she'd insisted and he gave in. The old smithy added that by the time the girl had got through flashing her calves at the boy, Marshall was lucky she wasn't demanding the whole stable because he'd have given it to her, and even helped her to carry it off. The stable boy protested with such a sweet jumble of vehemence and confusion as to confirm all that the smithy had said. But by then it was very late and Marshall was exhausted, so he went to bed.

At dawn on Saturday, Jenna awoke to find Marshall standing over her pallet in the wardrobe off Nancy's chamber. This man just cain't make up his mind, she thought, as she pulled the covers back to reveal her nakedness. Marshall turned his back on her. "Can you ride?" he asked.

"Sure thing, Mistah Marshall."

"Then get dressed and meet me at the stable immediately."

And so it was that Marshall's tender backside trotted out of Richmond at daybreak, accompanied by a tough girl who was riding bareback and feeling no pain. They rode a while in silence under the gathering clouds, until they came to a fork in the road, one way due west towards Cumberland, the other slightly southward towards the Appomattox River. Marshall reined in Jurisprudence, turning to face Jenna.

"Which way?" he asked.

A simple question, but one rarely asked of slaves.

"I doen know, suh. I jest go where you says," she replied.

"I say we go to Nancy."

"But I doen know where Nancy is, Mistah Marshall."

"I think you do," said Marshall. Jenna's insolent shrug told him that he was right. "And not only that," said Marshall, pulling himself to his full height in the saddle at the expense of his *derrière* so that he might tower over her, "you are going to take me to wherever that is, and you are going to do it *now!*"

Marshall barked the last word with such venom that he surprised both himself and the mare carrying Jenna, which reared up in fright, throwing her rider. And yet Jenna was not down, for as she was thrown she instinctively dived for the mare's neck, to which she clung with all her strength until the mare came down and Jenna was able to settle against its broad withers. Then she calmed the frightened animal with gentle sounds that might have been its own equine conscience, they were so light and familiar. When it was over, and she lay in silence against the mare's mane, Marshall knew he would not overcome this girl's will by sheer force. Better that he shift the contest to a field in which he clearly held the advantage.

"I am aware," he said, "that you participated in your Mistress's escape from lawful custody." Before she could protest he cut her off. "I spoke to the stable boy and the smithy, and they both confirm it, so it will do you no good to deny it." She shrugged her shoulders again as if to say "so what?" – but in fact said nothing. A lifetime of bondage had taught her well the virtues of silence, the one response that combined obedience and defiance, subservience and mockery, detachment and contempt.

"I understand that you did it out of loyalty to your Mistress, but you must realize that helping Nancy to escape did not in fact help her, but will end up hurting her." Marshall was pleased to observe that, with this last remark, he had finally caught Jenna's attention. "Escape," Marshall continued, "is not only a serious crime in itself, for which Nancy can be imprisoned for many years even if she is acquitted of murder, but it is generally treated by juries as an admission of guilt, so that if she is caught, as she will be, her chance of being acquitted of murder will be much smaller simply because she tried to run." Jenna listened intently. "In addition, as an accessory to the escape, you are equally guilty with your Mistress for this crime."

I'm what? thought Jenna. Oh Lordy, Miss Nancy dint say nothin' 'bout this.

"Unfortunately, though equally guilty, your degraded status does not permit equal retribution. For a slave to be convicted of such a serious felony would mean death by hanging."

Marshall paused to allow his words to have their desired effect. It did not take long. "I 'spect we should take dat road right dere," said Jenna, pointing towards the more southerly route. "She woulda gone th' other way so's she can stop in Cumberland last night, but den she'd head south fer Bizarre. If'n we make a beeline for Bizarre, mebbe we can head her off 'fore she lits out ta Kintucky, or some such place."

"You lead the way, Jenna," said Marshall with a smile.

2.

Bizarre's gatekeeper, Old Franklin, knew he must be dreaming when he saw Miss Nancy trotting down the lane, but no amount of blinking could dispel the vision. "Whoa, Chance," she said, as the dappled grey pulled up with a snort. She dismounted as the old man did his best to stand up. "Sit," said Nancy, "I can get the gate."

"No, Miss, dat's my job, you rest easy," and he sprang between her and the gate with unexpected quickness.

"All right," said Nancy, "you may get the gate for me, so long as you forget that you ever saw me, no matter who asks."

"Yes Miss, I ain't never seen you."

"And Franklin, do you happen to know if Syphax is here?"

"He ain't here, Miss."

"Do you know when he will be back?"

"No, Miss. Jedidiah might know, cause dem two been talkin' jest before he goes, but I doen know."

"Thank-you, Franklin," said Nancy, remounting. "How's your back?"

"My back's so good dat when I die I's gonna strap my wings to my head."

Nancy laughed. "I'm sorry it's been paining you. Have you tried a compress of comfrey roots?"

"No, Miss, I ain't."

"Why don't you have Georgeanne prepare one for you?"

"Thank-you, Miss, but I dunno. Least when I's bent over, dat field boss, he leave me be, y'know."

"Oh," said Nancy. "Well, you take care of the rest of yourself, then, and leave your back the way you like it."

"Yes, Miss."

Nancy trotted down the lane, turning right on a path into the woods before coming into sight of the hulking frame of the Great House. She followed the path over a rise and down into the sag occupied by Mudtown. Tying her horse by the edge of the wood, she traversed the last hundred yards on foot while the pigs grunted their annoyance. Quietly, she slipped into Jedidiah's shack, where the pungent odor of manure and slops met the equally pungent odor of sweat and tobacco. She stood stock still, not ten feet in front of Jedidiah's blind stare.

A smile came across his face. "Well, if it ain't Miss Nancy," he said, cool and easy as if she were expected for tea.

"How did you know, Jedidiah?"

"Dem hogs, dey talk ta me, Miss. Dey tell me someone's comin', an' I hear you comin' from da woods, not da house. An' I knows you's white, cause I kin smell dat stinky ole perfume, coverin' da sweat."

"It's a wonder you can smell anything in here over that nasty old pipe of yours."

Jedidiah just laughed. "Yessuh, dat's Miss Nancy. Set yerself down, girl."

Nancy was so tired that the dirty straw strewn about the earthen floor looked more inviting than the one rickety chair. As she settled down she wondered where to begin. She didn't know Jedidiah as well as she knew many of the other servants, since he kept to himself here in Mudtown and hardly ever mingled with the whites.

"Jedidiah, as I am sure you are aware, I am in a great deal of trouble right now. I was hoping perhaps that Syphax could help me, but I've heard he's away. Do you know when he'll be back?"

"I doen know, Miss Nancy, I doen think till tomorrah, anyways."

"Has Syphax or Jenna ever told you anything about me?" she asked, haltingly.

"Like what?"

"That I'm not like other white folks, that I am a special friend to your people?"

"No, Miss."

"Have you ever heard any reports of me mistreating any of your people?"

"You been kind as de law allows, Miss," he answered, testing his limits.

She ignored the sass. "Then will you trust me?" she asked.

"Ain't dat th' wrong question?" replied Jedidiah. "Ain't da question really, you gonna trust me? You's da one in trouble. I ain't in no trouble 'til I help you."

"Will you help me, please, Jedidiah?"

"No way, Miss. Nothin' personal, you understand. But no way."

Nancy saw that it was no use to beg. Tired, hungry, without blankets, food or water, she would not make it very far. She dared not approach the Great House for fear of Jack, but everything needed to survive was inside. Is this all it comes to, caught in Mudtown and dragged back to Cumberland to appease the hot God of scandal? Nancy lowered her face in her hands and cried.

Jedidiah, long since immune to any sorrows not his own, was surprised to feel a pang for this white girl. Maybe he was just getting soft in his old age. And maybe it was because Syphax really had told him that this one was special. But the bitter years had numbed him, and though his heart ached to reach out, the rest of him held still.

At length, Nancy pulled herself together. Jedidiah felt her hand touching his, something no white had ever done in kindness.

"I understand, Jedidiah. If I were you, I wouldn't get involved, either." Nancy turned to go.

"I doen believe dat, Miss Nancy. Mebbe some time I kin find a way ta help you."

She turned back and smiled once before going, feeling that it would not be wasted on this blind man. Then she poked her head out and stared up at Bizarre. Jack or no Jack, she would need supplies. That meant a visit to the Great House.

Fear sharpened Nancy's senses and quickened her step. She broke into a run across the open ground between Mudtown and the servant's entrance. Climbing the four steps to the stoop, she peeked in the back window, hoping to find Georgeanne in the pantry. The room was empty. Slowly, she pulled open the outer door, and then pushed up the latch on the inner door. With a snap the door opened and Cupid began to bark.

"Shut-up!" came Jack's voice, but the dog was running down the hall towards the pantry, barking furiously. Without thinking, Nancy quickly slipped across the pantry and into the buttery, closing the door behind her. She heard the skitter of dog claws just outside the door, so she slipped her hand out to appease him with her familiar scent and a few quick strokes.

"Cupid," boomed Jack's voice from just around the corner, "what is it, boy?" Nancy startled and nearly pulled the door shut on her hand as she snatched it inside. It was pitch black in the buttery, and the room smelled of onions. Suddenly she understood how Jedidiah, after years in darkness, could know so much of what went on around him. Over the pounding of her heart she could hear Cupid's whine, the kind he makes when he is worried about someone in the family, not the kind he makes to warn of a stranger, and she could see him so clearly in her mind's eye, straining to lead Jack to her. She could smell Jack over the onions, not a body odor, but the negative odor of indecision, poised between the heightened awareness of the hunt and the comfortable oblivion of daily routine. Then he made his choice.

"You want to go out?" She heard the servants' door opening. "G'won, get out of here!" And then the whimper of pain meaning that Jack's boot sent Cupid arching out the door. The boot and its burden retreated back across the pantry and beyond the range of Nancy's hearing.

Nancy waited an extra minute, just to be sure. Then she cracked the door, just enough to allow in some light. Finding a sack, she went to work. She packed salt pork, smoked mackerel, corn meal, flour, lard, hardtack, salt, sugar, tea and dried apples. These she left just inside the door to the buttery, before tiptoeing into the creaky pantry. In the cupboard she found the pot she wanted under three others, so she took the one on top in the interest of silence. She took a skin for water, a flint, and some candles. Deciding that she could get a horse blanket from the stable with far less risk than by attempting to go upstairs, she gathered her treasures and headed out the door.

This time, by pushing against the door while lifting the latch, she was able to open the inner door quietly. As she opened the outer door, hands burdened with her provisions, Cupid was there to greet her, tail wagging, jumping and licking, knocking her sideways so that her body no longer held the door and smack! it slammed back on its spring. She hurried down the stairs and was just able to get around the side of the house before the door flew open again.

"Who's there?" demanded Jack.

Damned Cupid at her feet. "Go!" she whispered, as fiercely as she dared for fear of being heard. Cupid just looked at her, unsure how to please, knowing in his doggy way that she needed him.

"Is that you making such a racket out here, Cupid? Get in here."

Cupid looked once more to Nancy. "Good boy," she whispered. "Now go!"

He sat.

"I said get in here, Cupid." Again the slam of the outer door. Footsteps on the back steps. One, two, three ... She could hear his breaths, just around the corner!

Cupid went. As did Jack, up the stairs, three, two, one, and then the door closed behind them. Heaving a sigh of relief, Nancy scooted across the field to the stables, grabbed a horse blanket and a bucket of oats, and ran all the way back to where Chance was tied. "Here you are, girl," she said, offering the mare some of the oats, which she ignored in favor of the fresh, sweet clover. As the horse ate, Nancy packed her provisions. But she could not bring herself to leave. Not quite yet. There was one more errand she had to perform, back on the other side of the Great House.

She had to say goodbye to Theo.

Once again the Great House loomed over her as she slinked around its haunches, and sped off on the far side towards the small cemetery. Three stone walls guarding three stones was all it was: Ryland, Theodorick, and Baby Boy Randolph, born to Richard and Judith December 12, 1790, died December 15, 1790. Nancy knelt down before Theodorick's stone, to read for the thousandth and last time its mocking inscription:

> Once I was as you are,
> Soon you shall be as I am.

She felt the first tentative raindrops on the nape of her neck. *And then a hand that froze her blood.*

"Such a beautiful inscription," hissed Jack as he stroked where her hair began. "You always preferred Theo's company to mine. Would you like to lie with him now? Be as he is, sooner rather than later?" Nancy was too terrified to speak. "I could strangle you now, and only be serving the law." His grip tightened.

"No," gasped Nancy, brushing one hand away only to feel it replaced by the other, this time squeezing even harder, hurting her so that she had to collapse to the ground to escape the pain. As she rolled over he lay down on top of her, pinning her to the grave. She tried to twist away, but her struggling only worked his wiry body deeper against her.

"Jack, no! Get off of me at once!"

He kissed her, long and deep, but when he pulled his child's face away and she was about to strike it, something stayed her hand. She just looked into that face, and saw that no blow she could strike could ever add to his pain. So she hugged him, not like a lover, but like the sister she was, like the mother he missed so, like the brothers he almost but never really had, and he was a child in her arms, weeping, kissing her lightly, curling up against her breast, promising never, never, to do or to say anything that would hurt his only, truest and best friend in the world.

And that is how Marshall and Jenna found them, in the cemetery, in the rain, fully clothed, quite proper, Jack with his head in Nancy's lap, Nancy sitting up straight against the headstone stroking his hair, Theodorick resting peacefully beneath them both.

Chapter 11

The Refracted Image

1.

Peggy Page was christened Mary Cary like a Christmas jingle, respectfully transformed into Mrs. Carter Page by Mr. Carter Page some eighteen years afterwards, but then and still a jangler. She was sister to Nancy's late mother, Anne Cary Randolph, but such a junior sister as to make her 'Aunt Peggy' in name only. She was pretty in a harsh sort of way, prone to the overuse of rouge to an extent that would have been indictable a century earlier, but which was now deemed trend-setting among that hard group of ladies who run with the pack. She wore her black hair curled, powdered, and enmeshed in various devices that impoverished the avian world without appreciably enriching humankind.

On this dreary Saturday, overhung with the promise of rain not yet fulfilled, Mrs. Page was a-flutter with the last minute preparations for the exciting week to come. Before going out to supervise provisioning for the expected stream of visitors lured to Cumberland by the promise of indecent revelations, Mrs. Page oversaw the work of her two maids-in-waiting in the selection of garments for Mr. Page and herself. For Mr. Page this was easy: simply select a half dozen frock-coats of drab and conservative cut and hue, match them up with an equal number of unremarkable breeches, stockings and undergarments, throw in some hats and cravats, impale the whole lot on a walking stick, and there you have it.

For Mrs. Page, on the other hand, the selection of the vestments for so important a campaign took on the difficulty of provisioning an army. First, and most importantly, there was the question of what to wear for the all-important day in which Mrs. Page was to stand front and center before Virginia society, as star witness for the prosecution. Scarlet seemed too controversial, purple too royal, pastel too vacillatory, white too naive, black too villainous, pink too bubble-headed, red too flirtatious. She settled, at last, on a queen's gown of forest green, or a navy blue lévite gown, the final choice to be reserved for the morning of the great event. Second, but also most importantly, there was the question of what to wear at the ball that she and her husband were hosting Friday next, at which she fully expected to be crowned Queen of the Commonwealth for her cleverness at exposing the murderous deeds of her wayward niece and the niece's adulterous accomplice. Once again the colors of the rainbow seemed alternately too modest, vulgar, parsimonious, matronly, irreverent, bawdy, affected, diffident, anemic, intransigent, or just plain common, to suit the exalted purpose, so once again she settled on either the queen's gown of forest green, or the navy blue lévite gown, depending on which she didn't wear on the day of her testimony. Third, and again most importantly, she selected her broadest folding metal panniers, a device resembling the unwound mainspring of a church clock tower, to be inserted under her gowns in order to expand her physical girth to match the exalted dimensions of her self image.

After completing these matters of state with diplomatic haughtiness, Mrs. Page left for Cumberland, just a mile from the steps of her plantation house, where she had a luncheon engagement with her sister Jane, wife of Thomas Randolph of Dungeness.

The Eagle Tavern of Cumberland was not up to the standards of Richmond's Blue Goose or Williamsburg's Raleigh Tavern. It was better described by the popular wisdom that "Heaven sends good meat, but the Devil sends cooks." Attractive on the outside, with a gambrel roof and broad entry portico, it was nonetheless a haven for overcooked steaks, soggy vegetables, and agglutinated sauces. Mrs. Page gathered up her petticoats and made a grand entrance.

"Jane, so nice to see you," said Peggy, and indeed it was, for these sisters shared that most intense family bond: hatred of the same relations. "Oh, Cedric, is that you?" asked Peggy, seeing a tall, pimply adolescent, half hidden behind a coat rack.

Cedric flashed his most dazzling smile. "Hello, Aunt Peggy, don't you look nice?" said Jane's little boy of nineteen, all blond and self absorbed. Jane's keeping a close watch on this one, thought Peggy, after that near brush with scandal. Indeed, there were still some who said that Cedric may have had more to do with the affair than had yet come out.

"'Thank-you very much, dear boy," answered Peggy, "and you are looking more handsome every day. But with such a pretty momma, I suppose it can't be helped." Jane smiled, knowing that it wasn't quite true, and that of all the Cary girls she, the middle one, had been least endowed by God's finer graces. When she was younger she'd envied Anne her beauty, but what had it gotten her? An early grave after an unhappy marriage to the Colonel, and a daughter in more trouble than she'd ever get out of.

It was fashionable to idle away an afternoon in chatter over lunch, and therefore regardless of the lowly cuisine, the Cary sisters loved the Eagle. Once seated in a private nook – but not so private that they couldn't see and be seen – they began to work their way methodically through the foibles and passions of half the County over a tray of relishes and crudités, pausing occasionally to offer a cautionary word to bored Cedric.

They were daintily sipping the catfish soup by the time they reached the subject of the trial. "So it's definite, is it, that you are to testify?" asked Jane.

"Oh, yes, no doubt about it. I talked to Mr. Binghamton just yesterday. He said that my testimony is most vital to the case." Peggy took a moment to savor her importance. "Of course, I've told you what I know, so I'd be interested in hearing what you think, Jane."

"Oh, well, there's no doubt about it, you and Cedric will blow the whole thing wide open."

"Cedric?" asked Peggy, discomfited to find that she might have a rival in the field of blowing the case open. "I didn't know that Cedric was testifying."

"Oh, yes," said Jane, delighted to be the bearer of a juicy tidbit, "he saw that devilish Richard visit Nancy's room one night."

"Mother!" protested Cedric, "you know what Mr. Binghamton said. We're not supposed to tell anyone."

"But this isn't anyone," said Jane, "it's your dear Aunt Peggy, and we can always tell her everything, right Peggy?"

"Of course," said Peggy, a bit stiffly. "Tell me, Cedric, when did you see this happen?"

"Oh, I don't know," said Cedric, "last January, I guess."

"You guess?" repeated Peggy with emphasis. "You're not going to survive some nasty lawyer's cross-examination by guessing. Either you saw it or you didn't."

"Well, it was dark. But I definitely saw someone slip into Miss Nancy's room late one night, and it must have been Richard."

Jane sighed. "I am really quite worried about him, for he's so unsure of himself that I fear he will be made a fool of. You know what I went through with that horrid breach of promise suit."

"Remind me," coaxed Peggy. "After all, that was twenty years ago, and I was just a child."

"Even now it is painful," began Jane. She took a big gulp of air, screwing up her courage. "When I was twelve, I met a young man of fine family at a ball in Richmond. He was fifteen at the time, and to me he seemed like a God. We courted, and then he promised to marry me when I was his age. After three years of perfect purity, waiting and thinking only of him, I called him on his pledge, but he refused.

"My honor was at stake, so Poppa brought a suit for breach of promise. My betrothed was represented by Patrick Henry – there's a snake in the grass, I don't care what anyone says! So he says to me, 'Miss Cary, is it your testimony that the defendant told you he would marry you when you were his age?' So I said yes. He pauses a second, and looks at me kind of funny, and I didn't know what to think. Suddenly, he shouts right in my face: 'The defendant is eighteen years old. Are you his age?' Well, I didn't know what to say," – here, Cedric could contain his laughter no longer – "Cedric, you stop that this instant. I'm telling this story for your benefit, so listen and profit from it."

Cedric muffled himself with a spoonful of fishy broth, and Jane turned back towards Peggy. "Where was I? Oh yes; I didn't know what to say, since of course I wasn't the same age as that scoundrel, that's not what he meant, at least I hadn't thought so, but that is what he had said. I tried to explain, but you're not allowed to, you just have to answer the questions, and by the time it was all over the case was dismissed and I was in tears." Jane clenched her jaw in anger. "I tell you this not to mourn old losses, but to caution you against the wiles of lawyers. I had a clear case, with right on my side, and never dreamt that it could be destroyed in an instant. Be careful what you say when you're on the witness stand."

Peggy Page shifted uncomfortably in her seat. "I'll take it to heart, Jane, and be sure to be most clear and definite about my testimony. At least," she said, "I shall not have Mr. Patrick Henry to contend with."

"Yes, that's something. And please, don't misunderstand me. I'm proud that Cedric will be testifying, but as a mother I am also worried for him. And I am proud of you as well, dear sister."

On this reassuring note, the two returned to the more mundane atrocities that were the stock in trade of their daily existence. This carried them through the Carthusian, an enormous pudding of savoy cabbage, beets and pig's feet, up to the one thing that was truly delicious on the Eagle's menu: strawberry pie. While they awaited the arrival of this delicacy, lost in conversation and uncharacteristically oblivious to all surrounding them, Cedric's drowsy demeanor suddenly perked up. The Cary sisters followed his gaze to the newest arrival, Mrs. Richard Randolph herself, looking drawn and pale, just as she lit upon their familiar faces and, with a smile of relief, headed their way.

The sisters just had time to exchange a look of perfect understanding, before Judith arrived at their table. "Aunt Jane, Aunt Peggy, it's so nice to see you both. It's been too long, really it has, since you've paid a visit to Bizarre. And you, too, Cedric, so good to see you," said Judith.

These warm salutations were returned, substantially chilled. Judith, blameless niece of these two fine ladies, was left standing by the table, and it was not for lack of chairs that she was not invited to be seated. After some uncomfortable shifting around, and the exchange of a few more cold wishes, the formerly champion idlers suddenly remembered a host of pressing engagements. By the time three fresh cut slices of pie arrived at their table, the Cary sisters and Cedric had rushed off to do the nothing that urgently awaited them anywhere but at the Eagle.

2.

Nancy slept most of Saturday afternoon, but when night fell she became restless. Finally, as midnight approached, she threw aside the downy coverlet, and padded barefoot from the wool carpeting of her chamber onto the chilly bare planks of Bizarre's airless ell-shaped hallway. With a nervous glance over her right shoulder towards Jack's chamber, she tiptoed silently past the Essex chamber, from which Marshall's snores buzzed as regular as bumblebees from a hive, to the master suite at the end of the hall. Slipping in, the door latched behind her with a snap that gave her goose bumps.

The room was deathly still. Nancy could just make out the form of a body illuminated by moonlight in the elegant sheer-canopied Queen Anne double bed in the center of the inner chamber. The upper part of the body protruding from the light comforter was bluish and still. "Judith, are you awake?" she whispered, as she tiptoed closer, past St. George's crib in the outer nursery chamber, past the sitting area near the arches between the two chambers, closer and closer, onto the circular hooked rug upon which the bedstead rested. Gingerly, Nancy extended her hand towards the blue flesh –

"Of course I'm awake," came the harsh voice, startling Nancy so that she jumped back, "I never sleep anymore." Judith sat up and twisted her haggard frame about to get a good look at her sister. "It is one of God's little jokes, when we are happy we sleep away our joy, but when we are miserable we stay awake to suffer every minute." Taking Judith's wan smile as encouragement, Nancy sat lightly on the edge of the bed.

Judith regarded that precious, familiar head of golden hair by her side, longing to take it to her breast and stroke it as she always had, but she did not move. "So many times we stayed up all night," she said, "especially when the moon was full, playing hide and seek in the boxwood hedge. Molly or Beth would always threaten to tell Father, but what did we care if he sent us to our rooms for the day? All we wanted was each other." Judith sighed. "Nancy, oh Nancy, I loved you so," and she began to cry.

"I love you still, Judith," said Nancy, reaching to stroke her face.

Judith's tone turned hard as she pulled back. "If you loved me, you would not have put me in this impossible position," she snapped.

"I never meant to, dear sister," said Nancy. "Please know, I have never wronged you."

Judith sat up. "I don't love you any more, Nancy," she said, but even as the poison passed her lips she knew it was not true. She wanted to snatch it back as she watched Nancy's diaphanous face wither and close like a flower in frost. "You'd best go," she urged, but Nancy did not move, and something about her smug assurance that despite everything she would always have a place in her big sister's bed ignited Judith's fury. Without warning, Judith shoved with months of pent-up rage, and Nancy fell hard to the floor.

"Judith, no!" but it was too late. Judith forced Nancy's head back with a handful of honey-colored hair.

"Let me tell you something, little sister," hissed Judith, "whether you care to hear it or not. I did not come by my husband, my home and my little family easily." St. George was awake and mewling in his peculiar way.

"Stop," cried Nancy, "you're hurting me." But Judith didn't stop, and Nancy could not struggle for fear that the hair would be torn from its roots. In the outer chamber, the night nurse comforted St. George as best she could, while straining to catch the drama.

Judith continued, oblivious to prying ears and Nancy's suffering. "Now by this I do not mean to say that I have the best home or family in Virginia. But that's all right with me, because I'm not so high and mighty as to forget that even the plain ladies have hearts and dreams, and even if we're not so quick-witted at the soirée, our hearts can break, and our dreams are not paper for your privy."

"I am innocent, dear Sister –" began Nancy, but Judith silenced her with a yank.

"Innocent is not how I would describe it." Judith spat the words. "Now be silent and hear me out. I will go to court and trade my honor for your worthless neck, which is more than Jack would have me do, but then I want you out of my home!"

Nancy gasped, frozen in the spectral light. Judith let go, and Nancy fell back into shadows. She could not speak, she just retreated deeper into her dressing gown, seeking comfort now that her second mother was dead to her. There, in the recesses of the gown, she felt the hard shape of the gift she had bought for Judith at Miss Hunter's. She considered whether to present it now, as she'd intended, even after this heart-rending turn of events. The old song rattled around in her brain, teasing her with a hollow longing: *"Judith and Nancy are sisters / Like the sun and the moon above…."* For the first time in her life, she couldn't remember the rest.

"I understand, Judith," her voice trembling and scarcely audible. "But I never laid a hand on Richard."

"Hand or no hand, your cat's eyes were enough," hissed Judith. "Now he stands trial for his life. Do you think he'd do as much for my plain brown eyes?"

"Richard loves you, Judith," whispered Nancy. "And, I pray, the day may even come when you'll long to embrace me again."

Judith said nothing.

Nancy swallowed hard. "In hopes that such a day will come, I will give you the gift I came in here to give," she said, rising, holding out a cylindrical package wrapped in waxed paper and a bit of ribbon, all festive and incongruous. "I got it at Miss Hunter's."

Judith, numb, took the package and unwrapped it in silence. It was a wooden cylinder with glass on either end, like a short telescope. She lifted it to her eye and watched through the little mirrors and tiny pieces of colored glass as Nancy refracted into dozens of rainbow shards. She looked long and hard at the dizzying Nancys.

"It is called a kaleidoscope," said Nancy. "Do you like it?"

"Yes," Judith replied, taking the glass away for a moment. "I look at you now, and see the little sister I loved more than myself. And then I put it to my eye," and she put it to her eye, "and I see your many faces."

CHAPTER 12

PRAYER AND DAMNATION

I.

"*Bonjour,* Robert," said the smooth-voiced mulatto James Hemings to his elder brother. "*Comment va tu? Assieds-toi, mon frère.*"

"Don't speak that Frenchie talk to me," replied Robert, surly as usual. "You know I don't get it." But he sat down nonetheless, put his feet up on the large round table in the kitchen of Monticello, and brandished a folded document bearing the master's seal. "I've been riding as long as I can remember just to get Patsy this here letter from Mr. Thomas, so feed me and leave me be."

"Oh, it's 'Patsy' now, is it?" said Patsy, her big feet slapping the bare stone of the kitchen floor. "Just because your sister Sally's a favorite around here doesn't mean I don't get respect from you Hemings boys."

The barely contained snickers of the brothers belied her. "James," she said, ignoring the insolence in deference to her Poppa's instructions, "you will serve poached eggs with goose ragout, croissants and grape juice for three in the dining room in one-half hour. Robert, you will get your boots off this table, give me the letter from Mr. Thomas, and then manage to find something to eat without getting in James's way. He was not trained in Paris to feed the help."

Robert lowered his feet, one at a time, but made no move to hand over the letter. "Very good," continued Patsy, as if she now had the situation firmly in control. "Oh, and as soon as you have eaten, help my husband get ready for the trip to Bizarre. We will be leaving immediately from the church, so be sure all the bags are packed within an hour. You may as well come along, since we could be there the whole week and may need the help."

Patsy snatched the letter from James's hand and exited through the underground passageway of the south wing back to the main house. Stepping over exposed beams and construction debris, she made her way to her second-floor chamber, flopped down into the alcove that snuggled her prim bed, and began to read.

My Beloved Patsy,

Fear not that your missive shall disappoint one who would be twice as disappointed if you did not consult him in times of greatest need. Why are there fathers, if not to lay troubles at their feet? Shall a father be but a cipher between horse and hat, a hairy thing to cook and sew for, a sort of glue to which the servants and household effects are stuck? I hope not, and if I ever become so, please box my ears and pepper my wig until I sneeze my way back to sense.

I am distressed to find my eldest and most sensible daughter contemplating the slightest deviation from the truth, although I fully understand that your motives are merciful. Mercy is for the Judge; the witness's only concern is truth. You cannot harm the defendants by speaking the truth in any way that they have not already harmed themselves by committing the deeds upon which it is predicated. But to lie, whom then shall you harm? First yourself, for I know the purity of your soul. Second, your family, for perjury is not merely a sin, but also a violation of the laws of man. Third, those unhappy defendants whose salvation would be your object, for if innocent, they rely entirely on the exact truth, with all its subtle currents and eddies, to save them; and if guilty, shall they be relieved of their guilt in the slightest by the knowledge that they have dragged their blameless and beloved sister-in-law down with them?

In a court of law, you answer the question asked, neither more nor less. As for this fellow Marshall, never admit to him a proposition tinctured in the slightest with uncertainty, for no matter how far removed from the point he seeks to establish, by having admitted the former he will demonstrate that you have admitted the latter. Why, if he were to ask me whether it was daylight or not, I'd reply, 'Sir, I don't know. I can't tell.' I had the duty of signing Mr. Marshall's license to practice law when I was Governor, and I am familiar with his qualities. He is an insensitive and unimaginative fellow, but these very flaws coupled with a sharp intellect and overweening ambition make him well suited for the practice of law. If anyone can extricate our unhappy relations from their present difficulties, he is the one to do it – and he'd be only too delighted to get there climbing over the back of a Jefferson, so keep your wits about you.

I have sent a separate letter to Maria to cover daily news and pleasantries. I leave you, my pious daughter, with this cautionary quotation from the Old Testament:

    The first wrote, Wine is the strongest.
    The second wrote, The King is the strongest.
    The third wrote, Women are the strongest:
    but above all Truth beareth away the victory.

Be strong, but be truthful, and all will come out as it should.

    With greatest affection,
    Poppa

Tucking this letter to her breast, Patsy prepared to enjoy the hospitality of her sister-in-law Judith, whose husband and sister her truthful testimony would surely help to hang.

2.

The gentlemen and ladies of Richmond clumped together like fish eggs on the graceful, sloping lawn of St. John's Episcopal Church. Gentle currents of status ebbed and flowed among them, here slightly tugging one down, there imperceptibly puffing another up. Tobacco and slaves changed hands, invitations were extended, snubs endured, cock fights arranged. Beardless beaus tussled and threw knives, making a grand show of disregarding the young ladies they sought to impress. Children, magnificently scrubbed and stuffed into starched breeches, scratchy tights, and frilly miniature gowns, wiggled and bit their tongues. Coach drivers and footmen sweated and squirmed in their ill-fitting homespun livery. Everywhere, there was the eager buzz of gossip, tall tales and small talk that greases a town's moving parts.

Of course the Brett Randolphs were present, as he was a vestryman of the Church, and could not miss a service even on excuse of the pending ride to Cumberland. Were that a valid excuse, half the congregation would be absent. But the Brett Randolphs had special reason to attend the trial, in view of their extremely close connections with the accused and their household. Brett was first cousin to Richard, and since he had indulged himself in the Randolph predilection for marrying first cousins, his wife, Anne Randolph of Curles, was also first cousin to Richard. These connections had, in the natural course of things, led to much visiting to and fro, especially by Anne, since she at nineteen years junior to her husband, liked to cavort with the younger set. Brett had never approved of the licentious air about Bizarre, and had warned Anne to stay away, but she would not listen. Now she had gotten her comeuppance for ignoring his advice: a subpoena from the prosecution.

"Anne, darling," cooed one of the pious ladies of the congregation, "you must be positively mortified by the thoughtlessness of your cousins, to have placed you in such a position. Do you know that I actually saw that young hussy just the other day, boldly strutting down the public way as if she'd nothing to hide."

"Perhaps she doesn't, Ma'am," replied Anne, a serious young woman with a slight build and pensive features, who was doing her best to remain polite. "After all, she has not yet been convicted."

"Come now, Anne, tell us the truth of what went on there. I've heard that the whole family shared a single bed, and that they cavorted about *au naturale* on warm days. Is this true? And what about Richard? Did he actually bestow improper attentions upon Nancy at the dinner table, right before Judith's eyes?"

"Oh, this is too absurd! Don't tell me you believe any of these slanders? I am sorry, but you really must apologize for these remarks."

"I will not," said the lady, indignantly. "I only know what I have heard from reputable sources, people of the best quality, people not distracted by a close blood tie to the source of the contagion."

Anne put her hand to her lips, to quell a retort she might later regret. "I think that will do," said Brett, efficiently maneuvering his wife through the predatory waters towards the refuge of their private pew.

The Reverend Jenkins felt it his duty to impose the day's homily on the distinguished congregation for twenty minutes or so, the subject of which was *The Law of God, and the Law of Man.* "There is no law, but finds its origins in the laws of God. The civil laws of Man derive their only just authority, in that they are rooted in concepts of good and evil derived from the teachings of Christianity. Thus, it is a sin to murder, and so it is a crime. It is a crime to commit adultery or incest, but first it is a sin."

Mrs. Brett Randolph blanked out before the drone of convenient truisms, platitudes in a consecrated hall that once rang to the thrilling refrain, "I know not what course others may take, but as for me, give me liberty, or give me death!" Anne's reveries were shattered when a porcine gentleman immediately to her right sneezed a hefty sneeze, only half into his hastily snatched handkerchief. *It's a sin to sneeze, and so it is a crime. It's a crime to sin, and so it is a sneeze.*

"It is right that it should be so," intoned the Reverend, clearly attempting to compensate for taking Jesus too seriously the week before. "Life for life, Eye for eye, Tooth for tooth, Hand for hand, Foot for foot, Burning for burning," thereby obliterating Jesus and his quirky concepts of mercy altogether by invoking the Old Testament. Snub for snub, Smirk for smirk, Lie for lie, Jab for jab, but this solves nothing, mused Anne. Poverty for luxury, Humility for haughtiness, Truth for deception, Understanding for ignorance, Forgiveness for vituperance, Gentleness for violence, isn't that Christianity?

"Each day we pray the Lord to deliver us from evil. He has answered our prayers by giving us the ability to make and enforce our own laws, laws that preserve and protect His kingdom on Earth. Blessed are the Courts, the Judges, the lawyers, and the jurors, and let us pray that in these difficult times their vision will be clear, so that they may do the

Lord's work in delivering us from evil; For Thine is the kingdom, and the power, and the glory, for ever and ever. Amen."

"*Amen,*" murmured the congregation in unison, satisfied to hear that their views in the matter were shared by God. Ah, *men,* thought Anne, always in need of God's permission to do what they fully intend to do anyway. Dear Lord, please deliver us from – from – *ourselves.*

As Anne left her pew the Colonel and Mrs. Harlan Beauregard Randolph of Tuckahoe left theirs in the Goochland Episcopal Church. Slowly they shuffled towards the exit where the Reverend Dumpkin was taking a last stab at the departing souls. When the Colonel finally reached the doorway the Reverend grasped both his hands with unctuous fervor. "My dear Colonel and Mrs. Randolph, I know that this will be an exceptionally trying week for you, and if there is anything that either I or Mrs. Dumpkin can do for you, you have simply to name it."

"God bless you, Reverend," replied the Colonel; *just let go,* he added in silent prayer.

"If you could sweep up your wayward daughter in the firm embrace of your own righteousness, Colonel, then all would be as it should be. I shall pray that all comes out well here on Earth. Thereafter, it will be for the One Unerring Judge to mete out the punishments as they are deserved."

The Colonel squirmed, still prisoner to the Reverend's clammy grip. "Thank-you," said Colonel Randolph, and mercifully the good Reverend released him. He and Gabriella quickly mounted their carriage for the ride to Mrs. Biddlesworth's. They pulled the curtains tight, and the coachman heard a mocking voice say, "Oh Colonel, if you'll jest sweep me up in the firm embrace of your righteousness, I'll do anything you want."

"Anything?"

"*Anything the Lord wants of me, I will do!*" cried the Harrisons, Mrs. Biddlesworth, and forty other impassioned Baptists at the Baptist Church of Sunnyside, near Cumberland, where the Grant Harrisons and Mrs. Biddlesworth were attending Sunday services. The Baptists, unlike the Episcopalians, took Heaven and Hell seriously. Their Sabbath was not principally devoted to socializing and commerce, but to fervent, rhythmical invocations of the gaping, sulfurous depths of damnation, the explicit details of each torment wreaked upon the unrepentant sinner, the endless variety of devious methods employed by Beelzebub to insinuate himself into the most innocuous forms of daily intercourse, the insignificance of human reason in the face of the imponderable wonders of creation, and the panacea of accepting Jesus. The Baptist Sabbath was a time for singing, fervent prayer, speaking in tongues, outing the Devil, shaking and sweating and cleansing oneself in the Blood of the Lamb. *Hallelujah!*

"If He calls on you to deliver up your firstborn son, what will you do?" thundered the Reverend John Weatherford.

"Deliver up our firstborn son," cried the assembly without an instant's reflection.

"And will you do it with pain in your heart?"

"No."

"And will you do it reluctantly?"

"No."

"For there are things in this world that are greater than the understanding of Man. There is evil in this world. The Devil lurks under each petticoat, over each bedstead, in the dirt between the floorboards."

This last assertion was at once so comical and yet so frightening that it could not have been carried off by a lesser bible thumper than the Reverend Weatherford, a legend among the preachers who had struck Virginia like a lightening bolt in the early days of the Baptist revival. The good Reverend had survived repeated imprisonments and other forms of persecution at the hands of the local guardians of orthodoxy, but these had only served to strengthen his faith in God and himself, which were perilously intertwined. Endowed with a voice like spun gold, resonant, flexible and powerful, and a broad, simple face that could at once hold all the longing, pain and ecstasy of life, he was a natural for the pulpit, or the bar. Patrick Henry himself had not only defended the man, but closely studied his style.

"And so I say to each and every one of you, be eternally vigilant, and fear not to shatter the complacency of everyday morality, for it is no morality at all, and it hides beneath its corpulent veneer a pu-tre-fy-ing wickedness." The Reverend squeezed every drop of slime out of 'putrefying,' and spread it across 'wickedness' with a long hiss. "Seek out the boils of evil wherever they erupt, and let your voice be like a lance to open the venom to the cold, purifying light of Jesus! *Hallelujah!*"

The air was lanced with Hallelujahs, loudest and most fervent among which was the Hallelujah of Grant Harrison. The Lord has called, he thought, and I shall not hesitate.

Mrs. Wood waited outside by the carriage, reading from her Bible and watching Elly crawl through the dandelions. She could not abide all that hollering and moaning in her religion. It seemed to her that the worst were always loudest in their piety. If God is worth his salt, he could be credited with a little dignity, to say nothing of a good enough sense of hearing to catch a whispered prayer. *Or footsteps on the stairs in the middle of the night.*

"Dear Lord," she whispered, "give me the strength to be honest and truthful, without malice in my heart, so's I may help the cause of righteousness in court. I trust in thee to be eyes to this poor blind servant." Out of the corner of her eye she saw Elly come within striking distance of the horses' hooves, and she snatched her back. Over Elly's frustrated cries she whispered "Amen. There, there, Elly, it's all right. We have to stay away from horses' hooves, that's all." And the sobs subsided as she sang this tune:

> *The fishmonger's wife ran free,*
> *Out on a summer's day,*
> *It smelled of fish in her old house,*
> *She had to get away,*
> *She boarded a ship and sailed the seas,*
> *To a land where fishwives go,*
> *Where roses smell like mackerel,*
> *But smelt smell rosy-o, ahh,*
> *The smelt smell rosy-o!*
> *And sing hey! for the bonny fishwife,*
> *She's happier than you think,*
> *Sing hey! for the bonny fishwife,*
> *For at last her hands don't stink*
> *Ohhhhhh*
> *At last her hands don't stink!*

"Mrs. Wood, have some respect for the Sabbath!" Mr. Harrison glared at her with disapproval. "Now come, we're going to Cumberland."

Everyone was going to Cumberland. Cumberland was growing this day by leaps and bounds, as if it had suddenly sunk to the core of the Earth, and all the people for miles about were sliding into the pit despite themselves. Mr. Peyton Harrison, Grant Harrison's cousin and an occasional visitor to Bizarre, slid off of his bar stool and stumbled eastward in the general direction of Cumberland from the Blood of the Patriot Tavern at Sprouse's Corner. From the West came a healthy chunk of Richmond and part of Williamsburg and Petersburg, including Jane Cary Randolph and her pimply son Cedric. "Now remember, Cedric, you are positive it was Richard that you saw."

"Yes, Mother."

"That's a good boy."

Hawkers of tin, silks, pottery, carpets, spectacles, patent remedies, barbecued and salted meats, smoked eel, spirits and ales, carved miniatures, toys of all kinds, and a host of other wonders never before seen in Cumberland, appeared out of nowhere and set up their stands on the green in front of the courthouse. A troupe of actors materialized, advertising Shakespearean wonders as seen by the Crown Princes of Europe for that very evening, but they were promptly closed down by Sheriff Dunby for violating the Sabbath laws. A troupe of wrestlers, made wiser by the example of the actors, advertised a gouging contest for the next evening. The law which prohibited the Bard of Avon on Sunday said nothing about tearing a man's eye from its socket on Monday, so the Sheriff left them unmolested.

The Carter Pages received family and friends all day long. Aunt Peggy in a magnificent scarlet gown gave each caller a warm embrace and a big kiss, and Mr. Page in black and white gave each caller, including his sister-in-law Jane, a perfunctory hug and a peck in the general direction of her cheek.

After church, Mrs. Biddlesworth spent a very satisfactory day turning away prospective customers who, despite membership in the best families, apparently lacked the ability to read the simple sign that she had posted: "No Vagrancy."

The Harrisons, Mrs. Wood, Cousin Anne, Aunt Peggy, former suitor Cedric, sister-in-law Patsy – all subpoenaed as witnesses for the prosecution. With so many called against Richard and Nancy, who was left to speak for them?

A man bent with age, but with the friendly blue eyes, aquiline nose, and wide mouth known so well to all Virginians, stopped his one-stick gig by a marsh, and crouched in the grass, quietly tamping down his powder. When the grapeshot was loaded, he picked up a stone and flung it to the far end of the marsh. Startled, several ducks flew away from the false danger, into a hail of hot pellets. Patrick Henry could still shoot 'em dead. Slinging dinner over his buckskin jacket, he continued on the road to Cumberland.

PART TWO
THE TRIAL

Chapter 13

The Defense Never Rests

I.

The breakfast table at Mrs. Biddlesworth's brought together an odd assortment of those best left apart. The merely curious were represented by Jean Pierre Blanchard, a little mouse of a man with sparkling black eyes and impeccable grooming who was said to be a displaced French nobleman. The partisans of the defense were represented by Judge Tucker and his second wife, Leila Skipworth Tucker. The partisans of the prosecution were represented by Peyton Harrison and Nancy's step-mother, Gabriella Harvie Randolph, who kept a secret prosecution subpoena tucked under her bodice. The defendant herself was balanced precariously between her squash-headed counsel and her father, picking listlessly at her bowl. Oblivious, Colonel Randolph greedily slurped at his porridge.

As Nancy sipped from the plain rainwater put out by Mrs. Biddlesworth, her eyes met Gabriella's. "Hello, Gabby, have you come to testify against me, too?"

"Don't be ridiculous, my dear. Your father supports you, and I support him."

"To look at you, one wouldn't think it possible," shot back Nancy.

"Miss Randolph!" scolded Marshall.

An audible silence filled the room. "Excuse us," said Gabriella, rising, and she looked to the Colonel, who looked from wife to daughter to porridge and back to his wife again. Gabriella marched out and, with a parting shrug to his porridge, the Colonel excused himself and followed.

Nancy immediately won back the table with her most contrite smile. "I'm so sorry, ladies and gentlemen - it must be the strain of the circumstances."

The little Frenchman jumped to his feet and executed a sharp bow. "I cannot speak for zee others, Mademoiselle," said Monsieur Blanchard, "but for me, I believe in you."

Marshall consulted his pocket watch for the tenth time in as many minutes. It was twenty-five minutes before nine. The trial upon which so much depended was to begin at nine. He had no appetite. If only he had gotten some sleep! All his many ideas for the defense were but a jumble in his fevered brain. "Excuse me," he said, bolting up and half running out the back way to relieve the twisting in his bowels.

Nancy looked up from her lumpy porridge to find the lumpy-headed Sheriff Dunby beckoning to her from the front hallway. She turned for Marshall's assistance, but he was gone. She went to the back doorway and called to him, in vain. Judge Tucker, who had been conferring with the Sheriff, came over to offer his arm, which she gratefully accepted. But the Sheriff insisted that more was required.

Marshall spent his final minutes of trial preparation behind the radiant carved sun of the gentleman's necessary house. While Marshall's pants were down, the Sheriff led his young client in irons past hundreds of pitiless gawkers to a holding cell in the courthouse. She held back her tears until there was no one to see.

2.

"Your Honor, this is an outrage!" railed Marshall to the back of Judge Archer Allen's head. The Judge, Marshall, Mr. Binghamton, Sheriff Dunby and Mr. Critch were gathered in Chambers at Marshall's request to hear certain motions, the first of which was for an order that the Sheriff not be permitted to bring the defendants into court in irons. While Marshall continued his impassioned plea, the Judge was brewing tea on the credenza behind his desk. "I turn my back for a moment, and this ruffian seizes my client," continued Marshall, gesturing with contempt towards the chinless Sheriff, "and parades her in chains before the crowds, including dozens of potential jurors. He may as well have hung a 'Guilty' sign around her neck."

"Your Honor," interjected Mr. Binghamton, "there is not a court in the Commonwealth that permits defendants, especially capital defendants, to run around loose."

"And do we still countenance trial by ordeal?" Marshall replied indignantly. "Shall we have the defendants snatch a stone from a pot of boiling water, to see if their hands are scalded? Shall we bind them and set them in a pot of frigid water to see if they float? Shall we have them swallow a feather to see if they choke? At one time courts in England followed these procedures, but were they proper? Change comes about when judges think for themselves, instead of blindly following the behinds of others."

Satisfied at last with his cup of tea, Judge Allen turned towards Marshall, who continued. "There have been major changes in the political circumstances of this Commonwealth since these barbaric procedures were employed. Under our Virginia Bill of Rights, the accused is presumed to be innocent until proven, by clear proof in open court, to be guilty."

Marshall rose and crossed the paneled chamber to plant himself beneath the portrait of Sir Thomas Dale, second Governor of Jamestown, a stern and deeply religious man who served as judge, jury and executioner for the fledgling settlement. "And from where shall the proof of guilt come?" asked Marshall rhetorically. "Why the Constitution says it: from the lips of 'the accusers and the witnesses,' not from the clanking of chains that know nothing of the events in question. Do we chain innocent people?" Judge Allen crossed his legs. "Chains undo the presumption of innocence," he cried, and the power of his words overcame the raspiness of his voice. "They are incompetent but eloquent witnesses for the prosecution, and they should therefore be barred from the courtroom."

As Marshall sat, the Judge slurped loudly at his teacup, then said, "Mr. Binghamton?"

"It would be quite improper and totally unprecedented –"

"I quite agree, Mr. Binghamton," said the Judge. "Motion denied. Now, shall we proceed with the trial before the defendants die of old age?"

"But Your Honor, with all due respect, I have another motion."

"Blast you, Marshall," shouted the Judge, but he seemed to think better of it, sat back down, erased all anger from his face, softened his tone, and emitted a nondescript, "proceed."

"A felony may not be proved solely by circumstantial evidence, Your Honor, yet that is what the prosecution intends to do here. The only witnesses to actual events are either the defendants themselves, who cannot, under our Bill of Rights, be compelled to give evidence against themselves, and certain colored servants, who of course are strictly forbidden by law from testifying. Most telling of all is the absence of a body, which, according to Sir Matthew Hale as quoted in Blackstone, requires dismissal of any charge of murder or manslaughter. All that the prosecution has to rely on are circumstances. For that reason, the case should be dismissed."

"Binghamton, what do you say?" asked the Judge, who, for the first time, seemed to be seriously considering Marshall's arguments.

"We have a body, Your Honor," exclaimed Binghamton with bravado, but then he thought better of it. "Well, not actually a body, but a white witness who saw a body."

"A body but not a body?" sneered the Judge. "What became of it?"

"We're not sure."

"Did anyone else see it?"

"The witness's servant, Your Honor. A trusted slave."

"In the eyes of the law, Mr. Binghamton, there is no such thing. Is the rest of your case purely circumstantial, as Mr. Marshall says?"

"Circumstantial evidence is inherently no weaker than direct because –"

"Nonsense," snapped the Judge, and he fixed the prosecutor with an angry stare. "I hope you have not troubled this Court by bringing before it a case based solely on inference, Mr. Binghamton."

"Of course not, Your Honor," said Mr. Binghamton, squirming like a worm on a hook, because he had.

"What direct witness shall you have?" asked the Court.

What direct witness indeed? "Why, the one just alluded to."

"Who cannot connect the body, if there was one, with the defendants," interjected Marshall.

"Anyone else?" probed the Judge.

"There shall be the defendants themselves," offered Binghamton hopefully, unsure why this was an answer, knowing only that if anyone had been at the scene of the crime, surely they had.

"But as Mr. Marshall correctly points out, they need not testify."

"But from their silence the jurors may infer –" having said the word he wished he could bite it out of the air and swallow it up, but he plunged on bravely, hoping against hope that it would go unnoticed, "– that they are guilty."

"And so I ask again, Mr. Binghamton," said the Judge, who had very distinctly noted the uneaten word, "what *direct* evidence will you have?"

Binghamton decided on a different tact. "Your Honor, at this time the case looks very strong, and there will certainly be direct evidence, but to reveal its nature would threaten its source. The Court should not be too hasty to dismiss a murder charge of such importance on a point of evidence until all the evidence has been heard. To do so would be a disservice to the many citizens of this Commonwealth who expect justice to be dispensed in open court, and indeed, would even be a disservice to Mr. Marshall's own client, who demanded a trial to clear his name."

"Political pressures ought not to change the applicable rule of law," responded Marshall. "No matter how much the mob may be clamoring for blood, if the case is purely circumstantial it must be thrown out. And as for what best serves my client, until he has retained you, Mr. Binghamton, I think I am better suited to speak for him."

The Judge regarded the two attorneys for a moment, before a sparkle of amusement came into his eyes. "Of course the Court would not be swayed for an instant by political considerations, Mr. Marshall. However, since this County still suffers from an old jail crammed into the basement of the courthouse, we can easily get the defendants in here to ask them whether Mr. Binghamton has misrepresented their desires in this matter."

"Your Honor –" objected Marshall.

"No, let's hear from them. Sheriff, bring in the defendants."

"Your Honor," said Marshall, "if I might have a minute to confer with my clients before this inquisition?"

"Mr. Marshall, if I had wanted to know what you would tell them to say, I'd have asked you," said the Judge, his quick eyes dancing with glee. "Bring them in!"

"But this is most irregular."

"Irregular?" parroted Judge Allen. "Mr. Marshall, this is one Judge who refuses to blindly follow the behinds of others."

There was the heavy sound of shackles dragging against the wooden planks, as the defendants were brought into chambers the back way, avoiding the courtroom. "You will remain standing," ordered the

Judge. "I have brought you in here because your clever lawyer has suggested a basis for dismissing the charges against you on a technicality. I might be inclined to grant his motion, in which case you would be free to go, but you would never have the trial you asked for to clear your name. Do you wish to stand on the technicality and force me to decide whether you must go free without a trial, or waive it and face trial?"

Stunned, Richard and Nancy sought direction first in the Judge's face, then Marshall's, then each other's. At last, Richard spoke. "Were it just myself, I would waive the technicality. But inasmuch as the Lady is involved –"

"No!" interjected Nancy. "We are not guilty, but our names are despoiled, which makes life unlivable. Trying one of us will clear us both, yet risk only one. Try me, and let Richard go."

"Absolutely not," said Richard. "Try me, and let the lady go free."

"That settles it," said the Judge. "The Clerk shall note that the defendants have each demanded to be tried. We shall try them both."

Marshall lunged at the Judge's writing table. "Your Honor, that's not what they meant!"

The Judge stood and faced him down, flexing the power of his office. "No more motions, Mr. Marshall, or we'll try you too. Now let's get to work."

3.

The courtroom looked magnificent, with the railing and the window sills bedecked in red white and blue bunting, the gallery brimming with brass-buttoned frock coats, satin collars, spit-shined leather boots, well-filled silk bodices, ribbons, ruffles and feathers. Beyond the seated gentry stood common farmers who, though they could ill afford to do it, had taken a few days off from plowing and planting to come see the once-in-a-lifetime spectacle of two Randolphs on trial. With the exception of the family and certain important gentlemen and their ladies, the spectators had stood in line outside the courtroom in the chill pre-dawn darkness in order to beat the crowd which was many times as large outside.

During the delay occasioned by the proceedings in chambers, the mood had turned from respectful and expectant to boisterous and impatient, and denunciations of the defendants had become more frequent and impassioned. "This is what comes from too much idleness," loudly exclaimed a woman in the second row; "I'd say it was the lack of piety," added her interlocutor in the fourth row; "It is the natural fate of those who mistake liberties for license," patiently explained a gentleman caught in between rows; "No, it is simply a failure of disciplined self restraint," corrected the gentleman at his side; "She's a looker, cain't deny it," shouted one of the farmers. Despite the glut of explanations, there was a remarkable shortage of forgiveness. In the time it took Marshall to present two motions, his clients were convicted twenty times over.

A sudden hush fell when the door to chambers opened. Mr. Critch crossed to his desk at the left as if he was routinely fetching a file from an empty room, oblivious to the rapt scrutiny. Next, the stenographer entered, took his place at the lowest tier of the bench, and began methodically lining up the dozen quills and ink wells needed to scratch the shame deep into memory. Then Binghamton emerged, acknowledging the crowd with a few handshakes to gentlemen of the bar who were close behind his table, projecting a confidence that gave no clue as to how near he had just come to losing his case before it had even begun.

There was a slight pause, followed by the clanking of irons that promised the crowd its first glimpse of the accuseds in court. First came the Sheriff, with something unpleasant clinging to his nose hairs, followed by Richard, his dark, handsome face looking straight ahead through glassy eyes. Judith rose, but she had to call to get his attention. Ignoring her outstretched arms, he smiled weakly as he walked by her to talk to Judge Tucker. The crowd murmured its disapproval. Then Nancy appeared on Marshall's arm, looking artificially virginal in white muslin, and the murmurings got louder and uglier. Nancy looked at her shuffling feet as she clanked towards the defense table, only to be redirected towards Judith by a little poke from Marshall. Judith's eyes kissed Richard as her lips pecked a prearranged kiss on Nancy's cheek.

Nancy fought back tears. She moved to embrace her sister, but the chains intervened. She was pale as the moon. Marshall led her to her seat for fear she would faint, but she refused to be turned back without a careful look at the many hostile faces arrayed against her.

"Murderess," "harlot," "witch," hissed the crowd. Somehow Nancy summoned a startlingly genuine smile. Dozens of eyes dropped or turned away, but a few stayed, softened, and a return smile or two took root in the rocky soil of the gallery.

Richard and Judge Tucker were engaged in a furious whispered consultation by the railing behind the defense table. As Marshall moved to join them, he heard the Judge say "– no choice but to go forward without him –" before the Judge noticed him and bit his tongue. "Ah, Mr. Marshall, Mr. Marshall," he said, startling Richard who spun on his heel with a guilty look. "Make 'em think up is down," said the Judge with a forced smile, and he gave Marshall a thumbs up.

"All rise!" and the crowd jumped to its feet to greet Judge Allen, whose flowing dark robes so upstaged his pale skin, thin lips and short graying blond hair, that it was easy to miss the man behind the judge. "*Oyez oyez oyez,*" intoned Mr. Critch in his native tongue, "the County Court for the County of Cumberland is now in assize, sitting in oyer and terminer upon the cause and matter of Commonwealth of Virginia versus Richard Randolph and Anne Cary Randolph, this Twenty-Ninth Day of April, year of Our Lord Seventeen Hundred and Ninety-Three, Honorable Archer Mather Allen presiding. *Oyez oyez oyez,* all who have evidence relative to the cause now under consideration draw near, and ye shall be heard. God Bless the Commonwealth of Virginia and the United States of America!" and with a whack of the Clerk's gavel court was in session.

The Judge spent a few moments arranging his papers, and then looked up. "Is the Commonwealth ready?" he asked perfunctorily, for if it was not there would be Hell to pay.

"Ready, Your Honor," said Binghamton.

"And is the Defense ready?"

Marshall stood but the voice answering was not his dry little buzz, but instead the resonant, confident voice of a man who had seen far worse odds and emerged triumphant. "The defense, Your Honor," said the square-jawed old man in the blood-streaked buckskin jacket who passed between parting waves of farmers as easily as Moses through the

Red Sea, "is now quite ready to lick this pathetic case put together by a prosecutor who has nothing better to do than to disturb the domestic tranquility of respectable families based on the titterings of niggers' tongues."

The crowd roared in laughter, then burst into applause, as this phoenix crossed the railing that separates the bar from the masses. Judge Allen pounded his gavel. "Order, order, there shall be order in the Court," he yelled, but there was none until the intruder himself turned to the crowd and drew his finger across his stubble-encrusted throat.

In the ensuing silence he turned his weathered face towards the bench and proclaimed, "Your Honor, my deepest apologies for disrupting the decorum which you so richly deserve by this tardy arrival, but the journey from my Long Island plantation is arduous, and I'm not as quick as I used to be. Nonetheless, Your Honor, Patrick Henry, Esquire, at your service," and here he bowed low as his stiffened old joints would permit, "engaged at Mr. Richard Randolph's behest as co-counsel with the esteemed Mr. John Marshall, on behalf of the unfortunate, unjustly maligned Mr. Richard and Miss Nancy." Turning to Marshall he winked one of his mischievous blue eyes. "Mr. Marshall, Sir, are we ready?" he asked in mock horror, before answering with contempt: "Are two bears ready to do battle with a hedgehog?" As he laughed, the crowd laughed with him, loving him, and thereby, by that process most human, preparing to love all whom he would enfold in his embrace.

Mr. Patrick Henry, former Governor, Member of the First Continental Congress, first Commander in Chief of the Revolutionary Virginia forces, embraced Richard, shook Marshall's unwilling hand, and kissed Nancy's manacled hand. "What's this?!" he roared. "We chain Ladies in Virginia? Is this what so many fought and died for during those dark days of the Revolution? Are we, a free people, afraid of this woman?" He strode to the bench, taking Judge Allen into his confidence, not to plead so much as to collaborate. "Surely Your Honor has overlooked this assault upon Southern Womanhood, else he would himself have removed the offending manacles. Your Honor, shall the Sheriff be ordered at once to unchain this woman, and Mr. Richard too, out of fairness and respect for his stature as a Gentleman?"

"Your Honor –" began Mr. Binghamton, but already the cries welled up from the crowd, "Unchain the Lady!" "Disgraceful!" and for fear of a riot Judge Allen nodded to the Sheriff, who was roundly hissed until he realized that his precious chains would have to go, and he went about removing them.

"Shall we proceed to draw a jury, Gentlemen?" asked the Judge, but Marshall had by then recovered sufficiently from the shock to find his tongue.

"Your Honor," he said in a voice pinched by rage, "if I may still be permitted to speak in this matter, you have addressed a question to *me* which is, as yet, unanswered by *me*. You asked if the defense was ready to proceed, and the most curious thing has transpired." Marshall shot a withering glance at Richard. "Although the defense was ready to proceed at the moment the question was asked, before I could answer it the defense became quite unready to proceed, indeed, the defense lost all sense of who directs it. Under the circumstances I must respectfully defer to my esteemed superior in both eloquence and audacity, Mr. Henry, to carry on as admirably as he has started. I hereby resign and withdraw my appearance."

"No!" "No!" "No!" cried Nancy, Judge Tucker and Henry with one voice, all leaping to their feet and yanking on Marshall's ill-fitting frock coat as he attempted to gather up his notes and scurry away.

Whack! went Judge Allen's gavel. "There will be a recess until one o'clock this afternoon while the defense attempts to determine who represents it. Until that time, Mr. Marshall, your withdrawal from this case is not recognized by the Court." Judge Allen strode out in disgust, as pandemonium erupted in the courtroom.

4.

Judge Tucker shrunk under Marshall's fiercest glare. "You gave me your word, Judge," was all Marshall said, but the tone of his voice and his glowering eyes spoke volumes.

The Judge just looked at his hands, tired hands, folded before him on the rough-hewn table in the conference room. Around that table were arrayed in civil war what should have been the army of the defense. Patrick Henry sat at one end, scowling at Marshall who was seated at the opposite end, while Richard and the Judge brooded off to Henry's right, and Nancy and the Colonel sat across on Marshall's right. What could the Judge say? "Perhaps it was not mine to give," he offered at last. "It is Richard who is on trial here, not me."

"Is your word available to be broken at the convenience of others?" snapped Marshall, the lack of sleep and shock of having this plum case pulled out from under him getting the better of his judgment. "Really, Judge, you astonish me!"

"He astonishes you?" burst out Richard, no longer able to contain himself. "He astonishes you? What of your lies to me, when you tried to trick me into confessing the very crime against which you are supposed to defend me? It is you who astonish us, Mr. Marshall."

"I was simply using my wits to try to draw the truth out of you, Mr. Randolph," countered Marshall testily. "I thought that was the point of this retainer - someone in this blasted family has to be able to rely on something other than the simple coincidence of birth."

"Now, just a minute Marshall," barked the Colonel, half standing and leaning forward on his hands so he looked like a bulldog about to pounce, "remember yo' place here. We've hired you to do a job, and as near as I kin tell, every time the going gets tough you git on your high horse about somethin' while someone else has to come in and bail you out. What have you accomplished here? I cain't think of a single thing other than to grovel for a big fee, which no gentleman would stoop to doing."

"Quite so, then, Colonel," replied Marshall, resigned to seeing his golden opportunity slip away, "as I have already indicated in open court, you have my resignation, and you shall have a full refund tomorrow." Marshall winced inwardly at his own bravado, wondering how much of the fee was already spent. He'd find the money somewhere. Above all, he was determined to salvage his pride; these people must see that he was no mere tradesman, not just another plodding country lawyer better suited to sorting out will challenges and disputed property titles. "It is only the Court's order that holds me now," he continued, "and I am sure that a clearly expressed preference by you for Mr. Henry as soon as court reconvenes will loosen that last bond. But before I go, I must warn my worthy successor, Mr. Henry, that I have already won this impossible case once, but once was not good enough for the clients, who are more determined to hang than Bing-hamton is to hang them."

"What's this?" asked Henry.

"The Court was prepared to dismiss the case as purely circum-stantial," answered Marshall, "but that was not satisfactory to our clients. Apparently they will only settle for a complete acquittal on the merits."

"That's not exactly right –" began Richard, but Henry cut him off.

"And well they should. A technical dismissal in a matter of this kind? Ridiculous!" Henry stood, and began pacing around the room, ever the orator, stalking his adversary, wooing his audience. "A techni-cal dismissal on charges of murder and adultery? What does that do to dispel the dishonor? Why nothing! Indeed, it confirms it. Would you care to go before your neighbors cleared of such a charge on a *technicality?*" Henry drew out the word in disdain. "I think not! This, Marshall, is not what we want to trade in, a petty search for the loop-hole and the lapse of logic."

"I do not recognize the meaning of this word, 'technicality,'" rejoined Marshall, testily. "Either it is the law, or it is not. If, under the law, my client should go free, he should go free."

"What about Chiswell?" boomed Henry. Marshall looked blank. "No, you wouldn't remember, before your time. He went free on a technicality, and ended up blowing out his own brains! The guilt and shame ate him up, and thus, for a technical liberty, he lost both honor and life."

"Sounds like a fool," said Marshall.

"A fool?" asked Henry, leaning close to Marshall to whisper, "or a man?" Then he stepped back and boomed, "A man with a heart, who values honor, who suffers no insults, who would sooner die than live a certain degraded kind of life. These are not matters for technical solu-tion, Marshall. They are matters that must be grappled with, fought over, we must sweat, we must cry, we must laugh and ridicule and scream with fear. Perhaps we will lose, I do not think so, but perhaps we will. But if we lose we will lose with honor, we will sow doubt, we will win friends, there will be jurors who will cry even as they cast their vote for conviction. We're not fixing a watch, you bloodless jeweler!"

Henry sat down, that old magic still there, the room sparkling with the effect of his rhetoric.

Somehow, Marshall drew the strength to stand his ground. "Mr. Henry," he croaked, sounding froggier than ever in comparison with the gossamer of Henry's voice, "by approaching the case with virtually no knowledge of the facts, you will almost certainly lose, and whether you lose with or without honor, the result will be the same for your unfortunate clients."

Henry scoffed at him, but Nancy raised her hand. "Pray continue, Mr. Marshall," she said.

"For Mr. Henry it is a game of dice," said Marshall. "He throws them and if they come up craps he moves on to the next game, leaving you to pay the price. For me, on the other hand, there is no chance involved. By approaching the matter rationally, I will convince the jury that the evidence does not show guilt, at which point they will have no choice but to acquit –" Here, Marshall stopped himself. "But what am I saying? I am out of it, and I wish you all good luck." Marshall rose and with a curt bow prepared to go, but he was stopped when Nancy reached out and took his hand.

"It is not just Richard who is on trial here today," she said softly. He moved again as if to go, but she held him as much with the autumn sadness of her eyes as with her touch. "Do not abandon me now, Sir, when I need you most," she pleaded, rising, placing herself between Marshall and the doorway. "Mr. Henry cannot do it alone, any more than you, I fear, could have done it alone. What is a heart without a head, or a head without a heart?" Her frightened gaze flicked from ungainly Marshall to craggy Henry, and back again. "We need you both, Gentlemen, and I pray you to put aside your differences for a few days, that our lives" – here she looked at Marshall – "and our sacred honor" – here at Henry – "may both be preserved."

Marshall hesitated long. Nancy's plea offered the fig leaf his wounded pride needed to permit him to continue. Marshall knew that if he walked away now he might never again be offered a case of such magnitude. He couldn't help thinking that this was all a stupid misunderstanding – that his days of careful probing and preparation would pay off if he was just given the chance – no, if he would just take the chance before him. Yes, he needed these despicable relatives, but they needed him just as much, if not more.

"Richard," he said at length, "we must start afresh if I am to stay."

Richard looked to Nancy, and she nodded. "If Nancy wishes it, it shall be so."

"I shall not be browbeating Jack Randolph about his past amours."

"Fair enough," said Richard, figuring he now had the man for the job.

"I shall cross-examine Grant Harrison," said Marshall.

"If you must," said Henry reluctantly, well aware that he needed Marshall for his knowledge of the details of the case. "I'll be interested to see what effect the powers of logic may have on that old zealot," he added skeptically.

"And, to ensure that my carefully wrought theory of the defense is properly presented to the jury, I shall be the one to present closing argument."

"Wait just a minute," protested Henry, "now you're infringing on my bailiwick. Closing argument is properly a time for persuasion, not your indigestible theories. I am afraid I must insist on closing personally."

"He's right, Marshall, he's right," said Judge Tucker. "With all due respect to your abilities, which you know I value very highly, no man in Virginia can equal Henry before a jury. Ask for anything, but not this."

But Marshall knew that if this case were to be remembered as his, and not merely the case in which he had assisted the great Patrick Henry, he could ask no less. "This is what I ask," said Marshall, a new steel in his voice. "This is what I demand. I assure you, I will not let you down."

The Colonel snorted. "Damn you, Marshall," he began, "that's just not gonna –" but Nancy cut off her father with a sharp wave of her hand.

"Mr. Marshall shall close for us," she declared, "and I have every confidence that he shall do so brilliantly." The Colonel scowled, but held his tongue. No one else said a word. It was settled.

– CHAPTER 14 –

IMPRUDENT FAMILIARITIES

I.

James Hemings rolled the fresh rosemary between his fingers slowly, savoring its earthy perfume before dropping it into the battered old pot with the lapin. His brother Robert, along with Jenna, Syphax, Junior, and Old Esau sat in the dirt behind the Eagle's cook shack, watching eagerly. Looking about to be sure no whites were in sight, James furtively produced a small flask from his pocket and splashed some burgundy into the pot. A rich and fragrant aroma encircled them, far superior to the thin, greasy odors wafting from the Eagle.

"Ain't dis th' life," said Syphax, leaning back, wearied from his two trips to Campbell County, the first to offer Patrick Henry two hundred dollars to join the defense team and, when he refused that, the second to double the offer. "Sun's shinin', white folks is too damn busy ta ride us, an' a French cook ta boot. I hope dis here trial lasts a good long while – afore dey find 'em innocent," he added, to make clear that his loyalties still lay with Richard and Nancy.

"What makes you think they will?" asked Robert. "From what I hear, most everyone wants to string 'em up."

"You hush," said Jenna, "dey ain't done nothin' ta deserve dat. Miss Nancy's a good girl, Lord knows, we ain't none of us perfect."

"Be ye therefore perfect, even as your Father dat's in heaven is perfect," said Junior. "St. Matchew," he added, as if this would ward off the snickers his piety had engendered.

"He's not my father," said James, "not unless he sleeps with the colored help."

"Aw, man, back off," said Junior. "Dere ain't nothin' wrong with the Bible 'cept you fornicators jest doen like what it's got to say."

"Who's a fornicator?" growled Robert, taking offense.

"Settle down, brother," said James, "there aren't any fornicators here, except maybe those white folks they're trying."

"They are not!" cried Jenna loyally, but she realized her mistake when all eyes focused on her.

"You were there, Jenna," said James. "Tell us what happened."

"Yeah," said Robert, "you was there. Are they guilty, or what?"

Jenna just looked to the sky. "Gonna get colder, I reckon, you think?"

"Aw, quit it, girl, we asked you a question," pressed Robert. "What'd you see that night at Ole Esau's?"

"Yeah, I doen mind knowin' myself," added Syphax. "Come on Jenna, what gives, girl?"

Jenna looked around at the circle of eager faces. "Dat stuff ready yet?" she asked James.

"Yes, I think we could eat now." He set the pot in the middle of the circle, and they each produced a spoon from the recesses of the rags on their backs.

Jenna took a big, steaming spoonful, and leaned back on a barrel just watching it cool. She sipped some of the juice, and then nibbled a chunk of potato. "Well, y'see, it was kinda dark, she din' want no candles or nothin', 'cause she says it hurt her eyes. But dere was some moon, and aftah a while my eyes dey got used t'da dark, an' I could see her lyin' dere, on the bed, knees up, legs spread wide, an her pink slit gettin' bigger and juicier by the minute."

Robert swallowed hard. Junior looked away, knowing he should not stay, trapped beyond his power to go.

"She heaved, and pushed, and groaned, an' screamed for what musta been a hour, with Mistuh Richard right dere by her side, and me jest waitin' to catch whatever was a-comin'. At last, I seen what coulda been a head, leastways I hoped it was, cause ain't no way she's gonna survive a breach with me midwifin' her. It gets bigger and den smaller, bigger and den smaller, out with each push, and slippin' back in again with each rest, and I think she's stuck, when all of a sudden wi' a great big heave dat tears her quim all bloody out it falls, and I near miss it cause its so heavy and slippery, but I hold on tight fer jest a second, an' den Mistuh Richard says give it here, and I do, and I never seen it again." Jenna eyed the stewed rabbit meat, and lowered her spoon. Everyone waited for her to continue, but she said nothing.

"And?" coaxed Robert.

"An' what?" said Jenna.

"And what was it? A boy or a girl?"

"White or colored?" added Syphax.

"A bear cub," said Jenna.

"A bear cub?" said Robert and Syphax together, and then Jenna shoved the rabbit in her mouth and laughed with her mouth wide open in a show of disdain.

"Why you bitch!" yelled Robert, raising his hand towards her, but Syphax caught it and twisted it back behind him until he understood. "Come on, Jenna," said Syphax, feeling that he had earned a claim on her confidence, "what really happened that night?"

"Nothin'," said Jenna.

"Nothin'?" said Junior.

"I don't believe that," said Robert.

"Who gives a toad's turd what you believe?" said Jenna. "Nothin' happened, and dat's th' end of it. I was dere, so's I should know."

Old Esau, a tall, leathery man with a few remaining wisps of white hair sprouting behind his ears, had been so quiet that the others had nearly forgotten he was there, but he had been listening intently. Now he spoke. "Knowin' an' sayin' ain't de same t'ing."

"Yeah, well what you know 'bout it?" asked Jenna, annoyed to have her absolute authority on the matter impugned.

"More'n you said."

"Well, as de whole County knows by now, it's a whole lot easier ta talk 'bout dis den ta know anythin' about it," said Jenna.

"I know dis much: th' Sattaday aftah Miss Nancy has her fits, when I go ta fetch some shingles to repair de smokehouse roof, I find me de body of a dead baby in dat dere shingle pile."

"Lord have mercy!" exclaimed Junior.

"You found th' body?" said Syphax, not quite believing his ears. "Then why ain't there been no body talked of before?"

"Well, I was so scairt I jest covered it back up an' went back about my business. Course, I been thinkin' bout it all night, an' finally I figure dat if'n I doen tell Mistuh Harrison pretty quick, someone'll find it an' blame it on our people."

"You mean it was black?" prodded Syphax.

"Cain't say," said Old Esau, with pity in his eyes. "Dat little babe was purple an' wrapped inna sheet, an' I jest took a quick little peek an' covered it right back up."

They sat for a minute, chewing the burgundy rabbit in silence. "But I still doen understand," said Syphax, at last. "If'n what you say is true, why's there no body ever been showed round?"

"I dunno," answered Old Esau. "I showed it ta Mistuh Harrison, an' den next thing I know'd, dat babe was gone!"

2.

"All rise!"

Judge Allen ascended the bench in three strides and then peered down his nose at the defense table, at which were seated, from his right to left, Henry, Marshall, Richard, and Nancy. "Is the defense ready now?" he asked with disdain.

Both Marshall and Henry rose, opened their mouths, glanced at one another, motioned each other to go first, and then said in perfect disharmony, "Ready, Your Honor."

The Judge snorted, unimpressed. "The Clerk will bring in the veniremen."

Richard watched as the prospective jurors were brought in, the meticulous with the rumpled, the foolish with the wise, the just with the venal. He had been distressed to learn earlier that two Carrington brothers were to sit in judgment upon him, since their father and his had been bitter enemies, and the enmity had seeped down to the next generation. Marshall had put in an objection on his behalf just before the afternoon session, but the Judge had put him off. They were watching him now, each wearing the distinctive Carrington smirk inherited from their father.

"Does the prosecution have any objection to the jury?" asked the Judge.

Binghamton stood. "May I enquire Your Honor?"

"Make it brief."

Binghamton puffed himself up like a bullfrog, squinted at each juror, and asked, "Gentlemen, are there any among you who are not familiar with the charges against the defendants?"

None responded.

"Are there any among you who have heard nothing of the events said to have occurred at Glenlyvar last October 1st?"

Again there was no reply.

"Do any of you hold scruple against the requirement of the law that a murderer shall hang from the neck until dead?"

The potential jurors met his gaze without wavering.

"These gentlemen will do quite nicely, Your Honor," said Mr. Binghamton, and he sat down.

The Judge turned to the defense table. "Is the defense content with the jury?"

Henry was nodding affirmatively as Marshall rose. "For the reasons previously communicated in chambers, Your Honor, we request the disqualification of-"

The Judge, looking impatient, cut him off. "You Carrington boys," he said, "is there any reason why you can't fairly and impartially decide this case involving Richard Randolph, not his father?"

"No sir," they both replied, without a moment's hesitation.

"Your request is denied, Mr. Marshall. Judge Carrington was a good man, he's got fine sons, and if the defendant's father had a quarrel with him, well, that's not sufficient grounds to assume that they will not hear the case fairly. Now, I ask for the last time, is the defense content with the jury?"

"Your Honor, I cannot say that we are," replied Marshall, as Henry fidgeted. "While I recognize that it has been the custom to select jurors from the neighborhood especially for their knowledge of the case, the most modern authorities are beginning to question this practice and to hold that jurors should know as little as possible about –"

Henry had heard enough. "Your Honor," he interjected, using Marshall to pull himself to his feet as he pulled Marshall down, "it has always been my experience that every Virginian is better than satisfactory; is indeed, exemplary. Wouldn't you agree, Gentlemen?" he asked, turning to the jury box, and the veniremen nodded in solemn agreement. "Well, Your Honor, this fine group is no exception to the rule, and I am sure that they will fairly judge our brother and sister Virginians, Richard and Nancy Randolph." Turning back to the potential jurors, he transformed them into actual jurors by saying, "Gentlemen, we are honored to be heard by you," and he sat down.

"Very good," said the Judge. "The jury will rise, raise their right hands, and be sworn by the Clerk."

"DoyousolemnlyswearinthesightofAlmightyGodtowellandtrulytry-thecausebeforeyouwithoutpartialityorfavortowardsanyperson?"

The jury grunted noncommittally.

"The jury is impaneled," decreed the Judge. "The Clerk will now read the charges."

"Your Honor," said Marshall, springing to his feet, "the defense waives reading of the charges."

Binghamton rose to protest, but there was no need. "The charges will be read, as is the usual practice," the Judge announced in a truculent tone.

"May we have a cautionary instruction to the jury that they are not to consider the charges as evidence?" asked Marshall.

"Mr. Marshall," the Judge scolded, "I am aware that some of the younger judges have recently been taking it upon themselves to tell the jury what it can and cannot do, but that is not my practice. As far as I am concerned, the jury knows its job, and can do it without our meddling." There was a pause, during which the jurors watched for further attacks upon their dignity by the apostate, Marshall. When none came, the Judge repeated, "The Clerk will now read the charges."

Mr. Critch, who had this entire colloquy during which he could have located the appropriate document, only began his search of the file at this moment. After much shuffling he produced a parchment, unclamped his upper tooth from his lower lip, and began to read. "By the Authority of the Commonwealth of Virginia," he intoned, as Nancy wondered if she made a mistake by keeping Marshall from resigning, but "upon information duly sworn" Marshall knew that it was all the fault of this biased Judge. "He did then and there have carnal knowledge of one Anne Cary Randolph, known as Nancy, his sister by marriage," and that might be hard to resist, thought the Gentlemen of the Jury, as they looked her up and down. "Willfully and wantonly, with malice aforethought," is just how this ridiculous co-counsel is setting out to destroy whatever chances we may have, lamented Henry, which are slim indeed if they did "choke and/or suffocate the newborn infant until it was dead." A shudder passed through the courtroom. "Against the peace and dignity of the Commonwealth of Virginia."

Rest in peace and with dignity, Richard and Nancy silently prayed.

3.

"Call your first witness, Mr. Binghamton," directed Judge Allen.

"The Commonwealth of Virginia calls Mr. Carter Page."

A prune in a black frock coat was brought in from the witness chamber in back, and made his way through the gate of the bar and past the jurors who inspected this familiar gentleman as if he was from China. Mr. Critch awaited Mr. Page, Bible in hand, so that it looked as if a convention of undertakers was about to begin.

"Raise your right hand, put your left hand on the Bible." Mr. Carter did as he was told.

"DoyousolemnlyswearbeforeGodalmightythattheevidenceyouare-abouttogiverelativetothecausenowunderconsiderationshallbethe-truththewholetruthandnothingbutthetruth?"

"I do."

"Be seated."

Mr. Binghamton stood and nervously ran his fingers through the space his hair once occupied, down to the remnants of some grayish-red fuzz. "State your name and where you live please, Sir."

"I am Carter Page, and I live at Lampshire Acres, on the outskirts of Cumberland."

"Are you some relation to the accuseds, by whom I mean Richard and Nancy Randolph?"

"Yes, Sir. I am an Uncle to them, through my wife, who was sister to Miss Nancy's mother, Anne Cary."

"Has this family connection brought you into contact with the accuseds?"

"Yes, Sir, there was the usual visiting between the families."

Binghamton, who had been safely ensconced behind counsel's table, now moved nonchalantly out towards the center arena, half way between the bar and the bench. "Let me direct your attention, if I may, to the period from 1791 through October of 1792. About how often did you see the accuseds together during that period?"

"I should say a half dozen times during each of those years."

"And tell the jury, Mr. Page," said Binghamton as he sidled over to the jury box, grabbed the railing, and looked them over, "during that dozen or so times that you saw Richard and Nancy Randolph together, did you ever notice anything out of the ordinary about their relations?"

Binghamton turned towards Mr. Page, the Judge turned towards Mr. Page, the jurors all turned towards Mr. Page, even his sister-in-law in the gallery, Jane Cary Randolph, who usually ignored him, focused intently on what he was about to say. "Now that you mention it, Sir," he remarked, as if there were some great coincidence that it had come up, "I did."

"What was it that you noticed?"

"I noticed, upon certain occasions, that there were, shall we say, imprudent familiarities between them." The gallery took a breath and leaned forward as if it were one great long-nosed beast.

"And by 'them' you mean?"

"The, um, accuseds, you know," he stuttered, wagging his index finger in their general direction, "Mr. Richard and Miss Nancy Randolph."

Binghamton turned to reclaim the center of the courtroom. "What sort of imprudent familiarities did you observe?"

The hand with the accusing finger quickly returned to Mr. Page's lap, where it was clenched tightly by its counterpart. "I saw them kissing, and fond of each other."

"'Fond of each other?'"

"You know," said Mr. Page, his ears turning crimson, "embracing," and he wiggled an incongruous wiggle, whether to free himself from binding garments or to dislodge the stuck word, it was unclear.

"Now, Mr. Page, did you observe anything else unusual about Miss Nancy Randolph, in particular, during the year 1792?"

Mr. Page looked perplexed. "As I said, there were familiarities."

"In addition to the imprudent familiarities, Mr. Page," and Binghamton came a few steps closer to the witness, sensing that he had forgotten, hoping that greater proximity could telegraph the response he sought. "Something that might indicate that she was with child?"

Marshall sprang to his feet. "Your Honor, the witness said nothing about this, and now Mr. Binghamton is trying to put words in his mouth."

"Quite right, Mr. Marshall. Mr. Binghamton, I won't have you leading the witness on a sensitive matter. Rephrase the question, please."

As Marshall sat down, pleased at last to have scored a point, Henry leaned over and whispered, "Congratulations. You've just alerted any dozing jurors to the importance of what follows."

"As I was saying, Mr. Page, did you notice anything else about Miss Nancy?"

"Come to think of it, I did," he said, as if he'd thought of it himself. "I noticed an apparent expansion in the size of her midsection."

The crowd all began talking at once. Judge Allen pounded his gavel. "Silence, silence in the Court!"

"Please tell the jury, Mr. Page, did you notice that expansion in Miss Nancy's midsection before or after you first noticed the imprudent familiarities between the accuseds?"

"After."

"No further questions. Your witness, Mr., uh Mr., well, you'll just have to fight that one out between yourselves, gentlemen," and a very satisfied Mr. Binghamton seated himself to a scattering of chuckles.

"Let me handle this," whispered Henry to Marshall.

"Fine," replied Marshall, "but be sure to find out when he first noticed the expansion in her midsection."

Slowly, Henry rose. He moved silently to the front of the defense table and casually leaned back against it, never for a moment taking his piercing blue eyes off his quarry. He had not said a word, but his extraordinary calm at the vortex of tension held the courtroom enthralled. At last he spoke. "Mr. Page, you're not what one might call a passionate man, are you?"

Those who knew him, which meant nearly everybody present, could not restrain their laughter, try as they might. And once it started it built, stoked by the sight of this prudish gentleman trying to make sense out of such a question, and then built further on the laughter of fellow spectators, until people were literally clutching at their sides, trying to keep from rolling off the benches. "Order, order, there shall be order in the Court," yelled Judge Allen, but even his thin lips were suppressing a smile. Finally, the crescendo gave way to a fluttering of chuckles, until the witness, with great seriousness, replied flatly, "No, Sir," and it started anew.

When at last the tumult died down, Henry stood. "You are not unduly free with your affections, I take it?"

"Absolutely not."

Henry moved one step closer. "Including your kisses and your hugs?"

This was too much. Determined to wilt this vagabond in the bloody jacket with a glance, Mr. Page sniffed down his nose in Henry's direction, and barely uttered, "Of course not."

With two more steps Henry closed the distance between himself and Mr. Page to a few paces. "You personally do not indulge in what you have called 'imprudent familiarities,' do you, Sir?"

"I should say not."

Now Henry leaned over Mr. Page, seeking to intimidate the truth right out of him. "But when your sister-in-law comes to visit, you have danced with her, have you not?"

It's true and she's sitting right there and I've sworn on the Bible. "Yes, but –"

"And you have embraced her?"

"I may have."

"You may have? Shall we ask her?"

Lord spare me from another encounter with this Jacobin monster, thought Jane, trembling in her seat.

"Yes, yes I have."

"And you have kissed her, haven't you, Mr. Page?"

"Yes."

Satisfied, Henry turned and strolled towards the jury box. Many would have left it at that, but Henry turned suddenly to ask, "Are we to infer, then, Mr. Page, that you have had criminal conversation with your sister-in-law?"

A scream came from the gallery as Jane stood, and then crumpled into a faint. Her husband Thomas and several other gentlemen attended to her.

"Mr. Henry," said the Judge, "there are limits of decency beyond which you must not transgress."

"I am aware of that, Your Honor," said Henry, "but it is precisely to point out that Mr. Binghamton would have this jury draw the same indecent assumption about my client that I have found it necessary to proceed as I have."

"The question is argumentative, Your Honor," said Mr. Binghamton, at last perceiving that an objection might be in order.

"That's all right, Your Honor, I do not insist upon an answer," replied Henry, and he went to take his seat. "I have nothing further."

"What about when he first noticed the increase in size?" whispered Marshall furiously.

"Leave well enough alone, Marshall."

"Your Honor," said Marshall, "there is one more question."

"I will not have you doubling up on the witnesses," cautioned the Judge.

"I must have an answer to this, Mr. Henry," whispered Marshall fervently. "My whole theory of the case depends on it."

"Oh, all right," said Henry loudly, visibly exasperated. "Mr. Page," he said, "before you step down and retire to the loving arms of your family," here the crowd began to titter, "my learned co-counsel wishes to know the answer to the question that is on nobody's lips but his own: tell us, when did you first notice an alteration in Miss Nancy's size?"

"In May."

Henry turned to Marshall. "He says in May. Shall I ask him whether the roses were in bloom yet?" The crowd roared, but Marshall simply made a note of it.

"No further questions."

"You may step down, Mr. Page," said the Judge, but he already had, and was half-way out of the courtroom.

4.

"Call your next witness, Mr. Binghamton."

"The Commonwealth calls Mr. Peyton Harrison to the stand."

This produced a watery-eyed scarecrow with thinning hair, who was so loosely jointed that he appeared to trickle forth rather than to walk, like flowing water. Having sputtered his oath, he settled himself with a practiced air, elbows on the platform before him, ready to quaff a few pints.

"You are Peyton Harrison of Sprouse's Corner, is that right?"

"Yep."

"Cousin to Grant Harrison of Glenlyvar?"

"Yep," and the cousin licked his dry lips. Thirsty work, this.

"Are you acquainted with the accuseds, Richard and Nancy Randolph?"

Harrison studied them for a moment, thinking it over. "Yep," was the product of his deliberations.

"Have you ever observed anything unusual in the relations between the accuseds?"

"Yep."

"What did you observe?"

"Well, last Spring, I observed whatcha might call an unnatural fondness between them."

"Was it like the fondness one might expect to see between brother and sister?"

"Objection!" Marshall sprang to his feet. "This calls for the witness to draw a conclusion about what kind of affection one might expect to see between brother and sister."

"Overruled," said the Judge, and, turning to Harrison, he added, "you may answer the question."

"Nope."

"In what way was it different?"

"Stronger."

Henry leaned behind Marshall and whispered to Richard, "How's this fellow treat his sisters?"

"And did you later learn anything more about the possible results of this unnatural fondness between the accuseds?"

"Yep."

"What did you learn?"

"Hasn't got any," Richard whispered back. "Only child, and a bachelor to boot."

"My manservant said –"

"Objection!" Marshall sprang back to his feet. "Hearsay, and, I might add, from an incompetent source."

"Sustained. We will not go into what Mr. Harrison might have learned from his servants."

"In that case, I have no further questions," said Mr. Binghamton, and he sat down.

"Experience is the best teacher, isn't it, Mr. Peyton Harrison?" said Henry as he rose, more as a statement than a question, so quick upon the close of Binghamton's last words that Harrison hadn't a moment to gather his wits.

"I 'spose so."

"You suppose so?" boomed Henry, moving quickly around the table. "It's a simple question. Is it or is it not true that we never really know about something until we have experienced it ourselves?"

The witness sat silent, fearful and disoriented. What is he getting at?

"Come, come, Mr. Harrison, do you prefer book learning over experience?"

"Nope."

"Do you think you can learn more about planting tobacco by watching your neighbor do it, or raising your own crop?"

"Well," said the cautious Mr. Harrison as his bones flowed away from the advancing Henry, "I 'spect you can learn something either way."

"Of course," said Henry, close enough now to smell Harrison's breath, "you can learn *something* either way, but to really know about raising a tobacco crop, you've got to do it yourself, right?"

It was either look like a fool, or get this behind him. "Yep."

"So you would agree with me that we never *really know* about something until we have experienced it ourselves?"

A most reluctant, "Yep."

Henry paused to retreat to the corner of the defense table nearest to the jury box. He turned. "You're a bachelor, aren't you, Mr. Harrison?"

"Yep."

"How many brothers and sisters in your family?" A nice wide open question, the kind you never ask unless you know the answer, or don't care.

"Two."

Damn you, Richard. No, wait a minute, think, think hard. "Let me rephrase that. How many who lived past childhood?"

"None."

Got him. "So you have no personal experience of the kinds of fondnesses that might properly go on between adult brothers and sisters, do you?"

He saw the trap at last, way too late. He shifted around, licked his lips. "Nope."

"Likewise, you've got no experience about the fondness that might properly go on between adult brothers and sisters-in-law?"

"Just what I've seen."

"Which is like watching someone plant tobacco," said Henry to the jury.

As Binghamton rose to object the Judge cut him off. "Counsel is here to ask questions, not chatter with the jury. The jury will please disregard this last remark by Mr. Henry." But of course they would not.

Henry, sensing the kill, plunged on. "As a bachelor and only surviving child, one might wonder whether you have had any personal experience with fondness, natural or unnatural, for any woman?"

Binghamton, who had been settling back down, sprung up. "Objection! The witness's private life is not on trial here."

"Your Honor," said Henry, "I am only attempting to establish whether the man, when he speaks of degrees of fondness between brother and sister, and man and woman, has any basis for knowledge of the subject."

The Judge paused, looking from Henry's cobalt eyes to the plea for mercy floating in the eyes of the witness. Such dissolution disgusted him. "Mr. Binghamton," he said, "in a matter of this seriousness, some latitude must be allowed on cross-examination. Proceed, Mr. Henry."

Henry impaled Harrison on his gaze. "Well, Mr. Harrison," who was doing his best to seep out the cracks in the floor, "have you had any fondnesses that might make you an authority on the subject?"

"I have not," he said at length, "but I know what I saw between Mr. Randolph and Miss Nancy."

"You saw it once?"

"Once was enough."

"On a social visit to Bizarre?"

"Yep."

"Morning, afternoon, or evening?"

"Evening."

"But haven't you neglected to tell us of an unnatural fondness of your own?"

The witness said nothing.

"One that, by evening time of most any day, would have impaired your judgment about the fondnesses of others?"

Still, the witness refused to answer. Henry came closer to him, and leaned over the railing to the witness box.

"You know the fondness of which I am speaking?" pressed Henry.

Nothing.

"Your unnatural fondness is for strong liquor, is it not?"

"No!"

"Then perhaps you would like to show the jury what makes that bulge in your frock coat pocket?"

"Objection!" yelled Binghamton.

"Overruled."

"Nope." But whispered.

"Or perhaps you would like to have the jury come over here where I am so they can smell your breath?"

The witness shook his head.

"Or would you like to tell them how your breath smelled that night when you were making fine distinctions about other people's fondnesses?"

Harrison said nothing. Binghamton rose, opened his mouth, and then sat back down when he saw the Judge's smirk. The courtroom was silent. Stepping back, with pity in his eyes, Henry said softly, "That's all right, Your Honor. His silence is answer enough. Mr. Harrison can go now."

"The witness is excused."

What little was left of this puddle of a man evaporated quickly.

"The Commonwealth calls Mrs. Brett Randolph to the stand."

Anne Randolph emerged from the witness room wearing a plain homespun gown and an air of great seriousness. She was not unattractive, with her long, chestnut hair falling in broad waves down her back, but her furrowed brow and pinched lips detracted from her natural allure. This suited her shy, pensive, bookish nature. As she passed the defense table she unknitted her brow in a nearly invisible gesture of apology. Then she placed her hand firmly on the Bible, and when she took the oath it was evident to all that she meant it.

"State your name please."

"I am Anne Randolph of Curles, wife of Brett Randolph."

"Mrs. Randolph, are you related to the accuseds, Richard and Nancy Randolph of Bizarre?"

"I am, Sir. Richard is my cousin."

"Did you and your husband visit the household at Bizarre?"

"I did, but often without my husband, who had business to attend to. I visited quite regularly, perhaps as often as once each month; some months more, some months less, but on average once a month."

"And what did you notice of the relations within that household?"

"The relations were always harmonious, with the exception of some occasional frictions involving Mr. Jack Randolph, Richard's brother. But among Judith, Richard, and Nancy, there was nothing but love and tenderness."

Mr. Binghamton stepped in front of the defense table, and pointed to the defendants. "You witnessed love and tenderness between the accuseds?"

"Perhaps you misunderstood," countered Mrs. Randolph, firmly, "I witnessed love and tenderness between husband and wife, between sister and sister, between brother and sister, and among them generally. I did not mean to single out Richard and Nancy."

"So you would swear that Richard's attentions towards Nancy were the same as those shown towards his own wife?"

Mrs. Randolph's brow bore down hard upon this question, and she was not entirely comfortable with what she discovered. "No, that is not so."

"I should hope not, Mrs. Randolph. A wife is due something more in that regard than a sister-in-law, is she not?"

"Yes."

"Yet a moment ago you implied that the sentiments shown were equal."

"Objection," said Marshall. "Your Honor, the prosecutor is leading his own witness."

"Sustained."

"I am sorry, Your Honor," said Binghamton, rubbing his pate as he crossed towards the bench, "but although I have called this witness, I fear that her sympathies lie with the defendants, so it is necessary to extract information from her through cross-examination."

"I've seen no sign of that, Mr. Binghamton, and the objection is sustained."

"Very well, Your Honor," said Binghamton, turning back to Mrs. Randolph. "Let me just clarify the record. Is it your testimony, Mrs. Randolph, that Mr. Richard Randolph paid equal attentions towards Miss Nancy and his wife, or that he paid lesser attentions towards Miss Nancy than towards his wife?"

"Neither." This elicited scattered murmurings from the gallery.

"Neither?"

"Neither, Mr. Binghamton. I am afraid that I must say, and of course this is just what I observed, but I must say that, at least beginning last year, Mr. Richard paid rather more attention to Nancy than to Judith." The murmurings got louder.

Binghamton, emboldened by this unexpected prize, strutted over to the jury box to bestow a knowing smile on the jurors. Then he asked, "Mrs. Randolph, did you see Miss Nancy both before and after October 1st of last year?"

"Yes, Sir. In fact, I was at Bizarre on that very day, and I saw them off in the carriage before leaving myself for Richmond."

"Did you notice, Mrs. Randolph, any alteration in Miss Nancy's shape during that time period?"

The truth, the whole truth, and nothing but the truth, so help you God. "Yes, Sir."

"What was the nature of that alteration?"

"She appeared, Sir, to have put on some weight over the summer and the fall, but I noticed on first seeing her several weeks after her trip to Glenlyvar that she seemed greatly thinned down."

"And would you say, Mrs. Randolph, that the changes you observed in Miss Nancy's shape would have been consistent with a pregnancy, followed by a birth?"

Marshall shot up. "Ob –"

"Overruled. Sit down, Mr. Marshall." Marshall sat.

"Do you have the question in mind, Mrs. Randolph?"

Mrs. Randolph, looking downcast but resolute, shook her head.

"The question is, would you say that the changes you observed in Miss Nancy's shape were consistent with pregnancy, followed by childbirth?"

With obvious reluctance, the witness nodded affirmatively.

"The Court requires a spoken answer," said the Judge.

"I'm sorry," whispered Mrs. Randolph. "The answer is, yes."

"No further questions," said Mr. Binghamton. He was satisfied but fearful until, to his relief, he saw not Henry, but Marshall, rise to cross-examine.

Unlike Henry, who never touched a piece of paper, Marshall rose trailing handfuls of notes, which he nervously shuffled as he stood rooted behind counsel's table. After an unnaturally long pause which allowed more than enough time for the witness's direct testimony to implant itself in the minds of the jurors, Marshall began. "Mrs. Randolph," he squeaked, "you have testified that, beginning last year, you noticed Mr. Richard paying more attention to Miss Nancy than to his wife, Judith, correct?"

"Yes, Sir."

"Was there any particular occasion on which you noticed that?"

"Particular occasion?"

"Yes. A visit in which that change in attentions was especially apparent to you."

"Well, Sir," said the witness, trying to be helpful, "I first noticed it at the beginning of the year."

"Could it have been February?"

"Yes, Sir."

"You did visit in February, didn't you?"

"I believe so, Sir." She thought a moment, and then added with greater conviction, "In fact, I'm certain of it, Sir, because that was the month of Richard's brother's funeral."

"And were you not aware that Miss Nancy and Mr. Theodorick Randolph had been close friends?"

"Yes, Sir, they were, now that you mention it."

"And in fact, didn't Miss Nancy take Theodorick's death quite hard?"

"Very hard, Sir."

"How did Richard take the loss of his brother?"

"He took it very hard, also. They had been quite close."

"Wouldn't it have been natural for Richard and Nancy, as fellow mourners, each of whom had been close to the deceased, to be especially solicitous towards one another?"

"Yes, Sir, that's right."

"Did you notice that Richard showed Nancy special attentions at any other time?"

"Yes, Sir."

"State, if you can, each of the dates on which you noticed this."

"I visited in March, but Richard seemed quite attentive to Judith and the new baby, so I can't say that I observed anything out of the ordinary that month. I think I visited twice in April, or maybe it was once in late March and once in early April, and each time I noticed that Richard was quite attentive to Nancy." She searched her memory, eager to provide some exculpatory tidbit. "Although I must add that Nancy had still not gotten over Theodorick's death, and Judith herself was quite worried about her, so that could explain it. We were away in May, and they were away in June, so I think that I next saw them in July, and perhaps again in August or September, and then at the end of September when I saw them off on the first of October. But try as I might, Mr. Marshall, I can't remember any specific incidents. I just have this general impression that Richard paid rather more attention to Nancy than to Judith at this time."

"An impression that may well be explainable by their shared sense of loss?"

"Oh, yes, quite definitely."

"And is it not also the case that Mr. Richard was a sort of surrogate father to Miss Nancy, in the sense that he took her in after she was shut out of her childhood home by her natural father?"

"Well, yes, that is my understanding."

"So their closeness may well have had a guardianship aspect to it?"

"Yes."

"Which leads to the conclusion that there are several independent explanations for special fondness between Miss Nancy and Mr. Richard, aside from an improper relationship, correct?"

"Yes."

"Now tell us, Mrs. Randolph, did you continue to observe special attentions between the defendants in the weeks and months after the rumors about their conduct began to circulate?"

"Yes, I did."

Marshall placed a check mark in his notes, as Henry cast an exasperated look his way. "Now, Mrs. Randolph, you spoke of harmonious relationships among the accuseds and Mrs. Judith Randolph, correct?"

"Yes."

"And you saw these three together at Bizarre just two weeks after the visit to Glenlyvar?"

"Yes."

"Were the relationships between and among Judith, Richard and Nancy just as harmonious then as they had always been?"

"Yes, Sir."

"There was no sign of strain between them?"

"No, Sir."

"And especially, there was no sign of strain between either Judith and Richard, or Judith and Nancy?"

"None, Sir."

"And that increase and diminution in size that you noted. Could that have been consistent with the gaining and losing of fat?"

Mrs. Randolph paused. It certainly had not seemed so, but could it have been? Well, anything's possible. "Yes, Sir."

"And could it also have been consistent with bloating accompanying an illness, followed by the restoration of health?"

"Yes, Sir, it could have been."

"One more thing, Mrs. Randolph," said Marshall, reaching into a box beneath the table to produce a daring full length winter coat of wool dyed bright scarlet, trimmed in fox. For the first time, Marshall moved from the spot where he stood behind the table, to bring the coat to the witness. "I show you this coat which has been marked as Defendants' Exhibit A. Take a good look at it, please, and tell the jury, is this the coat that Miss Nancy wore that first morning in October when you saw her off?"

Mrs. Randolph gave the coat a cursory inspection. "Definitely, Mr. Marshall. One does not quickly forget a coat like this. It was cold, she had it buttoned to the throat, and she looked quite stunning in it."

Marshall took the coat back and returned it to its box. "No further questions."

"Well, I have a further question, if you don't mind," announced Henry, rising.

Marshall gave him a look calculated to sour milk, but Henry was not affected. "Mrs. Randolph –" began Henry, but he was cut short.

"Objection!" cried Marshall.

"You can't object to me," protested Henry, "we're on the same side," and, with a wink to the crowd, he added disparagingly, "at least I know I am!"

"Gentlemen," said Judge Allen, "I will give you one minute to whisper between yourselves and solve this problem. The court will not permit two attorneys to cross-examine the same witness, but if Mr. Marshall wishes to enquire along the lines proposed by Mr. Henry, he may do so."

Henry and Marshall huddled. "She stayed at Bizarre after the carriage left that morning," whispered Henry. "Why? I'll bet it was to dally with Jack, who also stayed."

"We have no proof of that," snapped Marshall.

"Who needs proof? Suggest it, and she is discredited."

"Never."

"She hurt us badly, Marshall, and you've barely scratched her. Her husband is old enough to be her father, she often visited without him, and when the carriage pulled out that left Mrs. Randolph alone with a gentleman just her age. It's enough to create doubts."

Marshall looked at Henry, puzzled that such a satyr could be so successful in life and law, and so well liked to boot. "She has told the truth as best she can, fairly to both sides. I will not impeach her with innuendo."

"Your Honor," said Henry, rising, "I have important questions about why the witness, who constantly visits Bizarre without her husband, would have stayed behind with Jack Randolph last October, but –"

"Objection!" screamed Binghamton, but it was too late, the poison was out of the bottle. Mrs. Randolph turned bright red, her eyes searching the crowd first for her husband, who looked grim, then for Jack, who grinned back at her.

"Counsel approach the bench," said Judge Allen. They did so. The Judge leaned over as far as he could towards Henry. "Governor," he said, "you're too old and well-respected to spend time in jail for contempt, do you understand?" If Henry understood, he didn't show it, so the Judge whispered: "That means I may have to have you shot." He was joking, but he wasn't smiling. Then he turned to Binghamton, whose sweaty dome glinted in the late afternoon sunlight slipping under gathering clouds outside the courtroom windows. "Mr. Binghamton, what do you want to do?"

"We should give the witness a chance to clear her name, Your Honor."

"Fine. You may proceed to ask some additional questions on this point, as you deem appropriate."

But as they returned to counsel tables, Henry whispered something into Binghamton's ear. Binghamton stood there, looking at the witness, who sat, pale and trembling, unsure of what would come next. "The Commonwealth would simply request a cautionary instruction, Your Honor."

The Judge peered at him with an odd look, but said, "Very well. The jury is instructed to ignore that last vile remark by Mr. Henry."

The jurors engaged in a ritual nod.

"The witness is excused."

Gratefully, she stepped down, and immediately crossed to her husband, who took her by the arm and led her out.

Whack! "Court is adjourned until tomorrow morning at 9:00 a.m. All rise."

"What did you say to Binghamton?" whispered Marshall to Henry, as the Judge took his leave.

"That she had been truthful so far," replied Henry, "so he should not ask any questions to which he was not prepared to hear an honest answer."

– CHAPTER 15 –

THE GOUGING CONTEST

I.

The Sheriff's office had reclaimed custody of Nancy, assigning a regular deputy to the business of escorting her back and forth from Mrs. Biddlesworth's, so Marshall descended the courthouse steps accompanied only by his mental burdens. He was concerned by the evidence of inordinate fondness between Richard and Nancy, and the evidence of apparent pregnancy, but in an agreeable sort of way, as legitimate parts of the puzzle he had been hired to solve. It was Henry that really weighed him down, usurping his place, disrupting his meticulous strategy by interjecting the parlor tricks of a cheap conjuror, throwing everything into confusion – and, he had to concede, being so damned successful at it all. Was it the disruption or the success that chafed so? And why permit such useless ruminations to displace the weightier matters of evidence and argument that lay ahead? Under the sway of Henry's alchemy, Marshall's keen mind was vexed from gold to dross.

To make matters worse, as Marshall descended the steps he lowered himself into a seething carnival. The green was teeming with people of all stations and intents, hot from the day's revelations and too much holding still, intoxicated by the break from whatever routine numbed their days. The usually placid town had been turned overnight into an itinerant metropolis, people battening down the flaps on wagons and tents against possible rain, wood being split and toted, cooking fires lit, goods being traded and hawked, money changing hands, children underfoot, flirtations blossoming, pockets getting picked. Marshall steered into the crowd with the reluctance of a sea captain entering unplumbed waters, and immediately ran aground on Jack Randolph.

"Mr. Marshall," shouted Jack over the din, "you're just in time. Come with me," and he grabbed Marshall by the sleeve and began leading him through the winding alleyways of the tent city.

"In time for what?" yelled Marshall.

"You'll see," said Jack, "just ahead."

Marshall peered through the wood smoke and the cloud-covered light of a premature dusk, but all he could make out was a thickening of the mob. Jack began to push through, and Marshall followed with reluctant curiosity, his fine frock coat repeatedly defiled by the week's accumulation of mud and sweat caked to his countrymen. "Make way for Mr. Marshall," Jack was saying, "Counsel for the defense demands his prerogatives," until they were smack up to the front row, and Marshall could discern a platform of baled hay, atop which was perched a bear of a man, hairy, scarred, muscular and fat. His face was fierce and indifferent, with puffy half-closed eyes, and when his mouth opened his occasional rotted teeth seemed to dance about his tongue in mockery of the spectators.

Around this beast danced a dwarf with a misshapen head and angry eyes who smiled as he taunted the crowd, "Who'll challenge Golga? There's not a man among you, you're all cowards, look at Golga, he's fat, he's forty years old, he's dumb as a fart," at this the crowd howled, "but you're too timid to test him," and the laughter quickly subsided as the men looked to their souls.

The dwarf stopped talking, sensing his quarry, scurrying his full-sized torso about on insect legs, poking those truculent eyes at the faces in the crowd. When the dwarf reached Jack Randolph, Marshall glanced over just in time to see a flash of kinship, and to see the dwarf see it too, so that he quickly passed on to the other potential challengers who, for all their strength, lacked Jack's ferocity. Jack was clearly enjoying himself, watching the dwarf cajole the young bucks, preying on their pride and insecurities, their fetal nobility. Now the dwarf was collecting coins to form the reward for the gouging contest, jangling the ever-increasing jackpot in a large tin bucket as it quickly swelled to more money than a man could earn in a year of back-breaking labor. How easily the peaceful farmers of the county could be goaded into financing the maiming of one of their own. Throughout the crowd, farm boys whose perfect bodies knew nothing of fragility hungered for that jackpot, for the glory, and recoiled at the charge of cowardice.

"Let's go, Golga," said the dwarf, the bucket half-filled with gold, silver and copper. "This money's ours for nothing. Nobody here's got the guts to fight us for it." But their pretense of leaving was soon cut short by a shuffling, beardless boy with powerful rounded shoulders, and an aw-shucks grin hung loosely on his friendly face.

"Go get 'im, Randy," shouted his friends and neighbors, for many knew Randy from the county fairs where he always did well in the good clean wrestling matches sponsored by Cumberland's magistrates.

"It isn't fair," pleaded the dwarf, "you folks setting such a strong young bull against old Golga here, he'll murder him!"

But the crowd didn't seem to mind, and now it taunted Golga and the dwarf, "Give him the money, then, if you're too yella to fight!" and "Does Golga need his mommy?" and "Don't worry, we'll give him a nice funeral!"

But the dwarf was adamant. "We won't risk the near certainty that this young Sampson will tear out one of Golga's precious eyes for this paltry sum," and he held up the bucket and shook it at the crowd. "Fill this bucket to the brim, and then you shall have your match."

Jack was the first to produce his wallet, and carefully extract several coins from amidst its precious contents. Others quickly followed suit, until coins were pelting down upon the dwarf, stinging him as he scampered about greedily. "You're gonna be the richest man in the county," yelled a farmer to Randy, and Randy nodded and smiled as he considered whether to purchase the back ninety near Bear Creek, or some land on the James near Bremo Bluff that he'd had his eye on. But now, to the business at hand, for the dwarf's bucket was overflowing.

"Gentlemen," yelled the dwarf, holding up his man-sized hands, "silence!" An expectant quiet came over the crowd. "There are only two rules in this contest." He paused dramatically, relishing his power. "Number one: the winner takes all!" Wild cheers. "Number two: there are no rules! Everything is legal!"

"You see, Marshall," yelled Jack over the growing tumult, "here's the real law."

The boy stripped off his shirt, and crouched in a wrestler's stance. He approached Golga cautiously, but Golga seemed unaware of his presence. "Fighters, are you ready?" asked the dwarf. "On three." Randy relaxed a bit, and glanced at the dwarf. *"One!"*

"You are mistaken, Mr. Randolph," replied Marshall. "This is not law, but anarchy."

"*Two!*"

Golga lashed out with a kick to the boy's groin that flattened him instantly. The crowd protested. "No rule against it, no rule against it," screamed the dwarf, gleefully.

Everything is legal, thought Marshall.

Golga reached down towards the face of the curled boy, whose hands were cradling his genitals. "Cover your eyes," screamed the crowd, and with one hand the boy flailed against his opponent's sure fingers, the ones that had popped enough eyes from their sockets to provision the blind of all Virginia. Golga grabbed a fist full of hair, yanked the boy's head back, and jabbed his thumb into the socket of the boy's perfect right eye. With a sound like champagne uncorking, blood frothed forth, washing over the dangling eyeball. Randy's screams were heard by his mother half a mile away, but it was too late.

2.

Nauseated, Marshall lurched off through the crowd, drinking the darkening air without refreshment. The legislature must act to outlaw such scandalous exhibitions, he thought, looking at the faces of his fellow spectators, some laughing cruelly, some saddened, some angry about the money, but most just numb. What laws shall be made by such a people? Routine laws, laws that do nothing to confine the passions that scorch our bowels. Laws that distinguish between criminal assault, and voluntary submission to a sporting contest. Laws that permit charlatans to titillate, because we like to be titillated. Laws that direct our viciousness at the weak, the defenseless, the powerless.

Marshall found himself at last at the door of Mrs. Biddlesworth's, and he entered gratefully, exhausted and hungry. As he washed up and changed his jacket, he thought of how pleasant it would soon be to relax in the company of his peers, even at Mrs. Biddlesworth's simple table. He grabbed a bottle of claret and a tin of tansy pudding sent by Polly, and descended expectantly.

It was too quiet. This he knew already, as he pushed open the door to the dining room. There sat Patrick Henry, with Mrs. Biddlesworth brooding over him like a thundercloud. "Yes, yes," said Henry, "by all means, Mrs. Biddlesworth, go midwife the sow. But you can hold onto your barrel of salt cod; I've victuals enough without chewing through that stuff. Why, when I was a babe at Studley, I used to eat a barrel before every meal –"

"It's fine for you to laugh, Patrick Henry," retorted Mrs. Biddlesworth, "but some of us have to economize the best way we can. We don't all get paid for nothing, you know."

"And lucky you are for it, Mrs. B.," replied Henry, "since I see that nothing is what you'll contribute to this evening's fare."

"Seeing nothing's what you're paying, I only supposed you'd be wanting your money's worth!"

"With your lovely company added into the bargain," quipped Henry, "I'm due a refund."

"Well, I can't match witlessness with you, Patrick Henry, as I've got some real work to attend to."

"Come, come, my dear Mrs. Biddlesworth," mumbled Henry around a mouthful of sausage, "don't be modest. You can match witlessness with the best."

"Really! Well, I wouldn't think it worth the while, like some I know."

"If you have to think on the worth of witlessness, then witlessness has whittled your wit worthless," shot back Henry.

"Ohhh, you!" was all Mrs. Biddlesworth dared, before Henry's laughter chased her past Marshall and out into the yard.

"Mr. Henry!"

"Ah, Mr. Marshall, what have you got there? Wine? Excellent! Please," and he motioned to a seat directly across from himself.

"But what has happened to dinner, and –"

"–And what am I doing here?" finished Henry, chuckling. "Dinner has gone to the pigs, or piglets, anyway. Mrs. Biddlesworth is off to the sty to play midwife to Eugenia, her prize sow, so of course it is up to the guests, who are generally an inconvenience, but are an intolerable nuisance at a time like this, to fend for themselves. And as for me, for some reason the Colonel and Gabriella have removed themselves to Bizarre, which very conveniently leaves a room for me. Now come, sit down and share my humble repast, and your hopefully not so humble wine."

Marshall sat reluctantly, and though he was grateful for the food that Henry loaded onto his plate, he accepted it without thanks. "Come, come, Marshall, even we lawyers do not bite the hand that feeds us. I know you don't like me, but we have to put that aside for a few days, to see if we can make something of this case, all right?"

"Very well," said Marshall. "I suppose it is good that you are staying here, because it will be easier to coordinate our strategy."

"I'm very glad to hear you say so, Mr. Marshall, seeing as I'm here as your guest."

Marshall gagged. "My guest, Mr. Henry?"

"That's right. Mrs. Biddlesworth is convinced that the Colonel's wife insisted that they leave because she couldn't abide such close quarters with Nancy, and she said that you promised to cover any cancellations Nancy might cause; therefore, you're paying for my lodgings."

Marshall took a large swig of wine, but said nothing.

"So," said Henry, refusing to let Marshall sulk, "how'd we do today?"

How did we do today? thought Marshall. Honestly, now. "You did a nice job with Mr. Harrison and Mr. Page, I'll give you that much. How did you know that Mr. Page dances with his sister-in-law?"

"I didn't."

"You didn't? Do you mean to say that you risked an entire line of examination on pure chance?"

Henry chuckled. "No, Mr. Marshall, nothing so irresponsible as that. It simply did not matter whether he dances with his sister-in-law, or not. Either he does, which means that he engages in the same sort of 'imprudent familiarities' with which he accuses our clients, or he doesn't, in which case he's too much of a stuffed shirt to tell an imprudent familiarity from a handshake. He was doomed just for being himself. It didn't matter what he answered."

"Well, that was all right, I suppose," said Marshall, unsure now whether it was or not. "But the rest of your behavior today –" Marshall struggled to convey his disgust – "unspeakable!"

"Whatever do you mean, Mr. Marshall?"

"What do I mean? Can you be so blind? By the standards of the mob, I'd say that you did quite well with Mrs. Brett Randolph. But by the standards of the law and the code of behavior attendant upon the high office of attorney, not to mention gentleman, I'd say that you performed shamefully."

"Then next time we have a jury made up of angels, I'll change my tactics. But as long as they're drawn from the mob, as you call it, I'll stick with what I know to be effective."

"Is it effective?" countered Marshall through a mouthful of leathery meat. "Or do you merely furnish a moment's entertainment, forgotten as soon as it's finished?" He waved the meaty joint at Henry's head. "You have them in your personal spell, Mr. Henry, but you cannot go with them into the jury room. Once there, they must think for themselves about a matter of the utmost seriousness, and unless we have given them something of substance to think about that suggests innocence, they will not let murderers run free simply because you put on a good show."

"I've given them something to think about. They'll think long and hard about what Mrs. Brett Randolph was doing at Bizarre with Jack Randolph, and in doing so they will not be thinking about her testimony against our clients, which is the last thing in the world that I want them thinking about."

"But it's disgraceful," said Marshall. "You have no basis for smearing Mrs. Randolph's name."

"Mr. Marshall," said Henry, trying to contain his annoyance, "you may have noticed that Mrs. Randolph was a very credible witness, and that your logical examination did little to undermine that credibility. At the end of it, all we had was the simple testimony that Richard paid more attention to Nancy than to his own wife, that Nancy looked pregnant, and that both of these facts could be due to causes other than guilt. People do not hold too many things in their mind at once – present company excepted – and they may always be counted on to prefer salacious innuendo over the simple facts. While you may consider that to be disgraceful, it is nonetheless the way the world works."

"You know little of the case," replied Marshall. "Anne Randolph's testimony cannot withstand logical analysis during final argument."

"You know little of human nature," responded Henry. "If you let such testimony go without serious challenge, final argument may be too late."

"But what of the pure ethics of the thing?"

"This is not a game of cricket, Marshall. It is more like that gouging contest out there."

Everything is legal.

Marshall pushed his plate away, his appetite lost. "I cannot believe that. We do not need to tear out the witness's heart in order to expose the logical fallacies in the prosecution's case."

Henry looked down his nose at this earnest young man. "And what if there are no logical fallacies? What if our esteemed clients are simply guilty as Hell? What then, counselor?" prodded Henry.

Marshall pushed with his tongue at a stray piece of gristle stuck between his front teeth, but he couldn't get it free. *What then, indeed?*

– Chapter 16 –

Damaging Testimony

I.

It had turned sharply colder overnight, and a thin mist transported the chill from air to bone in an instant. The wheels of the carriage skidded in the muck, splattering Junior into a mosaic of earth tones, as he coaxed and bullied the horses along the discouraging road towards Cumberland. Behind him, in the relative comfort of the damp, cramped compartment, sat Judith, Jack, Patsy, the Colonel and Gabriella.

Only Gabriella had the heart to chatter, and chatter she did, consuming in a single bite the upcoming Governor's ball, the silly French nobleman with his hot-air balloon, the slave uprising in Haiti, poor awkward Mr. Marshall, the questionable evening perambulations of a vestryman's wife, and the suspicious bulge in the belly of a certain gentleman's house girl. As Gabby talked, Patsy sat with her head tipped towards the window, staring out into the mist, letting the dull passing shapes of things at once so familiar and alien slip by without recognition. Patsy expected to be called to the stand that very day, and her cares made Gabriella's innocent chatter feel obscene. How could she babble on, when such weighty matters loomed before them? Patsy noticed that Jack wasn't really listening, but whenever he sensed that Gabby was about to run down he stoked her with an inane question. Judith, poor Judith, sat at the receiving end of Gabby's blather, feigning attention as if this were just another ride in the country.

And what about me? thought Patsy. Is my brooding any better? I enjoy the hospitality of one of my sisters-in-law, so that I am fortified to aid in convicting another. Patsy removed the parchment from her purse, and looked at its fine calligraphy. What is the power of this subpoena *ad testificatum,* that it can turn mothers upon daughters, sisters against sisters, kith upon kin? Is it the parchment itself, formerly a living skin, now mummified into a force against life? Or is it the words so elaborately scratched into the dermis, *By the Authority of the Commonwealth of Virginia, You are Hereby Commanded...?* It is for God to issue commandments, not this fledgling civil state.

'*Thou shalt not bear false witness against thy neighbor.*' Nor in favor of thy beleaguered sister-in-law.

Patsy drew her cloak tighter about her neck, but it did not keep out the chill. Now Gabby waxed profound about the delights of whipped syllabub, and suddenly Patsy felt that it was neither the words nor the skin that made people comply against nature. It is our own unnatural hearts, she thought, sundered from God, lying bleeding and open to the contagion of law. The subpoena does not make us testify against our loved ones. We were ready to do that the day we were born. It merely tells us when and where to do the deed.

2.

"All rise." Judge Allen swooshed in, full of business and brisk decorum, but Nancy could not help noticing the gold buckles of his shoes peeking out from beneath the homogeneous black robes. What do these buckles mean? Is he daring and unconventional, ready to judge less harshly a deviation from the run of the pack? Are there poet's feet fastened to his calculating trunk, pulling at its orthodox judgments till they are tinged with remembrances of fields of wildflowers? Or are these buckles a flash of Cotton Mather, cruel, egotistical, a mark of the brutality born of fear?

"Are counsel ready?"

"Ready, Your Honor."

"Call your next witness, Mr. Binghamton."

"The Commonwealth calls Mrs. Thomas Mann Randolph, Sr., nee Gabriella Harvie."

Gabriella emerged from the witness chamber looking spectacular with her flowing red hair set off against an emerald silk gown and ivory lingerie bonnet. She glided through the gallery aglow with smiles and confidence, touched the hand of Grandpa Gabe in the front row, entered the gate to the courtroom's inner sanctum, and then startled everyone by pausing to bestow a light kiss on Nancy's cheek. Nancy recoiled and stiffened, then turned to glare at her father, who shrugged, palms upward, as if to say he'd no idea his own wife was to be called to the stand.

"You are the wife of Colonel Thomas Mann Randolph?" asked Binghamton.

"Yes."

"Which makes you step-mother to the accused, Miss Nancy Randolph?"

"Yes, Sir."

"And, Mrs. Randolph –" here Binghamton paused, seized by a sudden inspiration. "We seem to have so many 'Mrs. Randolphs' to contend with in the record, would you mind terribly if I called you 'Miss Harvie'?"

Now it was Gabriella's turn to stiffen. "Mrs. Gabriella Randolph will do," she said coldly.

Caught by surprise that his innocent suggestion had gone wrong, Binghamton sought to make light of it. "All right, then, perhaps Mrs. Randolph two," and he laughed to the jurors who were intently watching Gabriella's cheeks out-blaze her hair. Another damned mistake, Binghamton swore to himself, how does Henry do it so easily? "I am sorry, no offense intended, Mrs. Gabriella Randolph will do quite nicely." Shuffling notes, at once familiar and inscrutable, tongue cleaved to the roof of his mouth, Binghamton sought out a glass of water and took a gulp so quickly that some ran down his chin. "Directing your attention, Mrs. Gabriella Harv – ah, Randolph, I mean, excuse me – directing your attention to the year 1790, was that the year that you were married to Colonel Randolph?"

"Yes."

"And did you take up residence with him at that time?"

"Yes. I moved in to Tuckahoe in May, 1790."

"And was Miss Nancy Randolph in residence at Tuckahoe at that time?"

"Yes, Sir, she was."

"Could you describe for the jury the course of your relations with your step-daughter, Miss Nancy?"

Marshall rose. "Your Honor, may we approach the bench, please?"

"Whatever for, Mr. Marshall?"

You rogue, you know that this means I don't want the jury to hear a word of it, not even enough to tell you what for. "A matter of law, Your Honor."

"Very well," sighed the Judge, communicating to one and all that Marshall was wasting their time again. Binghamton, Marshall and Henry huddled about the bench for a whispered conference with the Court. Jurors whose attention had otherwise been straying to the next meal or to the upcoming task of transplanting the tobacco seedlings, suddenly focused all available mental resources on lip reading.

"Your Honor," whispered Marshall, "Mr. Binghamton is about to elicit a story from this witness about an alleged attack upon her by Miss Nancy, if I am not mistaken, which has no relevance to the charges before this Court, and which can only serve to unfairly inflame the prejudices of the jurors."

"Is this true, Mr. Binghamton?" asked the Judge.

"It is true that Miss Nancy has attempted on several occasions to kill her own step-mother, which bears quite directly on her murderous disposition."

"Your Honor," said Marshall, producing a sheet from his notes, "in *King v. Eastwick*, 1767, Lord Halvert of the King's Bench said, and I quote, 'Suffer not the Prisoner to stand for all the offenses, petty and grand, attributed to him by the waggling of the popular tongue, for what force and effect is left to the process of indictment and information if a man can be bound over and executed for any offense, real or imagined, charged or uncharged, that he has given or others may have felt, during his long passage through life? It is no crime to be a bad man, so the proof of it is not germane. Lacking direct proof of the offense charged, the character of the accused is too unreliable to substitute; and where direct proof is found, there is no need to resort to the vagaries of gossip.' Your Honor, on the strength of this persuasive precedent, we rest our motion for exclusion."

The Judge looked impressed, unused as he was to having actual law cited at him from out of the untamed Virginia woods. He turned to the prosecutor. "Well, what do you say to that, Mr. Binghamton?"

"Perhaps it is all right in Great Britain to hide the truth from the jury, but in this Commonwealth, Your Honor, a juror has the right to make up his own mind."

"That's right, Mr. Binghamton –" said the Judge, and Marshall's face fell – "based on all the evidence of this crime, not some other. Charge her with assault or the attempted murder of Miss Harvie, and then come back to me with this evidence. Otherwise, I do not want to hear it. Motion granted." Marshall beamed.

"But Your Honor –"

"Is this something new, Mr. Binghamton?"

"Well, not exactly, but –"

"Then why are you still nattering on?" The Judge looked at his pocket watch. "We have a trial to finish, gentlemen. Let's not dally."

Counsel returned to their places. Binghamton leafed through his notes, frantically searching out something to latch on to. "Ah, Mrs. Har – ah, Randolph …"

"Yes?" she leaned forward.

"Um." There was nothing. "No further questions."

"The defense has no questions," said Marshall, quickly.

Gabriella was a blaze of red against white knuckles straining to hang on to her pulpit. Suddenly, she could contain herself no longer. "But she's a harlot," she protested, looking first to the prosecutor, then to the Judge, then to the jury, and finally straight at Nancy, pointing a long, bony finger. "Harlot!" The Judge pounded his gavel, crying out for order, but there would be no order. "Step down, Miss Harvie, and contain yourself, or I'll have you arrested for contempt!"

Grandpa Gabe jumped up and into the field of battle. "Your Honor," he cried, "I appear on behalf of this witness." Sheriff Dunby and a deputy approached the interloper menacingly.

"Stay out of this, Gabe!" barked a stern voice – but it did not come from the bench. It was Colonel Randolph himself, lumbering through the swinging gate of the bar. He pushed Gabe aside and strode directly to the witness stand, grabbed his furious wife by the wrist, and half-led, half-dragged her from her perch.

Nancy glared daggers at Gabriella as she was pulled past the defense table, re-igniting the legendary family temper. Gabriella lunged at Nancy and managed to inflict a small scratch with her fingernail before she was restrained by Sheriff Dunby, who joined the Colonel to help drag Gabriella cursing and struggling from the chamber of justice, Grandpa Gabe hot on their heels.

Marshall knelt by Nancy's side and, with a flourish, proffered his handkerchief for her to dab at the trickle of blood. Then he rose. The courtroom was absolutely silent, but for the timorous sobs of the stricken defendant. "The defense requests a brief recess to tend to the vicious wounds inflicted by the prosecution's witness."

"Court will resume in twenty minutes."

Henry eyed Marshall with new respect.

3.

"The Commonwealth calls Mrs. Martha Jefferson Randolph."

Patsy emerged from the witness chamber slowly, bringing with her a much-needed air of dignity. Dressed simply but elegantly in a peach riding habit over a silk waistcoat and a full silk skirt, this big-boned, pious woman carried herself like a risqué novel, cover consciously inward. She did not look at the defendants as she walked by, and she took the oath with great seriousness. Then she sat, hands clasped tightly in her lap.

Nancy leaned over to whisper to Marshall, but he put his fingers to his lips, and slid a piece of note paper and a quill to her instead. She began scribbling.

Binghamton moved to dominate the center of the courtroom before beginning his examination. "State your name and relationship to the accuseds, please."

"Martha Jefferson Randolph. I am married to Miss Nancy's brother, Thomas Mann Randolph, Jr."

Another 'Mrs. Randolph,' thought Binghamton. What shall I call this one? "Uh, Mrs. Jefferson Randolph," he began, stumbling over the syllables, "please tell the jury –"

"Excuse me, Mr. Binghamton," interrupted Patsy. "'Mrs. Jefferson Randolph' is such a mouthful. 'Miss Jefferson' will do quite nicely, if it would be easier."

Binghamton, who could have kissed her, merely thanked her. He then proceeded to establish that she was a very frequent visitor to Bizarre, while Marshall's attention turned to his client's note:

> I forgot to mention that Patsy told Judith & me about gum guiacum for colic last Sept., and she sent me some at my request shortly before Oct. last. It can produce abortions, but I took it only for colic.

Marshall braced for the worst, silently cursing clients who keep secrets from their lawyers.

"Miss Jefferson," Binghamton was saying, "based on your familiarity with the defendant, Nancy Randolph, I would like to know if you noticed any unusual alteration in her size last year, prior to October 1st?"

Patsy thought carefully before answering, "I do not believe so."

"Well, then, Miss Jefferson, did you see no indication of pregnancy?"

"I saw none."

"So it is your testimony, under oath, that you did not believe Nancy to be pregnant?"

"I saw nothing to indicate pregnancy."

"Did you or did you not believe Nancy Randolph was pregnant?"

Patsy took a deep breath and replied, "I suspected that she might be." It did not escape the attention of several of the jurors that Nancy's and Richard's eyes met at just this moment.

"And what was the basis of this suspicion?"

"It had no basis."

"Well, it must have had some basis."

"Call it intuition, then. It was just a feeling that I had."

"Whatever its basis, you did believe your sister-in-law, Nancy Randolph, to be pregnant?"

"I would not say that I believed it, since that implies too great a certainty. I would leave it that I suspected it might be so."

"Very well," said Binghamton, willing to make do with that since, if Polly Page was reliable, he knew that he could get finer nuggets from Miss Jefferson. "I would now like to direct your attention to September of last year. Did you visit with the Bizarre household during that month?"

"Yes, Mr. Binghamton, I did."

"Do you recall a conversation that you had concerning a certain medication?"

Patsy looked to the ceiling as if it held the answer. "I have had many conversations concerning medication, Mr. Binghamton."

Binghamton took a step towards the witness. "I do not doubt that, Miss Jefferson, but this was a very particular conversation, in that it involved the defendant, Nancy Randolph."

"Objection!" shouted Marshall, "we don't even know yet that there was a conversation, and already Mr. Binghamton has placed the defendant in it."

"Can you rephrase the question, Mr. Binghamton?" enquired the Judge.

"Yes, Your Honor. Miss Jefferson, did you have a conversation with Nancy Randolph at Bizarre Estate last September, that would be September of 1792?"

"More than one. We are sisters by law. I visited for an entire week."

"Did one of those September conversations between you and Nancy Randolph concern medication for colic?"

Patsy turned the question over in her mind, and then answered with a deliberate, "No."

Binghamton looked surprised, but he pressed on. "Isn't it true that you had a conversation about medication for colic at Bizarre last September?"

Absent-mindedly straightening a lock of hair that could get no straighter, the witness answered, "Yes, Mr. Binghamton, that's true."

Her father taught her well, thought Henry, chuckling to himself.

"So then," continued Binghamton, feeling now that he'd gotten the matter cleared up, "it is true that you spoke with Nancy concerning colic medication last September?"

"No."

Now Binghamton was puzzled. "Then with whom did you speak?"

"I spoke with Judith Randolph on the subject."

"And not Nancy?"

"No, Mr. Binghamton, not Nancy."

"Very well then, what did you tell Judith about colic medicine?"

"That would be hearsay, Your Honor," objected Marshall.

"It is merely offered to show its effect on the state of mind of the defendant, Nancy Randolph," pleaded Binghamton, "and not to establish the truth of anything that was said."

"I do not see how it could have had an effect on Miss Nancy's state of mind if she was not party to the conversation," countered Marshall.

"Mr. Marshall is right," said the Judge. "Sustained."

Binghamton looked harried, but he took a lucky stab in the dark. "Was Miss Nancy Randolph present in the room when you had this conversation with Judith Randolph?"

Patsy looked tenderly at Nancy, cradling her against the impact with her eyes. "Yes, Mr. Binghamton," she whispered.

"Speak up, please."

"Yes; I said yes."

"So she could have overheard what you said to Judith?"

"Objection! Calls for a conclusion."

"Overruled."

"I repeat: so she could have overheard what you said to Judith?"

"Yes, Mr. Binghamton."

"How near to you was she?"

Patsy looked down. "Quite."

"So she almost certainly overheard your conversation with Judith Randolph?"

"I would think so."

"And what did you say to Judith with Nancy Randolph close by?"

"Object –"

"Overruled, Mr. Marshall."

"You may answer, Miss Jefferson."

"I told her about gum guiacum; that it is an excellent remedy for colic."

"Is that all?"

"No, Mr. Binghamton, that is not all. I also cautioned her, as a married woman, that gum guiacum is not to be taken during pregnancy, as it has been known to induce abortion."

"Do you recall the precise day of that conversation?"

"I am not sure. A Wednesday, I think."

"And did you return home shortly thereafter?"

"Yes. I returned home that Friday."

"Two days after warning Judith, within Nancy's hearing, of the dangerous properties of gum guiacum?"

"Yes, Mr. Binghamton."

"And how long after your return home was it before you received a visit from a Mrs. Carter Page?"

"Mrs. Page visited me on Sunday."

"Four days after Nancy overheard your description of gum guiacum?"

"More or less."

"What did Mrs. Page want?"

"Gum guiacum."

"For herself?"

"No."

"For whom, then?"

"For Miss Randolph."

"Mrs. Judith Randolph?"

"No, not Judith." She put her hand to her hair and tugged on it. "For Miss Nancy Randolph."

Several jurors turned to take a hard look at Nancy, who was biting her lip. The murmuring of the crowd was like a Greek chorus. It was the sound of convictions forming.

"Did you give Mrs. Page the gum guiacum for Nancy Randolph?"

"Yes."

"I have no further questions. Thank-you, Miss Jefferson."

The witness nodded curtly.

Marshall rose to cross-examine. "You are Richard Randolph's sister-in-law?"

"I am."

"Does he greet you with affection?"

Patsy looked fondly at Richard, who sat straight and proud before her. "Yes, Mr. Marshall. Richard is a gentle, affectionate man."

"In what ways does he show his affection towards you?"

"He hugs me and kisses me, with my husband at my side, and no one has ever thought ill of it. He dances with me. He takes my hand and escorts me to dinner."

"Let's talk about this visit from Mrs. Page. First, what evidence do you have that Nancy sent Mrs. Page to you?"

"That is what Mrs. Page said."

"Do you have any other evidence that Mrs. Page came on Nancy's behest?"

"No."

"And I take it that you have no idea what Mrs. Page did with the medication after you gave it to her?"

"That's right."

"So you do not know if she gave it to Nancy Randolph, used it herself, or threw it into the James?"

"I do not."

"In addition, if the medication was in fact sent for by Miss Nancy, and was in fact received by her, you would have no way of knowing whether she in fact took any of it?"

"That is correct, Mr. Marshall."

"Miss Nancy Randolph suffers from colic, does she not?"

"I believe so."

"And therefore if she took it, then she may well have been taking it to treat a perfectly innocent ailment, namely, colic, isn't that right?"

"Yes, that's right."

"How do you feel about abortion, Miss Jefferson?"

"I do not approve."

"And yet you say you sent a known abortifacient to your sister-in-law whom you suspected of being pregnant?"

Patsy's heart raced at the question. Just tell the truth, Poppa had said, and he was so right. I stretched the truth, and now he's got me. "It was only a small quantity," Patsy heard herself answering.

"Even so, Miss Jefferson, had you truly suspected pregnancy, you would not have sent it, isn't that right?"

Oh, you foolish man, how little you know about a woman's heart. "I have known more to be given to a pregnant woman without adverse effect."

Marshall was puzzled by her indirection. "Are you saying that you sent a dose that was insufficient to induce labor?" he asked.

"I am saying that the dose I sent may or may not have been sufficient."

Marshall blundered forward. "Well, then, either you don't object to abortion, as you claim, or you didn't believe Miss Nancy to be pregnant, as you claim, or you wouldn't have sent such a dose of medicine, as you claim. All three cannot logically stand together, can they?"

"I suppose not, Mr. Marshall." Her eyes begged him to stop.

"Which is it then? Which is false?"

Patsy swallowed hard. "I am afraid, Sir, that I would act logically. I love Nancy."

Marshall was stunned. He staggered back to familiar territory. "But the dose you sent, if taken, could have been taken without inducing labor?"

"That is correct."

"I have nothing further."

"You may step down, Miss Jefferson," said the Judge.

Patsy would willingly have contributed her humiliation to the cause of those she loved. But it was Marshall who skulked to his seat.

4.

This was really too much, thought Peggy Page. She and Cedric were left to languish in the antechamber reserved for witnesses with nothing to do but watch the hands on the clock mock them by refusing to move. *Eleven-ten.* Of course she'd worn the queen's gown of forest green, only to be humiliated to find Gabby Randolph adorned in a gown of similar cut and color. If that Mr. Binghamton had any sense, such matters would be arranged in advance, but no, she had not even been able to go see him to ask permission to rush home to change, and now here it had been over two of the longest hours ever to pass since creation so she could easily have made it home and back, and she cursed herself for not indulging this morning's sudden urge to dare to wear purple which had been nipped in the bud by Carter's reproachful look.

In the back of her mind she had to confess that Gabby cut quite a figure, sprightly imp that she is, but she hasn't got any breasts to speak of, she's built like a little girl, which apparently suits the Colonel just fine. Her own fleshy ladies were quite different, more along the lines of what tickled most men's fancy. She looked down to admire how they swelled nicely over the ruffles of her plunging Medici collar with the prim bow to barely avert infamy, pleased that she could fill a gown and still have enough cleavage to get the jurors to sit up straight. Even Patrick Henry is not too old to notice a pair like these, she thought. Maybe if she wiggled oh so slightly at just the right moments he'll lose track of those devilish words of his, and remember that he's not a gentleman. A lascivious smile twisted Peggy Page's rouged lips as she crossed her legs. *Eleven-eleven.*

The movement attracted Cedric's notice though his eyes had been shut and he was half dozing. His momma had nearly fainted yesterday when that Mr. Henry burst in, and she'd spent half the night trying to decide whether they ought to skip out on the subpoena, never really deciding not to, just working herself into a sort of paralytic fit. Cedric didn't see the problem, he'll just tell them, there's no question whatsoever that it was Richard I saw going into Nancy's room that night at Bizarre. As long as you stay clear and definite there's nothing a lawyer can do about it; it's only when you start hemming and hawing that they can chew you up. What's Mr. Henry going to say, anyway? He wasn't there, he doesn't know how dark it was.

But wait a minute, does he have some proof of what the moon was that night, there wasn't much, was there? Damn, he couldn't remember. He thought there'd been a moon the night before, when he and Nancy took that walk, that beautiful walk, down to the river. She'd been crying over some trifle, and she took comfort in his arms for a change. Yes, he could see the moonlight now, caressing Nancy's skin.

But wait, no! He'd better forget all that, and focus on the matter at hand. Did it cloud over the next day, blocking out the moon? Think, think. But he couldn't remember, his mind was too languid, he was getting so bored, locked away with nothing to do, nothing to look at but God-awful Aunt Peggy, nothing to read but a well-thumbed Blackstone and a sheaf of desultory statutes. Grandpa clock, what do you say?

Eleven-twelve. Nearly noon and dark as dusk. Chilly and damp, but thank God for that, what else is there to keep a boy awake but the chill? Do the lawyers plan it this way? Lock the victim in a bare room, deprive his brain of all stimulation, while their predatory minds are fired in the crucible of the courtroom till, by the time the witness is dragged before them, he's stupid and dull and an easy mark.

The chamber-stick! That's it, to Hell with the moon, he could say that he could see Richard's face clearly by the light of the taper in his hand. But which hand? *Do you mean his face was towards you,* they'll ask. *Then how is it that he did not see you? And if he could not see you, does that not mean that his face was not towards you?* Oh Lord, he didn't know, too many possibilities, but it was Richard, that's all, stick with that, it had to have been Richard, *it certainly wasn't me,* wait, no, better not say that.

Eleven-thirteen. Perhaps they'll break for lunch before they get to me, thought Peggy Page, and then I'll have time to change my dress. Of course, several ladies had seen her in the forest green this morning, but that's all right, she would simply have to wear something else for the ball on Friday. She could send the chocolate spice girl back to bring the dress here, but knowing that foolish maid she'd probably bring the wrong shoes or drag it in the mud. Anyway, she couldn't very well change right here in the witness room while the trial was going on, because it would not do to be called to the stand suddenly wearing nothing but a corset and her panniers!

It would be wonderful if they broke for lunch, because Jane and Carter could fill her in on what was said, so that she'd be sure not to get anything wrong. But she'll be careful, that Mr. Henry won't trip her up because she'd figured out how he does it. He takes advantage when a witness hasn't made her testimony perfectly clear, so she planned to make her testimony so clear they'll need to squint against the glare of it. Oh yes, when she is done testifying that Mr. Henry will know what kind of a hussy his client is, and he and everyone else will know that when Peggy Page says something is so, it's so.

She looked at the clock. Still *eleven-thirteen.* From there she looked to the window, at the fractured trees seeping through thick blown glass and raindrops. Her eyes were heavy, she was so sleepy. She watched the trees dance, jiggling to and fro through misting drops.

The door flung open with a crack! "Mrs. Carter Page," insisted the bailiff, and she stood rather too quickly, banging her knee on the underside of the table, her heart pounding as she veered past the clock, *eleven-thirty-four* – good Lord, she had fallen asleep! – towards the brightness and warmth of the courtroom. Calm now, calm yourself, she thought, surreptitiously wiping a dribble of drool from the corner of her mouth, disoriented by the instantaneous jolt from sleep to the scrutiny of hundreds.

She had meant to stride in proudly, but her throbbing knee and tenuous equilibrium would not permit it, so she substituted stiff dignity. There was Jane, how good to see her face, everyone else was looking at her with unaccustomed suspicion. And Carter, where was Carter? She couldn't find him in the crowd, darn that man, why couldn't he have sat by Jane like she'd instructed? Oh, he would hear about that later, nothing to be done about it now; what a long, long walk to the witness stand. She fumbled with the gate to the bar, then Mr. Binghamton sprang to her aid, Carter should be doing it and she turned to find him and cluck her disapproval but couldn't find him still so she clucked at the whole gallery instead. Now where should she go? Over here, hand on the Bible, it feels slimy, does she solemnlyswearhmmhmm damn! she forgot to smile at the jurors and give them a little wiggle on the way by, oh well, she'll do it right now while Critch blathers on. *There boys, how's that?* Oh, yes, now Mr. Critch awaits an answer, "I do, I do," *do I ever want to sit down, I feel so trembly.*

"State your name and your relationship to the accuseds, please."

Mouth full of cotton. Good, a water glass. She took a drink, spilled a bit, dabbed at her mouth with her handkerchief. All right, here goes. "I am Mrs. Carter Page of Cumberland."

"And your relationship to the accuseds?" pressed Binghamton.

What? He needs more? All right, bothersome man! "As everyone here already knows, Mr. Binghamton, Nancy Randolph's mother Anne was my eldest sister, God rest her soul, so Nancy and Judith are my nieces."

"Have you enjoyed a close relationship with your nieces, and particularly with Miss Nancy?"

"Oh yes, very close," answered Mrs. Page. "Nancy has always affectionately called me 'Aunt Peggy,' and we visit frequently." Nancy blanched despite herself.

"Tell us, Mrs. Page, did you find the relations between Mr. Richard Randolph, his wife Judith, and Miss Nancy Randolph, to be harmonious?"

"Oh yes, yes indeed, I always have."

"Did you ever observe any friction between the accuseds, and Mrs. Judith Randolph?"

"Well, Mr. Binghamton, you have to know that Judith is one of the kindest, gentlest ladies in all Virginia, and she is quite devoted to both her husband and her sister, so I would never expect to see Judith angry towards either of them, and I never did." Peggy paused, and just as heads were turning back to Binghamton, she added, "But she did say something of interest to me back in March of last year." Marshall began to rise, but Henry pulled him down. "I remember we were sitting by the fire and she was nursing that poor little baby St. George, her son, who you know isn't really doing very well, but he was just a newborn at the time and not even christened, and so we didn't know how he'd come along –"

"Yes, Mrs. Page?" prompted Binghamton.

These lawyers, always so impatient! "Well, Judith said to me, 'You know, Aunt Peggy, these days it seems that Nancy and Richard are only company for each other.' But she never complained." Peggy looked sweetly at Judith, who looked away. "She wasn't like that."

"What about you, Mrs. Page, did you notice any improper familiarities between the accuseds?"

"I must honestly say, Mr. Binghamton, that I did notice a special fondness between them in March or April of last year, which made me suspect criminal conversation. Of course, they weren't together all the time, for Richard was frequently out on his plantation, while Nancy was often in her chamber, but when they were together," she paused, closed her eyes, and lifted her hand in pirouettes towards General Washington's countenance above her, "sparks flew." Judith looked towards Richard, who looked towards Nancy, who looked down.

"How did Miss Nancy appear to you in May of last year?"

"She appeared melancholy, and complained of colic. I offered to examine her, but she refused to undress in my presence, and would not allow it. Nonetheless, I was able to detect a definite increase in the size of her midsection. This led me to suspect pregnancy."

"Were you able to see anything more that excited your suspicions?"

"When Nancy visited us in June she wasn't much bigger, but I do recall seeing her look down at her waist, and then cast her eyes up to Heaven in silent melancholy."

"Did you ever receive a request from Miss Nancy for some gum guiacum?"

"Yes, Sir. Well, not exactly from Nancy herself, but from her girl, Jenna, who said it was for Nancy."

Marshall had tried to beat the hearsay, but it was too late. "Forget it," whispered Henry, "this one's mine. I won't be needing any fancy objections."

"Did you know what the gum guiacum was for?"

"I was not familiar with the remedy, but the girl said it was for Nancy's colic, and that it had been recommended to her by Mrs. Patsy Jefferson Randolph. I was on my way to Monticello, so I was happy to get it for her. Of course, if I'd had any idea what she was going to use it –"

"Objection!" This time it was Henry. "You don't have any idea whether or how she used it, now do you, Mrs. Page? Shame on you!"

"Sustained. The witness will kindly stick to the facts."

"Yes, Your Honor. I'm sorry. I didn't mean anything by it." *He wants facts, that Mr. Henry? I'll give him facts.*

"Did you obtain the gum guiacum for Miss Nancy?"

"Yes, Sir, I got some from Patsy Randolph, and I handed it to Nancy's girl."

"When did you hand the gum guiacum to Nancy's girl?"

"It was the last week in September, last year."

The timing was tight and uncomfortable. Binghamton paused to let it sink in, before launching into his prize dirt. "Now, Mrs. Page, did you make any observations about Miss Nancy's condition after June of last year?"

"Yes, I did. I visited Bizarre again in August, during which time Nancy kept to her room constantly. I became suspicious, so I went up to her door, which was locked, and I could hear her talking to her maid. I couldn't quite make out the words at first, so I had to put my ear right up to the door, and when I did so I found not only that I could make out the words, but that by pushing slightly on the door I could make a crack to see through."

"And what did you observe through the door to Miss Nancy's chamber?"

Everyone held their breath, as if in fear of being caught eavesdropping.

"I saw Nancy in a state of near-complete undress, with her hand below her belly. She seemed to me to be obviously pregnant. She asked her girl whether she thought she was smaller today, but the girl replied no, she thought she was bigger, at which point Nancy put her hand to her brow, said she felt unwell, and fell upon the bed. As it appeared that the servant might go to fetch something, I retired immediately, and saw nothing further."

"Naturally," agreed Binghamton, approvingly. "And was that the last you saw of Miss Nancy prior to October 1st?"

"Yes, Sir. But I did see her when the rumors of the birth first began to circulate, towards the end of October. I confronted her with what I had heard, and told her that I wished she would put it in my power to contradict these rumors by permitting me to examine her body for signs of a recent birth."

"Did she permit this examination?"

"Alas, she did not. She became quite indignant that her denials alone would not satisfy me. I am sad to say that we parted on unhappy terms at that point." Her unctuous glance at Nancy was met with a defiant stare. "Since then I have had no further intercourse with this ungrateful niece, whom I only wished to help." Peggy shifted her gaze to the jury, where it was received sympathetically. She leaned forward so that her breasts strained at her bodice, and smiled a little wounded smile.

"No further questions."

Henry rose and Peggy retracted her chest.

"We'll break for lunch for one hour only," interjected the Judge, and his gavel sent the multitudes scrambling for a quick bite, wondering how even God Himself could get those two off now.

5.

Marshall leaned across his bowl of peppery gristle and turnip stew, the Eagle's contribution to the bleakness of their predicament. "I have made careful notes, Mr. Henry, which may be of some assistance to you."

"Hmph. Do you think so, Marshall?" Henry was ignoring both the indigestible stew and his indecipherable dining companion.

"Yes, I do. If you will permit me, perhaps I could make some suggestions for the best ways to undermine Mrs. Page's testimony."

"Hmmm. Yes, all right, go ahead."

"Well, Mr. Henry –"

"Call me 'Patrick'."

"What? Oh no, I couldn't, Sir."

"All right, then call me 'Angus,' but my name's Patrick." He laughed mirthlessly, just as two men dressed in homespun tentatively sidled up to the table, hats in hand.

"Excuse us, Gov'ner," said the older of the two, "I know you two's busier thenna dog in a cathouse, but I jest wanted my boy here to be able ta say he'd shook Patrick Henry's hand."

Henry leaned back and took a good long look at the older man before saying, "Sir, I recognize that face of yours, though it's a bit the worse for wear since I seen it last. Didn't you stand with me against Lord Dunsmore after he stole our powder?"

The old farmer sprang to attention, and saluted. "Yassir."

"Crawford, that's it, Corporal Robert Crawford!"

"Yassir," said the old man, near bursting into a jig as he shook Henry's hand and tried to talk to his son at the same time. "Didn't I tell you he'd remember me, yassir boy, there's no man on the face of the earth like Gov'ner Henry, never was an' never will be agin. Dunsmore, that ole British windbag of a fake Gov'ner, stole the Commonwealth's powder right from under them Tidewater gent's noses, and farts like Peyton Randolph are all tippi-toein' around like they gotta apologize for bein' robbed. But not Mr. Henry here, he called up 'bout 300 of us upriver boys, the kind that kin hit a rabbit at a hunnert paces, an' marched us right at Williamsburg till it scared the wig right off'n that British toad, an' he paid up fer what he took, £300 cash on the barrel. Gov'ner, I'd be pleased if you'd shake my son's hand."

The sinewy ragamuffin extended a hand that could sprout potatoes from each cuticle, but Henry grasped it firmly. "My pleasure, Mr. Crawford. Son, your father's a good man, he wasn't afraid to stand up for liberty back when it wasn't so fashionable. I hope you'll do him proud."

"I'll try, Mr., uh, Gov'ner Henry, Sir."

"What's your name, anyway, boy?"

The young man looked down, as if he wasn't sure it was right, but after a gentle prod from the old man he looked proudly into Henry's eyes. "Why, Patrick, Sir, named after you."

"Well, I'm real pleased," and it was clear that Henry was touched. Those years of service, of risking safety and neglecting personal affairs, bear fruit in unexpected ways.

As the Crawfords moved on, Marshall felt his opinion of Henry shift despite himself. Damnable rascal that he was, he was undeniably a man of importance. He'd touched a lot of lives. Marshall knew he couldn't do that the same way Henry had done it, but still, he saw that it was something worth doing.

"About those suggestions for cross-examination, Mr. Henry?"

Henry focused again on his gangly dining companion. "I'm going to call you John even if you don't call me Patrick," he said, a bemused twinkle in his eye.

"The cross-examination?"

"All right," said Henry, "what do you think?"

Marshall washed down the last lumps of gristle with a large swig of cider, and pushed his bowl away. "Well, as I see it, there are two principal areas of damage: first, the observations concerning pregnancy, and second, the gum guiacum story. The gum guiacum is easy. She has no direct knowledge that Nancy asked for it, or that Nancy ever received it, having dealt exclusively with Nancy's girl, Jenna."

"That is precisely correct, John old boy."

"Thank-you, Mr. - er, Patrick."

"Yes," said Henry, smiling, "it is precisely correct and about as useful as wings on a pig, because not even you actually believe that Jenna did not faithfully deliver the potion to her mistress. But excuse me - do go on."

Marshall frowned, seeing that Henry was only toying with him. "Well, we have to point out each little hole in the case, in the hopes that they will add up to something bigger. Anyway, it is the first area of damage that is the more problematic. The silent melancholy and looking towards Heaven is easy enough, since she could have been upset about any of a number of things: an innocent illness, a social slight at a ball, the loss of her girlish figure. The May thickening can be attributed to overeating, or to illness-related bloat. The unwillingness to be examined is not unusual, since it is natural to desire privacy, and to fear learning of one's own infirmities. This leaves only the incident at the door to Nancy's chamber, which, I must confess, leaves me stumped." Marshall spread some notes on the table. "Her words were, and I quote, 'she seemed to me to be obviously pregnant,' which is a conclusion, so you could pick at the basis for the conclusion, which is probably no more than an enlarged midsection. This, even *in extremis,* is consistent with Nancy's complaint of illness and her swoon. Perhaps we could suggest some sort of intestinal blockage?"

"And perhaps we could suggest that Miss Randolph had swallowed a cannonball," said Henry.

Marshall winced. "This is not a time for jokes, Mr. Henry."

"I'm not joking, John, I am trying to get you to see that not every problem can be solved with logic. Ask yourself instead, 'What would it take to persuade me to acquit, if I were in the jury box?' As you see it, there are two areas of damage: the gum guiacum, and the direct evidence of pregnancy. This is not, however, the way I see it, because I am interested in the process of persuasion, not logicians' proofs."

"And how do you see it, Sir?"

"I see only one area of damage: a nosy aunt who has turned against her own niece. If we destroy the aunt, we destroy the testimony."

"Another opportunity for an *ad hominum* attack?" snorted Marshall. "I warn you, Mr. Henry, I will not tolerate these sorts of tactics as part of a defense that bears my name. I may still be forced to withdraw."

"Don't be a fool, Marshall," said Henry, abandoning the pretense of camaraderie. "This woman is poison to us, and you expect me to go in there with nothing but meek blabber about a possible intestinal blockage? What's so high and mighty about that? It's pure fabrication, and you know it."

"I am not saying we should offer testimony that Nancy had a blockage. I am merely saying that you should force Mrs. Page to acknowledge that the facts she witnessed are consistent with conclusions other than pregnancy. There is nothing improper about that, and it is far superior to an attack on the witness's honor."

Henry's eyes turned to blue ice. "You don't want to win this case, do you?"

"Of course I do," cried Marshall, his voice breaking; how desperately he wanted to win this case, needed to win this case, Henry could never guess. But he wanted to win it with honor – not by doing just anything, but by being right, by being smarter than the prosecution, by using the majesty that was the law, not by defiling it. If he were ever to achieve a moment in which someone approached him in his old age just so his son could say, "I shook John Marshall's hand," it would not be by leading the charge on the armory, but by devotion to the rule of law itself.

Suddenly, Marshall's voice was smoother and stronger than Henry remembered ever hearing it. "Of course, Patrick, we must win this case. On that we are united. But if lawyers kill to win, what have they won? Not an acquittal, which is a creature of the law. A brawl, or a gouging contest, to use your words, but not an acquittal. So, maybe you can win this gouging contest and blind the court to the truth. Is that what you have trained for all these years? Is that what your brilliant mind, your eloquence, your passion for liberty and justice, are placed on this earth to achieve? To inflict pain and injustice by brute force and trickery? I pray to God that it is not so, and that a man of your stature and wisdom knows, deep down, that our calling is not so ignoble."

Henry fidgeted with his spoon, standing it straight up in the cold, uneaten stew. He was chastened, and it made him surly. "We'd better get back," was all he said as he rose.

"What about Mrs. Page?" prodded Marshall. "You'll stick to the evidence?"

"Like a dog to its droppings," snapped Henry.

– CHAPTER 17 –

"OUT DAMN'D SPOT"

I.

Peggy Page sashayed past the jurors, and smiled as Mr. Critch jumped to hold the swinging gate to the witness box for her. She lowered herself like a giant spider on tin pannier legs that flexed gradually as her bottom settled on the witness chair. Then she struck a pose of dutiful virtue, which gained in artifice with each unflinching minute.

"All rise!"

Judge Allen strode in and bounded to the bench, looking neither left nor right. "You're still under oath, Mrs. Page," he brusquely reminded the witness. "The defense may proceed."

Aimless as a ship's passenger, Patrick Henry sauntered towards the front of the defense table. Mrs. Page defied the laws of nature by growing even more still. Her stillness spread to the jurors, who sat in rapt attention, daring anyone to dispel the weight of the morning's testimony. From there it spread across the bench, stifling the stenographer's frenetic quill, freezing the Judge's impatient breath so that he mirrored, for an instant, the avuncular features of Washington nailed to the wall above him. Next, the spectators fell under the trance, suffering itchy noses, blocked views and hard seats without wiggling, keeping their pithy insights to themselves, swallowing the tickles in their throats, barely daring to blink for fear of attracting attention away from Henry and his quarry.

"I am really only interested in one minor detail of your extraordinary testimony, Mrs. Page," began Henry, "which is, the door to Miss Nancy's chamber. Would you describe that door for us?"

Perfect clarity. *If I am perfectly clear, I will be safe.* "It's a plain door, Mr. Henry, made of wood, but of what kind of wood I could not say."

"Just an ordinary door, like one might see anywhere?"

"Yes, that's right."

"Was it in good condition?"

"Yes, I think so."

"Not cracked?"

"No, Sir."

"Did it have any windows in it?"

"No, Sir."

Henry began to stroll about, stroking his chin, as if perplexed. "No windows?" he repeated, almost to himself. "Then a transom above, perhaps?"

"No."

"No cracks, no windows, no transom," muttered Henry. "A peephole, then?"

Really, now, this was too much. "No, Mr. Henry, no peephole. As I said already, by pushing against the door, I was able to make a crack to see through."

Henry slapped his hand on his knee. "Oh yes, by Zeus, you're right, you did say that." Turning towards Binghamton, he added, "What a fine witness, sharp as a tack." Peggy beamed, relaxing. As Henry turned back towards her, she even let him see a little cleavage. "So it was this crack that you peeked through, and not any window or peephole or anything?"

"That's right."

"You are quite sure of that?" he asked, his gaze moving from her eyes to her breasts and back to her eyes.

She was pleased to see him succumb to her charms. She leaned forward, and smiled. "Absolutely sure, Mr. Henry."

Henry, apparently sated, walked back towards the jury box. "But now, Aunt Peggy, you must tell me, what kind of lock did this door have?"

Aunt Peggy? Well, he's a rogue, she thought, but he's my rogue now, so I suppose it's all right. "An ordinary lock."

"An ordinary door with an ordinary lock, how splendid. Do you mean the kind that locks with a key?"

"Yes, Sir."

"And that therefore has a keyhole."

"I suppose."

Henry pounced. "You suppose? Is your memory on the subject less than clear?"

"Oh no!"

"Then tell us, did Miss Nancy's door have a keyhole, or not?"

"It had a keyhole."

"And yet you chose not to look through this keyhole, but instead to push open the door enough to make a crack?"

Aunt Peggy shifted uncomfortably. "Yes."

"Do you always seek out the more difficult solution to a problem?"

"Oh, no, not at all."

"Why do it on this occasion?"

"But I didn't."

"Didn't you?"

"What else was I to do, Mr. Henry? The key was in the other side of the lock. I could see nothing through the keyhole."

Cross-examination is invariably fatal to either the witness or the examiner. Henry, though wounded, staggered forward on instinct.

"So now we know why, Aunt Peggy," he said, grasping to retain the offensive, "but we would still like to know –" he paused, seeking the thread – "how?"

"How?" she sniffed, as one might speak to a backward servant. "Excuse me, but I do not follow your question."

"If I recall your morning's testimony, you said that the door was locked, isn't that right?"

"Yes, that's right."

Now she spoke confidently, knowing that this old man could be beaten. Henry saw her hubris, and immediately incorporated it into his plans. "What I am trying to say – and I know you are trying to be clear, and that it is probably just my own failings that are preventing me from seeing this – is that now we know why you had to make a crack to look through, but we still do not know how it is that you were able to make a crack in a locked door."

She barely deigned to answer. "I told you, Mr. Henry, I pushed on it."

"Hmmm." Henry just stood there, in front of the jury, chin in hand, brow furrowed. Then his face lit up, as if he'd just had a brilliant idea. "Aunt Peggy, I'm sure you will agree that it is important that we understand this, so would you mind demonstrating it for us?"

She rolled her eyes at his stupidity. "Of course." And to think, a moment ago she had feared his cleverness.

"With your permission, Your Honor?" asked Henry, solicitously.

"Any objection, Mr. Binghamton?"

"No, Your Honor."

Of course not, thought Marshall. What's Henry up to? Is he trying to discredit her, or to implant her story so soundly in the jury's mind that nothing will ever shake it loose? These are the dangers of an unplanned examination.

Aunt Peggy rose, and dragged her panniers through the gate and down to the floor in front of the jury box, presenting herself to Henry as if for an obligatory waltz with an unwashed uncle. "I am most grateful to you, Madam," said Henry, and he took her hand with great decorum, and turned her towards the jury box. She felt the jurors' eyes on her body, over her breasts, down her corseted waist, under the great billows of her gown, and she knew that they were hers so long as she did not falter.

"Now, Aunt Peggy, what I would like you to do is to imagine that this –" and Henry swept his big hand through the air between her and the jury box, " – is the door to Miss Nancy's room, locked as it was on that August day that you claim to have seen her through the crack. Can you do that for us?"

Aunt Peggy looked, seeing only the intent faces of the jurors. "I'll try, Sir, but what you ask is rather difficult."

"Everything depends on this," said Henry, his voice dropping dramatically. "You must be perfectly accurate in your descriptions. Do you understand?"

"Yes, of course."

"It is August, it is hot, you come upstairs to lie down, you see the door, an ordinary door, and from behind it you hear the muffled voices."

"Yes, that's right," Aunt Peggy said, and suddenly she really could see the door, that dark paneled door, enticing her to learn more. "I wanted to hear what they were saying, I was curious–"

"Of course you were," coaxed Henry.

"–so I pressed my ear to the door."

"Show us, Aunt Peggy, show us how you did it."

Aunt Peggy bent slightly, her right ear cocked towards the jurors, listening for those remembered voices. Then she raised her right hand.

"What are you doing now, Aunt Peggy?"

"I'm trying the doorknob," and she tried it, "but it's locked."

"So what are you going to do, Aunt Peggy? How can you see what's going on in there?"

"I have to push, like this," and she pushed with her right shoulder against Henry's hastily extended arms, "but it won't budge."

"That's because it's locked, of course it won't budge."

"Ah, but you see, here's where I outsmarted her," said Aunt Peggy, lost in the charade, proud of her ingenuity. "You see, the lock bolt goes in here," and she pointed to a spot belly-high, "so I got down to the floor like this," and she squatted down before the jury box on all fours with her panniers splaying up in the air behind her like a mechanized peacock on display, pressing her face to the floor so that the jurors in back had to stand to see it, "and then with a little push I could see through the crack between the bottom of the door and the threshold!"

Peggy turned her head to look up in triumph at the jurors, who were craning their necks for a good look at the Aunt with her rump in the air and her breasts squished flat to the floor. Henry stepped back to leave her helpless, and his voice changed in an instant from solicitude to icy sarcasm. "And tell us, *Aunt Peggy,* while you were groveling at your niece's doorstep, *which eye did you peep with?*"

Peggy's face turned crimson, as she suddenly realized that she had been made to play the fool. Peals of laughter erupted in the courtroom, over which boomed Henry's last disparaging remark: *"Lord save us from busybodies!"*

2.

"Come with me, Cedric!" commanded Jane, and he stood despite himself.

"But I'm next, Mother. What if I should be called while we are away?"

"This is no time for questions, young man. Come along." She ushered him out of the witness antechamber and down the circular steps in a flash, and he had all he could do to keep his balance along the inside track where the steps narrowed to a fraction of their proper width. He could see his mother's jaw set firmly as they approached the entry way with its press of soggy onlookers, and he noticed that she had been crying. A deputy was stationed by the door, but his mission was to keep out those who wanted in rather than the contrary, so with heads bowed they slipped past undisturbed. Suddenly it dawned on Cedric that they were not going back, that he was running out on his subpoena, and he stopped one step above the mud.

"Mother, we can't," was all he said, and when she pulled on him slightly and he would not budge, she turned from her perch in a mud puddle first to command him, then to implore him.

"Cedric, listen to me, please, it's not even human in there, there is no dignity, there is only viciousness. I can't let you go before that monster, he'll destroy you."

"He won't destroy me, Mother," replied Cedric cockily, "I'm grown now, I can handle myself."

Inside the courtroom a voice cried out: "The prosecution calls Mr. Cedric Randolph."

"Two out, two in," said the deputy behind Cedric, and as the crowd began to jostle for position, a bull of a man shoved in between Cedric and his mother, pushing Cedric backwards against the next step. He grabbed the man to regain his balance, but the man took it wrong, seized Cedric by his oversized lapels, and hurled him into his mother. Jane tried to save her baby, but he really was grown even if he couldn't handle himself, and they both went down in a splatter of muck.

"Gentl'm'n or no, you don't climb over me!" and the big man squared off, ready to do battle.

The bailiff blinked into the empty antechamber, craned his neck to look behind the door, and then shuffled through to check the hallway.

Cedric rose up like a Spanish galleon raised from the depths, soiled from his ivory breeches to the brocade of his silk jabot. He raised his fists and began to circle his attacker warily, and the bored crowd formed a natural ring around them, happy for the diversion. The man flexed enormous arms that were thick as Cedric's waist, and prepared to enjoy himself. Jane weighed the competing dangers, then cried out to the deputy who, upon learning the value of this soiled tatterdemalion, snatched him from the clutches of the large predator.

Back up the winding stair, with Momma whispering in his muddy ear. "Don't let him pin you to a particular word or phrase. Always be certain, but leave a way out. Don't consent to demonstrate anything for him. Watch out for his sarcasm. Don't agree with him about something that seems innocent and unrelated. Stay noncommittal. Say as little as possible. Explain yourself clearly. Don't let him take something you said out of context. Make sure he doesn't get away with suggesting anything improper tying you to Miss Nancy. Don't tell him how much you had to drink at Glenlyvar that night. Be polite. Don't let him get you angry. Smile at the jury. And," as he was pulled off into the crowd at the back of the courtroom by the deputy, "oh, Cedric, do be careful."

The bailiff shuffled to the front of the bench. "Your Honor, the witness is gone!"

"Not quite, Your Honor," announced the proud deputy from within the crowd. "I found him mixin' it up wi' a lumpkin out front. Here he is!" And he flicked the stringy blond stray cat into sight, where he suffered the jeers of the assembly with a bowed and dripping head.

"Mr. Randolph," said the Judge, "what have you got to say for yourself?"

Haltingly. "I just wanted a breath of air, Your Honor. I didn't know I was called. I was close by, Your Honor. I'm sorry."

"Take the stand."

His feet squished in his riding boots as he took the oath. He sat, and his teeth began to chatter. It's from the damp, he thought. Or is it? Then he knew what he would do.

"State your name, please," began Binghamton.

"Cedric Randolph."

"And your relationship to the accuseds?"

"I am Miss Nancy's cousin."

"You were a frequent visitor to Bizarre Estate during the years 1791 and 1792, correct?"

"I think so."

This equivocal response elicited a raised eyebrow from Binghamton, but he dismissed it as an anomaly, and pressed on. "During this time period, did you notice anything untoward about the relationship between the accuseds?"

"Possibly."

The other eyebrow ascended Binghamton's smooth summit. "Possibly? Either you did or you did not, one would think."

"I had thought so in late 1791, but had dismissed the possibility by the summer of 1792."

"Tell us, then, Mr. Randolph, upon what incidents did you base your original suspicions?" pressed Binghamton, growing annoyed.

"I can't recall." His mud-caked mother gave a little nod from the back of the courtroom.

"Come, come, Mr. Randolph, if you suspected improper familiarities between the accuseds, it must have been based on something."

"If so, I cannot recall what."

Binghamton weighed the options in his mind. He could impeach him here and now with his prior statement, but in the process of battling a recalcitrant witness the revelation could lose much of its impact. He decided to try a gentler course. "Well, nonetheless, you are quite sure that you had such suspicions?"

"No."

"No? Didn't you just say you had?"

"Yes, but now you're asking me if I'm quite sure that I had them. I think I had them, but I'm not positive."

Binghamton lost his temper. "Don't play games with me, young man!" he cried, as he strode to the witness box. "Is it or is it not your testimony that you thought the accuseds were too familiar with one another in 1791?"

"I think that I believed that to be so, correct."

"All right. And you said that you later changed your mind. What caused you to change your mind?"

"I can't recall anything in particular."

"So for all you know, your original belief may have remained valid?"

"It may have, but that was not my impression."

"For no reason?"

"For no reason that I now recall."

Binghamton strode off towards the jury box, shaking his head. "You do recall, I hope, accompanying the accuseds to Glenlyvar on Monday, October 1st, 1792?"

"I do."

"And did you observe any change in Miss Nancy's size at that time?"

She was no taller and no shorter. "I did not."

"You did not?" asked Binghamton, obviously surprised. "Are you certain?"

"I am certain that I did not notice such a change. Whether there was a change or not, I could not say."

Henry raised his hand to shield a chuckle.

"So for all you know, there may have been such a change?"

Marshall began to rise, but Henry stopped him. "He's doing his best not to hurt us, so just leave well enough alone," he whispered.

"Perhaps," Cedric conceded.

"What do you recall of that first night at Glenlyvar?"

"Nothing."

"Nothing?" thundered Binghamton. "Do you expect us to believe this?"

"Anyone who has ever enjoyed the better part of a bottle of rum in a single evening could well believe it, Sir." There was scattered laughter from the crowd. Yes, they certainly could believe it.

"Do you recall anything of that visit to the Harrisons? You were there for five days, were you not?"

"Yes, Sir."

"And did you see Miss Nancy in that time?"

"She kept mostly to her chamber, on complaint of illness. But I believe it was on Thursday, the 4th, that she passed through the room in which I was sitting, so I saw her then."

"And what was her condition?"

"Quite weak. At her request, I assisted her up the stairs, to her chamber."

"Did you notice anything unusual in her chamber?"

"Aside from a peculiar smell, nothing."

"A peculiar smell? Can you describe it for us?"

"Just a smell. Not an agreeable one, but not overpowering either. I don't know what it was. I hadn't smelled it before and I haven't smelled it since."

"Do you know anything more about this matter?"

"No, Sir."

Damn, I cannot let him off so easily. "Did you not stay at Bizarre in January of 1792?"

Cedric's discomfort was not solely due to the muck on his stockings. "I'm not quite sure of the dates."

"But certainly you stayed there around that time?"

"Yes."

"During the night, after everyone had gone to bed, what did you see in the hallways of Bizarre?"

Everyone leaned forward in eager anticipation.

Cedric looked off into the distance as if straining to remember. He wrinkled his brow, pursed his lips, squinted his eyes, put one hand to his pimply chin, even emitted a faint hum, all in the cause of conveying concentration. At length, his attention returned to Binghamton. "Nothing that I can recall right now, Sir."

"Now wait just a minute, young man," thundered Binghamton, unimpressed by the display. "Do you recall speaking with me just last week at your home?"

"Yes, Sir."

"And didn't you tell me then –"

"Objection!" thundered both Henry and Marshall simultaneously. "The witness is available to testify under oath to the whole truth," continued Marshall. "What he may have said when he was not under oath is hearsay, and totally irrelevant."

"It bears on whether he truthfully cannot recall, or whether he simply refuses to testify," responded Binghamton.

"But regardless of whether the witness will even agree that last week's gossip is true, by merely asking the question, the prosecutor will reveal it to the prejudice of the defendants."

"Overruled. We'll allow the question, in light of the witness's obvious recalcitrance."

"A further objection, Your Honor," said Marshall. "The Court should not be commenting on the witness in such a manner."

"That's enough, Counsel," Judge Allen barked. "In view of the witness's obvious recalcitrance, and the frivolous nature of your objections, we will allow the question." Marshall opened his mouth. "One more word out of you, Mr. Marshall, and I'll hold you in contempt!"

Marshall sat, furious.

"Proceed, Mr. Binghamton."

"Mr. Randolph, is it not true that, just last week, you told me that you saw Mr. Richard Randolph go into Miss Nancy Randolph's chamber at night?"

"I don't recall."

"You don't recall?" asked Binghamton, his voice heavy with sarcasm. "You don't recall what you told me just last week?"

"No, I do not recall the incident you refer to."

"But you did tell me, just last week, that you saw Mr. Richard Randolph go into Miss Nancy Randolph's chamber?"

Cedric looked for some way out, but saw none. "I may have suggested something like that, yes."

"At night?"

"At night."

"In January, 1792?"

"Or thereabouts."

"No further questions."

Marshall rose, and looked long and hard at the quivering spatter of mud in the witness box. "Mr. Randolph, have you ever been Miss Nancy's suitor?"

Cedric looked towards his Mother, fear in his eyes. "I don't know..." he began, but Marshall cut him off.

"Come, come, young man, don't tell us you don't know whether you offered love to this pretty young lady!" he snapped, and there was muffled laughter as a muddy blush suffused Cedric's face.

"I suppose I did," he allowed, "but she refused me." Marshall would not give him the chance to disclaim bitterness over the refusal; he had what he needed for closing argument.

"Regardless of what Mr. Binghamton may have understood you to say about Mr. Richard last week, when you were not under oath, it is your testimony now, under oath, that you cannot recall any such incident, correct?"

"That is correct." I saw someone who *looked like Richard,* but I cannot be sure that it was Richard.

"Your Honor, in view of the witness's obvious lack of memory, about which he has been commendably candid, nothing would be gained by questioning him further."

3.

"Call your next witness, Mr. Binghamton."

"The Commonwealth calls Mrs. Grant Harrison."

The Harrisons and Mrs. Wood had arrived only a few minutes before, so Mary Harrison had suffered none of the monotony which had hung so heavy on the faculties of prior witnesses. She strode to the stand, crisp in starched linens that had miraculously avoided the soggifying omnipresence of mist. Confronted with Mr. Critch's oatmeal version of the oath, she clarified it by responding that "Wild horses couldn't keep me from telling every drop of truth I know about this, so help me God." By the time she sat down and cast the fire of her lantern eyes across the unworthy jurors, it seemed that the Good Lord himself was raptly attentive.

In response to the prosecutor's preliminary inquiries, she revealed herself indeed to be Mary Harrison, wife of Grant Harrison, of Glenlyvar. Mr. Binghamton got down to business.

"Now, Mrs. Harrison, I would like to direct your attention to Monday, October 1, 1792. Do you recall that day?"

"As if it were yesterday, Sir."

"Did you have visitors that day?"

"Yes, indeed. We had Mr. and Mrs. Richard Randolph, Miss Nancy Randolph, and Mr. Cedric Randolph, who all arrived that day."

"About what time of day did they arrive?"

"Late in the afternoon. Perhaps four o'clock, or four-thirty."

"And did you greet your guests?"

"Of course I greeted my guests," snapped Mrs. Harrison, mistaking the formalities of direct examination for an accusation. "Mr. Harrison handed them out of the carriage, and I met them at the door."

"Did you notice anything unusual about Miss Nancy?"

"Miss Nancy had on a heavy coat, so it was hard to tell much about her size. She did not want to remove it, and started in complaining right off. Soon as she got through the door, she was doubled, holding her stomach."

"How did you respond?"

"I laid her down on the settee just inside the door, where she could be comfortable. I offered her some tea, but she only wanted to be left alone. Judith sat with her for a spell."

"What happened next?"

"Next, we all had a fine meal of stewed rabbit – well, not all; all but Miss Nancy." Mrs. Harrison deigned to look at Nancy for the first time since beginning to testify. Her eyes glinted so briefly that one could mistake it for a trick of light. My God, thought Nancy, she's enjoying this.

"Nancy was called for supper, but declined," continued Mrs. Harrison, disapprovingly. "Instead, she went to bed just before supper. Mr. Richard and Nancy's girl helped her up the stairs."

"Mr. Richard helped her?"

"Yes."

"And then what happened?"

"After supper Judith and I went up to see how Miss Nancy was getting on."

"And how was she?"

"Not well. Her girl was there, and she looked scared. Nancy was moaning and tossing, with her knees pulled up and her hands under the covers clutching at herself."

"Could you see her body at this time?"

"No, Sir, she was just a bundle of quilts. And there was only one candle and the light of the fire to see by."

"What, if anything, did you do for her at that time?"

"Miss Nancy asked Judith for some medicine, and I went to fetch laudanum."

"Did she take the laudanum at that time?"

"Yes."

"When was that?"

"About eight o'clock."

"Did she take any other medication?"

"Not when I was there."

"What happened next?"

"We went back downstairs, and pretty soon we all went to bed. Mr. Cedric slept downstairs across from Mr. Harrison and me, and Richard and Judith retired upstairs, to the chamber outside Nancy's. I was distracted a bit by my own little one, Elly, who was a mite under the weather herself."

"Nothing serious, we hope?"

"No, she's a strong, healthy little girl, thank the Lord."

"Was that all you heard of Miss Nancy that night?"

"Oh no, no Sir. Perhaps an hour after we'd gone to bed, we woke to the most awful screaming. I took the chamber-stick and a bottle of laudanum and went upstairs. I didn't even knock, not very polite, but the screams were so horrible that I just had to go and silence them, or do something, and so I just pushed through that outer door without a thought."

"What did you see when you went in?"

"Only Judith, sitting up with a candle by her bed, and the white quilt pulled to her neck. She said, 'Why, it's Mrs. Harrison.' She said it real loud, like she was talking to someone else."

"Was Mr. Richard there with her?"

"No, Sir, Mr. Richard was nowhere in sight."

"What did you do then?"

"I asked Judith what was the matter with Nancy, and she said she didn't know, but she supposed it was some sort of hysterical fit. She said it wouldn't be the first. I thought she was remarkably calm considering the screams, which had just then subsided into a kind of awful moan, but I did not tarry with Judith. Instead, I crossed straight to Nancy's chamber, but when I tried the door I found that it was bolted from the inside."

"Were you able to get in?"

"I knocked, and heard a bit of whispering and bumping about, and then the bolt slid back and the door was opened just a crack. There was Mr. Richard in a nightshirt and dressing gown, his black hair wild and tangled, looking agitated."

"Did Mr. Richard admit you to the chamber?"

"Not right away. He said that Miss Nancy's eyes were sensitive to the light, and she would like it better if I'd leave my chamber-stick outside before entering. I thought this peculiar but did not argue, I just did it, and then I was admitted."

"And what did you see in Miss Nancy's chamber?"

"Well, nothing at first, since it was quite dark, with only a few embers from the fire to light the room. But as my eyes got used to the light, I could make out the forms of Richard and Jenna, both kneeling by the bedstead, and the knotted covers revealed the shape of Miss Nancy, all curled up in a ball, sobbing as if she would expel her soul in a single breath."

"Did you see any signs of a birth?"

"I cannot say that I did or did not. I was not looking for a birth. She seemed to be having spasms, and whether they were contractions or just nausea, I do not know."

"What did you do?"

"I offered her the laudanum, but she paid no attention to me. Richard took it, poured rather a large dose, and gave it to her." Then a thought struck her. "And, Mr. Binghamton, I've just remembered, do you know how you asked me whether she had any other medicine?"

"Yes."

"Well, when Richard set the bottle of laudanum down on the night stand, he set it down next to another bottle that looked like some kind of medicine."

"Do you know what kind it was?" probed the prosecutor, hoping against hope for the kind of break that could make a case.

"I read the label, but it was not anything I'm familiar with. Gur, gun, gum something, perhaps." She smiled nervously.

"Could it have been gum guiacum?"

The lantern eyes flashed. "That's right, that's what it was."

Binghamton looked proudly towards the defense table. *Take that, Mr. High-and-Mighty,* he seemed to be saying to Patrick Henry. *You'll never get this sharp young woman to crawl around on the floor.* He had planned to ask a few more questions, but a good lawyer knows when to stop. "No further questions."

Because Marshall had been to Glenlyvar, it fell to him to cross-examine. He rose slowly as he contemplated where to begin, and how much to risk.

"Mrs. Harrison, at the time the events were occurring, did you suspect that Nancy had given birth to a child?" That was risky, but if she did, she would have to say why, and every basis she might have for such a suspicion would also be attributable to innocent causes. He watched her turning the question over in her mind, examining it for barbs and traps, weighing her recollections against her desires.

"I did not at that time."

A good start. Marshall moved on quickly before she could explain why she is now convinced of it. "Tell us, Mrs. Harrison, if you suspected that your sister was having a child by your husband, how would you feel?"

"This is disgusting!" cried the witness. "Aren't you going to object?" she demanded of Binghamton who, still reveling in the gum guiacum revelation, had not been listening.

"Objection?" Not very convincing. He had no idea why he was making it, but the Judge saved him from further embarrassment. "Sustained. Mr. Marshall, the Court will not tolerate such disagreeable tactics."

My tactics disagreeable? What about Henry over there? Marshall couldn't believe it. Henry gets away with ridiculing the witnesses for no reason, while he gets a scolding for asking a directly relevant, hypothetical question! Is it because he wears a frock coat while Henry wears that smelly frontiersman's buckskin?

"Mrs. Harrison, would you agree with me that a wife who finds that her husband and sister have engaged in criminal conversation would be justly enraged?"

"Yes, Sir."

"And that such a wife might justly be resentful and uncharitable towards that sister?"

"Yes."

"Yet when you burst in upon Judith Randolph on the night that her sister was supposedly having her husband's baby, you described her as," here he checked his notes, "I believe your words were, 'remarkably calm,' is that right?"

"Yes, Sir. But who knows what she knew about it."

"Probably a good deal more than you knew then or now, wouldn't you agree?"

Binghamton, still dreaming, did not object. Mrs. Harrison reprimanded herself for indulging in an off-hand remark. "Yes, Sir, I would suppose so."

"And yet Mrs. Randolph showed none of that justifiable rage that we both agreed a wife might be expected to show, correct?"

"No, Sir."

"And during the following four days, while they were at Glenlyvar, did you detect any resentment between the sisters?"

"No, Sir."

"Any nastiness?"

"No, Sir."

"Or resentment between husband and wife, Richard and Judith Randolph?"

"No, Sir."

"And all this would tend to indicate that Miss Nancy was not delivered of a child by Mr. Richard as charged by the prosecution, would it not?"

Mrs. Harrison pursed her full lips. "I suppose."

"And against this we are to weight what? Screams, a bolted door, and a bottle of strange medicine. Is that all?"

The witness thought a moment. "No, Sir. There was also the fact that Mr. Richard did not want me to bring in the candle, and the fact that Miss Nancy was having contractions."

"Which you yourself said may have been just nausea."

"Yes, well, I remember now, they were like regular pains."

"Cramps?"

"Yes."

"Are not women prone to cramps at certain times?"

"Objection, Your Honor, most indelicate."

"Your Honor, really," said Marshall, "I am not aware that the law recognizes indelicacy as a sound basis for the exclusion of evidence. If it does, then we shall have to move to strike the entire web of insinuations against our clients put forth by the prosecution, for it is most indelicate."

"The objection is overruled. Can you answer, Mrs. Harrison?"

Mrs. Harrison, bright red, merely nodded in the affirmative. Marshall, sensing that she would be happy to end the entire discussion of contractions versus cramps, gave her the opportunity. "And so, what-ever these pains were that you witnessed, they were entirely consistent with innocent female conditions?"

"Yes."

"Which leaves the screams, the bolted door, the strange medicine, and the request to keep out the candle, correct?"

The witness thought hard, but did not answer.

"If there is anything else, please do not hesitate to add it."

"No, that's right."

"But of course all these circumstances are entirely consistent with innocent illness, are they not?"

"Only the screams, I think, if it were a severe illness."

"You yourself administered laudanum to Miss Nancy earlier in the evening. Does it not tend to make one sensitive to the light?"

"I have heard that complaint, though I have never experienced it."

"But you concede that it apparently has that effect upon some?"

"Yes."

"And therefore that effect could explain the request to keep out the candle?"

"It's possible."

"So all that is left is the bolted door and the other medicine, cor-rect?"

"No, all these things that I testified to are true."

"Yes, but none of them points only towards guilt, the way the har-mony between Judith and the defendants points only towards inno-cence."

"Why bolt the door if you are innocent?"

"I was hoping that you could tell us."

"I can't."

"Are you sure?" pressed Marshall, and as his cool eyes extinguished her lanterns she remembered his visit and how she had caught him inspecting that very same door, and she knew that he knew.

"Oh," she said, as if it had just crossed her mind, "perhaps it is because that door is slightly warped, and the latch doesn't catch very well."

"Aha!" said Marshall, "the door is warped, so it must be bolted to keep it closed at all?" He was willing to pretend that this was a surprise to him.

"Yes."

"So it is true, is it not, that everything you saw or heard can be explained without guilt."

"Except the gum guiacum."

Marshall's sensors went up. "Didn't you know that it is commonly used for colic?"

"But it is also used for abortions, Mr. Marshall."

Marshall uncharacteristically dropped his notes and scrambled up to the witness box. "Excuse me," he said, "perhaps I misunderstood. What did you say?"

"I said, gum guiacum is also used to produce abortions."

Marshall stepped back so he could project his astonishment to the jury. "That's what I thought you said, Mrs. Harrison. I have only one more question. How is it that a woman who was so unfamiliar with, and I quote, 'gur-, gun-, gum-something' on direct examination, could suddenly pronounce it perfectly and know its exact qualities?"

Everyone saw her mistake, and an awful silence fell upon the courtroom.

Mrs. Harrison froze in her seat. What could she say? Should she admit here, before the whole world, that which she hadn't even told her dear husband, that which she'd barely even admitted to herself since it happened over ten years ago? It's not fair, she really did see the gum guiacum in Nancy's room, and to her undying shame she knew just what it was. To cover that shame, she'd pretended to be unfamiliar with it. But an explanation now was out of the question; they'd say she's no different from Nancy, though what she did was done long before quickening.

"Well, I mean, we all know about it now." She laughed her nervous laugh again. "I really did see it, there, on the night stand."

"No further questions."

4.

A shaken Mrs. Harrison was supplanted on the witness stand by her confident domestic.

"You are Mrs. Wood, household servant to the Harrisons?" asked Binghamton.

"That's right, Sir."

"I have only one question for you, Mrs. Wood. When you changed the linen in Miss Nancy's chamber on October 2nd, did you notice anything unusual?"

"Yes, Sir, I did."

"What did you notice?"

"There was quite a large bloody area on the sheet, Sir."

"I have nothing further."

Marshall and Henry conferred hastily, while this new information impressed itself on the minds of the jury and onlookers. "Gentlemen, we are waiting," prodded the Judge.

Marshall rose. "Mrs. Wood, how do you know that the stain you saw was a blood stain?"

"It was reddish-brown, and it looked like a blood stain, Sir."

"But it could have been a stain from any other source, such as spilled medicine, correct?"

The witness thought about it. "It started half-way down the bed, Sir. It's not a likely place to spill your medicine. And it was so big." She shook her head. "It's possible, Sir, but I doubt it."

"It could have been caused by some sort of illness-related hemorrhage?"

"I suppose, but in this case I doubt it."

Don't ask why. "How long have you been a domestic, Mrs. Wood?"

"Twenty-one years, Sir."

"How many households have you served in that time?"

"Let's see now," and she did some figuring in her head. "That would be four, Sir, not counting one job that only lasted a few weeks."

"In that twenty-one years, Mrs. Wood, have you ever seen a stain you took for blood upon a sheet?"

"Oh, yes Sir, many times."

"It's fair to say that barely a member of these four households could escape conviction if a stained sheet were all it took?"

"Oh, but Sir, no, no, this was different."

Don't ask why; she'll kill you. "But it is true, is it not, that a blood-stained sheet is commonplace?"

"Yes."

"And is often perfectly innocent?"

"Not this one."

Don't ask why. "Such stains are often attributable to the female cycle, isn't that true?"

Flustered, but determined. "I expect so, Mr. Marshall, but not this one."

Don't ask why. "You already conceded that it was possible that this was not even blood, correct?"

"There is that small possibility," said Mrs. Wood with reluctance.

"So surely it is also possible that this stain, if it was blood, was attributable to innocent causes?"

"No."

Don't ask. "Why not?"

"Why not?" exclaimed the witness. "I'll tell you why not," and suddenly Marshall wished she wouldn't. "Because someone tried to wash it out, that's why not. It looked like she had made an unsuccessful effort to scrub out the blood in the washbasin, which I hardly think *a lady* would bother to do unless she's feeling guilty about it. I've never seen that before in twenty-one years of handling other people's dirty linen, I can tell you!"

"'Out damn'd spot, out I say!'" shouted an erudite old man from the gallery, and others took up the chant as Judge Allen attempted in vain to gavel them down. "'Here's the smell of blood still,'" thought Richard to himself, his thorough classical education compelling him to complete the quotation against his will. "'All the perfumes of Arabia will not sweeten your little hand,'" and as Richard covered his face in his hands, his nostrils were sickened by the sanguineous air as the deeds of yesterday mixed with the promise of blood on the morrow.

"The next man to speak shall be removed in irons!" shouted the Judge, and the hateful noise became a hateful silence. "Proceed, Mr. Marshall."

Proceed? Where could he go from here? "Mrs. Wood, there was a slave girl called Lou at Glenlyvar, was there not?"

She was expecting that question, but before she could answer Binghamton was on his feet. "Objection! Beyond the scope of the direct examination."

"Sustained."

Marshall fidgeted, unsure how to proceed. A good lawyer knows when to sit down. "No further questions." Marshall sat, five minutes too late.

5.

"The Commonwealth calls Grant Harrison."

The clouds had just broken. A ray of sun peeked through the west windows to anoint Mr. Harrison as he ascended the mount. His close-cropped hair betrayed the slightest flecks of grey, his jaw bit down on certitude, and his pin-point eyes were locked on salvation. He stood before the witness box straight as the barrel of a Kentucky rifle, until Mr. Critch held out the Bible, which he bent to kiss. After a fervent oath, he was seated.

Mr. Binghamton was determined to carry the day with this, his star witness. Leaving all notes aside, he took up a strategic position at the center of the courtroom to begin the examination.

"Are you Mr. Grant Harrison of Glenlyvar?"

"Yes, Sir, I am."

"Was it your home that the accuseds, Richard and Nancy Randolph, visited last October 1st?"

The witness nodded in the affirmative. "To my never-endin' woe, Sir."

"How did that visit start out, Mr. Harrison?"

"Like any other. I woke at dawn an' went out to the barn, and there was Lemon, she's my retriever, and Old Esau, he's my best hand, and we commenced upon our mornin' chores."

"If we could just skip that, and get straight to the arrival of the accuseds."

"All right. They come in about four-thirty claiming to be tired though they hadn't done a lick o' work all day. I handed them outa the carriage, and right away Miss Nancy was complaining of feelin' poorly, some sort of female thing, so I left that to the Missus to take care of."

"Did you observe any mark or sign of pregnancy?"

"She appeared to be mighty big around the middle. Wouldn't surprise me, the way she'd been carryin' on."

"Carrying on?"

"Yes, Sir. We'd visited at Bizarre in March and again in August, and Miss Nancy was all over Mr. Richard, and he weren't exactly pushing her away, neither."

"Would you say this affection could have been just the normal attentions between brother and sister-in-law?"

"At the time I had too high an opinion of them both, so I didn't suspect nothin'. Now, looking back, I realize it was there plain as day."

"What was there plain as day?"

Suddenly Harrison's voice took on a vehemence it had lacked a moment before. "It was plain all along that these two were fornicators, damned to Hell!"

"Objection!" cried Marshall, springing to his feet. "Your Honor, the witness must be instructed to stick to facts, and to leave such judgments to Our Lord."

"Them there's the facts," snapped Harrison before the Judge could get a word out.

"Overruled, Mr. Marshall. We'll let the jury decide for itself what to make of Mr. Harrison's descriptions. Continue, Mr. Binghamton."

"Thank-you, Your Honor. Mr. Harrison, directing your attention back to the night of October 1st, at about what o'clock did the company retire?"

"We stayed up kinda late that night, later than suits me, anyhow. 'Bout nine o'clock, 'ceptin', of course, for Miss Nancy, who'd retired jest before supper."

"Did anything unusual occur after you had retired?"

"Only the most terrible screamin' an' howlin' you ever heard in your life. Comin' from upstairs, it was. Only time I ever heard anything like it was out in the Ohio territory, when I seen a soldier take a scalp off a live Shawnee, and it didn't sound no different."

"When did this screaming begin?"

"I don't rightly know. Woke me up."

"What happened next?"

"The Missus goes up to see what's the matter, and after a while she comes back down, and when I ask her what in tarnation's goin' on she jest shakes her head and kneels down to pray. Well, then the Missus gets into bed, so's I figure everything's all right, an' I start to doze off again. That's when I heard it."

"Heard what?"

"Footsteps, heavy ones, like a man's tread, comin' down the stairs. We jest lay there and listen, real quiet like, and we hear the door creak, but not slam, like someone's bein' real careful, and then 'bout ten or so minutes later we hear the door open up again, and the same kind of tread going back up."

"Did you get up to investigate?"

"Nah. We jest figured it was Mr. Richard, sendin' for the doctor."

"Was the doctor sent for?"

"No, Sir."

"Did you hear or see anything further that night?"

"No, Mr. Binghamton, nothin' till I went in the next morning to lay a fire for Miss Nancy."

"What did you see at that time?"

"Not much. Miss Nancy was a-bed, and she had the covers pulled up tight, out of modesty, I figured. She was whiter than her pillowcase, and I noticed a disagreeable flavor to the air, but nothing more."

"Did you suspect anything untoward at that time?"

"Like I said, Sir, it was all there to see, but I had too high an opinion of them both to know what I was lookin' at."

"Did there come a time when all that changed?"

"There most certainly did."

"When was that?"

"The next Friday, four days after that night."

"What happened on that Friday?"

"My field hand come a-runnin' up to me, acting like he's seen a ghost or somethin'. 'Massa,' he says –"

"Objection, hearsay."

"Excuse us, Your Honor," said Binghamton, eager not to get drawn into a debate over legal niceties at this dramatic moment. "Just say what you did and saw, Mr. Harrison, not what your boy said."

"Well, I follered him around to the back of the house and down the path to the edge of the woods, where I keep a pile of cedar shingles. He wanted me to look in under the shingles, so I walked 'round behind, and bent down, and then I seen somethin' there that I wish I'd never seen."

"What did you see, Mr. Harrison?"

Harrison pointed to the floor in front of the jury as if the gruesome sight lay at their feet. "There, half covered by shingles, wrapped in a sheet, I seen a dead baby, a white boy, perfect in every way, 'ceptin' I couldn't see his poor little face, 'cause his head had been twisted round so far."

One women shrieked and collapsed as the crowd erupted in horror. "Murderers, murderers, murderers," began the chants, and no amount of gavel pounding and threatening by the Judge could silence them. Nancy buried her head in her arms, hands over her ears, in a fruitless attempt to shut out the rhythmical accusations. Richard just sat, rigid and erect, frozen like a marble statue. Finally, Judge Allen adjourned court and angrily stomped out, buckles flashing gold in the gaslit gloom.

– CHAPTER 18 –

SYPHAX CASTS A SHADOW

I.

"I'll just leave you here long enough to let your lynch mob disperse," the Sheriff said to Nancy, guiding her by the arm into the cell next to Richard's. She was in no hurry to mingle with those who had passed judgment even if they could be persuaded to refrain from immediate execution. In these cells it was cool and dark, and for company she had only herself, a few spiders, and Richard.

"Richard," whispered Nancy, loud enough that her voice might carry around the wall to the adjoining cell, but not so loud that it might be heard through the door to the Sheriff's office, which had been left ajar. "Richard, do you hear me?" she repeated.

"Nancy, oh Nancy," came his tremulous reply. "You poor dear, I'm so sorry, wasn't it horrible?"

"Yes, Richard. It is so humiliating. As if they're any better than us. Ha! Why I know enough about those hypocrites to scandalize the Devil, but do I gossip about it? Of course not!"

"It is your good nature," observed Richard.

"Thank-you, dear, but what difference does it make? We're doomed, it's obvious to everyone, and no matter how clever our lawyers are there is nothing they can do to save us. One, two, three witnesses, yes, it can be put off to 'innocent causes,' as Mr. Marshall likes to call it, but this barrage of family and friends? Oh, Richard, I'm afraid it bodes ill." Nancy pressed herself against the corner closest to Richard, seeking comfort, finding only stone and iron.

"Do you think so?" said Richard. "I thought, all in all, that things went fairly well today." But his words rang hollow.

"Richard, don't patronize me."

"I'm sorry, damn it, but it's that blasted Marshall's fault. He's just not good enough, not like Patrick Henry."

"Oh Richard, don't be like that. He's doing as well as a man can do. We haven't given him much to work with." She paused for a moment, barely daring to breathe. "I know you say you are not afraid to die, but all the same, wouldn't it be better to live? You could still save yourself."

"And what about you?" He reached through the bars towards the adjacent cell. He could feel the stone, and the pain of his arm pressing against the bars, but nothing more.

"Me?" came the abstract reply, as if Nancy were speaking of stranger. "I am no longer eager to live in this hateful world. Everyone I ever loved is lost to me, even Judith, so all that still matters is to protect our vows. I will face death, if that is what is required."

"Don't say so, Nancy." They were quiet for a minute, each lost in thought. Then Richard broke the silence. "Reach towards me, and perhaps we can touch."

Nancy pressed her arm through the bars, and crept with her fingernails along the stone to the limit of her reach, and then stretched further, fingertips wavering in the air near Richard's trembling fingertips, white and bloodless, aching not so much from exertion as from the need to touch and be touched. They could not quite reach. Tingly and useless, their arms collapsed.

"Will I ever touch you again?" Who said it, who merely thought it? Their tears were interrupted by whispering from beyond the cell window.

"Mistuh Richard?"

"Syphax?"

"Yessuh, it's me. I's wonderin' if you need anythin'?"

"How about a miracle, Syphax?" It was Nancy, pressed to her window for a glimpse of her friend.

"Why Miss Nancy, how'd you do, Miss?"

"I've been better, you old crow," laughed Nancy, heartened to see him at last as he moved his strong frame back into the view of both cells. "You know, I came calling on you just last Saturday, but you were out. It's not polite to jilt a lady," she teased.

Syphax glanced quickly at Richard, dropped his eyes, did his best shuffle, and said, "Shucks, Miss Nancy, I's on a job for Mistuh Richard."

"And you can stop idling around here and do another one," said Richard, a little too harshly. "Catch!" and without warning Richard tossed an object at Syphax, who caught it with a quick stab at his shoe-laces. "That's the key to the wine cellar. Bring me back enough port so I can forget about this whole sorry world for one blissful night."

"Yassuh!"

"And Syphax!" shouted Nancy at the retreating form.

He stopped and turned. "Yes Miss?"

"I forgive you."

Syphax smiled. "Yes Miss," he said. Imbued with fresh determination, he straightened up and strode fiercely towards his waiting mule.

Nancy returned to the front of her cell and listened for Richard, who was listening for her. Neither was quite willing to say the first word, their frightened hearts telling all though their tongues were silent as the stone wall between them. Footsteps approached, and with them the quarreling voices of their counsel.

"But it's my idea," said Marshall.

"And a brilliant one it is," agreed Henry. "But only I can bring it off."

"Sheriff," said Marshall, "see to it that this subpoena *duces tecum* is executed by tomorrow morning!"

"But, Sir –"

"It's your commission, Sheriff," barked Henry, "and don't think I couldn't block it!"

"Aww, yes Sir, Gov'ner, all right. Tomorrow mornin'. I'll send a deputy right now."

"Good," said Henry. "Now leave us be, so we may have a word alone with our clients before you move Miss Randolph."

"I don't know what there is to talk about," said Marshall. "A deal is a deal, and the deal was that he was my witness."

"He may be your witness, but it's their lives," was Henry's last rejoinder as they came through the doorway to the cell area, closing the heavy wooden door behind them. "Richard, Nancy, if I may be so bold – but you'd better not start calling an old grandfather like me 'Patrick' or I'll put you both over my knee and wallop your backsides – how are you? Feeling a bit better, I hope?"

Henry was like a shooting star in the gloom, and the fact that Marshall was its lugubrious tail did little to dampen the cheering effect.

"Yes, thank-you, Mr. Henry," replied Nancy, smiling, "you give us strength." Marshall's brow darkened even further, until Nancy added, "As do you, Mr. Marshall."

"Well, that's good," said Henry, patting Nancy's hands through the bars and then stepping back to where he could see them both, "because I know it wasn't easy for you in there today. But tomorrow," he looked them in the eye, one after the other, "tomorrow will be our day. We'll have Judith, who will be marvelous. And we'll take that righteous little crusader, Harrison, and hang him out to dry."

The defendants' hearts lifted to hear that. "But how?" they asked in unison.

"By exploiting a particular logical inconsistency in Mr. Harrison's story," said Marshall. "It is one that completely escaped the notice of my learned co-counsel until I pointed it out to him."

"Yes, it was Marshall's idea," conceded Henry magnanimously, "and it's a damn good one, but it will be tricky to pull it off, so that's where I am needed."

"But I was assured that I would be permitted to cross-examine Mr. Harrison," said Marshall.

"Well," said Nancy, "why don't you tell us the details, and then we can decide." So Marshall explained his insight, and even Richard was impressed.

"This is not for us to decide," said Nancy, when Marshall was finished. "We have already promised Mr. Marshall that he could cross examine Mr. Harrison, so it is his decision to do it or to relinquish it to Mr. Henry, as he thinks best." Marshall beamed, the big smile filling his little head making him look rather clownish. "But," continued Nancy, looking straight at Marshall with eyes soft as magnolia blossoms, "just as it is your peculiar gift to conceive of this strategy, it is Mr. Henry's gift to be able to exploit it to its fullest effect. Please consider this – and consider me, who has always stood by you – while you make your decision."

The big smile faded, but it was replaced by something more dignified, as Marshall suddenly saw his capabilities and limitations as one. "I'm sorry," he said, but there was no need to apologize. He turned to Henry. "Patrick, go ahead. You may examine Mr. Harrison tomorrow." He paused, then added with a faint grin, "Just don't bungle it!"

"I'll try not to, John," replied Henry in his humblest tone.

2.

By the time Syphax reached Bizarre it was dark, yet ahead of him he still had the return ride to Cumberland by the light of a waning moon half hidden by clouds. He passed the deserted gates with a shiver at the memory of his humiliation by Jack. On he pressed, down the curving path towards the deep gloom of the Great House, glowering at him through an occasional window. He turned off towards Mudtown, tied his mule, and treaded carefully back towards Bizarre's shadow, the new grass of the back field feeling soft and comfortable against his bare feet. There was a light wind, and Syphax melded into it, a seedling aloft. Not even the raccoons by the slops behind the cooking shed noticed the passage of this night-skinned man.

The wine cellar was reached by way of a hatch leading to a slippery old wooden stairway that descended between stone walls into a subterranean chamber. The hatch was closed, but when Syphax bent down and pulled he found it was unlocked. Gently, he lifted the weight of the hatch door, stepped down beneath it, and then closed it over him with a soft sound like an expensive casket. Though he saw and heard nothing, he sensed an alien presence. Silently, he felt his way down the stairs in complete darkness to a second door at the bottom. This door was also unlocked, and after slipping through it he stood perfectly still for a moment to allow his eyes to adjust to the dim light of a single distant candle.

Catlike, Syphax crept across the bottle-lined cavern. Jack, totally absorbed in rearranging the bottles of tawny port on the top shelf, was oblivious to the dark man's approach. Syphax studied the feminine curve of Jack's nape where his ponytail was pulled to the side, and he realized that he could snap that thin neck in an instant. But if it was to be done he'd have to act fast, before Jack turned to go and saw him. He felt the Ashanti blood coursing through his veins as he lifted his arms to strike. His hands, unfeeling as the hands of a marionette, dangled in the air as he pondered the sure swift punishment for attacking a white man. His festering humiliation burned hotter than any powder blast against his heart as he lowered his arms and backed silently away to hide.

Not like this, Mistuh Jack, not like this, he said to himself as he crouched behind a wine cask and watched Jack retreat with his liquid comfort. *It's coming, but not like this.*

As soon as he was sure that Jack was gone and he heard both doors close, Syphax rose from his hiding place and began to trace the rows of mysterious bottles with his fingertips, until he found the still-warm candle and rekindled it. By the flickering light, he admired the variety of labels covered in tantalizing script that whispered of unknown wisdom. He did not need to read to fetch the port, since Richard had long ago marked the different varieties with whimsical pictures so that his slaves could fetch them: roses for beaujolais, hearts for red burgundy, stars for white burgundy, the jolly roger for rum, a lightning bolt for whisky, a cherry for sherry, an anchor for port.

There, right where Jack had been standing, was an anchor. Syphax reached up and removed the bottle in front, and the next bottle, and then, as he reached for the third anchor in back, his fingers brushed an unexpected object, not a bottle at all, but something square and hard. He removed the third bottle, and then reached way back to bring down a plain black box from its place of concealment. It was locked with a small latch, nothing formidable. Syphax looked about for a tool, and his eyes settled upon a corkscrew kept dangling from a piece of twine for the convenient sampling of the stock. He inserted the tip of the corkscrew under the latch, and with only a few twists of his powerful hands, the lock gave and the box popped from his hands spilling upon the dirt floor a locket and several robin's-egg blue sheets of the family writing paper.

What treasures or trash were these? Like a novitiate stumbling upon holy relics, how could he know? He picked up the locket, opened it, and gazed upon a tiny likeness of Richard's mother, the young Frances Bland. This he returned to the box, for it was of no use to him. Then he gathered the papers and stared in reverence at the script, written in two different hands. It was curly and inscrutable, like the lettering on the wine labels. Tucking the papers into his shirt, he closed the box, returned it to its hiding place, grabbed three bottles of port, let himself out with Richard's key, and fled towards Mudtown.

"Dat you, Syphax?"

It was Jedidiah, the one man on earth not even death could sneak up on. "Yeah, Jedidiah, it's me. Thought you might share a drink wit' a ole pal, an' help him out some."

Syphax produced one of the bottles, and Jedidiah ran his appreciative fingers over it and sniffed the cork. "Smells like a good port ta me," he said. "What you hafta do to get dis, Syphax?"

"Nothin', it's all right, Richard give me the key, tells me to git him somethin' to drink. So's I did, but he doen need to drink it all hisself, I figure."

They laughed, had a few swigs, and passed the bottle to Junior, the only other person in the shack who was still awake. He declined on account of God, but without any preachiness. "So what you need mah hep fer?" asked Jedidiah, leaning back, lighting his pipe off a faggot from the stove. "You's up to yer snot in white man's business agin, ain'tcha?"

"I s'pose I just cain't leave it be till I get even with Jack-ass."

"Or git yerself kilt."

"Well, lissen," said Syphax, ignoring the caution. "I found me some papers dat need readin'. I figured if I just copy the letters in yer hand, you can tell what-all dey say."

"Worth a try," said Jedidiah, laughing, shaking his head at this rascal Syphax, his laugh turning into a bad, deep cough that was only relieved by Junior pounding just the right spot on his back, followed by another long draw at the port. Then Syphax pulled up close to the stove so that he could see the letters on the first sheet by the flickering firelight cast through the damper. Jedidiah held out his palm, crowded already with half-remembered hunts and ceremonies, lost embraces, lashes, chains, hoes, bales, weeds, pitchforks, pipefuls of bitter tobacco. Into this crowded, trembling page Syphax recorded the dancing letters faithfully, transforming that leathery old palm into a delicate eye.

At last, the translation was done. One document was a three-page letter from Frances Bland Randolph to her son, Jack. This he would put back. The other was a single page letter in Jack's own hand; one he had never found the courage to send.

"Dat dere's pretty hot stuff," laughed Jedidiah.

"But damn," muttered Syphax, "I thought it might be da note from Richard that Jack took offa me."

"I know'd it wouldn't be," said Junior, mysteriously.

"God tell you where it is?" ribbed Syphax, a little annoyed.

"No," replied Junior patiently, "Georgeanne did. He keeps it in his wallet, an' sleeps with it under his pillow."

"Well, ain't that sweet," said Syphax, setting aside the bottle. "The rest's for you, Jedidiah." Then the night-skinned man floated silently back towards the darkened hulk of the Great House.

The airless ell at the top of the stairs again. Jack slept a conscience-less sleep in the thin moonlight. His dreams were as empty as the bottle on his nightstand, boxes without color, surfaces without substance, things to be touched but not felt. He barely stirred when a shadow fell between the moon and his pillow.

CHAPTER 19

BAD DOG

I.

It had rained more during the night, but now the sun steamed the earth dry. The foggy brightness outside revealed no earthly forms, but transported the packed courtroom off the planet to a realm of its own, with its own laws, its own mysteries, its own morality. Inside, Grant Harrison sat straight in the stand, a living vision of clarity against the mist.

It was from the fog itself that Patrick Henry drew his strength, standing to the left of the jurors by the first large window, hands thrust into the pockets of his buckskin jacket, a great pagan wrapped in the hide of a beast, calling upon the powers of Beelzebub to slay the crusader. Henry's bright blue eyes drank the mist through the glass, watching it hiss and dissolve under the sun's torments, waiting for a sign of some sort, indifferent as to whether it came from above or below.

How he stares, thought Judge Tucker, shifting nervously in his seat. He squeezed Judith's hand, but she did not squeeze back. She was as near to mist herself as a living woman could be. "Are you all right, my dear?" he whispered.

"It's nothing," she sighed weakly. "Palpitations."

He patted her hand. "Don't fret, don't fret, my dear, just tell the truth, and there isn't a thing that they can do to you."

This advice did not calm Judith. "All rise," came the Clerk's call, but the woman of mist slipped the other way, Judge Tucker neatly catching her as she fell. Having left to a commotion, Judge Allen was in no mood to return to one.

"Your Honor," said his other Honor, "I am afraid that the lady has fainted."

"Then remove her at once, and let's get on with the trial."

"Yes, Your Honor," and with the help of another gentleman, the star witness for the defense was spirited out.

"Mr. Grant Harrison," said Judge Allen, "you're still under oath."

"As always, Your Honor. The Lord sees all."

That's your misfortune, thought Henry, scanning in the sun-speckled green with smoldering eyes.

"Proceed, Mr. Binghamton."

Binghamton stood. "We have nothing further of this witness, Your Honor."

The Judge glanced over to the defense table, noting, for the first time, the complete absence of any defense counsel. Spotting Henry by the windows, he enquired, "Why, Mr. Henry, so good of you to join us. And where's your friend, Marshall? Did you push him out the window?"

Henry turned slowly to face guffaws from the gallery. "No, Your Honor, quite to the contrary, we're getting on so well now that he has entrusted me with the start of this morning's examination."

"Then please, let's move along."

Henry's gaze turned nonchalantly towards the witness, who sat even straighter, bracing himself for the onslaught of wickedness. The onlookers held their breath in anticipation of the first vicious thrust and parry.

"Lovely weather we're having, isn't it?"

That was all, mundane and disorienting. Well, yes, it was getting rather sunny now, the last of the mist was lifting, but really, what has this to do with anything? He'll not make a fool of Grant Harrison so easily.

"I don't follow," was the disdainful retort.

Hesitating just a beat, Henry moved in from the window to press his meager point. "The weather, Mr. Harrison," and he pointed back towards the sun-streaked windows, "outside; it's rather nice now that the rain is over," and he added, as one might add to a simpleton, "wouldn't you agree?"

"So what?"

"So, is it, or is it not, a nice day?"

"What's the relevance, Mr. Henry?" asked the Judge.

"I want to see if the witness is capable of reporting on what he sees."

"I'll allow you just the briefest moment to tie this in, out of respect for your station, Sir."

"Is it a nice day, Mr. Harrison?" continued Henry, ignoring the Judge's threat.

"It's warm enough. We've had some rain, and now the sun will help the crops. Yep, pretty nice."

"Shirt weather, isn't it?" asked Henry, casually resting on the corner of the defense table.

"Yes."

Then he slipped it in just like it was still part of a chat about the weather. "Warmer today than that day last year when the Randolphs came to visit?"

"Yep, I'd hafta say so."

"That wasn't a very nice day, was it?"

"No, Sir, it was cold and gray. 'Course, I don't question what the Good Lord sends us."

"But that was coat weather, right?"

"Yep." It was just dawning on Harrison that the focus of the conversation had changed, but it was too late to do anything about it.

"Nancy was wearing a scarlet-colored coat, wasn't she?"

Harrison paused. Well, she was. No harm in admitting it. "Yes."

Henry pulled out the coat from the box under the table. "This is it, correct?"

He didn't want to look like a fool. He figured someone else had probably already identified it, so he'd better just say yes. What harm could it do? "Looks like it. What of it?"

"Nothing," said Henry, dropping the coat back into the box. "Marshall told me to ask you, so I asked you. Makes no sense to me, but then, I'm not as smart as my co-counsel," and he winked at the gallery as he wandered back towards the window to the left of the jury box, but deep inside he was beginning to believe that it might be true.

The jurors craned their necks to watch Henry, hands thrust back into his pockets, staring out the window again. Had he lost it? Was he too old? Coat weather, shirt weather, what's the difference? There was a dead infant in amongst the shingles, and Henry is rambling on about the weather!

"When were you last in the Ohio territory?" asked Henry, his back rudely turned.

"Maybe nine, ten years ago."

"You saw a scalp taken off a live Shawnee?"

"Yes."

"Are you a father?"

What? How this man flits from here to there. "Yes." The jurors' necks snapped as they tried to watch both the examiner and the examined as Henry suddenly accelerated the pace of questioning.

"Boy or girl?"

"Girl."

"Where was she born?"

"Glenlyvar."

"Who assisted in the birth?"

"Our housekeeper and a slave girl."

"I s'pose you were out attending to chores?"

"No, Sir. I set myself right outside her door, the whole time." By now all eyes were on the witness, and Henry was just a disembodied voice.

"Did you hear anything while you sat there?"

"Well, course I did. Ain't no one gives birth all quiet."

"When was your baby born?"

"August. August last year."

"About two months before Miss Randolph's visit?"

"Yep." So what?

At last Henry saw the sign he'd been straining to see, flashed from the green, and he spun away from the window. His quick movement after such detachment drew everyone's attention. "Now isn't that strange, Mr. Harrison?" Harrison sat still as a lizard on a rock. "Two months before you heard the sounds you heard last October 1st you sat outside the door of an actual childbirth, yet you have to reach way back to a scalping in the Ohio territory ten years ago to describe what you heard that October 1st. Must have sounded different, didn't it?"

The jurors' heads snapped back to find Mr. Harrison impaled on his seat. He thought a minute, then realized thinking only gave the question more force, so he gave the only answer he could. "No, Sir. Sounded about the same."

Henry picked up the first piece of paper he'd touched all trial, made a show of donning a pair of spectacles, and then leaned in towards the jury box as he said, "But that goes against your own testimony, Sir. Didn't you testify just yesterday, and I quote, 'Only time I ever heard anything like it was out in the Ohio territory, when I seen a soldier take a scalp off a live Shawnee,' end quote? Didn't you say that?"

Harrison shrunk down in his seat. "Well, not the only time."

"But yesterday you testified, under oath, that it was 'the only time,' isn't that right?"

They all heard me. They're sitting right there. I can't deny it. "If'n you say so; could be."

Henry's indignation blotted out the sunlight. "Then tell us, Mr. Harrison, were you lying to us then, or are you lying to us now?"

This age-old cannonball of a question ignited Harrison as Henry hoped it would. "You demon!" he cried as he arose. He turned to the jury. "Don't you see, he's twistin' words, he's usin' the power of Satan to cover the wickedness of Satan's minions." Judge Allen tried to gavel him down, but Harrison was in the thrall of a Higher Court. "We must destroy Satan in any guise. You think you're so clever, Patrick Henry, but you are tiny and wretched in the eyes of God –" Harrison stepped towards Henry, heavy with menace.

"The witness will return to the box!" ordered the Judge.

The witness did not return to the box, but stood there menacing Henry. The Sheriff moved in, fearing trouble.

"Objection!" chimed in Binghamton at last. "The question is argumentative."

"You set down, Codfish!" shouted Harrison. "He wants an answer to his connivin' little question, I'll give him one; then I'm headin' home. I come up here to tell the truth, not be insulted by some heathen."

"The objection is sustained," said the Judge, "you don't need to answer."

"I ain't walkin' out of here accused of lyin'. I never lied, do you think I would risk my immortal soul for scum?" And he spat towards the defendants.

The Judge whacked his gavel. "Sit down, Mr. Harrison, or I'll throw you in jail for contempt of court!"

"No, Sir, I ain't done answerin' his filthy question." He took another step towards Henry, and planted himself so they could smell one another's teeth rot. "You snake oil lawyer," he snapped, "you bet I heard that sound before, it was childbirth sure as I'm standin' here, but not the same as my sweet baby girl 'cause this here was the cursed labor of unholy fornication, a bastard's birth, and a bastard's murder!" As the words reverberated through the hushed chamber, Harrison pushed towards the gate, bumping Henry hard on the way past.

"Sheriff!" ordered the Judge, "restrain this witness, he is not excused!" Both the Sheriff and a deputy closed in, blocking off Harrison's avenue of escape. But it was Henry's words that stopped him.

"What have you to fear, Mr. Harrison?" boomed Henry in his most heretical style. "If you run, we'll all believe the worst of you, that you have profaned against the oath you took on God's Holy Bible." The accusation locked onto Harrison, twisting him back towards his tormentor like a trout on a hook.

The moment was ripe for Marshall's gambit. The zealot was prepared for the ancient ritual of trial by ordeal.

"I'll make you a deal that will save you from going to jail and losing your new crop," Henry mildly suggested. "I won't drag you through each scrap of testimony, if you'll be willing to meet me out on the green for a little test of your truthfulness –" Henry genuflected towards the Judge – "with the Court's permission, of course."

Seeing that this might be a quick way to diffuse the sticky problem of a non-compliant witness, the Judge said, "The Court is willing to permit it, if Mr. Henry thinks it would expedite matters. Mr. Binghamton?"

All Binghamton wanted was a chance to keep his star witness out of jail. "No objection, Your Honor."

Henry stared down Harrison, challenging him and coaxing him at the same time. "How about it, Mr. Harrison? We can settle this whole thing right now. Do you believe in your own sworn testimony enough to put it to the test?"

Whether he did or not, he could not say no. "Of course."

Presiding from a chair on the very porch where Richard had made his impassioned speech not one month earlier, Judge Allen was ruler of a very unruly kingdom. Beyond the fidgety witness and puffed up jurors was a gaggle of the noble Lords and Ladies of Democracy, powdered and perfumed against the stink of the first generation of sovereign pig farmers in history, who crowded in behind. Beyond them all lay the commons, which by now was more hospitable to the pigs than their masters, acres of filthy wagons and carts, woodpiles, rags, peddlers' stands, cooking vessels, and temporary privies, all strewn about and glistening darkly in the new sunshine like trolls driven from under a rock. From this unlikely neighborhood a familiar figure emerged, and the crowd parted to allow a somewhat soiled Mr. Marshall through to join his colleague at the defense table.

Judge Allen whacked the wall of the courthouse with his gavel, and a splinter of hickory ricocheted into the crowd. "Court's in session!" he barked, ignoring the damage he'd done. "Proceed Mr. Henry. And Mr. Harrison, you're still under oath."

Henry rose, backed as far from the witness as possible without falling off the porch in order to ensure that he and the witness would have to speak loudly, and began. "You say you found a dead baby in your shingle pile?"

"Yes." Harrison had no intention of uttering one word more than was absolutely necessary.

"Four days after October 1st?"

"That's right."

"You don't know how it got there?"

"I got a pretty good idea."

Henry cut him off sharply. "But you don't *know*."

"No, I don't know," mocked Harrison. "But I 'spect Mr. Richard put it there the night of October 1st."

"Well this is a very significant development," Henry taunted back. "We now have a witness who claims to have seen what the law calls a *corpus delicti*. Of course, you didn't keep such a serious and shocking discovery to yourself, now did you?"

Harrison began to say something, then thought the better of it.

Henry bore in, moving closer to the witness. "What's that, Mr. Harrison? You were about to tell us something more about this astonishing find?"

"Well, I didn't want to upset the womenfolk," was all Harrison could choke out.

"Of course not. So what did you do? Bury it yourself?"

"No." Harrison was fighting back. "I sent for the Sheriff."

"Now isn't that interesting," said Henry. "Tell us, then, why is it that there isn't any evidence that the Sheriff, the prosecutor, any responsible official or, for that matter," Henry added sarcastically, "even any irresponsible official, ever saw this devastating piece of evidence?"

"You can sneer if you like, Lord knows it's your nature, but this here's the gospel truth. When the Sheriff came next day, there was nothin' left but a smear of blood on the shingle where the baby had been. It was gone!"

"You mean you left that poor thing out there, Mr. Harrison?"

"I didn't want to disturb the evidence."

"That poor little babe, you just left it there?"

"Objection," croaked Codfish.

"Sustained," ruled the Judge. "He's stated his reasons. Move on, Mr. Henry."

Henry turned to play the crowd. "So, Mr. Harrison," he mused, "that poor babe vanished into thin air, did it now? Lying in the shingles undisturbed for four days after the dastardly deed, but gone the next day?"

"Yes, Sir."

"Do you have a dog?"

What now? "Yes."

"What's her name?"

"Lemon."

"What kind of dog?"

What's he after? Better play it careful. "Bird dog."

"Got a good nose on her?"

"Not bad."

"Not bad? She gets everything, doesn't she?"

"I dunno 'bout that. She's all right."

"Didn't you tell Mr. Marshall here that she gets everything, and then prove it by shooting down a bird that she retrieved?"

What in tarnation is he after? "I don't rightly remember. Mebbe. What of it?"

"What of it?" exclaimed Henry, spinning around to confront the witness again. "Well, did you take your dog and look for it?"

"Look for what?"

"The corpse, of course! The vanishing corpse!"

Oh, so that's what he's after. Harrison relaxed. "No point in it. She'd a dug it out if it was around."

"So she's that good a retriever?"

Suddenly Harrison had a funny feeling in the pit of his stomach. "She's all right, but she's gettin' old."

"But you just said that if a corpse had been around, Lemon would have dug it out."

"I ain't so sure."

Henry leaned in close, but he spoke in that golden voice that carried out across the field of intent faces to the farthest corner of the green. "Fact is, Mr. Harrison, that you know she would, which means that no corpse could possibly have sat in that shingle pile for four days like you say it did."

Harrison fought back desperately. "No way. She's gettin' old."

Henry played his trump card. "Shall we put her to the test?" He gave a signal to the deputy, who knocked on the courthouse door. It opened, and out ran the freshly subpoenaed Lemon, straight to her master's side, where she sat, wiggling and wagging delightedly. Harrison sat rock still.

"Your Honor," said Henry, turning to the Judge, "Mrs. Biddlesworth's prize sow gave birth to a dead piglet, which she kindly permitted Mr. Marshall to bury this morning, over across the green." He turned back to Harrison. "Tell her to fetch."

Harrison was trapped. He looked deep into Lemon's wise brown eyes, knowing that she would do anything a dog could do for him, but that no dog knows how to lie. She cocked her head, eager for the command, sensing some new emotion in her master, determined to redouble her efforts to sate this mysterious longing. "Fetch," said

Harrison in a strained voice, a wounded voice, a voice that more than ever needed the loyal service only Lemon could bring to Master.

She left the porch like a shot, and the crowd jostled and scrambled to get out of her way. Go baby go, thought Nancy, rising up to watch the amazing show, knowing that her life was riding on nostrils that could smell the difference between April 30 and May 1. Nose to the ground, Lemon circled the first few wagons, weaving in and out of sight in search of the quarry. She came upon the remains of someone's breakfast, and tarried among the pans.

My God, thought Marshall, I failed to account for the sloppiness of the campsites; she'll never find her way through such filth.

Blessedly, Lemon moved on quickly, long familiar with the distinction between man's cookery and his uncooked quarry. Some children playing on a knoll began calling to her, and threw a stick, whether at her or for her was not clear, but she dodged both peril and temptation to do her master's bidding.

The green was huge and rife with smells, enough to bewilder even the blunt noses stuck on humans as an afterthought, let alone the delicate, finely-honed canine organ. The minutes passed as she scuttled among the wagons and woodpiles, mud occasionally blocking her airways, so that she would have to stop and sneeze before she could continue on her desperate mission.

All is lost thought Richard, and the crowd was getting bored, beginning to wisecrack, "Henry's folly," "He's gone to the dogs," "His star witness is a bitch," when suddenly Lemon began digging furiously near a distant woodpile, and the crowd quieted so that it could hear her growl and yip as she tore at the last impediments between her and her quarry. Now Lemon had it, gently cradled between her muddy jaws, and she held it high for all to see as she proudly returned through the crowd, and laid the dead piglet at her master's feet.

"Bad dog," hissed Harrison, so that Lemon, tail between her legs, shrank down in confusion and wounded supplication, and licked at his bootlaces.

3.

Back inside, Binghamton moved quickly to shore up Harrison's credibility. "The Commonwealth calls Sheriff Dunby to the stand."

The chinless sheriff bit off his oath with a cocky smile, secure in the knowledge that there wasn't a man in the jury box with whom he'd not caroused the liquid hours from dusk to dawn.

"State your name, please."

"Donald Dunby."

"And your position?"

"Jeez, Codfish, you know me as well as the resta these folks. I'm sheriff for the same county you prosecute for."

Binghamton's pate flushed as the crowd got a laugh at his expense. A small price to pay. "Sheriff, were you called to Glenlyvar by Mr. Harrison last year?"

"Yep. October 5th, jest like he says."

"What was the purpose of the trip?"

"Investigation of possible crime. Message I got was –"

"Objection!" Marshall was on his feet. "Hearsay."

"This goes to the *res gestae* of the investigation, Your Honor."

"We'll take it."

"Go ahead, Sheriff."

"Message I got was that Mr. Harrison had found a dead baby out there."

"Did you look for yourself?"

"Yes, Sir. October 6."

"Did you find any signs of a dead infant?"

"Well, I didn't find no body. But in the shingle pile, right where he said it'd been, I saw blood stains on the shingles."

"No further questions."

Marshall rose. "You saw dark blotches on the shingles?"

"Blood stains."

"Stains, but you really have no way of knowing whether they were caused by blood?"

"I seen a lot of blood. This was blood."

"If it was blood, Sheriff, you certainly don't know where it came from, correct?"

"Well, he told me –"

"Not what he told you, Sheriff," corrected Marshall, sharply. "We've heard his testimony. I'm asking you what you know, based on what you saw. Now, based on that, you don't know where those stains came from, do you?"

The Sheriff shrugged. "No, I s'pose not."

"In fact, if it was blood, you don't even know whether it was raccoon blood, porcupine blood, gopher blood, or some other kind of blood, isn't that right?"

The Sheriff thought about it for a minute. "Nope."

"No further questions."

Binghamton stood. He had nothing left. "The prosecution rests."

It was the same courtroom, but not the same courtroom. It was the same Judge, the same jury, the same spectators, yet they were not the same at all. They no longer stared with condemnation in their eyes. They no longer merely pretended to listen. Their eyes had been pried open, their attention commandeered despite themselves, so that now they were actually wondering, were we wrong about these two all along? The defense had not yet won, but it had taken the first, most important step: it had shattered the complacency, sown doubt. Now the jury was ripe for harvesting, provided the defense could do what every law book in the country agreed that it had no duty to do: *prove the defendants innocent.*

CHAPTER 20

TAILORED ELOQUENCE

I.

"The defense may proceed."

Marshall stood. "The defense calls Mrs. Richard Randolph to the stand."

Judith was back in the courtroom, although still perilously misty. After an uncomfortable pause, she floated to the witness stand. Had there been a slight headwind, she might not have made it. She had been crying, and her face was puffy and dazed. Mr. Critch proffered the Bible, and she laid her hand gingerly upon its cover, jerked it back, and then laid it down again, this time more easily.

"DoyousolemnlyswearbeforeGodAlmightythattheevidenceyouare-abouttogiverelativetothecausenowunderconsiderationshallbethe-truththewholetruthandnothingbutthetruth?"

Mr. Critch's boredom rescued Judith. It was difficult to tremble when the sword of divine retribution was wielded by so phlegmatic a messenger. "I do," she replied, straight into Critch's indifferent eyes.

"Tell the Court and jury who you are, please," began Marshall, all business.

There was another long pause, and many spectators rearranged themselves in embarrassment, suddenly cognizant that they were will-ing participants in a ritual of public humiliation. "I am Mrs. Richard Randolph of Bizarre Estate," she said at last, in a manner that recalled the time when it was an honorable thing to be. "It is my husband and my sister upon whom you sit in judgment," she added with a trace of bitterness.

Marshall noted her fragility, and sensed the need to get what he needed quickly. "Mrs. Randolph, I know this has been a most difficult time for you, so I will be brief. What were the circumstances of Miss Nancy coming to live with you and your husband?"

"Our father married a young woman, and then asked Nancy to leave. Nancy was barely sixteen. She needed a place to live, so we took her in."

"During the entire time Miss Nancy lived under your roof, did you ever notice any improper familiarities between her and your husband?"

Judith swallowed once. "No," she whispered.

"You'll have to speak up, Mrs. Randolph," ordered Judge Allen.

She cleared her throat. "No," she repeated, barely louder.

"I direct your attention to the night of October 1, 1792. On that night, what were the sleeping arrangements?"

"Mr. Randolph and I slept in one chamber upstairs at Glenlyvar, and Miss Nancy slept in another." Then she added in a catty tone, "Glenlyvar isn't much, it really isn't. Politely, one might call it a cottage. To get into Nancy's chamber upstairs, you had to go through the chamber occupied by Mr. Randolph and myself."

"And therefore," added the meticulous Marshall, "anyone or anything trying to get out of Nancy's chamber had to go past you?"

"Yes."

"What about the windows?"

"They were covered over with hides nailed fast."

"Why is it that Mr. Randolph attended upon Miss Nancy, instead of you doing it yourself?"

"He did it at my request, since I was also somewhat indisposed." Then, firmly, she made her point. "He did it out of consideration for me." Here, for the first time, she really focused on the gentlemen of the jury, determined to persuade them that it was she whom Richard loved.

"Were you awake throughout the time that your husband nursed your sister?"

"Yes, Sir."

"Could anything have been brought out of your sister's chamber that night without you seeing it?"

She felt chilled, her tongue thick. "No."

"Did your husband or anyone else carry a baby out of your sister's chamber that night of October 1st, 1792?"

She was watching herself down there, clutching the witness chair, stretched taut between her oath and her vows, and she noted how like Lemon she was, willing and even eager to fetch and hold the disgusting thing between her lips. She took a moment of comfort in Richard's smooth face, till her eyes slipped past it to its blood parody, Jack.

"Excuse me, Mrs. Randolph," said Marshall, gently chiding her with raised eyebrows. "Did you understand the question?"

"Oh yes, I beg your pardon. Was there a baby?" She took a breath. "There was no baby."

"You are quite certain?"

She nodded affirmatively, tight-lipped.

"You must speak, for the record," prodded Marshall.

"I am certain."

"No further questions."

Marshall sat anxiously, feeling his future prospects balanced on Judith's precarious composure. The tension was palpable. The Judge nodded to Binghamton.

The prosecutor began to move before he began to speak, slowly circling the outer perimeter of the field of battle, sniffing the air, flexing, preening, probing for weaknesses and finding nothing but. Better to go slowly nonetheless, he thought, for this examination could well decide the verdict.

"Mrs. Randolph," so soft, silken, comforting, "I am sensible of the fact that you have suffered much already, and I shall endeavor to discharge my duties with honor and respect for a greatly wronged lady. If there are any questions that you do not understand, please be sure to ask for clarification before answering, and I shall be pleased to rephrase them. Otherwise, I shall assume from the fact that you have responded that you understand the question. Is this agreeable?"

"Not to me, it isn't!" said Marshall, rising. "Either Mrs. Randolph or the jury may decide that she didn't understand a question any time they choose, same as for each other witness who has come before." He turned on the prosecutor. "Now quit pretending to be her friend, Mr. Binghamton, and get on with the examination."

"Mr. Marshall," said the Judge, "if you have an objection, it must be directed to me. I will decide whether counsel needs to be cautioned."

"Then I object to his making speeches, when he ought to be asking questions."

"Generally correct, Sir, but a modicum of civility towards the witness does not strike me as an abuse. Overruled. Proceed, Mr. Binghamton."

"Attaboy," cheered Henry in Marshall's ear. "You're learning." Marshall winced out of habit, but secretly he was pleased.

"Now, Mrs. Randolph," continued Binghamton, "you are at the advantage over the other witnesses we have had here in that, due to your close family connection, you have been permitted to sit in and hear what the other witnesses have said, correct?"

"It is correct that I have heard what they have said. Whether this is to my advantage or not, I cannot say."

Good show, thought Marshall. *She may yet prove to be our star.*

"But the point is, Mrs. Randolph, that you must have heard both Mr. and Mrs. Carter Page, as well as Mrs. Brett Randolph, Mr. Peyton Harrison, and Mr. Grant Harrison, all attest to the improper familiarities that they observed between your husband and your sister?"

Judith's brown eyes reflected an inward pain, but she fought to keep it from spreading. "I heard their testimony, Mr. Binghamton."

"So you did hear the part about the improper familiarities?"

"That may have been their perception, yes."

"Was it your perception, also, as the wife in the household, that, in words already attributed to you, 'Richard and Nancy were only company for each other?'"

She made her voice hard. "No."

"But you did say that? 'Lately, Richard and Nancy are only company for each other?'"

"No." This time not hard; brittle, rather.

"You are saying that your own Aunt Peggy lied under oath in attributing that to you?"

Oh dear, will she get in trouble if I say so? I suppose I may have said something like that. "No. I mean," *what do I mean?* "I may have said something like that in a moment of frustration. But I didn't mean anything by it."

"Of course not, as a loyal wife you try not to comment on your husband's misdeeds, correct?"

"Yes. I mean, no. I mean, I wouldn't call them misdeeds."

"But in fact his attentions towards Nancy had become so clearly manifest, that even you could no longer hold your tongue, isn't that right?"

"No."

Stepping closer, Binghamton began circling, jabbing with questions at an ever-accelerating pace.

"But you just admitted that, though you tried not to comment on Richard's improper conduct, in this case you finally had to."

"There was nothing improper in it."

"There was nothing improper in it, or you wished that there was nothing improper in it?"

"Familiarities, yes. We are a close family. But improper familiarities, well, I just didn't observe any."

Binghamton would take it either way. "Despite the fact that five other witnesses, watching the same couple, observed the contrary?"

"Despite that."

"Then perhaps you have chosen to overlook this delicate matter, Mrs. Randolph, to protect your own sensibilities?"

"I think I have been as observant as anyone; perhaps, in light of my station, more so."

"Well, then, let me ask you this. Miss Jefferson suspected pregnancy. Mrs. Brett Randolph, Mr. Page, and Mr. Harrison, all detected an increase in your sister's girth consistent with pregnancy. And Aunt Peggy saw Miss Nancy's pregnant belly, unobscured by garments. Would you, Nancy's own sister, agree with these observations?"

"No."

"You did not observe any signs of pregnancy?"

"No."

"And yet you claim to be as observant as anyone?"

"Argumentative," objected Marshall.

"I'll withdraw it," said Binghamton. "What about the gum guiacum? Is it true that Miss Jefferson told you last September that it was a good remedy for colic, but warned you of its tendency to induce labor or abortion?"

"Yes."

"And is it also true, as she said, that your sister was in the room at that time?"

Judith thought back. "I'm not sure."

"You didn't notice?"

"No –" then seeing the trap – "I mean, I must have noticed then, but I don't recall."

"You have memory problems?"

"No, Sir. I'm not a fool, Mr. Binghamton, and I'd appreciate it if you wouldn't treat me like one."

Binghamton quickly retreated and executed a short bow. "My humblest apologies if I was misunderstood. I would never intimate anything of the sort." The trick, of course, was to carve her up so deftly that the wounds are bloodless. A bloodied wife on the stand attracts sympathy, and he certainly didn't want sympathy interfering with the kill. "Did you or your husband administer gum guiacum to your sister Nancy on the night of October 1st, 1792?"

"No."

"Really? Well, then, can you tell us the nature of your sister's malady that night?"

"Colic. Extreme, but she had been given to such attacks before. Colic, and her monthly female troubles."

"And when you and Mrs. Harrison looked in on Nancy, you administered laudanum, correct?"

"Yes."

"But the laudanum made her no better, correct?"

"Apparently not."

Binghamton stroked his chin. "Then I fail to understand why it is that you did not administer gum guiacum, knowing it to be a good remedy for colic."

"Because of the danger –" she bit her tongue.

"Go ahead, Mrs. Randolph, you were saying?"

"Because of the danger of mixing medicines."

"Ah," Binghamton looked knowingly towards the jurors, "*that* danger. Had you given your sister any gum guiacum at any time since learning of it from Miss Jefferson?"

"No."

"In fact, you had refused to make your supply available to her, knowing that she was pregnant, isn't that correct?"

"No."

"That is why she had to go to the inconvenience of obtaining some from Miss Jefferson?"

"I have no knowledge of that."

"Then why would she send away for it when you had a supply at Bizarre already?"

Marshall was on his feet. "Objection. There has been no evidence of any other gum guiacum at Bizarre."

"That is correct, Mr. Binghamton," said the Judge.

"Excuse me, Your Honor." Binghamton turned back to the witness. "It is true, is it not, that you acquired a bottle of gum guiacum immediately after speaking with Miss Jefferson about it?"

What should she say now? If she lies, she must create an entire world in which to fit the lie, but she is not God, she lacks the omniscience needed for such a boundless task. But if she tells the truth ... "No."

One eyebrow shot up, and it seemed that in the absence of a hairline it might go right over the top and down the other side. Binghamton hurried to his table, and grabbed a large book, to which he referred as he formulated the next question. "I put it to you, Mrs. Randolph, do you deny that on or about the nineteenth of September, 1792, you purchased from Dr. Robert Jensen of Farmville a decoction of gum guiacum?"

Judith trembled, tried not to tremble, and the effort to control her body wiped her mind clean. She should back off the lie, but how? Her tongue was fat and sluggish as a possum, making an eloquent retreat virtually impossible. She struggled to think, as hundreds of eyes recorded even the pulse at her neck. He's bluffing, if I back off I'll look a fool for certain, against the chance of escape if he's bluffing. I have to stand firm.

"I do not recall buying any gum guiacum."

Binghamton brought the book to the witness stand with the pomp of a crown-bearer, and set it before the witness. "What is this, Mrs. Randolph?"

Judith looked at the large book. Her heart fluttered. "I – I've never seen it before."

"What does it say it is?"

Marshall started to rise, but Henry pulled him down. "Let him finish it up," he whispered. "He's doubtless got Dr. Jensen in the back room, so there's no point."

Judith read the cover inscription. "'Dr. Jensen's Apothecary – Business Ledger – 1792.'"

"Please open to the marked page."

The pages felt like slate as she pushed them back.

"What is the heading for that page?"

"September 19."

"Do you see the marked entry?"

"Yes."

"What does it say?"

"'Mrs. Richard Randolph. 3 ounces Burdock; one container arnica ointment; one bottle decoction gum guiacum. 48¢, paid in full.'"

Binghamton took away the ledger book and slowly brought it back to his table, as the impact of the impeachment took hold. He turned to face her from across the room. "Now, Mrs. Randolph, isn't it true that you acquired gum guiacum on September 19th of last year?"

Judith withdrew into herself. "Yes," she whispered. "I'm sorry, I must have forgotten."

"Yet your sister had to send to Monticello for some, because you wouldn't let her use yours, isn't that right?"

"No." Quiet and sullen.

Binghamton ignored the denial. "And the reason you wouldn't let her use yours is that you suspected her to be pregnant, isn't that right?"

Silence.

Binghamton moved in, dominating her with his presence. "Isn't that right, Mrs. Randolph?"

Judith looked at him quizzically. "Whatever are you thinking, Mr. Binghamton?" The intense quiet in her voice was riveting. "Do you believe I would withhold the chance to abort from my own sister if I thought she was pregnant with my husband's child? Is that the theory of your case? That I would withhold even an elixir of hemlock from her under such circumstances is preposterous. If she obtained her own gum guiacum, as you say, it is happenstance only. She never asked if I had any, and I never thought to offer it."

There were murmurs throughout the courtroom. Binghamton cursed himself for allowing her to wriggle free, and vowed not to let it happen again. "But there was a baby born that night, wasn't there, Mrs. Randolph?"

"I saw no baby."

"Oh, that's right. Unlike five other witnesses, you saw no improper familiarities, correct?"

"That is correct."

"And unlike five other witnesses, you saw no signs of pregnancy?"

"That is so."

"And now you say you saw no baby?"

Silence.

Binghamton didn't care. He'd gotten his point across. "Mrs. Randolph, it is your testimony, is it not, that your husband went to your sister's aid that night out of consideration for you. How do you know that it was out of consideration for you, and not out of consideration for your sister, that he did so?"

"Because he doesn't love her. He loves me."

"Are you quite sure of that?"

"Yes, Mr. Binghamton. If he and I are the only ones who are sure of it, that is enough."

"Because you love him very much, isn't that so?"

Judith tried a quick reply, but was overcome with a welling of emotion. "Yes," she managed to say, "I do ..." She produced a little hanky embroidered with butterflies, and dabbed at her eyes.

"You would do anything for him?"

"Yes, of course."

Binghamton pressed himself close to the witness box, his breath stinking of onions. "Including perjuring yourself to save him from the gallows?"

Judith froze. What does he know? She looked past Richard to Jack's thin smile. Oh, she felt so sick. Her stomach, her head. *No!* she has to answer. Everything was spinning, there was Nancy looking frightened, why not? And Poppa, do you even care, just so long as it doesn't reach you, *No!* that's what she has to answer, the same word she'd screamed while fighting off Poppa's clumsy hands, but no one had heard then, why should they hear now? *No!* would protect Nancy once again, like she protected her from Poppa, say *No!*, say it quickly, the quicker the better, it may already be too late, *No!* and then look what Nancy did, she threw it all away, say *No!* now, before they all begin to laugh at you, they'll say she's plain and dumb, not like her sister, but she's not dumb, *No!* is the smart answer, she's just angry like she's got every right to be –

"Yes! Mr. Binghamton, yes, a thousand times, yes!" she cried. Binghamton turned to gloat at the jury, but his move was premature. Emboldened by his retreat, Judith added defiantly, "But I'm not lying now. There was no baby."

Binghamton swung his head like a cobra ready to spit. "Just as you bought no gum guiacum, Mrs. Randolph?"

It was too much. She had failed. She had said the words, the right words, over and over, just as she always had as a little girl, but again no one heard her, no one believed her. It was her fault, she began to sob and could not stop, but again Binghamton pressed forward, determined either to have the truth, or to have her soul. "If there was no baby, Mrs. Randolph, what was it that you saw your husband bring out of Miss Nancy's chamber that night?"

Judith saw it again through the tears, but not as she'd seen it then, for now it stared at her through anthracite eyes that burned her own. *Go away, you're not there, you're nothing, nothing at all,* and when she shook her head to clear the vision it really was nothing, nothing at all. "I see now," she whispered, and Richard tensed, "nothing, nothing at all," and she sat, shaking her head, repeating, "nothing, nothing at all," for a full minute, until everyone was quite sure that she was no longer answering questions of this world.

"There is no point in questioning this witness further," said Binghamton.

"You may step down, now, Mrs. Randolph," coaxed the Judge, but Judith did not move. Marshall had to lead her from the stand, and as he passed her to Judge Tucker's arm, she was still in a world of her own, muttering "nothing, nothing at all."

Marshall set in motion his last, desperate gambit. "Your Honor, the defense has no more witnesses, but it has a demonstration to be presented for the jury."

"What sort of demonstration?"

"I would like Miss Nancy Randolph to put on the scarlet coat that Mr. Grant Harrison and Mrs. Brett Randolph have identified as the one that she was wearing on the carriage ride to Glenlyvar, this past October 1st."

"Mr. Binghamton, have you any objection?"

Binghamton smiled his most disingenuous smile. "Of course not, Your Honor. If the defendant wishes to testify in this manner, we will be delighted to cross-examine her."

"Your Honor," interjected Marshall hastily, "this is hardly testimony. The testimony tying this coat to the events of this case has already come from the lips of the prosecution's own witnesses. All I ask is that Miss Nancy be permitted to put on the coat in question in the presence of the jury. She will do so in silence, and therefore her privilege to remain silent ought not to be deemed compromised."

Binghamton was determined not to let this point slip away. "She might not speak words, Your Honor, but by donning this coat she will have communicated to the jury."

Henry leaped up. "On the prosecution's theory, no defendant has a right to avoid the stand if he appears clothed in court!" Laughter competed with sanctimonious cluckings, but Henry pressed on. "Indeed, were the defendant to appear unclothed, that would apparently be such a statement as would rob her equally of the protection of our Virginia Bill of Rights, for which so many brave patriots laid down their lives."

Judge Allen wagged a bony finger at Henry. "Mr. Henry, you are out of order! I'll only hear from one counsel for the defense at a time."

"Your honor, they said I was out of order to take up arms to defend our Commonwealth, but I would do it again. Either the Bill of Rights means something, or it was not worth fighting for. The defendant has the right to confront the witnesses against her, so she can hardly be held to a waiver of her other rights based solely on the clothes she chooses to wear while in court confronting them."

"Mr. Henry," said the Judge, "I'm warning you."

Henry sat.

"Your Honor," said Marshall, "I hereby adopt each and every word spoken by my learned colleague."

"But Your Honor," said Binghamton, "what Miss Randolph chooses to wear is of little consequence unless and until it is made an exhibit that has been identified by the witnesses. Then it is quite a different matter."

"I am inclined to agree with that, Mr. Binghamton."

Marshall moved quickly to avoid an adverse ruling. "But then of course," he mused out loud, as if it were already a part of the judge's order, "the cross-examination and the extent of the waiver of the right to remain silent, can extend no further than the coat itself, which is the only subject to be covered by the demonstration."

"But Your Honor, we do not question the authenticity of the coat!" blurted out Binghamton. "It is to the heart of this matter that we would direct our inquiry."

Marshall pounced on Binghamton's error. "If Mr. Binghamton does not question the authenticity of the coat, then he has stipulated that no cross-examination is required."

"The Court will rule that Mr. Binghamton has the right to cross-examine as to the authenticity of the coat, but no further. Proceed, Mr. Marshall."

"Excellent," whispered Henry to Marshall. "One more such victory, and he is vanquished."

But Nancy would not budge. Marshall bent to urge her up.

"This means he'll question me?" she whispered.

"Only about the coat," reassured Marshall, "nothing significant."

"I won't do it."

Marshall hadn't shaken that mule-stubbornness in ten days, how was he to do it now in ten seconds? "If you back out now, under the jury's gaze, they'll hang you in a minute."

"I don't care."

Marshall could think of nothing. He looked up, and his eyes met Richard's. Richard leaned over to Nancy. "Our vows are better served by taking the chance, and doing as Mr. Marshall says," he whispered.

Nancy rose.

Marshall took the scarlet coat from its box, and led his client into the center of the courtroom. His clumsiness was a perfect foil for her grace, as he positioned her towards the jury and held up the coat. It was a beautiful coat, stylish with its dyed fox trim and broad flair just below the waist to accommodate the panniers. Nancy slipped it on and began the tedious process of buttoning the two dozen black velvet buttons that ran from the neckline to just below the tummy. With each button, her figure stood out more clearly, a swan's neck, breasts ripe but not pendulous, and then the alluring flatness of her young belly offset by the flair below. Parisian perfection, each stitch enlivened by its kinship with the lithe flesh beneath. Not a breath wasted. Not a crimp, not a gather, not a bulge.

And certainly no place to hide a baby.

"Your Honor," said Marshall, after allowing the irrefutability of this evidence to impress itself upon the courtroom, "we have no questions."

"Mr. Binghamton?"

What could Binghamton say, confined as he was by Marshall's rules? Is that the coat you wore that night? He knew that it was, and to ask again would only make matters worse. "No questions," he said.

"The defense rests," announced Marshall triumphantly.

Chapter 21

A Warrior's Revenge

I.

"Let us drink," proclaimed Richard, raising his pewter goblet to his fellow jail-cell diners, "to the finest lawyers in Virginia!" Nancy, Judge Tucker and Colonel Randolph all raised their wineglasses. Jack, sitting apart in the corner, poked at a plate of cold pig's tongue pudding while holding his own sharp tongue.

"No, no," said Henry, tipping his own glass towards Marshall, "to *the* finest lawyer in Virginia."

Even the Colonel inclined his head in respect. Marshall glowed, visions of wealth and honors obscuring his usual caution. He raised his milk on high. "Thank-you, Patrick. I can only say that I've learned from the best." They drank, and the warm curds sobered Marshall quickly. "But let's not get ahead of ourselves. We've battled them to a draw is about all I can say. Now, at law, that ought to mean acquittal, but as my friend Patrick is fond of observing, what follows logically is not necessarily what follows in life."

"Quite right," said Jack through a mouthful of tongue, "there's always the unexpected element."

The others exchanged nervous glances. "Yes," ventured Judge Tucker, seeking to sound out Jack as nonchalantly as possible. "Although the prosecution probably won't have any rebuttal witnesses, it is to the unexpected flourish in a closing argument, or the human element in the jury's decision-making process, that Master Jack refers."

Jack chewed thoughtfully, but said nothing.

"Come on, Jack," said Richard, "join us in a drink. To acquittal!"

Marshall raised his milk again, and met the wine goblets held aloft. He feigned enthusiasm for the fatty secretion in his mug, but the gnawing at his stomach was not quelled. Jack had not joined the toast.

Henry stepped in to ease the awkwardness. "Did I ever tell you, Richard and Jack, that I had the honor of knowing your father, John of Matoax?"

Jack showed genuine interest for a moment. "Did you really? What was he like?"

"It's good you should ask, Jack," replied Henry, "because I see something of him in you. In fact, he was about your age when I knew him, as he used to come by the Hanover Tavern where I tended bar. Now, that's not to say he was a drinker; he could hold his own but never went over the line. What I remember best about him is that he could size a man up in a minute just as if he could see right through into his head, the way you do, Jack." Jack nodded, momentarily placated by flattery. "And the thing he always said to me was 'Patrick,' he says, 'family's the secret of life. Damn the rest of 'em, but stand by your family.'"

Jack saw through the ruse. "Lotta good it did him, dead of the fever at thirty-three," he muttered bitterly. "But you're right, Governor – like my father, I can see right through into your head right now. And what I see is fear."

"Not fear, young man," replied Henry. "Call it compassion for a fellow loner."

"You are family, Jack," added Judge Tucker. "True, it can't keep you from dying like your dear father when the Lord says your time is up, but it can keep you from dying alone."

Jack shot them both a vicious glance. "I don't need your pity." He looked around the rickety table in the jail cell. "I don't need anybody's pity. I'd pity you, is what I'd do."

"Oh, Jack," said Nancy soothingly, "no one pities you, we love you, that's all. Perhaps you mistake it for pity. You'll see, when we are acquitted, we'll all be back together again, just the way it was before," but as she said it she realized that it might not be Jack's heart's desire, so she added, "only better."

"'Just like it was before, only better?'" Jack mocked in falsetto as he leapt to his feet, upsetting his bowl so that chunks of tongue wagged about his boots. "Exactly which part will be better? The silences when I enter the room? The sneer behind my back? The orgies from which I am excluded? The false smiles? The hands pulled back in revulsion?

The kisses that land short of my cheeks? Oh, what a fool I've been. I gave you your chance, Richard, but you were too soft to take it. Why should I stand by and watch silently as my torment is revived by perjury? Sheriff!" he cried. "Come let me out! I need to see old Codfish."

"Wait!" cried Richard, holding Jack back by the sleeve. "Please, Jack! You're angry at Nancy, but how can you do this to me, your own brother? What of Judith, and St. George? What of the memory of Theodorick?"

Jack faced Richard. "And what of the memory of our sweet mother, who charged you on her deathbed to watch over Theodorick and me? You spit on that when you chose this hussy over that solemn promise. Our mother must surely be looking down from heaven in horror. SHERIFF!" he shouted, ripping his sleeve free of Richard's grasp.

"It was you who chose Nancy, not me," said Richard. "Now be a man, and let her go."

Jack turned to face them all down, full of teeth and bluff like a cornered badger. "There was never anything between Nancy and me," he spat in a feral voice, "and there never will be." He looked at her with self-loathing. "She's a tramp, a whore, she parades around the house half-naked, who would believe a word she says?"

He was down before anyone could stop Richard, indeed, before Richard himself could control the blow. The Sheriff ran to the cell and began fumbling with the keys. "I'll see you all in Hell," cried Jack, bleeding at the mouth, as he dragged himself out the door.

The room echoed with stunned silence. "Excuse me, Gentlemen," said the Colonel, who hated to be associated with failure. "Looks like up is down, after all." And he waddled out past the Sheriff.

As soon as the Sheriff was gone, Marshall turned to his clients. "The deceptions have gone on long enough," he said firmly. "It may already be too late, but we need to know what to expect. What will Jack say?"

Richard and Nancy stared hard at one another. At last Nancy, seeing that Richard would not speak, began. "Jack knows –"

"Nothing," said Richard. Nancy fell silent.

"Well," said Henry, "whatever it is, we'll find out in a few minutes. You let me handle the cross-examination, John. If ever a fellow deserved me, Jack Randolph's the one."

"Very well," muttered Marshall glumly, his bright future fading before it even began.

2.

Henry spent the rest of the lunch recess learning what he could of Jack's overtures towards Nancy, while Marshall sought out Jack. The lawyers met in the courtroom just before the hour appointed to reconvene.

"Any sign of him?" asked Henry.

Marshall nodded grimly. "Nothing."

"Well, then, there's nothing left to do." Henry smiled and began chatting with onlookers as their clients and the jury were brought in, and Marshall marveled to see him looking as untroubled as a dying priest. Knowing that an effort to coax a smile out of his own dour lips would only attract suspicion, Marshall feigned interest in his notes.

The buzz of conversation ceased abruptly as Judith entered, clutching tightly to Mrs. Henry St. George Tucker's arm. Together they shuffled to their seats, Judith's eyes downcast and distant, Mrs. Tucker plainly leading the way. All the probing stares revealed nothing definitive, just a loyal wife in impossibly humiliating circumstances, possibly mad, possibly just exhausted.

Nancy felt Critch's gavel as a blow to the gut, and watched as the Judge with Binghamton and Jack appeared simultaneously from the door to chambers. The Judge's buckles flashed cruelly for an instant, before disappearing into the bench, followed by Jack's polished riding boots as he crossed in front of the bench and ascended to the witness box.

"Proceed with your rebuttal case, Mr. Binghamton," said the Judge, clearly apprised of what was coming.

"The Commonwealth calls John Randolph, Junior to the stand."

Jack placed his left hand on the Bible, his longest fingertip covering the middle b. He raised his right arm in such a fluid, undulating fashion that for a moment it seemed not an arm at all, but a serpent poised to strike. Like a serpent, Jack swallowed the oath whole.

"State your name, please."

Jack licked at his swollen lip. "John Randolph, Jr.," he said.

"What is your relationship to the accuseds, Mr. Randolph?"

"I am Richard's brother. I have the misfortune of being a distant cousin to Miss Nancy Randolph."

"Now, Mr. Randolph, is it accurate that you and I have had no discussions whatsoever touching upon this matter, until you sought me out at my luncheon table, not fifteen minutes ago?"

"Yes, Sir."

"And that when you did so, you addressed a serious allegation to me?"

"Yes, Sir."

"What is that allegation?"

"That my brother's wife, at the behest of my brother, did commit perjury when she denied that she saw a baby being carried through her chambers."

The shock of hearing spoken from the stand what so many had already privately concluded sent a murmur through the courtroom, followed by a silence so viscous that it seemed to suffocate the defendants.

"And how is it that you know that Mrs. Randolph perjured herself?"

"Two ways. First, she told me –"

Marshall could not wait for Henry's dulled reflexes to respond, if ever they would. "Objection! Hearsay! It cannot pass as an admission, for Mrs. Randolph is not on trial here."

"But Your Honor," faltered Binghamton, "it will become admissible if we press charges, so the court should take it now when the harm can be mitigated."

"A poor argument, Mr. Binghamton," noted the Judge with annoyance. "However, we'll take the evidence for impeachment purposes."

Damn, he's smarter than Codfish, thought Marshall.

"You were saying, Mr. Randolph?"

"I was saying that Judith told me that she saw a baby that night, but that she would hold her tongue because it was mixed breed."

"That's a lie!" screamed Judith, rising up like a revenant from the grave.

"Silence!" shouted Judge Allen, but she looked right through him.

"It was Jack Randolph who wanted me to claim it was a mulatto, a vile and false calumny!" continued Judith.

"One more word and you will be arrested!"

As Mrs. Tucker pulled Judith down, Richard rose to take her place. "That's right," he said. "Jack urged me to tell the same lie, but I refused."

"Sheriff, chain and gag that defendant!" ordered the Judge. The Sheriff and a Deputy sprang to work, and no amount of remonstrance by Henry could achieve anything greater than to narrowly avoid Henry's own arrest for contempt.

"There will be order in this court," warned Judge Allen, when Richard was firmly secured. "The next person to speak out of turn shall be arrested for contempt of court. Proceed, Mr. Binghamton."

"Thank-you, Your Honor. Now, Mr. Randolph, you said there were two reasons that you know Mrs. Randolph was not truthful with this court. What is the second?"

"The second is a note from my brother to his wife in which he urges her to save him by saying that she saw no baby."

"Do you know where that note is now?"

"Yes, Sir."

"Where is it?"

"I have it right here," announced Jack with satisfaction, producing his wallet. "I have kept it safely in a special compartment of my wallet since receiving it, always on my person, or tucked under my pillow at night." Jack fished around for a moment in his wallet, and produced the folded sheet of the family's robin's-egg blue writing paper, which he carefully unfolded and began to hand to the prosecutor. At the last instant, however, his eyes widened and he snatched it back with such urgency and alarm that it could have been his own death warrant. Hurriedly, he rifled through his wallet, spilling banknotes and a lovely silhouette of Nancy that floated off the stand and alighted at the foot of the jury box like a swan on a quiet pond.

"I'm, I'm s-sorry," stammered Jack, "m-most clumsy of me, but, but I appear to have, um, misplaced it. You know, I checked it again just this morning, b-but I didn't unfold it, and, well, it seems to have been switched."

"Switched?" repeated Binghamton blankly.

"Yes, damn it, switched!" cried Jack, fear in his eyes. "You have my word, however, under oath," and he looked up furtively, "that's enough." All the while he was trying to stuff the blue sheet he'd snatched away back into his wallet with trembling hands.

Henry rose. "Your Honor, this man has made a most serious accusation, and then slinked away from his proof like a bird dog from a polecat. I demand to see the paper he has produced, this so-called evidence against my clients."

"Never!" cried Jack, and he began to shove it into his mouth.

"Seize it!" ordered the Judge, and the Sheriff and Deputy were all over Jack in a second, jamming their fingers into the hinge of his jawbone, crying out as their fingers got bit. After a brief struggle, Dunby emerged with the document, somewhat torn and bloody, but largely intact. He gave it to the Judge, who pieced it together and then studied it intently. The Judge passed it to Binghamton, who cringed so while reading it that his entire bald pate wrinkled. Binghamton reluctantly passed it to Henry, who read it with the jaundiced eye of one who'd been expecting every word, as Marshall craned over his shoulder like a pirate's parrot.

"Your Honor," said Henry, "I move that this document be published to the jury."

"Any objection, Mr. Binghamton?"

Binghamton shrugged, a beaten man. "Hearsay?"

"Overruled. Go ahead, Mr. Henry."

Henry cleared his throat, and his clear voice trumpeted words meant only to be whispered, words so sensitive that the writer never even brought himself to send them:

> My Beloved Nancy,
>
> Can it be only two days since that hot night beneath the west portico when I pressed my breast upon yours and hoped you would press back, but hoped in vain? To me it feels an eternity. I have spent the time reliving the seconds, but perfecting them for the better. That you prefer another to me you have made plain, but the why of it remains obscure. I cannot imagine that you are one of

those simpletons impressed with virility to the exclusion of all else. Why women should measure men by that quality in which donkeys are unquestionably superior eludes me. If, however, as I believe, you are truly like me, you should see that together there is no plantation we could not own, no reputation we could not eclipse, no power we could not wield. There is so much petty fear and propriety in this world that we few who are truly fearless can do as we please with the rest. Unite with me, please, because I love you, you are all that I need, I thought I needed nothing but I was wrong. And although you do not realize it, you need my relentless strength to enable you to attain the heights you deserve. My passion for you is cold and unwavering, not hot and transient like that of the common boys with whom you trifle. Come to me now, and you will never regret it.

Your servant and master,
Jack

During the reading of this extraordinary document, the author edged off the stand. Now, suddenly, he bolted out the door to chambers and down the back way before the Sheriff could catch him.

Syphax watched as Jack burst from the courthouse into the unrelenting light of day. Sighting the wretch down the imaginary barrel of his index finger, he pulled the trigger, then laughed an Ashanti warrior's fierce laugh.

Chapter 22

Closing Astonishment

I.

Marshall began to rise, but Judge Allen cut him off before he could open his mouth to speak. "All the usual motions are deemed made, denied, and exceptions reserved. Mr. Binghamton, the Court will hear your final argument at this time."

Binghamton rose ceremoniously, pulled his waistcoat down over his belly, and cleared his throat. "Thank-you, Your Honor."

He turned to confront his audience. "Learned Brethren; Gentlemen of the jury. Throughout the course of this proceeding, there have been times when passions have run high, when eloquence or trickery have confounded simple facts, and when ridicule has replaced analysis. However, where matters of life and death are involved, it is well that we confine ourselves to that most reliable of human faculties, the faculty of reason. Let us strip away the showmanship, and look simply at the evidence."

Now Binghamton was warming to his task. He began moving about the room, emphasizing points with a sweep of the arm. "When this is done, you will see that four facts are established beyond any reasonable doubt: first, that there were improper familiarities between the defendants; second, that Miss Nancy Randolph was pregnant last year; third, that Miss Randolph took gum guiacum and gave birth while at Glenlyvar on October 1st of last year; and fourth, that she and Mr. Richard Randolph did their best to conceal this birth by various means, including murdering the poor, defenseless infant, and hiding the body in a pile of shingles."

Nice and clean, thought Henry; I just hope Marshall can do as well.

"The improper familiarities are attested to by no fewer than five witnesses: Mr. Carter Page, who noticed kissing and embracing; Mr. Peyton Harrison; Mrs. Brett Randolph; Mrs. Carter Page, who noted that when the defendants were together, 'sparks flew'; and Mr. Grant

Harrison, who noted that in March and August of last year Miss Nancy was, and I quote, 'all over Richard, and that he certainly wasn't pushing her away.' Against this, we have only the loyal wife's refusal to characterize the familiarities as improper, but even she could not deny that there were, in fact, familiarities, and that the defendants were, in her own words, 'only company for each other.' Is it any surprise, then, that in January of 1792, Mr. Richard was seen entering Miss Nancy's room at night? And how many other times did he slip in, unobserved?" At this, several of the jurors turned to scrutinize Richard, as if the answer were carved in his forehead.

"The most imprudent of the familiarities are, of course, the ones well hidden," continued Binghamton, "the ones for which our only direct evidence is the effect they produced. I refer, of course, to pregnancy. Once again, no fewer than five witnesses attest to signs of pregnancy. Mrs. Martha Jefferson Randolph suspected pregnancy. Mr. Carter Page noted an alteration in the size of Miss Nancy's midsection, as did Mr. Grant Harrison. Mrs. Brett Randolph reported not only an increase in size consistent with pregnancy before October 1st, but a concomitant decrease in size only two weeks later, which would be consistent with childbirth on the first." Binghamton rushed towards the jury like a fast-moving thunderstorm. "But most damning of all and, I might add, the point at which the defense stooped to the most base parlor tricks and failed to produce any logical refutation, Miss Nancy's own Aunt Peggy saw her niece's obviously pregnant belly with her own eyes, naked and unobscured. No wonder Miss Nancy would cast her eyes from her belly to Heaven with an anxious sigh." Pointing to the ceiling, Binghamton bellowed in righteous indignation: *"God above was not deceived; nor should you be!"*

The prosecutor dropped his voice momentarily, all the better to bellow again. "That there was a birth at Glenlyvar and that these contemptible co-conspirators snapped a poor innocent babe's neck in an effort to conceal it, requires little argument to establish." Marshall stifled his astonishment that the most speculative points would require the least explanation. "Perhaps most damning is the fact that the defendants chose not to take the witness stand to deny it. Would an innocent person, charged with so foul a deed, let the accusation pass unanswered?"

Binghamton paused to allow the devastating effect of this question to linger, before continuing. "Viewing the testimony of those who did come forward, we may conclude that Miss Nancy did not expect the labor so soon and, perhaps, having successfully concealed it from her sister to that point, she could not ask to turn the carriage back based on what she might then have passed off as travel sickness. Having arrived at Glenlyvar, and finding that her condition had not improved, her only hope was to pretend that it was colic, and to abort quickly with the gum guiacum." Now Binghamton's words rushed forth as if urgency could supplant doubt. "When her supply of gum guiacum proved to be too small a dose to kill the fetus, her wicked confederate, Mr. Richard Randolph, snapped its neck, as is evidenced by the position in which the corpse was found by Mr. Harrison. Richard then smuggled the murdered babe past his wife, who claims to have seen nothing, but whose powers of observation in this delicate matter have been proven by the testimony of no fewer than five disinterested witnesses to be woefully inadequate. Richard went down the stairs to hide the incriminating burden in the shingle pile, returning a few minutes later. The murderer's footsteps on the stairs were noted by his hosts, and reported to you from the witness stand. But this was merely one part of the plot to conceal this crime. These conspirators in lust –" pointing straight at Nancy and Richard whose faces should respond in anger, sorrow, terror, or some human emotion, but were instead held impassive on strictest orders of counsel, thereby inadvertently communicating monstrosity – "bolted the door, sought to keep out the light, and tried to wash out the stain of their foul deed, all conduct which bespeaks a consciousness of guilt, as does Miss Randolph's unwillingness to permit her trusted Aunt Peggy to examine her."

Binghamton paused a moment to permit all this to sink in, before launching into his grand climax. "It is true that we do not know what became of the poor murdered child that Mr. Harrison saw in the shingle pile. Mr. Richard may himself have stolen back to remove the corpse to some unknown place at which, to this day, it languishes in unconsecrated earth." Binghamton's voice peaked in a devastating crescendo. "It is for God to have mercy on such adulterous fornicators, such cruel murderers, not for us poor mortals. We can only look upon the evidence with horror and cry out *'Guilty, guilty as charged!'*"

2.

Binghamton removed his handkerchief, mopped his sweating dome, and sat heavily. "Counsel for the defense may close," said the Judge matter-of-factly, but the room was still in the thrall of Binghamton's fervor, and Marshall's mousy little head perched on his bric-a-brac skeleton seemed a paltry counterforce against the emotions that had been awakened.

Marshall pushed his notes aside. "If it please the Court, my learned colleague Mr. Binghamton, and the esteemed Gentlemen of the jury," he began in his thin voice, but his black eyes met the jurors, one by one, over and over, never wavering. "Mr. Binghamton speaks of that most reliable of human faculties, the faculty of reason, and urges you to reach your decision in this matter by the exercise of reason. In this, I heartily concur." Henry winced. "I am mystified, however, in what way imprecations to the Deity, and the use of nasty epithets such as 'vile conspirators,' 'adulterous fornicators,' and 'cruel murderers,' further the reasoned solution of this case. It is your job to determine whether or not the Commonwealth has proven beyond any reasonable doubt that this gentleman and this lady who sit before you, who indeed have been known to you all your lives, are guilty of the crimes charged. The Commonwealth cannot prove its case by shouting epithets while pointing at the defendants, any more than you or I could change fallow land into fertile by calling it such. Were I to attempt to do so, you would reach down, feel the soil between your fingers, and judge it for yourself. You can do no less with the evidence upon which the lives of these two Virginians depends."

There is a certain compelling clarity to it Henry had to admit to himself. Marshall's manner was as if he had met an old friend on the street and was simply chewing over the daily gossip, yet he had gained everyone's attention. He was easy to listen to. As he spoke, he seemed to give voice to one's own thoughts.

"But before I ask you to scoop up some of the evidence in your own hand, I need to pause to discuss a very distressing point relied on by my brother at the bar, one which cannot help but interfere with the reasoned analysis of this matter that he has asked us to make. That point is the exercise by my clients of their rights under section 8 of the

Virginia Bill of Rights, to refuse to give evidence in a case against themselves. That the Commonwealth would seek a conviction because this lady and gentleman chose to exercise rights that you and I fought to preserve is almost inconceivable, and should alone be reason enough to scorn Mr. Binghamton's argument. Is it a crime to exercise a natural and legal right; a right which is recognized by the Constitution of the Commonwealth of Virginia, the constitutions of each of the other states of this proud Union, and by the newly-enacted Bill of Rights to the United States Constitution, which the wise people of Virginia – led by my esteemed colleague, Mr. Henry, I might add – demanded as a condition of Union? We should tremble ere we see the day it becomes so; I have faith that you will not permit it to be today."

Marshall paused to take a drink of water. He had not yet raised his voice, he had not yet even moved from behind the defense table, but he had made his mark. It was he to whom their trust now shifted, not that unpatriotic prosecutor.

"Turning to the evidence, Mr. Binghamton claims that it establishes four basic propositions, which he charitably calls 'facts', but which I suggest to you are merely suppositions that he has been unable to prove. Supposition number one is that the defendants engaged in various improper familiarities, and, I think, the emphasis here must be on the word 'improper', because I would think that anyone must concede that these two were well within their rights to engage in the usual sort of familiarities that might pass between brother- and sister-in-law, especially when the sister lived in the brother's household; indeed, we might think them peculiar not to.

"Common experience teaches that there is no gentleman in whose household a young lady lives who does not, from time to time, pay her attentions and fondnesses, which a person prone to suspicion might consider as denoting guilt. Thus, it is important that you weigh the actual evidence of what was witnessed – scattered kisses and hugs, all in plain sight – against the motivations of the witnesses to reinterpret what they saw in light of the current atmosphere of suspicion. For example, it is most significant that several of the witnesses who reported improper familiarities, conceded that what actually went on was not different in kind from what they themselves have engaged in; and it is also significant that Mr. Grant Harrison, despite his current impatience to condemn the defendants, conceded that at the time he witnessed the familiarities he did not think them improper. If these familiarities passed muster under the eye of such a devout and scrupulous judge at the time they occurred, how can we now condemn them? The actual evidence, in short, does not support the conclusion being claimed for it.

"If this is true even without considering the circumstances of the defendants at the time, it is even more apparent when one considers those circumstances. Miss Nancy, a creature raised to every indulgence, and with nothing but the finest prospects in life, was cast from her childhood home because of the arrival of the new step-mother, and was taken under the protective wing of her elder brother-in-law, Richard. They suffered a common loss together of Richard's brother Theodorick, to whom they were both quite attached. With the exception of the highly qualified testimony of Mr. Cedric Randolph, whose memory was murkier than his attire, all witnesses date the attentions of Richard towards Nancy to the period of mourning following Theodorick's loss. The comforting of a mutual loss between family members is not improper, and those who would ascribe other than spiritual motivations to it are simply speculating. We have a known cause, which is Theodorick's death; there is no need to concoct another cause, such as an illicit affair, for which there is no independent evidence. The natural human fondness for scandal might be thus satisfied, but Mr. Binghamton has enjoined us to use the faculty of reason, not passion, in solving this puzzle. Reason does not support it.

"If this is not enough to convince your reason that the first of the prosecution's suppositions is merely speculation, then I ask you, what is the first inclination of a guilty love? Is it to parade its affections before Aunt Peggy, Uncle Carter, devout Mr. Harrison, and every other Tom, Dick and Harry who should happen by? Or to parade it in front of one's own wife or sister? Or is it more the inclination of guilty love to conceal itself from view, fearing the just condemnation of a Christian society? If you think the latter, as surely one must, then these alleged familiarities were not guilty, and the prosecutor is wrong as an uphill stream. Recall, if you will, that I asked Mrs. Brett Randolph whether the familiarities she witnessed continued even after the rumors of an illicit affair began to circulate, and she said that they did. What criminal is so brazen as to continue the crime in the open after it has been detected? Reason cannot comprehend this; if it is reason we are to apply, we can only say that the relations between Mr. Richard and Miss Nancy must have been proper."

Marshall took another sip of water, and then startled everyone by stepping out in front of the jury box. It's wonderful, thought Henry, he's so parsimonious with physical display that, eventually, three steps seem like fireworks.

"I have dwelt so long on the first of the prosecution's suppositions because it is the only one that can claim even a shred of credibility. I do not, of course, ask you to accept my labels any more than you should accept the prosecutor's, so let's test the soil in which is rooted his claim that Miss Nancy was pregnant.

"The coat you have seen. It was identified both by Mrs. Brett Randolph and Mr. Grant Harrison as the one Miss Nancy wore on that fateful October 1st. You have seen for yourself that such a coat does not permit a pregnancy. It is closely and expertly tailored to a point below the waist, and it could not have been buttoned by a pregnant woman. But how shall we square this with Aunt Peggy's testimony? I cannot; nor will you be able to. You must decide: will you accept the evidence as told to you by Aunt Peggy, or the evidence of your own eyes?

"There is a special reason to accept the evidence of your own eyes over Aunt Peggy's testimony, aside from the obvious reason that seeing is believing. Mrs. Brett Randolph, who saw Miss Nancy on October 1st, testified that the bulge she saw was consistent with bloating or ordinary weight gain. Similarly, Mrs. Grant Harrison, who saw Miss Nancy on that same day, testified that she couldn't tell if Nancy was pregnant. Yet if you will recall, I had my recalcitrant colleague, Mr. Henry, ask Mr. Carter Page when he first noticed an increase in Nancy's size, and Mr. Page responded that it was in May, which is the same month that his wife first noticed the increase." Suddenly, Marshall stepped right up to the jury box, and leaned in. "Now I ask you, Gentlemen, if Miss Nancy began to show a pregnancy in May, how is it possible that she had not grown sufficiently by October to enable Mrs. Brett Randolph to distinguish it from fat, or Mrs. Harrison to even see it at all? I put it to you that it is not possible, and that, once again, reason will not permit you to draw the conclusions that the prosecutor would have you draw."

Marshall turned briskly and marched back to his spot in the center of the room. Binghamton mopped his dome, helpless before the onslaught. But Marshall had not yet raised his voice.

"The prosecutor called it two but then he mixed it all as one final supposition that he would have you call fact: that my clients, Mr. Richard Randolph and Miss Nancy Randolph, the lady and gentleman seated before you at counsel's table, snapped the neck of a poor innocent babe, and took various steps to conceal the deed, including hiding the body among the shingles. A terrible deed if true, but, we must not forget, an equally terrible injustice against these two if not true. What evidence can we hold in our hand, and test for the truth of this question?

"First, the prosecutor says that there is evidence that Cedric Randolph saw Mr. Richard enter Miss Nancy's chamber. That is false. The only evidence is that Cedric Randolph, himself a disappointed suitor to Miss Nancy, had the temerity to make such an accusation to the prosecutor while not under oath, but refused, as properly he should, to repeat it before God and under penalty of perjury, in open court. Whatever Mr. Cedric was malicious or foolish enough to say in private, he was at least man enough to retract in public, and that the prosecutor would ask you to find an illicit rendezvous based on this fellow's attempt to retract the claim that one ever occurred, is contrary to the reason he invokes, and the justice that we seek.

"From this point forward, the prosecutor's case gets weaker still. He asks us to conclude, through the exercise of reason, the following points which defy all reason:

"First, that Miss Nancy, desirous of causing an abortion in herself, would wait until pregnancy was near full term, as it would have been by October if it showed in May, rather than acting before quickening, as would any sensible woman;

"Second, that Miss Nancy, who did not trust her busybody Aunt enough to permit her to examine her in May or October, trusted her to act as messenger for the abortifacient agent in September;

"Third, that Miss Nancy, supposedly knowing herself to be near term, would embark on a full day's carriage ride to Glenlyvar, or would even step out of the house into public view at all;

"Fourth, that Miss Nancy would not turn back on claim of illness, when she realized the possibility that she was going into labor;

"Fifth, that contrary to the evidence of our own senses, the supposed corpse languished in the shingle pile for four days, unmolested by Lemon or any other creature;

"Sixth, that after sitting for four days undisturbed, it coincidentally disappeared on the fifth day, just as the Sheriff was about to find it.

"Gentlemen of the jury, I put it to you plainly, how does this soil feel to you? What can you grow in it? Not what does the prosecutor say he has grown in it, but what can you really grow in it? What does the faculty of reason that the prosecutor invokes tell you now of his supposition that Miss Nancy suffered not from colic, but from childbirth, that ill-fated night at Glenlyvar?"

Marshall paused for another drink, and caught a look of admiration from none other than Colonel Randolph himself. But so consumed was he in plying his trade, that he did not pause to calculate the advantage to himself.

"That the alleged concealments by the defendants were not in fact concealments, I need hardly mention. The bolt served the place of the broken door latch; the candle left outside the sick chamber was due to the laudanum's effects on Miss Nancy's eyes; the washing of the sheet is attributable to common embarrassment. The value of gum guiacum for treating the innocent ailment colic has already been established, so whether Miss Nancy used it or not that night is immaterial to the question of pregnancy, except to the extent that it tends to show she was not pregnant, since she would be most unlikely to take it if she had been, and thereby risk an abortion outside of her own home. There is simply no evidence here of any concealment by the defendants; to the contrary, they were forthright in their conduct, as has already been discussed.

"But, you may well ask, what of Miss Nancy's refusal to be examined by her Aunt, if not in May, then certainly in October? That this refusal was imprudent, viewed in the hindsight of the gravity that these rumors have assumed, cannot be denied, but we must not examine this refusal from the perspective of a courtroom trial that an innocent girl would not have foreseen last October. Fairness requires that we view it instead from the perspective of the time and place in which it was made; that is, from the vantage point of the girl who refused to be examined when the rumors first sullied her virtuous ears. We all know that the heart conscious of its own purity resents suspicion, and the resentment is all the keener when the suspicion comes from family. This pride of innocence explains the refusal.

"There is another piece of evidence which bears so powerfully on the issue of concealment that I am surprised that the prosecutor, in his zeal for a rational verdict, could have omitted it. It is not a fact in evidence, but it is one of which you are all aware in your capacity as jurors out of the neighborhood. I refer, of course, to the fact that, for six long months after the rumors of this alleged crime began to circulate, the Commonwealth apparently thought so little of them that it refused to act against my clients, and that it was not until Mr. Richard Randolph himself, proclaiming his innocence, came to the steps of this courthouse and demanded to be tried in order to clear his name, that this prosecution was brought. Now ask yourselves, quite frankly, are these the acts of a man engaged in a conspiracy to conceal the truth? Of course not!

"The only conspiracy to conceal that is present here, Gentlemen, is the Commonwealth's conspiracy to conceal the only logical conclusions that can possibly flow from the facts as we know them: first, that the evidence of the alleged crime is riddled with inconsistencies and therefore not worthy of your belief; second, that what has been proven shows absolutely no concealment; and third, that the defendants have not in fact been devious in their conduct, but have, to the contrary, been commendably forthright."

Henry mentally retracted every silent curse he'd ever laid on his ungainly colleague's head, as he watched him slurp again at his water. And to think, he has yet to raise his voice.

"This leaves only the question of Mrs. Richard Randolph's testimony, and the shameful appearance of Mr. John Randolph. If it is true that, by one's accusers, you may judge the character of a person, then Mrs. Randolph must be deemed a saint. That she was candid about the fact that she would lie to save her dear husband certainly does not mean that she was in fact lying when she said that no baby was brought past her that night. Indeed, were a dedicated wife to swear under oath that she would not lie to save the life of her husband, it would be all the more cause for suspicion. In saying this, I by no means condone perjury, but one must be realistic about the power of an oath where ties of the heart bind, and the gallows lay beyond.

"So, having candidly admitted that she might lie to save her husband, but having steadfastly maintained that she saw no baby brought past her that night, we may well ask ourselves whether this is one of the lies she might have told out of love for her husband? I believe that it could not be, and the reason is plain: the fact that the witnesses observed continual harmonious relations between the wife, the husband, and the sister, and the fact that to this day she obviously loves her husband so much, makes it unthinkable that she should have seen him pass before her carrying an illegitimate child sired on her own sister. Love and all vestiges of domestic tranquility would have been destroyed by such a scene, yet the evidence shows that neither has suffered.

"As for this fellow Jack Randolph's motivation to attack Mrs. Randolph and, thereby, Miss Nancy, it is too obvious to require discussion. He is proud, but he exposed his vanity to the most severe wound that a man can suffer, that of unrequited love. In his bitterness he will stop at nothing, including concocting this dreadful tale of mulatto birth, which conveniently exculpates his brother while further inculpating the woman he hates. If this vicious allegation were true, it would require us to believe that Mrs. Randolph had it in her power to speak a truth that would have saved her husband, but that she chose not to do so. This alone is not credible. So, inasmuch as Jack Randolph had a motive to lie, and what he said is unbelievable, his testimony is not worthy of a shadow of consideration."

Marshall paused to drink, but found that his glass was empty. Outside, the shadows were lengthening against the coming of evening. Marshall smiled, half to himself, still on that street corner having a chat with an old friend.

"You'll forgive a lawyer who talks too much, but life is long, and it is precious when you're only twenty-three and eighteen years old as are Mr. Richard and Miss Nancy, so I felt that they deserved a thorough explanation of the flaws in the case against them. My colleague Mr. Henry says that I'm too concerned with logic and not enough concerned with passion, and I'm sure that he's just itching for me to raise my voice and get you gentlemen all fired up about God, and judgment, and fornication, the way Mr. Binghamton did. But you see, I believe in you gentlemen too much to do that. I also believe too much in the system of law we've come up with in this country, where the government, represented here by Mr. Binghamton, can't take the lives of two of its sovereign people no matter how much it rants and raves, unless it persuades twelve good men such as yourselves that taking their lives is absolutely necessary; that it is fair, and just, and required by the evidence, carefully and reasonably evaluated here in open court.

"So I'm only going to shout one thing, and I'm going to shout it at you now, and then I'm going to sit down. When you go back to the jury room to sift through the evidence together, before you vote I WANT YOU TO THINK, USE THE BRAINS GOD GAVE YOU, AND DECIDE FOR YOURSELVES WHETHER THESE CHARGES MAKE A LICK OF SENSE!"

The panes in the big windows rattled and Marshall's voice echoed out over the green hills like a clap of summer thunder as he sat down sheepishly, afraid he'd astonished his audience. And he had.

Chapter 23

The Verdict

I.

Now came the time of helplessness, as they sat together in the defense conference room awaiting a verdict. Judith, eyes pressed shut, rocked and moaned softly. Nancy held her hand, Richard paced, Marshall sat with pursed lips pressed against tented fingertips, and Henry sat with his legs stretched in front of him and his hands folded behind his head, beaming at Marshall.

Richard stepped out for a moment, crossed the hall under the Sheriff's watchful eye, checked the clock, and returned. "They've been at it an hour," he said.

"It should be a while," said Henry. "They've a great deal to chew over."

"What's to think about?" burst out Richard, nerves taut as a bowstring. "Didn't they hear what Marshall said? There's nothing to the case against us!"

"If they heard what I said, they will think," remarked Marshall, dryly. "Now calm down, Richard. The conventional wisdom is that the longer the jury is out, the more likely they will return with a defense verdict. The defense prevails by sowing doubt, and doubt doesn't come to people as easily as certainty."

"So we are consigned not merely to languish in purgatory, but to hope for an extended stay?" asked Nancy through a wan smile.

"I fear it is so."

"Then perhaps," said Nancy to Richard, "we can get a doctor to look at Judith?"

"I've already sent for the doctor," he replied. Then he raised his voice and said haltingly, "Do-you-hear-that-Judith? I've-sent-for-the-doctor-for-you."

Judith opened her eyes but said nothing, nothing at all.

A sharp knock on the door. "We have a verdict!" announced Mr. Critch.

Marshall looked worried. "So soon!" gasped Richard, as his stomach knotted. He looked at Nancy, whose green eyes mirrored his fear.

"Come, come," said Henry, "don't be frightened. I've never heard a closing argument so fine. If the jury was in the same county, you've nothing to fear."

The Sheriff was at the door to take charge of the prisoners. Nancy felt his rough hand around her upper arm, but for once she was grateful for the support. One foot in front of the other. Eyes straight ahead. What would it be like to walk to the gallows? I will do it myself, I will not cheat myself of that last opportunity to feel the power of my own limbs, to move across this sweet earth. But perhaps ...

This is the moment that separates lawyers from clients, thought Marshall. We fight this fight together, steeped in confidences, sharing hopes and fears, but judgment cannot be shared. Even if the verdict is guilty, Marshall knew he would go back to a comfortable office, there to pluck a new client with new hopes, while Richard and Nancy go to the gallows, the end of hope. In this moment they sit side by side at counsel table, but they are worlds apart. And yet Marshall could feel their dread, the coldness, the terrible finality of this approaching stain called judgment.

Nancy watched the jurors come in, one by one, looking at their feet, giving nothing away – or perhaps everything by this unwillingness to look her in the eye? All rise for the Judge, Marshall holding Nancy up, Henry doing the same for Richard. Will Judge Allen rise for us if we are acquitted? thought Nancy. Will he polish our boots, prepare our meals, empty our slops, the law's penitent representative, atoning for these indelible scars? Or will he simply call the next case, the next in an inexhaustible supply of carrion for the law?

"Be seated," croaked Mr. Critch, and Nancy's feverish brain wondered how there could be a Hell to rival this courtroom. That's it! She must have forgotten; she has already been convicted, executed, and *this is Hell.* But no, holding fast to Marshall's arm, this all seems solid enough. A man like Marshall could never end up in Hell, Marshall who asks only that we think. Of what? Of how beastly we can be to one another? Of how, if the jury spares our lives, life after this trial will be Hell on earth? Of the eternal nothingness of death? Of the beloved, stone cold and laid in earth's fallow soil?

"Gentlemen, have you reached a verdict?" Oh yes, we've reached a verdict. We find that life is squalid and precious, law unjust and necessary, truth unknowable, love hateful and ennobling. We find that the more we think, the less we know; the less we know, the more certain we grow in our folly. We find that the trial is a charade, a random event that could as easily have come out this way as that, and would if repeated again and again. We find that law is a convenient illusion to enrich lawyers and pacify the bloodthirsty multitude.

Have we reached a verdict? "Yes, Your Honor."

"What is your verdict?"

What, indeed, thought Richard. Shall we become like you, quick to condemn? Shall we suppress the longings of our hearts all the days of our lives, so that we die bitter, empty, and respectable? Or, wise jurors, hope against hope, is there room in this land of the free for passion and compassion?

"On both charges, we find the defendants to be *Not Guilty.*"

There was a moment of stunned silence, in which all the world seemed to pivot sharply around that Cumberland Courthouse. A few scattered hurrahs rang hollow against the general hush. With tears in their eyes, Richard and Nancy embraced most imprudently under Judith's unflinching gaze. Remembering his place, Richard stepped back from Nancy, and vaulted the railing on an impulse, landing before his wife. Judith stared into the eyes that were so like the fathomless midnight sky. As the arms she had craved for so long enfolded her at last, she felt a terrible chill.

2.

"Patrick, you rogue," said Marshall as he extracted a large, green bottle from among the garments and boxes of papers strewn across his bed at Mrs. Biddlesworth's, "I have here a rare treat, a bottle of genuine French champagne, Chateau D'Auboissant, 1776, a good year if ever there was one. Would you be so kind as to join me?"

"Well, John, I don't usually drink with Federalists, but I suppose I can make an exception in your case," laughed Henry, as he pulled over a side chair, and eagerly grabbed a drinking glass. Marshall propped the bottle between his legs, began prying at it with his bony thumbs. This having failed, he leaned over and grabbed the cork in his teeth.

"Whoa!" exclaimed Henry. "Hold on there, young man, I wouldn't recommend that unless you've a hankering to swallow that cork!" Marshall looked up, puzzled. "Don't tell me you've never had champagne before?" Marshall's embarrassed silence confirmed it. "Why, you're just a plain woodsman after all, a man after my own heart. Come on, give it here, and when we're through we'll wash out the sticky sweet taste with some Virginia beer!"

Henry exchanged his glass for the bottle, and with two thrusts of his powerful thumbs the cork whizzed within an inch of re-parting Marshall's slicked down hair, ricocheted off the wall and the ceiling, and returned to shatter the glass in Marshall's hand. "Holy Mother of God!" cursed Marshall, leaping up in alarm, "what sort of French cannon is this?" But Henry just laughed and lifted the foaming bottle so that it cascaded over Marshall's head, and as the bubbles ran down his face Marshall began licking the intoxicating nectar and laughing along with him.

"If it isn't our dignified counselors!" laughed Nancy from the hall, and even Jenna was smiling.

"Come on in and join the party," boomed Henry, "but watch out for broken glass." Nancy motioned towards the glass as she entered, and Jenna bent her sturdy frame to the work at hand, sweeping away the shards with two halves of a discarded sheet of writing paper. Fresh glasses were brought, and Henry poured three generous libations.

Nancy raised her glass. "I must toast you both now, truly, as the most magnificent lawyers, and the finest gentlemen, ever did God create."

"If God makes lawyers," interjected Henry.

"A lawyer to the end," gibed Marshall. "See how he cross-examines even your delightful compliments?" And they touched glasses and drank.

"So, what are your plans now, Miss Nancy?" asked Marshall.

"Miss Nancy, fancy and free," added Henry, in his most scurrilous tone. "If I were just a year or two younger ..." and he winked at her.

"Oh, I have no plans," said Nancy, gulping down the tingly champagne, feeling its delightful tickle behind her eyes, "except to pack up my clothes and be out of here before nightfall. Other than that, I will simply enjoy having my life back."

Marshall rummaged through the debris on his bed. "If you're packing up you should take this," and he handed her the precious scarlet coat. Nancy blanched at the sight of it, then took it gingerly between her thumb and forefinger.

"What is it, Miss Nancy?" asked Marshall. "With all that coat's done for you, I'd think you would be happy to see it."

"On the contrary, gentlemen," Nancy replied, "I'll never wear it again." Nancy saw dear Jenna arise, dutiful Jenna, moving, as always, from one job to the next, and the urge to brighten her day was irresistible. "Here, Jenna," she said, as she handed over the Parisian coat, "it's yours."

Jenna's eyes grew wide. "Mine to keep, Miss Nancy?"

"Yes, Jenna."

Overcome, Jenna threw her arms around Nancy. "Oh Miss Nancy, you's so sweet, I'll jest let dem buttons back out agin' an' it'll fit me jest right!"

Nancy stiffened, then pushed Jenna away so hard that she nearly fell. The bewildered girl started to speak, but a firm shake of her mistress's head silenced her.

"'Again?'" echoed Marshall blankly, all gaiety evaporating from the chamber. Henry hustled to close the door, for fear that any hint of this might escape. "You moved the buttons on that coat?" demanded Marshall.

"I didn't, no," said Nancy, her voice constricted with fear.

"DON'T LIE TO ME!" thundered Marshall in a voice he used just once during the entire trial, and then he swung at her with the back of his hand, and she was down before Henry could save her. Jenna dropped the precious coat to rush to her aid, but Nancy shook her off and stood on her own power, a nasty welt rising by her right eye. She did not strike back; she did not cry. She stood her ground and waited.

Marshall sat in a lump upon his bed, head lost in his large hands. He groaned, and began to think out loud. "My situation is an impossible one. However unwittingly, I have helped to perpetuate a fraud upon the court. I will, of course, have to bring this matter to Judge Allen's attention. Whether he can set aside the jury verdict at this point or not, I do not know, but I must leave it in his hands."

"But John," protested Henry, "Binghamton had a chance to question on the coat, and he declined. You know how the system works. The fault, if any, is his." He paused to gauge the response, and then added, for good measure, "Besides, you sliced the prosecution's case up twenty ways even without the coat. The result would not have been any different had Binghamton exposed this."

"We cannot possibly know that," said Marshall sternly, "and even if you're right, you're missing the point. This is not a question of whether the outcome would have differed. This is a question of cheating the law of a chance to work its way to an uncorrupted decision."

"And what could that decision be?" pressed Henry. "To hang this poor girl because proper people don't get caught in their indiscretions?"

"I'm sorry, I can assure you that I would not welcome that. But," and he avoided Nancy's eyes, "I cannot be responsible for her any more."

"Oh, but you are responsible, and you will be even more so if you go to the Judge," spat Henry, waving a calloused finger in Marshall's face. "You'll be just another sanctimonious stuffed shirt who cares more about half-baked ideas than about real people's suffering."

"Save it for the jury, Mr. Henry," shot back Marshall. "You of all people should understand that it is thanks to those 'half-baked ideas,' as you call them, that we are a free people." Marshall rose, determination spreading like a dark stain across his face. "Now," he said, glaring at Henry, "I'm going to see the Judge, and no one's going to stop me."

There was a time when Henry could have, and even now, in the autumn of his years, he measured himself against Marshall's hulking frame. Awkward though he appeared, Marshall was the only one at Valley Forge who could leap a board held at his own height; he was powerful in unexpected ways. Henry stepped aside; Nancy, broken and despondent, stepped aside; only Jenna did not step aside.

"Mistuh Marshall."

"Out of my way, girl."

She backed her muscular torso up against the door. "Mistuh Marshall, I ain't movin' till you hear me out."

"Insolent girl!" he exploded, but he did not strike out a second time. "Make it fast."

"Dis thing got started with da slave talk, right?"

"What of it?" Marshall snapped impatiently.

"So's if'n yer pants ain't on fire to hang a innocent girl, I figure you oughta know what us slaves is sayin' right now."

"What do I care –" began Marshall, but her impudence in the cause of saving Nancy's life knew no bounds, and she cut him off.

"I know you care 'cause you treat me right. And 'cause us slaves, we been talkin' to people who talk to people who talk to Lou."

"Lou? From Glenlyvar?" The sound of the name drained some of Marshall's fire. "Go on," he said, beginning to listen.

"Ole Esau, he says dat dere was a body out ta da shingle pile, but he doen know if it was a white or black body. 'It's purple,' dats all he says. Den he shows it ta Mistah Harrison, and next thing ya know, it's gone. Wonder why, huh?"

"Why?" asked Marshall, but the answer was already dawning on him.

"Well, I been pokin' round, and the word is dat Mistuh Harrison laid with Lou an' put her wit' his chile."

"Lou," repeated Marshall, as half-conscious intuitions crystallized.

"Yessuh, Lou. She either give birth or aborted right around the time dat Miss Nancy visits, an' she tries to cover it up by dumpin' the body in dem shingles an' runnin' off. When Ole Esau found dat poor thing out dere, Harrison he blames the whole thing on Miss Nancy here jest ta save his ass from the Missus, an' Ole Esau he doen know no different, but me, I sho' do. Course, he gotta get rid of the body, else it be pretty clear dat it ain't no white babe, so dat's why it ain't dere fer the Sheriff. Then he lets Lou run off; heck, he doen never wanna see her face agin."

Marshall stood stunned in his tracks. The clear truth of a moment past was suddenly nothing but lies; worse than lies, it was a dangerous trap door through which his innocent clients could drop with a noose around their necks.

"I was dere," continued Jenna, "and I tell you, Miss Nancy had the bloat, dat's all, she was feelin' poorly, so she needs more room around the belly, dats why we be movin' dem buttons from time to time. But dis girl Lou, she's da one wit' the baby, Mr. Marshall, Lord strike me dead if it ain't the gospel."

Everyone was silent as they watched the effect of Jenna's story on Marshall. Surely it was possible – the most righteous are often the biggest hypocrites. Besides, what if Marshall were to suddenly turn on the whole Randolph family? What would be the effect on his own fortunes, on Polly and the children? Right now, the future was brighter than it had been in years. He was back in the public eye, but even more importantly, back in the good graces of people who could make a difference. Those people would not forget his service – nor would they forget if he suddenly turned on them. These were practical men, men who distrusted zealotry in any form.

Marshall was 38 years old. Now, at the very moment of triumph, was a poor time to throw it all away based on some foolish speculation. Henry was right, Codfish could have questioned about the coat, but he didn't. That was how the system worked; it wasn't Marshall's job to prosecute. If he was ever to escape the grind of mortgage foreclosures and wills and petty disputes over the sale of livestock, now was the time.

But did he really believe this black girl, or was he just grateful for a clever and glib excuse to do what's convenient? To allow murderers to escape based on falsified evidence he'd produced. *Was he willing to do what was necessary?* That had been the question all along. It wouldn't wait. Now, right now, Marshall had to answer it.

All eyes were upon him. They saw him struggle, as he retreated from the doorway to his bedstead, where he sat and then changed his mind and rose again. He approached Nancy, who was huddled in a corner looking frail as a frozen sapling, took her proud chin between his thumb and forefinger, and brought her mercurial eyes to his. She let him enter her through the eyes, let his hard gaze ravish her most secret memories. Satisfied, he knelt down, and kissed each hand just once, ever so precisely. His head looked smaller and more forlorn than ever as he looked up at her and croaked, "Forgive me?"

Nancy helped him to his feet and embraced him, as he squirmed and bumped his elbows on the surrounding boxes. Then she gave Henry a quick kiss, grabbed Jenna by the elbow, and ran out of the room without a word.

Marshall looked over at Henry, who was pouring out the last of the champagne. "And I really thought I had this case figured out, Patrick," he said.

"I'm sure you did, you clever young man," said the old campaigner with a chuckle, as he passed Marshall a refreshed glass of bubbly. "And you probably still do," he added with a wink.

PART THREE
POST-TRIAL MOTIONS

- CHAPTER 24 -

SISTERS MOON AND FIRE BREATHER

I.

In the soft light, it was as if Nancy could reach out and touch his sweet face. She could reach out and touch his sweet face. She touched him, first with trembling fingers, then with her lips. His eyes, so soft, expressive, intelligent. She could see herself in the light of his eyes. She wanted to live in his eyes. "Ricky," she sighed, as she pulled him on to her, kissing him deeply, wanting him so. It was right, she could feel it, it was how it should be, this business of peeling away the garments to reach the essence. She pressed his body into hers, so that they might defy the fates and live inside each other forever and ever, bathed by nectar, delicious sticky rushing exotic nectar –

Mrs. Gouverneur Morris awoke with a start, disoriented by the lingering sweetness. After more than twenty-two years, she still dreamed of him. She snuggled deep into the rococo linen print of the easy chair where she sat nursing her babe, Gouverneur Junior, as she watched over the uneasy sleep of her nephew, Judith's younger son, Tudor.

The last light of evening crept into the commodious bedchamber so that the linen bed hangings and intricately carved whitewashed cornices glowed like decorative slices of moon. As the babe suckled, Mrs. Morris shut her green and gold eyes, and let her mind drift back to the nightmare years, when she was just Miss Nancy, alone and friendless. She remembered what it had been like just after the trial, shut up with Judith, Richard and Jack, in the Great House of Bizarre, the house with no visitors. Day by day, Judith and Jack had cut her off, first from the stables so she could go nowhere, then from Richard so she could get no comfort, and finally from their table so she could barely even get sustenance beyond what Jenna smuggled to her.

She smiled to remember her salvation: the long hours she spent in the nursery with St. George and then Tudor. Judith, consumed in her own personal purgatory, seemed to forget about the children completely for long stretches at a time, so that their only real mother was their Aunt Nancy. St. George, poor thing, could neither hear nor speak, but he always understood her gentle touch, and answered it with perfect clarity. Then Tudor was born in 1795, a sickly, brilliant waif whose feverish mind strained to devour his frail body. Nancy poured out upon them her boundless affection, and was grateful for the chance to do it. Without her the boys could not have survived, and without them, she would have died from unrequited love.

Nancy leaned forward and lit a candle, but even the ruddy glow could not give color to Tudor's sunken cheeks as he lay, cut down by tuberculosis in the prime of his junior year. The cruel illness had robbed Harvard of the boy who would have been valedictorian of the class of 1816. Nancy remembered with bitterness the day, after seven years of constant loving care, that Jack forbade Tudor to speak with his Aunt Nancy. It was just a few years before Jack and Judith threw her out of Bizarre altogether. Seeing that his nephew had at last reached a useful age, Jack took Tudor under his wing to teach him the manly arts of riding, hunting, and hatred.

How she had cried! It had been as if they had stolen her own child and turned him against her. Unlucky child! To have never known so noble and sweet a father as Richard, and to fall prey to such a caricature as Uncle Jack.

But the fates shift and now, once again, she had gladly scorned expense and risk of contagion to try to nurse Tudor back to a semblance of health. Nancy leaned forward to dip a cloth into a basin and wipe at Tudor's ashen brow. "For you I do this," Nancy whispered, as much to the ghost of his father as to the shade of her stricken nephew.

Now hot tears pulsed like blood from a wound as Nancy remembered that horrible night in June, 1796, when Richard lay abed in the grip of stomach cramps, and she nursed him with compresses while Judith rushed to the apothecary's. What was that look in Judith's eye when she returned to find them together on the bed? She'd only just sat down beside him and begun to massage his abdomen to relieve the pain.

Nancy remembered the chill of Judith's hand as she took from it the prescription. When she questioned the accuracy of the notation, "10 gr. tartar emetic," Judith had shrieked that "I suppose his own wife knows how to care for him," so Nancy mixed the prescription just the way the paper said, and administered it with her own warm hand.

Nancy would never forget Richard's calm, trusting eyes as he drank the potion. Tudor's rattling breaths are nothing compared to the moans that came from Richard's chamber all that hellish night, but Judith would not permit her to send for the doctor, even barred her from sitting with Richard on pretext that the vigil was his wife's duty.

A week later, with Richard cold and under ground, Nancy came upon the crumpled prescription in the pocket of her dressing gown. Examining it more closely, she noticed for the first time that the zero in "10" appeared to be squeezed unnaturally between the "1" and the abbreviation for the word "grain." She could not bear to investigate further, and threw the prescription into the fire. She never told a soul, aside from her husband.

Time, like water, washes away the blood, leaving only stains. Tomorrow, thought Nancy, tomorrow's the day that Judith and Jack will arrive, and she promised herself that she would welcome them without bitterness.

Little Gouv was nestled warm and snug in Nancy's arms. "Dear Lord," she prayed, "may our family at last find peace."

2.

Sixty-one year old Gouverneur Morris's peg leg forced him to wait at the crest of the long stairway leading up to the entry pavilion of Morrisania, his grand estate overlooking Long Island Sound. Nancy, still unrestrained by her forty years, rushed down the stairway, dragging her ivory silk gown all the way, so that she could be there to meet the phaeton before the guests' feet touched the ground. Judith disembarked first, and was immediately aware that her riding habit over a full petticoat and muslin dress was frumpish next to her sophisticated sister's stylish gown. Nancy embraced Judith warmly without regard to the effect on their costumes. Judith let it happen, wondering how hard a squeeze it would take before she could feel it. She dutifully brushed kisses into the air by each of Nancy's cheeks before pushing her away.

Then came Jack, now styling himself, "The Honorable John Randolph of Roanoke," in light of his new estate and his ascension to Congress. He peered lecherously into the scoop collar of Nancy's canezou, and planted his kiss firmly on her delectable lips.

"Welcome," Nancy said to him, thinking back to how sad she had felt when Jack bested a senile Patrick Henry in a campaign debate just three months before Henry's death in 1799. The voters had nonetheless favored a shade of Henry over Jack in his prime, but when the doctor opted to treat Henry's stomach cancer with a vial of liquid mercury the seat suddenly became vacant, and Jack purchased what he could not win fairly. Nancy took Congressman Randolph's hand on one side, and Judith's hand on the other, and led them up the stairway to her waiting husband.

3.

The dining chamber at Morrisania was truly extraordinary. Its lengthy expanse could be entered from either end via arched doorways topped by fanlights into which the family coat-of-arms was embedded in stained glass. A huge rectangular 16th century Persian vase carpet – so-called for the motif of Chinese vases interlocked with archaic flowers – covered most of the floor, leaving a burnished border of deep-grained mahogany around the room. This border was set off by the gray paneled dado skirting the walls, which were papered in an exquisite Chinese wallpaper drawn in green, white, rose and silver with tree peonies, bamboo, nightingales, peacocks, and hummingbirds. These flowered and flew upwards into an elaborately ornamented pink and blue cornice, suggesting the sky in early sunset. Huge marble slab side tables supported Chinese vases and gold candelabra, supplemented by eight gilt bronze wall branches and three crystal chandeliers, reflected in two pairs of looking glasses, and framed in walnut with gilded carvings.

At the head of the great cherrywood table sat Gouverneur Morris, with a ring of flowing white hair cradling his bald dome like clouds around Olympus. A mere silver fork now occupied the very hand which had once held the quill that authored the preamble to the Constitution. His mild blue eyes and long patrician nose nestled confidently atop cherubic cheeks and a double chin confected of a love of French sauces and the women who served them. Nancy sat to his right, her luminous eyes set like opals in a face made more beautiful by the softening brush strokes of time. Judith, who at forty-two looked fifty, flabby, and immeasurably sad, accepted the chair on Morris's left. Jack, puffed up from years of self-importance, perched by Nancy like one of the wallpaper peacocks incarnate. Tudor, exhausted by the day's visit, had retired to his chamber to rest for the journey back to Virginia.

It was sweetbread and oyster pie, a dish coveted by Gouverneur Morris as a tonic for his virility, which had sagged after Nancy's pregnancy. Nancy detested the dish, and ate eggs and bacon instead. Jack and Morris talked on interminably about the war, decrying the burning of the President's House; applauding Macdonough's Victory at the Battle of Plattsburgh "without which," noted Morris, "we'd be dining with the Redcoats today"; and disagreeing sharply over the New England secessionist movement.

Barred from the conversation by convention which the years had taught her to honor, Nancy had a chance to reflect. How things have changed, she thought, as she looked across the table at her sister's sad countenance. After years of penniless wanderings and the humiliation of hiring herself out as a domestic, Nancy found herself the respectable wife of the esteemed Federalist diplomat and signer of the Constitution. She had her family, her security, and her fortune. But even as her star rose, Judith lost everything. Even the Great House of Bizarre from which Nancy was driven nine years before, had fulfilled Ryland's prophecy by burning to the ground, leaving Judith a supplicant, dependent upon Jack's parsimonious charity.

Nancy put her fork down and pushed away her plate, angling for a lull in the gentlemen's declarations. Catching the meaningful look in her eye, her husband announced that the gentlemen would retire to his study for cigars and brandy. As soon as they were gone, Nancy leaned across the table, though it was too wide to permit actual contact. "Judith, dear," she said, "why don't you rest here for a month or two? You are quite welcome, and I haven't seen you in such a long time." Judith looked about blankly, trying to focus on the portent of these words. "Besides, it would do Tudor good not to have to travel so far so soon."

Judith's hound dog eyes found her sister, and her lips trembled slightly as she pushed them into a bit of a smile. "Thank-you, Nancy," she whispered, then she took another in a series of large, unladylike swallows from her wine goblet. "Thank-you," she repeated in a stronger, gravel-toned voice, "but not in mid-October. This is one Southern lady who is not equipped to endure your Northern winters. Perhaps…"

Nancy waited, but Judith could find no possibilities to express.

"Yes?"

"Perhaps," whispered Judith again, but she was overcome with regret, and could not finish. Nancy rushed around the table to comfort her. She circled her arms around Judith's heaving breast.

After a time, Judith blew her nose on a butterfly handkerchief. "You once said," she caught her breath, stifling the sobs, "you once said that there might come a time when I would long to embrace you again," she stuttered between trembling gulps of air. She took a deep breath and cried, "That time has come at last," before her voice shattered like surf on the rocks, and she held fast to Nancy to avoid the powerful undertow.

"Then won't you stay, please?" asked Nancy, trying to kiss away her sister's sorrow.

"No, dear," said Judith, trusting herself with only a glimpse at her sister. "Whatever you owed me, I have taken, and more."

"But this isn't a matter of sums, Judith!" cried Nancy. "I love you."

"And I love you too, dear," said Judith. "But we know too much of one another. To have spoken these words together is the most we could dare to hope for."

Nancy put her head in Judith's lap, and Judith stroked it gently. Soon Judith was humming softly, then singing:

> *Judith and Nancy are sisters*
> *like the sun and the moon above,*
> *We'll love each other till our days are done*
> *like moonlight sweetens the fiery sun.*
> *To Heaven we'll rise together:*
> *Sisters moon and fire breather.*

Nancy's breathing became calm and even. Together like this, Judith felt close to Heaven again, if only for one night.

– CHAPTER 25 –

THE LETTER

I.

Nancy knew something was wrong when the servant told her that her husband wished to see her in his study. Gouverneur Morris's study was his sanctuary; a smoky, dark, mahogany-paneled bastion of masculinity, walls hung with large paintings of Roman Legions battling the barbarians.

On this sparkling January day, Nancy had been practicing minuets on the fortepiano in a pool of sunlight in the solarium, so the transition to her husband's lair temporarily blinded her. She saw the dark silhouette of another gentleman, perched like a bony mule in a stiff armchair on the edge of a Roman battlefield, but at first she could not make out his identity. Then, even before she recognized his squashed, quizzical face, she knew from the jut of his elbow and the disarray of his spindly legs that it was the Chief Justice himself, Mr. Marshall, his thinning hair flecked with the snow of passing years, but otherwise looking robust. Marshall had been a steady though distant light throughout the difficult years of wandering; indeed, it was he who had recommended Nancy to Gouverneur Morris's service in the first place. The press of his weighty duties and the isolation of her domestic tranquility had kept their paths separate for more than five years, since her wedding on Christmas Day, 1809.

Though the gentlemen stood when Nancy entered, neither offered her a chair. The greetings that should have been warm were restrained, and she wrapped her paisley shawl tight around her shoulders for comfort against the calamity that this well-intentioned reaper must have brought to her doorstep.

"I've had a letter, Nancy," began Morris, stiffly.

Her queasiness was not solely due to cigar smoke. "Yes?" she prompted.

"From John Randolph of Roanoke."

Jack. Of course.

"I received it last October, shortly after he left Morrisania."

My God, thought Nancy, for three months this tumor has gnawed at my home, and not a word to me! Such treachery – when Jack had departed with Judith and Tudor that crisp, rainbow-hued October morning, he had expressed nothing but fondness, had placed a second, more fraternal kiss upon Nancy's lips, and had slipped a friendly note into her husband's hands agreeing that Judith and her sons might visit next summer.

"I did not know what to make of it, so I consulted Judge Marshall, in light of his familiarity with the case."

The case. She bit her tongue. *You consulted the Chief Justice of the United States before you consulted your own wife?* She was beginning to tremble.

"The Chief Justice's duties did not permit him to get away until now," and with a solicitous glance towards the gawky eminence he added, "but I am grateful that he could come at all."

Marshall nodded, but said nothing.

"It seems," continued Morris, "that on the road through the city Jack's carriage overturned on Courtland Street, cracking his bones, but worse yet, agitating his malignant nature. As his bones healed his anger festered, until he took pen in hand and wrote the most poisonous letter ever to blacken paper." Morris held out two pages of that familiar robin's-egg blue writing paper emblazoned with the Randolph crest. "Out of consideration I spared you this till now, but the Chief Justice suggests that you are entitled to see it."

The letter hit Nancy like a fist to the gut. It was in Jack's slashing scrawl, but every word jumped from the page quite clearly. He had addressed it to her, but he did not have the decency to send it to her. Instead, he sent it directly to her husband, covering it with a note that stated, "I wish that I could withhold this blow, but I must do for you what, under a change of circumstances, I would have you do for me." As she read, all that ancient desperation and fear came rushing in upon her at once, tightening her throat so that she had to struggle for breath.

Greenwich St., Oct. 21st, 1814
Madam:

I would hold my tongue did I not observe the carrion glint in your eye as you looked upon the carcass of your generous husband. The blood of at least two is upon your soul, along with promiscuity and miscegenation untold. So long as I have breath, no more victims shall fall to your deceptive enticements. What role you played in Theodorick's demise shall be ever shrouded in mystery, but a more dangerous nursemaid I cannot imagine. And what of your father – how did you "love" him? Did you add patricide to your list of sins, too? I always thought it strange that the Colonel should die but four months after the conclusion of the trial. But this is speculation; what I know for certain is that in early 1792 you found yourself with child, if "child" such an incestuous progeny can be called, so you needed assistance to cover up the fruits of your lewd amours, and what better place to seek it than from dear, gullible Richard? But how was his sympathy to be gained? The same as always: through harlotry, shameless and cunning. He fought, but what mere mortal could resist the serpent's kiss? You told him the child was his, and he passed his word that he would guard your honor, a pledge that was redeemed at the hazard of all that a man can hold dear – domestic peace, reputation, life itself!

You took a potion to kill the babe and lied to Richard that it was born still. Or did you twist the neck beneath the sheets while modesty compelled him to avert his eyes in that dark, dark chamber? It matters not, the result was the same: you killed your babe and used my brother under false pretenses to dispose of the body. It was only due to your sister Judith's perjury that you two conspirators did not swing on the same gibbet. She has never recovered from the shock of foreswearing her holy oath, and dreads the coming of Judgment night and day.

What proofs do I have? I have heard from the second Mrs. Harlan Beauregard Randolph. I have received Judith's confession. You know that I saw the letter from Richard meant to confess his sins to Judith, and swear her to silence. Did your Othello, Syphax, steal it from me in return for your favors? <u>I am sure he was well satisfied.</u>

But you were never satisfied to let live one who knew so much, though he was your marionette. Thus, my second beloved brother died suddenly in June, 1796, of the "cramp" in the stomach, after taking medicine from your Stygian hand!

When I heard that you were at last placed as housekeeper for Mr. Morris, a respectable man of the world who had resisted the most beguiling European temptresses, I thought at last you would be kept under control. The idea of his marrying you never entered my mind. <u>Another connection did.</u> When the news arrived that you had insinuated your way to the altar with this aging gentleman, I put it out of my mind in disgust. But Tudor's illness has thrown you again under my gaze. What do I see? A vampire that, after sucking the best blood of my race, has flitted off to the North to strike its harpy fangs into an infirm old man. But before this reaches you it will have been perused by him to whom, next to my unfortunate brothers, you are most deeply in debt, and whom, next to my brothers, you have most deeply injured. If he be not blind and deaf, he must unmask you now, unless he too is to die of the "cramp in the stomach" – you understand me!

John Randolph of Roanoke

Nancy's hands were shaking so hard that she folded one upon the other and pressed down with all her strength until a large, bloodless patch appeared. She dared not raise her eyes to meet her husband's. "I'll go, of course," she said to the blackened parquet floor.

"Not on my account," said Morris. He took her folded hands like the wings of a wounded bird, and warmed them against his cheek. She began to swoon, and he guided her into a chair, rearranged the shawl about her neck, and then nodded to Marshall.

The Chief Justice cleared his throat, but still it came out scratchy. "Mrs. Morris –"

"Nancy," she corrected, her voice distant and ethereal.

"Miss Nancy, then," he said, seeing her once again as the proud, frightened filly he had rescued so long ago. "Miss Nancy, I have informed your husband of Jack's creed – 'Do unto others before they do unto you' – and advised him not to believe a word from this rogue. How can we believe a man who testified under oath that the infant was of mixed breed, when he now attributes paternity to a white man? It doesn't follow."

Nancy smiled weakly. She was relieved to find Marshall still trusting his logical nose. "Your husband," Marshall was saying, "who is most understanding, has expressed to me his confidence in you." Here, Nancy snuggled against the pink old man who stood by her chair, cradling her in his puffy hands.

"At your husband's request, I have studied this letter carefully," continued Marshall. "Mr. Morris shared with me your suspicions about Judith's role in Richard's death. I felt duty bound to refer both your version and Jack Randolph's accusations to the Prince Edward County prosecutor."

Nancy stiffened at the prospect of becoming enmeshed in a new round of legal machinations.

"The prosecutor has performed an investigation," Marshall went on, "which has led nowhere. Judith has denied altering the prescription, Dr. Jensen has passed away, and the prosecutor has been unable to unearth sufficient evidence of wrongdoing to warrant a charge. Since you are beyond the reach of his subpoena power, he has consented to accept your affidavit in lieu of testimony, with the assurance that, if it is consistent with what you told your husband, he will consider the matter closed both as to yourself and your sister."

Nancy managed to incline her spinning head, sending ringlet curls brushing past her cheeks to land upon the amber paisley of her shawl. "It seems, Mr. Marshall, that I shall be forever in your debt."

The Chief Justice chose this moment of vulnerability to rise up, transforming familiar dishevelment into looming intimidation. "Your troubles are not so easily ended, Miss Nancy. Jack is trumpeting this whole gruesome story around Virginia, and even here in New York." Nancy gasped and fell back. "Your husband has authorized a suit for defamation, but it cannot proceed until we know the truth." Marshall stabbed at her with the obsidian glint in his eyes. "Have you ever told it, Miss Nancy? Have you ever told it to this day?"

Nancy stared past him to the dark wall, spattered with the blood of fallen gladiators. She brushed the hair from her face as she rose, crossed the chamber, and then turned suddenly to face Marshall. "No, I've never told it," she said, "but it seems I'll never be rid of this curse until I do." Her voice was an oratorio. "I'll tell you, Mr. Marshall. Oh God, at last, I'll tell the whole world the truth!"

2.

At first it was hard to speak the words she had blocked from her lips for so long, but as she built momentum she felt lighter with every word. "That my departure from my childhood home was an unhappy one, and my relationship with my father also unhappy, you both know, although perhaps you are unaware of the depths of that unhappiness. Mr. Marshall, you have seen the kind of woman that my father allowed to despoil my mother's memory, and I never forgave him for that. But my anger towards him runs deeper, as shall presently become clear to you." Here she paused, girding herself against Jack's nauseating charges. "Ours was not, however, an improper relationship. When my father was drunk he was violent, and it seems that he may have exceeded the bounds of propriety with my long-suffering sister Judith, but he never touched me in that other way."

Nancy paused to draw courage, then plunged on. "The same cannot be said of Jack. You know about Jack's unwanted attentions that long ago night under the portico, but what you do not know about that night is that he tried to take me by force."

"No!" cried Morris, and he went to hold Nancy, but she slipped from his grasp.

"You want the truth, Sir?" she asked with a hint of venom. "Sit down, and you shall have it." Morris backed away haltingly, then crumpled into the very chair where he had comforted her not five minutes before, his fingers fumbling at his linen cravat.

"Jack was not successful that night. But it was only his own physical incapacity that prevented him from using me most cruelly. He has never forgiven me for the sin of witnessing his failure. I believe it is this shame that motivates his attacks on me."

Nancy paused, and then knelt down before her husband's drooping face. "I must speak of things now from my youth, Gubby," she whispered, "things that happened long ago and which have nothing to do with us." He looked up at her, but said nothing. "I will continue as your companion and as a mother to your child for as long as you want me, just as we agreed." She paused, then whispered, "You know that I have never pledged my love." Morris jerked his head once to signify assent, then looked away.

Nancy rose, now addressing herself more to Marshall than to her husband. "I fear that I have misled you as to the depth of my affection for Theodorick. Theodorick and I were in love, and our visit to Tucka-hoe in December, 1791, was intended not merely as a family visit, but to seek my father's consent to our marriage. To my astonishment my father refused to consent, based on the barest pretext that Theodorick's fortunes were too precariously encumbered – this, despite the fact that he had already consented to Judith's connection with the very same family fortunes. We fought bitterly, but he was drunk and reckless, and finally he had the audacity to propose, directly to my beloved Theodorick, that if he truly loved me he would urge me to marry a man of substance, a man who could support me in accordance with my station in life, a man such as Gabriel Harvie! You know the rest, Mr. Marshall. I insulted him and his young wife with a remark calculated to wound, and it was only Theodorick's hand that stayed me from inflicting physical wounds to match."

Marshall recalled the insult well, and he hoped that Morris would never hear it. How ironic that Nancy should ultimately be driven into the sort of marriage she had once mocked so savagely.

"It was too late to depart," continued Nancy, "so I had to spend one more night in that hateful house. But even in my bedchamber I was not safe, for after I retired my father staggered in, calling me an ungrateful whore and other wretched names, cursing me for defying him. What else he would have done I dare not think, had Theodorick not heeded my cries for help. You used to marvel at my hatred for my father, Mr. Marshall, but what kind of a father would deprive his daughter of her best chance at happiness?"

For the first time, Marshall saw beneath the veneer of beauty in Nancy's eyes, to the wounds underneath. Nancy sank into a chair in the far corner of the room, but she did not falter in her account. "Of the fatal chill Theodorick caught on the carriage ride home, you know. I nursed Theodorick – my dear Ricky I called him – day and night. With my father's attitude, there was no hope of legal solemnization of our love for each other. But I was determined that he who had sullied holy matrimony by marrying a vixen should not despoil our pure love.

"As Theodorick sank deeper and deeper into the grip of illness, we could both see that time was short, though we did not admit it to one another. Finally, in desperation, Ricky and I performed our own wedding ceremony." Marshall's eyebrows shot up in surprise. "Yes, Mr. Marshall, we took solemn vows before one another, and God." Nancy's eyes were brimming wet, but her cheeks were hot with defiance, not tears. "When our ceremony was finished, I slipped under the sheets, and with Ricky's last strength, we consummated those vows. Theodorick Randolph was my first husband, gentlemen, till death parted us, and I honored him and was faithful to him always." Morris wiped away a tear, and even Marshall felt his eyes moisten.

"The marriage was to be secret. Theodorick would not otherwise have agreed to marry without proper sanctification, since he said that it would destroy our prospects in life – though of course, he meant my prospects, knowing his were so soon to be cut short. On his death bed, not yet knowing that I was pregnant, he enjoined me again to absolute secrecy."

Now Nancy's pale lips quivered, but still she held the tears. "When I told him I needed a confidante, Theodorick called in his brother Richard, swore him to secrecy, and then told him everything. After Richard left, I laid down with my new husband – poor frail Ricky, it seemed as if the candlelight shined right through him – and the two of us slept in one another's arms." The room was so still, their heartbeats were like footsteps of the dead. "He never awakened," gasped Nancy, and then her tears poured forth.

"So it was Theodorick's child that you bore?" asked Marshall, gently.

Nancy nodded.

"And therefore," continued Marshall, "there was no adultery."

"And, God strike me dead, no murder either," exclaimed Nancy urgently, as she sprang from her chair and crossed the chamber to her interrogator. "I would sooner have taken my own life than that of the last fruit of Ricky's seed." A despondent cry escaped as she knelt, pleading before him. He squirmed with embarrassment and looked to Morris, who merely nodded. With short haphazard strokes, Marshall patted Nancy's honey hair.

"Alas, it was not to be," Nancy sighed. "I kept my pregnancy a secret from all but Jenna, and her crafty alterations hid it as well as might be expected, save for the occasional lapses of which you heard in the courtroom. Judith was so busy with her own newborn that I was able to mostly conceal it from her, although she surely suspected something by the end. Though Richard knew of the vows, I didn't tell him about the baby until that awful night at Glenlyvar, for fear that he would urge me to abort – what else could he have done; how could we explain a new child at Bizarre when Judith had just delivered in February?

"I went to Glenlyvar – seemingly against all logic, as you so deftly pointed out at the trial, Mr. Marshall – out of fear of being left alone at Bizarre with Jack. It was, as you know, a terrible mistake, but perhaps not worse than to have stayed. My labors began of their own accord, and were merely expedited by a small dose of gum guiacum, clearly not enough to injure the fetus, according to Patsy's advice. But, to my profound sorrow, Ricky's last chance for an heir was born stone dead, never a breath in him." As the memory caught at her own breath, she managed to stammer, "Despite everything that happened, and despite what may still lie ahead, it was, and will remain, the saddest moment of my life."

"But you are not guilty of murder, dear Nancy," said Marshall, puzzled. "Why did you refuse to testify?"

"Our vow of silence was made to Theodorick *on his death bed*," cried Nancy. "I could not testify, without compromising my beloved Theodorick's honor, and this sacred death-bed vow. I tremble to think that I have cast aside that vow so casually as even to have shared these confidences now, over twenty years later, but I fear that if the truth is not told soon, another household will be destroyed by the deception."

"Do not tremble on my account, dear Nancy," said Morris. "You have been true to both of us in your fashion. How could I punish you out of jealousy for an unfortunate boy who died so long ago?"

Nancy crossed to the old man with a graceful step, and kissed him tenderly on the brow. Then she turned towards Marshall, alight with conflicting passions like a fiery sunset reflected in a still pond. "And you, dear Mr. Marshall, my first and best lawyer, shall you turn against me now?"

Marshall sat, testing the soil in his curious way. It was like none he had ever touched, nor ever would again. It was fallow, yet it brought forth a cornucopia of twisted flora. It made no sense. What would Henry do?

He would ask himself, *what do I feel in my heart?*

Then Marshall knew that he believed her, and that he would stand by her always.

3.

That night Nancy burned the letter Syphax had retrieved for her. Why had she saved it all these years? As the blackness curled around Richard's delicate script, she thought for a moment that she heard a faint cry.

AFTERWORD

Taking up her pen the next day, Nancy wrote a scathing reply to Jack's letter, copies of which were delivered to many of the best families in America. In it, for the first time, she publicly confessed to the world her youthful betrothal, her father's objections, and her consummation of unsanctified vows in the arms of her dying love, Theodorick. But in telling her side of the story, she told the whole story, ruthlessly exposing Jack's lewd advances, his betrayals of his brothers, his violence and his lies. Noting that by reviving the tale in northern cities, where it had hitherto been little known, he blackened Richard's reputation along with her own, she asked, "What must be the indignation of every feeling heart to behold a wretch rake up the ashes of his deceased brother to blast his fame? Who is there of nerves so strong as not to shudder at your savage regret that we did not 'swing on the same gibbet?'" Marveling that Jack would leave his beloved nephew for three months in the care of a woman he believed to be guilty of fornication and murder, Nancy borrowed from the Bard of Avon to dismiss Jack's accusations as "a tale told by an idiot, full of sound and fury, signifying nothing!"

Tudor, who was eulogized by one of his professors as "perhaps the most promising young man who has been at Cambridge within my knowledge of the institution," was never to fulfill his promise; he died of tuberculosis in his senior year. Then Judith died, in March, 1816, bitter and alone, having refused Nancy's many offers of assistance. Blow followed blow, and in November of that same year Gouverneur Morris died after a short illness, but he left Nancy a life estate in Morrisania and a good income, with the remainder to their son. At last, after suffering these losses, Nancy was freed from the bittersweet entanglements of family to live a comfortable and quiet life, which she did until death found her in 1837.

John Marshall sat as Chief Justice until his death in 1835, and during that time he laid the foundation upon which American Constitutional law is built. St. George, the end of the Matoax blood line, grew a long, white beard, and lived to a ripe old age on the steps of the Charlotte County Courthouse in Virginia. Jack Randolph's aptitude for deception was not wasted: he continued to serve in the House of Representatives, and even briefly in the Senate, until 1829. He died four years later, mouthing through wasted lips his final words: "Remorse, remorse!" Found out, at last, in death, his will was denied probate as the product of a madman.

"Though this be madness, yet there is method in't."

Acknowledgements

First, I would like to thank my beloved wife, Carol, whose keen editorial eye and encouragement contributed immeasurably to the finished product. I would also like to thank the Virginia Historical Society for providing copies of John Marshall's trial notes, and sundry related correspondence and newspaper clippings. The slave song "Sun, you be here and I'll be gone," is reprinted from Howard Zinn, *A People's History of the United States,* p. 191 (Harper & Row, 1980). Many thanks to my dear friend John Sessions, who has believed in my writing and helped to support it in many ways. Special thanks to Celeste Bennett, my publisher, who has repeatedly demonstrated her belief in this project by going above and beyond the call of duty. Appreciation is also due to Nancy Attwell, fellow historical novelist, who provided insightful editorial comments and publishing advice. And thanks to my former agents, Ray Powers and Bob Goldfarb, who believed in this story before it was even *Just Deceits*. Kudos to professor and author Jocelyn Moody for providing advice on slave dialect, to Julian Riepe and Bob Dugoni for reading and appreciating the manuscript, to Esther Fiddes for equine advice, and to Robert Moulthrop for encouraging me to co-author a stage adaptation. Last but definitely not least, much love to my daughters, Ava & Nellie, who encourage me to dream.

About the Author

In addition to writing novels, Michael Schein of Seattle is a poet and practicing attorney. From 1988–2003, Michael taught American Legal History at the University of Puget Sound School of Law and then Seattle University School of Law, where he became interested in this footnote to the career of Chief Justice John Marshall. Michael is Artistic Director of the annual LitFuse poetry workshop held in Tieton, WA, has served on the boards or as executive director of a number of nonprofit organizations, and is on the speaker's bureau of the ACLU of Washington. Michael's poetry has received various honors, including two Pushcart nominations. To learn more or to contact Michael, please visit www.michaelschein.com